The Fabulist
Play Cycle

Also by the author

Extreme Dentistry
Why I Hunt Flying Saucers and Other Fantasticals
The Progressive Apparatus and More Fantasticals
The Hard Side of the Moon

The Fabulist
Play Cycle

A radio play collection

Hugh A. D. Spencer

Milton, Ontario

Brain Lag Publishing
Milton, Ontario
http://www.brain-lag.com/

Cover artwork by Catherine Fitzsimmons; interior illustrations © Emily O'Brien

"Calling Occupants Of Interplanetary Craft" by Terry Draper and John Woloschuk

Copyright © 1976 by Magentalane Music Limited.

Administered by Southern Music Pub. Co. Canada Ltd for the World.

Copyright Renewed. All Rights Reserved. Used by Permission.

"After You Get What You Want, You Don't Want It" music and lyrics by Irving Berlin

ISBN: 978-1-998795-05-5

Library and Archives Canada Cataloguing in Publication

Title: The Fabulist play cycle : a radio play collection / Hugh A.D. Spencer.
Other titles: Radio plays. Selections
Names: Spencer, Hugh Alan Douglas, author.
Identifiers: Canadiana (print) 20230497284 | Canadiana (ebook) 20230497292 | ISBN 9781998795055
   (softcover) | ISBN 9781998795062 (EPUB)
Subjects: CSH: Radio plays, Canadian (English) | LCGFT: Radio plays.
Classification: LCC PS8637.P47 A6 2023 | DDC C812/.6—dc23

Content warnings: Car accident, death

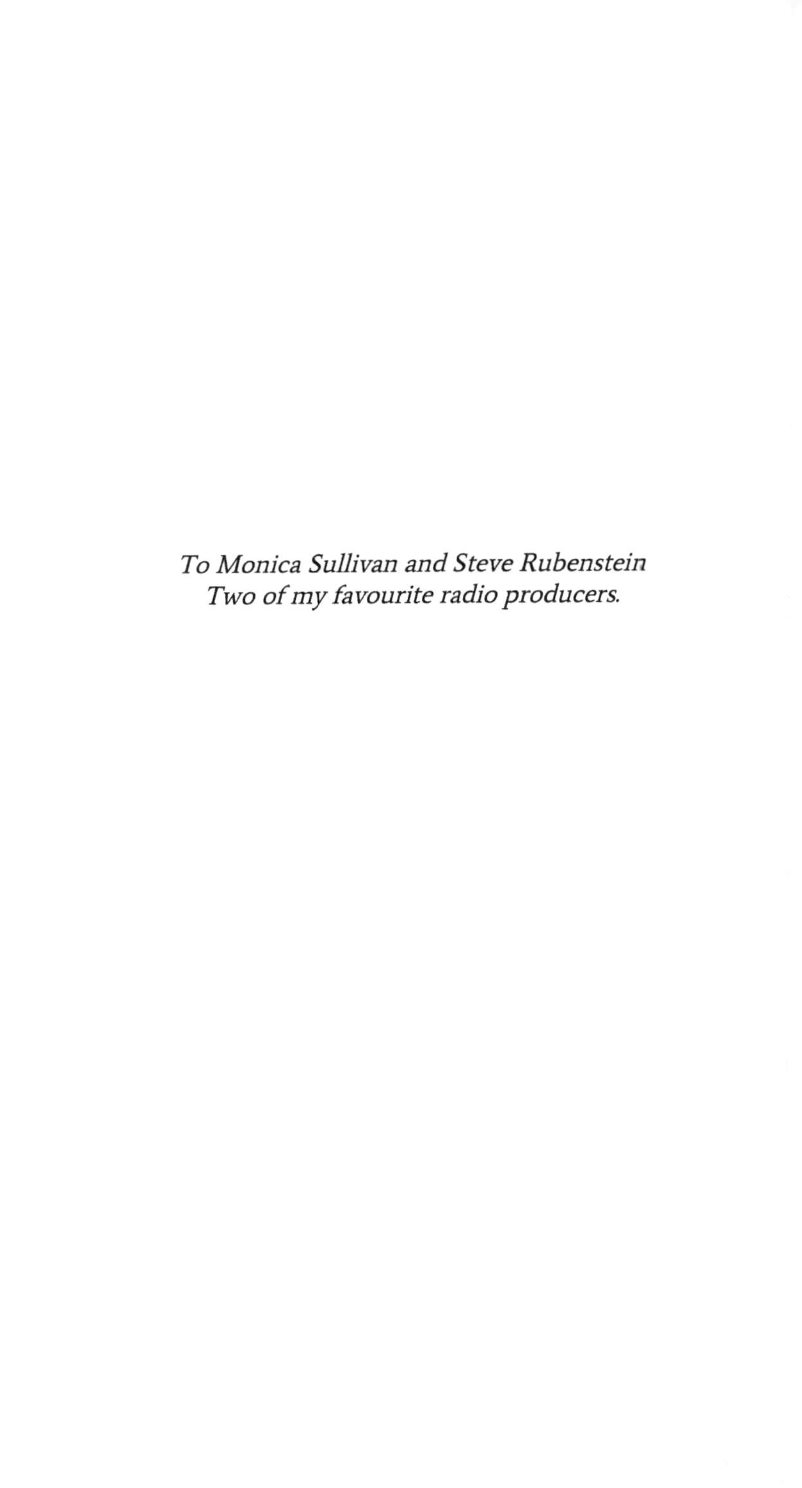

To Monica Sullivan and Steve Rubenstein
Two of my favourite radio producers.

Contents

You Laugh But In A Very Uncomfortable Way

In his fiction, Hugh A. D. Spencer has frequently dealt with popular culture in its many expressions. His approach is often humorous, as he satirizes a range of popular culture tropes and phenomena, from urban legends to science fiction in various media. In his story collection *Why I Hunt Flying Saucers and Other Fantasticals* (2016), for instance, Spencer skewers accounts of alien abduction (the collection's title story), millennial cults ("When Bloomsbury Fails"), fast food ("The Z-Burger Simulations"), and science fiction's countless uncontrollable robots ("The Robot Reality Check," a riff on Isaac Asimov's Three Laws of Robotics). He loves to write about the SF pulp magazines and television shows that so many of us grew up on, like *The Twilight Zone* and *Star Trek* (Rod Serling even makes a cameo appearance in "Astonishing Failures"), and that made us fans and Fans of the genre. He has made frequent use of his training in anthropology and his wry wit to create marvellous, hilarious, and affectionate send-ups of beloved but philosophically and artistically flawed science fiction. He cannot help being attracted to the charming optimism behind many Golden Age and TV visions of the future, particularly the incurable belief among some that advanced technology can only bring about a Utopian society. After all, we have been so good at handling our own creations since Mary Shelley's *Frankenstein*, what could possibly go wrong if we gain control over the very underpinnings of reality?

More recently, Spencer has turned to radio drama as a favourite medium, although his interest in radio expressions of the fantastic dates back many years. For example, when we were putting together the National Library of Canada's exhibit on Canadian science fiction and fantasy, "Out of This World," in 1995, he took on the task of exploring and identifying Canada's rich legacy of fantastic creation in radio as well as in other media. His Media Resource List, although never published, is an important bibliographic resource for knowledge of what Canadian playwrights and other media artists were up to during most of the twentieth century. On the creative side, Spencer has written scripts for quite some time, and one of them, a radio play called, "A 21st Century Scientific Romance," was published alongside the short stories in *Why I Hunt Flying Saucers and Other Fantasticals.*

The Fabulist Play Cycle is a suite of eight linked radio plays about the authors and the pulp magazines, paperbacks, TV shows, and movies constituting what has meant the world and the Otherworld to us since the 1920s. Four of them form parts of *Amazing Struggles, Astonishing Failures & Disappointing Success* and the other four are episodes of the connected "Cult Stories". The entire sequence can be seen as what we might call a *drame à clef:* that is, the characters, the magazines and TV shows, and even the titles of the two parts are direct allusions to and fictional representations of actual figures and elements in the history of media science fiction. The title of the first set includes a reference to *Amazing Stories,* which, as many readers of SF know, Hugo Gernsback founded in 1926 as the first all-science fiction magazine. Arguably even more influential was *Astounding Science Fiction,* which began in 1930; when John W. Campbell, Jr. became the editor, he created a "stable" of authors comprising the leading authors of American and British science fiction, including Isaac Asimov, Arthur C. Clarke, Robert A. Heinlein, L. Ron Hubbard, and Henry Kuttner, to name only a few. Stewart D. McReady in Spencer's plays is a thinly disguised portrait of Campbell, and Sheldon Isaacs is not-so-loosely based on Asimov. The young writers in "Amazing Struggles" desperately want to join McReady's stable of those writing for *Tremendous Stories of Super Science.* Implausible heroes and villains, and equally implausible forms of technology, will be these budding scribes' tickets to pulp stardom. Later, *Space Spanners* appears both alongside and as a parodic version of *Star Trek,* complete with a lascivious and politically self-righteous Captain.

The key reality-based figure throughout the cycle, however, is Donald H. Evanston, who is a satirical depiction of L. Ron Hubbard, founder of the Church of Scientology—here represented by the Temple of Mentotechnics. Hubbard influenced Campbell just as Evanston does McReady, and both the Church and the Temple set up headquarters in California. Spencer even incorporates a truncated reference to John Travolta in "Disappointing Success II". There are a number of other parallels, and it should be noted that Spencer knows whereof he speaks as he researched the Church/Temple as a graduate student, in much the same way that his avatars in the plays, Lambert and Daniels, have done.

On the other hand, it would be mistake to see Spencer's satire as directed solely at the people and institutions of pop-culture science fiction. How SF has fit into the United States's culture more generally, particularly in promoting and promulgating American ideology, is Spencer's larger interest. At one point during a confrontation with an alien species in "Disappointing Success", Captain Hughes asserts that their way of thinking is "completely... *wrong*!" and informs Elder #3:

> You fail to recognize the sacred right of every individual to pursue their personal economic happiness in a democratic free-enterprise system based on self-respect and the values of fair play and open competition, where all men (and some women) are free to choose to live in a heterosexual monogamous man-wife relationship. (pauses briefly for breath)
>
> Only when you surrender to the altar of individual choice, and convert to a monotheistic sect based on basic rights and truths... and only then... will your vile and degraded society crawl out of the sub-human barbaric totalitarian slime... and slowly progress towards the dignity and honour and goodness...

In the *Space Spanners* universe, aliens just need to have their eyes opened by an American starship commander to see the error of their ways. Less humorously, and more distressingly, in this capitalist cultural realm some of our idealistic young authors eventually sell out in order to achieve the professional success they have sought.

Spencer deals with other issues as well, such as McCarthyism, corruption in Hollywood, and academic politics. What we see in the world of science fiction in Spencer's plays reflects the materialism, corporatism, and degeneration of human relations in society as a whole. Pulp fiction may often be silly, Spencer shows, but there is an innocence to its approach to the future that gets lost when ego and bigger economic and social forces come into play.

The Fabulist Play Cycle is thus funny and tragic at the same time. That is the hallmark of satire: it makes you laugh but in a very un-comfortable way. Spencer knows his material, and he simultaneously appeals to our nostalgia and our sense of the way the world really works.

Allan Weiss
August 2023

Amazing Struggles

Play One:
Amazing Struggles

Characters – In Order of Appearance

SOLAR POLICEMAN ALEXANDER STEEL	A character from stories created by Bob Clyde and Sheldon Isaacs.
EVIL ALIENS	Also part of a story written by Clyde and Isaacs.
SHELDON ISAACS	An aspiring science fiction writer. He is a member of a writers group known as the Fabulists.
BOB CLYDE	Our protagonist and narrator. He is also an aspiring science fiction writer and one of the Fabulists.
MRS. ISAACS	Sheldon Isaacs' mother.
STEWART D. McREADY	Recently appointed editor of *Tremendous Stories of Super Science*. In his early thirties.
ELAINE WILLIAMS	McReady's secretary.
GERALD MITCHELL	A writer in his early twenties. Also one of the Fabulists.
DONALD H. EVANSTON	A science fiction writer in his early thirties. The most popular and prolific contributor to *Tremendous Stories*.
JAY E. CROSS	A science fiction writer in his late twenties. Self-taught philosopher and the second most popular writer for *Tremendous Stories*.
DAVID POOLE	An occasionally published writer. A

	member of the Fabulists.
FRANCIS FREEDMAN	An aspiring science fiction writer in his late teens. A member of the Fabulists.
ROLF DENSEN	An aspiring science fiction writer in his mid-teens. A member of the Fabulists.
ED SILBERBERG	A science fiction fan.
AL WARREN	A science fiction fan.
JACK WEISS	A science fiction fan.
HAL ZUCKERMAN	A big name science fiction fan.
STEVE MILLER	A science fiction fan.
WILL GRUNWALD	A science fiction fan.
ELECTROSTATIC COMPULATOR	A machine intelligence.
JOHN STEADMAN	Founder and CEO of Samuels and Steadman Publishing. In his late fifties. He is McReady's boss.
RAY ANN SPARKS	A member of the Young Communist League and also an aspiring science fiction writer. In her early twenties, she is not quite a member of the Fabulists.
FAN #1/FAN #2/ FAN #3/FAN #4	Even more science fiction fans, attending the First World Science Fiction Convention.
JACK WEBB	An FBI agent.
BEN JOHNSON	Another FBI agent.
NAVIGATOR	On the aircraft Enola Gay.
PILOT	On the aircraft Enola Gay.
BOMBARDIER	On the aircraft Enola Gay.

Scene One

Events alternate between fictional caverns on one of Jupiter's moons and a small bedroom in New York City. It is late afternoon, August 1937.

SOUND:　　THE ROAR OF ROCKET SHIP ENGINES GROW LOUDER AND THEN SUBSIDE AS WE HEAR ITS MASSIVE LANDING FINS DIG DEEP INTO THE ALIEN SOIL. THERE IS A HISSING SOUND AS THE HULL OF THE ROCKET COOLS AND A DEEP METALLIC ECHO AS THE MAIN HATCHWAY OPENS.

STEEL:　　(to himself) So here I am on one of Jupiter's moons...

SOUND:　　A SOFT CRUNCH AND DUSTY FOOTSTEPS AS STEEL JUMPS DOWN AND WALKS OUT ONTO THE SURFACE OF THE MOON.

STEEL:　　...I just hope the readings from my mentaloscope are accurate. Otherwise...

EVIL ALIENS:　　(a bunch of them) Die, terrestrial scum!

SOUND:　　TINY DYNAMOS POWER UP AS STEEL ACTIVATES HIS WEAPON.

STEEL:　　Get back, you inhuman, slavering hordes! I have an atom blaster here—capable of imploding your nucleic structure even from distances exceeding 700 zardons...

EVIL ALIENS:　　We have no fear of your pathetic human toys!

SOUND:　　AN EERIE HOWL RISES AS THE EVIL ALIENS MOVE CLOSER.

STEEL: In the name of Science, I'm warning you! Stay back, you mutated monstrosities, you!

ISAACS: (echoes) ...even though... it seemed as if certain doom...

SOUND: <u>THE SOUND OF SLOW, HUNT AND PECK TYPING IS HEARD IN THE BACKGROUND.</u>

ISAACS: ...leaked from every... fissure... of... the Jovian caverns... Space Patrolman... Alexander Steel... felt fear... sorry! Felt... *no*... fear... As a leader of the... United Earth States... Solar Police... he knew he... could fail... damn! Could *not*... fail...

STEEL: *Die, subversive beings!*

SOUND: <u>RAPID BURSTS OF ATOMIC FORCE AS STEEL FIRES HIS BLASTER. THE ALIENS SCREAM AS THEY IMPLODE.</u>

STEEL: Such is the fate of all who oppose the rule of Technology!

SOUND: <u>THE SOUND OF THE TYPING RISES A LITTLE OVER THE CONTINUING SCREAMS.</u>

ISAACS: ...and with each sweep of his blaster beam... powerful bursts of... charged particles emerging from... (suddenly sounds very confident) ...a miniature controlled fission reaction would stream out, striking the bad... no... no... the insidiously vile... aliens... causing them to dissolve into... into... pools of a soup-like... pus...

CLYDE: Pus? That's disgusting!

ISAACS: ...their death agonies... rendering fearful payment... for their hideous crimes against... against... everybody...

CLYDE: (sarcastic) Oh, that's good.

ISAACS: ...um... how about... against... man... I know... scientific man! Glancing down... at the smouldering pool of extraterrestrial gunk.. Alexander Steel reminded himself that the defence... of the Interplanetary Republic... could sometimes... be a dirty business...

STEEL: (grimly) But now, I have another mission to attend to...

MRS. ISAACS: (distant) Sheldon! Sheldon Isaacs! What are you doing up there?

ISAACS: (mutters) Aw, geez. (calling) Nothing, Ma!

MRS. ISAACS: Come down here and help your sister! You can play with your friend later!

SOUND: ISAACS PUSHING HIMSELF UP FROM THE TABLE AND WALKING TO THE DOOR.

ISAACS: I have to go. Finish this one, okay?

CLYDE: Sure.

SOUND: DOOR CLOSES, CLYDE STARTS TYPING... WITHOUT MUCH HESITATION BECAUSE HE CAN TOUCH-TYPE. DRAMATIC SPACE OPERA MUSIC STARTS TO RISE.

CLYDE: Steel's mission was profoundly dangerous with certain death lurking in every corner. It was a difficult three-part assignment, only given to the bravest and most intelligent Space Patrolmen. Steel would have to: 1) Baby-sit his little sister; 2) Finish his homework; and 3) Run some errands for his mother. But Steel was supremely confident. He knew that he was up to the challenge. Soon the women of Earth would forget all about that bed-wetting problem of his...

SOUND: HEROIC THEME STOPS SHORT.

STEEL/ISAACS: (in unison/horrified) *What?!*

Scene Two

Somewhere beyond time and space.

SOUND:

STRANGE OSCILLATIONS THAT INDICATE NARRATIVE NON-TIME.

CLYDE:

(VO, mature) That's essentially a true story. Sheldon was living vicariously through this ultra-phallic, totally represented superhero we created. And somehow he was sure that together, we could get someone to publish the adventures of space-dork here. I didn't know any better, so I agreed to help.

ISAACS:

(B.G., still a teenager) ...just a minute... just a minute...

CLYDE:

The trouble was that he got so obsessed with the project that he wouldn't let me do any of the writing unless he absolutely had to.

ISAACS:

...but I've really got to get these ideas down...

CLYDE:

So I did what any idealistic and reasonably articulate adolescent would do. I waited until he was vulnerable and I tried to humiliate him.

ISAACS:

(upset) Hey! What did you write this silly stuff for?!

SOUND:

SHIFTING FORCES OF NON-TIME GROW FASTER AND MORE COMPLEX.

CLYDE:

This story is pretty much autobiographical. It has aliens, spacecraft, mind control, dreams of galactic conquest, movie contracts and divorce settlements that cover property acquired over the last three billion years. You know, post-modern social realism.

This part of the story takes place in New York City.

It is the year 1937. I'm 17 years old and my friends and I are all aspiring, but unpublished, writers in the artistic field that will some day be referred to as science fiction. We were strange kids—with our thick glasses, bad clothes and haircuts and acne— we were prototype geeks who really worried about what would happen to us if the Earth were suddenly sucked into a galactic whirlpool. We called ourselves "The Fabulists" and we kept ourselves going by self-publishing in these mimeographed newsletters called "fanzines" while we waited for human intelligence to evolve to a state where others could understand the true merit of our work.

Scene Three

The office of Stewart D. McReady, editor of *Tremendous Stories of Super Science*. A few days after the events at Sheldon Isaacs' home.

McREADY: Miss Williams, have you seen my cigarette holder?

WILLIAMS: Is it on the crystal radio?

McREADY: No, I already looked there.

WILLIAMS: How about under your microscope?

SOUND: <u>SHUFFLING OF OBJECTS AND PAPERS ON MCREADY'S DESK.</u>

McREADY: No, not there.

WILLIAMS: Try the gyroscope.

McREADY: Good god! What's it doing there?

SOUND: <u>MCREADY LIGHTS A MATCH AND INHALES.</u>

McREADY: I wonder what it was doing there.

CLYDE: (V.O., mature) Then this gentleman appeared on the creative landscape: Stewart D. McReady, the new editor of *Tremendous Stories of Super Science*. McReady was one of our favourites. He wrote about space ships bigger than New Jersey, Brain Stealers from Saturn and cities on the Moon powered by the energy from thought itself. This guy wrote about stuff that really mattered! We Fabulists knew that McReady was our big chance.

McREADY: Would you like to play with my electric gyroscope, Miss Williams?

SOUND: <u>WHIR OF THE GYROSCOPE.</u>

McREADY: It really is quite a remarkable apparatus.

WILLIAMS: No, thanks.

SOUND: <u>WHIR OF THE GYROSCOPE DEEPENS AND RATTLES A LITTLE AS MCREADY SETS IT ON HIS DESKTOP. THE WHIR CONTINUES IN THE B.G AS MCREADY SPEAKS.</u>

CLYDE: (V.O.) Here was a guy who would appreciate our genius.

McREADY: Very well, let's resume dictation. (inhales on his cigarette) Where were we?

WILLIAMS: (reading back from her notes) "...I regret that I cannot consider your manuscript for publication in its present form..."

McREADY: Right. (in a more formal voice) Although your story does manage to avoid any gross scientific or technical errors, the future society you postulate is implausible in the extreme. Frankly, these problems go beyond mere implausibilities and I can only regard them as outright predictive *howlers*. (inhales) Miss Williams, I want you to underline the word "howlers" throughout this letter. Do you understand?

WILLIAMS: Yes, underline "howlers".

McREADY: Now, these *howlers* include the idea that the United States will enter another World War in the near future. This will just not happen, Mr. Mitchell, America will never enter another foolish European squabble and the world of the future will be too rational and well ordered to allow war to escalate to this extent again.

SOUND: <u>MCREADY PAUSES TO TAKE A LONG DRAG OF HIS CIGARETTE. HE THEN EXHALES FOR AN EQUALLY LONG TIME.</u>

McREADY: Besides, the horror of poison gas is simply too great a deterrent to the all-out war experienced in

	1917 and '18. Today, no one nation could ever emerge as the clear winner, etc. etc.
WILLIAMS:	Do you want me to type in the last five paragraphs of your letter to Mr. Heinlein about right here?
McREADY:	Yes, but be sure to underline the "howlers" from there as well.
SOUND:	A SMALL SWITCH IS FLIPPED. THE WHIRRING SOUND GROWS FASTER.
McREADY:	Look, Miss Williams, I can increase the gyroscope's speed.
WILLIAMS:	Yes.
McREADY:	(back in his dictation voice) Another thing, Mr. Mitchell, why do you always make the fascists in your stories look so bad? Personally, I don't know why people are so bothered about Hitler. As far as I can see, all the man wants to do is establish a rational society. This thing about race and anti-Semitism is just a public relations problem—
SOUND:	SUDDEN AND DULL THUD. THE GYROSCOPE FALLS OFF MCREADY'S DESK AND SPINS ACROSS THE FLOOR AND OUT THE DOOR.
McREADY:	Miss Williams! You kicked my desk!
WILLIAMS:	Sorry, my foot slipped.
McREADY:	Well, try to be more careful. (back in dictation voice) Don't believe everything you read in the papers, son. And I want to make science fiction the literature of ideas. So why don't you write me a story where the Nazis get to be the good guys?
SOUND:	THE RECEDING WHIR OF THE GYROSCOPE AS IT INSANELY WHIZZES DOWN THE HALL.

Scene Four

	The Clyde family kitchen. One week after the events in McReady's office.
McREADY:	(V.O.) ...and one last comment: I can't quite nail it down, but there's a creeping sentimentality in your prose. Now, I've nothing against sentiment—golly, if some professor of literature sent me the right yarn, I'd print it in a microsecond. But such a thing ain't happened yet. The tone of *Tremendous Stories* is...
MITCHELL:	(reading from McReady's letter, fades in over the editor's voice) ...a hard-nosed, brass-tacks, no-nonsense, both-feet-on-the-ground peek at mankind's next few billion years. The weak and backward-looking perspective of today's poets and philosophers just don't cut it; you have to approach the future like an engineer!
CLYDE:	(in awe) Jeez!
SOUND:	MITCHELL LOUDLY CRUSHING THE LETTER IN HIS FIST.
MITCHELL:	(enraged) *Moron!*
CLYDE:	Did you see all the hyphenated words? I've never seen so many in a single sentence. That's got to be some kind of an achievement...
MITCHELL:	(even angrier) *Absolute* moron!
CLYDE:	Don't sweat it, Mitch.
SOUND:	CLYDE UNCRUMPLES THE LETTER.
MITCHELL:	*Crash and die on Saturn's rings!*
CLYDE:	I don't think you can crash into them, Mitch. As-

	tronomers seem to think the rings are gas or ice crystals or something.
MITCHELL:	*Shut up!*
CLYDE:	Hey, Mitch, its not like this is a standard rejection letter here. He's put a lot of effort into this letter. McReady must figure you're a pretty serious talent.
MITCHELL:	(getting progressively angrier) That's crap. The man's obviously got no life and he must be some kind of compulsive. What you've got in your hand is the toilet paper used to deal with (now completely losing it) *Stewart D. McReady's verbal diarrhea!*
SOUND:	<u>MUFFLED THUD AND AN ODD METALLIC "SQUISH".</u>
CLYDE:	Hey! Don't hit the typewriter!
MITCHELL:	*Ouch! Hell!*
CLYDE:	*That's my mom's!*
SOUND:	<u>A LONG PAUSE WHILE MITCHELL'S BREATHING SLOWS AS HE CALMS DOWN.</u>
MITCHELL:	I'm sorry, Robert. Allow me to make amends.
SOUND:	<u>AS MITCHELL SPEAKS WE HEAR SOFT "PINGS" AS HE RELEASES ALL THE TYPEWRITER KEYS HE JAMMED DOWN WITH HIS FIST.</u>
MITCHELL:	Not only did the man not like my story... he didn't like the premise... he didn't like the social commentary... and... I don't think he likes the author!
CLYDE:	Oh, come on.
MITCHELL:	Further, it is very likely that Mr. McReady has never liked anything the author has *ever* written... (grows progressively angrier again) ...*may* write in the future, or even *think* about writing *throughout the infinity of time and—*

CLYDE: Hey! Don't hit the typewriter!

MITCHELL: Sorry... sorry...

CLYDE: Well, it looks like you fixed it.

MITCHELL: I really am sorry. I didn't want to deprive you of your means of production.

CLYDE: But I think you're wrong. Even if McReady is a flaming A.H., he wouldn't have time to put this amount of effort into a writer with no potential.

MITCHELL: Actually, I doubt it was much work at all for him. There's barely an original word in the whole damn letter.

CLYDE: Now, how can you know that?

MITCHELL: He's been singing the same brown shirt song to Poole and Freedman.

CLYDE: (shocked) You mean, you guys are comparing rejection letters?

MITCHELL: Yes, it's been very informative. I'm trying to invent a new form of collective bargaining.

CLYDE: I thought you said you were an artist.

MITCHELL: I am. But we Fabulists are obviously the lowest class in the creative hierarchy, so we need all the group action we can get.

CLYDE: Maybe so, but we can't force anybody to publish us.

MITCHELL: Do you know he even criticized the typeface on the manuscript. This man doesn't like your mother's typewriter! I bet he doesn't like your mother, either.

CLYDE: (a little hurt) You're welcome to use someone else's machine if you can do better.

MITCHELL: (strangely cheerful) Not at all, Robert. For a bourgeois, your mother is a fine person...

SOUND: <u>MITCHELL LOADS A SHEET OF PAPER INTO THE TYPEWRITER AND ROLLS IT INTO POSITION.</u>

MITCHELL: ...and this device should suit our purposes very nicely.

Scene Five

A diner in New York City. That evening.

CLYDE: (V.O., mature) We Fabulists had an active interest in the careers of our fellow artistes, and we were very understanding. We rarely allowed the fact that some of them had prostituted themselves by actually getting paid for their stories influence our opinion of them.

SOUND: <u>SHUFFLING OF SEATS, RATTLE OF CUTLERY AND MURMERED CONVERSATIONS IN THE DINER.</u>

CLYDE: (V.O., cont'd) We are now moving into the realm of the Pros.

SOUND: <u>DINER SOUNDS RISE.</u>

EVANSTON: Three and a half hours? That's a long meeting. Was he after some big re-writes?

CROSS: He required no changes in words.

EVANSTON: You mean he didn't buy the story?

CROSS: He bought the stories. McReady always buys my stories.

EVANSTON: So what were you two talking about for three and a half hours?

CROSS: He wanted to discuss my interest in Applied Semiotics.

EVANSTON: (with disbelief) What for?

CROSS: He behaves in ways that suggest fascination. To quote him: "I can't believe a mind like yours came from the backwoods of Canada."

EVANSTON: My god, at times I can't believe how provincial McReady can be.

CROSS: Perhaps. He was certainly mistaken; to be accurate he should have said the prairies.

EVANSTON: Right. (pauses to take a drink of something) On the other hand I know all about Saskatchewan—from my travels with the Cree.

CROSS: The Cree Indians?

EVANSTON: That's right. (another pause to drink) Did I ever tell you how I rode across the north with Edmund Curtis? As part of my graduate studies with Franz Boas?

CROSS: I have no recollection of you saying that. Was this before or after your assignment on the submarine in the Atlantic?

EVANSTON: (coughs) In between tours, Jay. That's why I didn't finish my doctorate. Boas said they committed a crime against ethnology when they called me back into service.

CROSS: Thank you for the additional information.

SOUND: EVANSTON CUTTING HIS FOOD LOUDLY.

EVANSTON: (mouth full for part of this) Now, I've never met with McReady for more than five minutes running. He just phones me up and invokes the "Three B's".

CROSS: Three Bees? Please explain.

EVANSTON: The Three B's. McReady's Laws of Editorial Technology: Beg, Buy and Bugger Off! (laughs) Developed by said McReady to exploit the creative energies of his most reliable contributors.

CROSS: (still uncertain) Thank you for clarifying.

EVANSTON: Of course, since I'm McReady's most popular and prolific writer, you'd think that he'd want to hear all about *my* theories of scientific philosophy.

CROSS: I don't understand your statement.

EVANSTON: Well, like that Applied Semiotics stuff you keep putting into your stories. My logical universal hypothesis of science and things is also the background for my work.

CROSS: I was not aware of that.

EVANSTON: Are you kidding me?

CROSS: No, I have been unaware of any underlying meaning in your written work.

EVANSTON: (annoyed) Are you meaning to tell me that you didn't think that "Plight of the Moon Maidens", voted by readers as the most popular *Tremendous* story of 1935, was a profoundly philosophical work?

CROSS: Um, let me process—

EVANSTON: Hell, man! I'm an important thinker! I've studied hypnotism with the Lamas of Ceylon!

CROSS: No hostility was intended. I convey my apologies. Perhaps I had difficulty in assimilating the fundamental constructs in your narratives.

SOUND: EVANSTON TAKES A LONG DRINK.

EVANSTON: Yeah, that must have been it. (sighs) Still, I shouldn't condemn my fellow writers. Besides, I do know that I've been an unconscious influence on your work.

CROSS: (suddenly very serious) Please clarify and detail the exact nature of your unconscious influence on my mind.

EVANSTON: Uh, well... uh... well... obviously you picked up some of the ideas from reading some of my stories... Hey! What are you doing with that notebook?

CROSS: Objectifying data. Now, you are saying that the printed configuration of letters, words and sentence units in your stories, in some manner—ma-

	nipulated my thought processes?
EVANSTON:	Uh, sure. Of course! Like I said, you must have picked up a couple of minor ideas from my ongoing research.
CROSS:	Please explain how your research activities manifest themselves.
EVANSTON:	Well... well... well... ever since my induction into the South African Brotherhood of the Yak, I've been working on some really detailed studies of the true meaning of the universe and the human condition. That's why I write science fiction, to fund my more serious work.
CROSS:	Have you documented your efforts to quantify and laterally externalize your inquiries into human existence into physical reality?
EVANSTON:	Have I...? Oh, do you mean, have I written any of it down? (relieved) Why, yes. Yes, I have! I've been putting together a major collection of real learned essays. The present draft draws heavily on my Asian travels and my time as a theology student at Cambridge.
CROSS:	How have you organized this datum?
EVANSTON:	The working title of the book is *Ultimate Argument.* I'd let you see it, but in its present form you might find it too, ah, *intense.*
CROSS:	Please define the word "intense" in this context.
EVANSTON:	(whispers) Jay, three editors and an Oxford don have been driven mad just by reading the manuscript. It's very, very strong stuff.
CROSS:	Please define the words "driven mad" in this context.
EVANSTON:	Mad, nuts, cuckoo, around the bend and out the window. None of them got past the middle of chapter four.

CROSS: (voice quivers a little with excitement) I am experiencing a very subjective emotional state: excitement. Therefore, my next statement may not be semantically precise: Please state the main thesis of your research project.

EVANSTON: Evanston's "Three M's", man! Mind, Matter and Manipulation! Stewart D. McReady may think he's the great technocrat of the future, well, I've plotted out the mechanics of the human soul

Scene Six

"Camp Fantastic"—the shared NYC apartment of Fabulists Rolf Densen, Dave Poole and Francis Freedman. Evening, a few days later.

SOUND: <u>DENSEN TYPING, POOLE LOADING PAPERS INTO A GESTETNER MACHINE. IN THE B.G. A GRAMOPHONE IS PLAYING A 78 RPM RECORDING OF "VENUS" FROM HOLST'S *THE PLANETS.*</u>

POOLE: I've got the letter column ready to go.

FREEDMAN: So print it out. We can do the layouts for the other pages later.

SOUND: <u>ROLLING DRUM OFF THE GESTETNER, PICKING UP PAGES AND THEN SPITTING THEM OUT.</u>

POOLE: Gawd, I can't believe Mitchell had the guts to write this!

DENSEN: It ought to shake a few people up.

MITCHELL: (V.O.) An open letter to the Camp Fantastic Leader-Post and Revelational Bulletin...

MUSIC: <u>THE MUSIC ON THE GRAMOPHONE GRADUALLY BUILDS INTO THE *"MARS: THE BRINGER OF WAR"* MOVEMENT FROM HOLST'S COMPOSITION, IN POWERFUL SURROUND SOUND!</u>

MITCHELL: Readers of science fiction, Awake! Arise! We have been betrayed!

SILBERBERG: (cont'd) Science fiction is the natural province of youth; its stories of imagination are the clarion of social progress and often the warning signs of disaster!

WARREN: (cont'd) We are the ones who must challenge the injustices and crises of today, and have the courage to live in the fantastic world of tomorrow!

WEISS: (cont'd) But none other than Stewart D. McReady has cruelly undermined us! A man we once believed to be a thinker and an editor of the highest principles!

ZUCKERMAN: (cont'd) Here is a man who claims to espouse the values of Science, Reason and Technologically-Based Democracy!

MITCHELL: (cont'd) Here is a man who is a liar!

MILLER: (cont'd) McReady is nothing more than a posturing, bellowing fascist! As the Mussolini of the Scientific Romance, he represents nothing more than the perpetration of ignorance, economic dominance and mental enslavement of the masses!

GRUNWALD: (cont'd) McReady has mercilessly and systematically censored and suppressed the work of some of our most talented and courageous young writers!

ALL: (in unison) McReady's reign of literary terror must end!

MITCHELL: (cont'd) At the First World Science Fiction Convention in New York City, the best and brightest of America's youth will assemble and together we shall proudly proclaim the true purpose of science fiction:

ALL: (in unison) *To be the vanguard in the creation of a scientific socialist world state!*

SOUND: THE MUSIC OF *"MARS: THE BRINGER OF WAR"* BLARES TO ITS STRANGE BUT TREMENDOUS CLIMAX.

Scene Seven

Somewhere beyond time and space.

SOUND: <u>STRANGE OSCILLATING SOUNDS THAT INDICATE NARRATIVE NON-TIME.</u>

CLYDE: (VO, mature) A little social history here. There was more to the 1930s than a lot of black and white movies of guys in overcoats and hats standing around in bread lines. We had massive unemployment, and people like Hitler and Stalin seemed to be on the rise. These things were damned bizarre, but they weren't science fiction. No, they were the realities we had to live with.

SOUND: <u>ODD ELECTRONIC BEEPS AND TONES AND THE CLATTERING OF TICKER-TAPE AS CLYDE PUNCHES NUMBERS INTO THE COMPULATOR KEYBOARD.</u>

CLYDE: Now, I'm going to use this Electrostatic Compulator, a period science fiction version of a super-computer, to give you a better sense of the context people like the Fabulists were living in.

SOUND: <u>MORE BEEPS AND CLATTERS AS CLYDE INPUTS INFORMATION.</u>

CLYDE: Let's calculate the probability of a kid in the 1930s—about my age, temperament and background, growing up to be more or less normal—getting a college education, having a productive, satisfying career, and enjoying a long and happy marriage... and in a society governed by justice, prosperity and general good will.

SOUND: <u>RAPID TICKING AS THE COMPULATOR "THINKS".</u>

COMPULATOR: (mechanical voice) For-get it!

CLYDE: So, for kids like us Fabulists, the possibilities offered by the conventional world looked pretty limited. Getting a job or a girlfriend was about as easy as strapping on your jet-pack, flying to Neptune and waging war on the King of the Gecko People. And the Neptune option certainly sounded more interesting than working in your parents' grocery store for the rest of your life.

SOUND: A SET OF FOOTSTEPS APPROACHING CLYDE AND THE COMPULATOR ACROSS THE DEPTHS OF NARRATIVE NON-TIME.

CLYDE: Still, even under these circumstances, a lot of science fiction fans were pretty strange. Allow me to demonstrate.

SOUND: THE FOOTSTEPS STOP.

ZUCKERMAN: Hello.

CLYDE: I would like to introduce an old associate of mine, Mr. Stanley Zuckerman. Now Stanley never joined the Fabulists—because he never wrote any fiction. But he was a well-known B.N.F.—Big-Name Fan for you outsiders. As such, Stanley was a pretty important fixture in my personal and professional world.

ZUCKERMAN: Of course.

CLYDE: And we're looking at Stanley as I knew him in 1937—essentially his intellectual and physical peak. This is a prime time to explore his inner universe.

SOUND: CRACKLE OF SMALL ELECTRICAL DISCHARGES, FAINT HOWL OF RADIO STATIC.

CLYDE: Are you ready, Stanley?

ZUCKERMAN: Yeah, yeah.

SOUNDS: HOLLOW CLUNKING AND RUSTLING AS CLYDE PLACES A LARGE METALLIC HELMET ON ZUCKERMAN'S HEAD AND STRAPS IT ON.

CLYDE: You're going to love this, Stanley—it involves exotic technology...

ZUCKERMAN: (now enthusiastic) Hey, great!

CLYDE: You're wearing an electro-hypno-mental-lo-transmitter.

ZUCKERMAN: (still enthusiastic—the word "kewl" hasn't been invented yet) *Really?*

CLYDE: Really. Now, I'm going to ask you a few questions and the transmitter will feed your answers into the compulator which will apply the god-like powers of Mechanized Science to determine the perfect and eternal truth embodied in your answers. Pretty neat, huh?

ZUCKERMAN: *Yeah!*

CLYDE: I'll just speak into the machine's microphone here...

SOUND: BRIEF HOWL OF FEEDBACK.

CLYDE: (cont'd, voice now distorted through a small speaker) Let's start with something simple. Stanley Zuckerman, where do you live?

ZUCKERMAN: I have an apartment in New York City.

SOUND: RAPID CLICKS OF TICKER TAPE SHOOTING THROUGH A MACHINE.

COMPULATOR: (flat mechanical voice) He-lives-with-his-mother.

CLYDE: Well, we're off to a fine start here. (into the microphone) Stanley, what do you do for a living?

ZUCKERMAN: I'm self-employed as a literary critic and intellectual commentator.

COMPULATOR: He-is-un-employ-ed.

CLYDE: (laughs a little) Okay... Stanley, so what are your career goals and professional aspirations?

ZUCKERMAN: To be a respected artist and devote my life to scientific education.

SOUND: <u>MORE RAPID CLICKS.</u>

COMPULATOR: This-person-will-never-earn-more-than-$500-a-year.

CLYDE: Inspiring stuff, isn't it, folks? Remember this demonstration when you see those "earn big bucks as a science fiction writer" ads in *The Times Literary Supplement.* So, Stan: what about your education? Are you attending college? Have you cultivated a life-long love of learning?

ZUCKERMAN: (proudly) I have a recorded I.Q. of 187. Conventional schooling was stifling me. Therefore I am pursuing a program of self-education.

SOUND: <u>MORE RAPID CLICKS.</u>

COMPULATOR: His-in-telli-gence-quo-tient-is-one-hun-dred-and-eight-y-seven-how-ever-lack-of-dis-ci-pline-and-low-self-es-teem-forced-him-to-leave-school.

ZUCKERMAN: (furious) *The hell with you—you damned tin can!*

CLYDE: Speaking of which, how's your emotional life, Stan? Any exciting romantic entanglements these days?

ZUCKERMAN: I have been involved in a number of intimate liaisons with different women.

COMPULATOR: In-correct-this-per-son-has-se-vere-prob-lems-with-social-en-counters-with-the-oppo-site-sex-often-re-sulting-in-out-breaks-of-facial-blem-ishes.

CLYDE: I'm getting different stories here. Who should I believe?

ZUCKERMAN: Your machine's gone wacky.

COMPULATOR: This-man-will-die-a-vir-gin.

CLYDE: Hm. Let's just table that line of questioning for a while. So, Stanley, where's your life heading? What's your destiny? What are your greatest potentials?

ZUCKERMAN: (suddenly very excited) To become a superior being! Did you see the last issue of *Astounding Stories*? The novel *Slan* by A.E. Van Vogt—it says it all!

CLYDE: Really? And what's the big revelation?

ZUCKERMAN: (emphatic) Fans! Science fiction fans! Fans are slans! We are mutants with superior mental powers. *Fans are slans!* Someday in the near future we will reveal ourselves and step forward as *the next step in human evolution!*

CLYDE: I see. I can't understand why I didn't spot your awesome superiority right away.

ZUCKERMAN: I admit I have a way to go in my evolutionary development.

CLYDE: (into microphone) Compulator, what do you make of all this? What is Stanley Zuckerman's ultimate destiny?

COMPULATOR: Pro-cess-ing... sampl-ing-fu-ture-time...

SOUND: FRANTIC RATTLING OF SWITCHES AND TICKER TAPE.

COMPULATOR: He-will-con-tinue-in-this-life-pat-tern-un-til-1942-when-he-forges-medi-cal-doc-u-ment-s-and-joins-com-bat-forces...for-ideo-logical-rea-sons...he-will-die-soon-after-ward...

Scene Eight

The action alternates between Camp Fantastic and the Editorial Head Offices of Samuels and Steadman Publications. It is about ten days after the publication of Mitchell's letter in the Fabulist Bulletin.

SOUND: <u>DOOR OPENS AND CLOSES QUIETLY.</u>

McREADY: (uncertain) Mr. Steadman?

STEADMAN: Just a moment, Stewart... (pause) ...just let me make a note here. There! Good to see you again. Have a chair.

McREADY: Thank you. I understand you wanted to see me right away, Mr. Steadman.

STEADMAN: That's right, Stewart. We're just pulling together the financial report for this quarter and we'd like to chat with you about one or two small things.

SOUND: <u>POOLE LOUDLY STAPLING SHEETS OF PAPER ON A CARD TABLE. THEN, SHARP KNOCKING AT THE DOOR OF CAMP FANTASTIC.</u>

POOLE: (calls) Enter ye, and abandon all virtue and sanity!

SOUND: <u>DOOR OPENS. FOOTSTEPS AS RAY ANN SPARKS MARCHES IN.</u>

SPARKS: Hello. I hope I'm in the right place.

POOLE: Of course you are. (pause) So, where are we?

McREADY: Sir, I think the sales figures show that my new editorial policies are working. Our circulation...

STEADMAN: (sighs) To be blunt, Stewart: 25% of 00.8% of our

total monthly distribution outlay does really comprise a major fiscal pillar in the corporate edifice.

McREADY: (shaken) Well, I suppose if you want to cast everything in terms of absolute numbers...

STEADMAN: Still, I do have to admit that you have managed to turn your little corner of the pulps division into a pretty tight operation—and the graphic quality of the magazine is much more consistent...

McREADY: Thank you.

STEADMAN: Mediocre, but consistent.

McREADY: T-thank you, sir.

STEADMAN: Now, Stu, do buck up! No one is suggesting that *Tremendous Stories'* less than tremendous performance is in any way your fault. We just have some tiny little questions about your long-term future at this company...

SPARKS: (strident) I'm here to join the Movement!

POOLE: So, I guess you're not here to help me staple these newsletters, huh?

SPARKS: That wasn't my first plan.

POOLE: I see, so what movement are you so keen to join?

SPARKS: (earnest) The *Mitchellist Movement!* I'm here to struggle to create a modern utopia based on scientific values. So, where do I sign up? What are we supposed to do?

POOLE: Besides stapling? Well... (pause) ...listen, how did you find out about Mitchellism?

SOUND: SPARKS RUMMAGING THROUGH A MASSIVE BACKPACK. LITTLE THUDS AS SHE DROPS A SERIES OF PULP MAGAZINES ON THE CARD TABLE.

SPARKS: My old boyfriend got me reading this stuff. I found I couldn't put them down... now where is it? I found this one issue with a story by a guy named Weinbaum, then this guy Heinlein, and a real weirdo named Van Vogt...

POOLE: (a little cool) Yeah, sometimes there's some pretty good stuff in *Astounding*.

SPARKS: Well, to be blunt, a lot of the prose reads like it was written by gorillas, but the concepts... (very excited) ...incredible! Do you know that we are on the verge of a new era of advanced consciousness for the human race?

POOLE: Well...

SPARKS: (very serious) Now, did you?!

POOLE: ...that does sound a little familiar to me.

SPARKS: Aha! There it is—issue four of the Camp Fantastic Leader-Post and Revelational Bulletin! Another one of my boyfriends brought this to a Party social. He thought it was funny, but he's a materialistic cretin. I think it's amazing! And so progressive!

POOLE: (a little surprised) Really? You think so?

SPARKS: (passionate) Yes, I do! I must meet Gerald Mitchell and his Fabulists! *They are the wave of the future!*

McREADY: (shaken) My future?

STEADMAN: Well, it's only fair that you know that we are concerned. We're starting to wonder if there's a real market for scientific romances anymore, and we even have some doubts about whether a publishing firm of our reputation should even be in the business of selling such peculiar (with mild disdain) *genre* fiction.

McREADY: You mean, you're thinking of dropping your line of pulp magazines?

STEADMAN: Oh, not *all* of them. Anyway, my understanding is that a lot of the young people who are so enthusiastic about this scientifiction stuff don't even buy the magazines anymore; they prefer to print their own, I'm sure quite dreadful, stories.

McREADY: (rallies a little) That's a slight misconception, sir. Most of my reader mail comes from people who print those fanzines... and regular fans like that are an important part of my readership.

STEADMAN: And do I misunderstand the rather peculiar content of some of your readers' mail, Stu?

McREADY: What do you mean, sir?

STEADMAN: My understanding is that a significant number of our so-called fans are organizing a letter-writing campaign. Attacking you personally...

McREADY: It's just a few cranks, sir.

STEADMAN: I understand that this is the most mail *Tremendous* has ever received. And we see these as very serious letters. Some of them are calling you a Nazi, and they are casting doubt on the patriotism of Samuels and Steadman, old chum.

McREADY: (suddenly furious) *That's a filthy lie!*

STEADMAN: I say, steady on, Stewart.

McREADY: (ranting) And you can't let them stop me! Not when I'm on the verge of finally breaking through! Those punks may hate my guts, but they praise my writers in the same letters. *They love my writers!*

STEADMAN: Now, Stewart...

McREADY: (still ranting) Some people don't like me very much. That doesn't bother me, and it really shouldn't bother you, Mr. Steadman. You want to know why? Because I am cultivating, *carefully cultivating*, a stable of the very best science fiction writers, and soon, *very soon, Tremendous Stories* will be the world's greatest magazine of its type. Which even for a (with conviction) *genre* publication will be a damned impressive achievement!

SOUND:	MCREADY BREATHING HEAVILY AS HE TRIES TO CALM DOWN. HIS BREATH IS A LITTLE THICK AND FORCED.
STEADMAN:	I see.
McREADY:	Sir, I-I'm sorry. My allergies tend to flare up a bit at times like this…
STEADMAN:	Probably over-work. Well, far be it for me in my minor role as chief executive and co-owner of this organization to interfere with your grand design.
SOUND:	STEADMAN LIGHTS A MATCH AND INHALES ON A CIGAR. MCREADY SNIFFS AND COUGHS A LITTLE.
STEADMAN:	All right, Mr. McReady. You keep tending to your stable and we'll see how things work out.
McREADY:	(subdued) Thank you, Mr. Steadman.
STEADMAN:	That's all, Mr. McReady.
SOUND:	MCREADY'S FOOTSTEPS HEADING TO THE DOOR, TURNS DOOR KNOB AND PULLS DOOR HALFWAY OPEN.
STEADMAN:	And one last thing: clear up this nastiness with the post. It's starting to look silly in the mailroom.
McREADY:	(still subdued) Yes, sir. I'll take care of it.
SOUND:	SHUFFLING OF OBJECTS BEING MOVED AROUND ON THE CARD TABLE.
SPARKS:	What are you doing?
POOLE:	Looking for my cigarette. Look, I really don't know how to say this, but we really aren't all that organized around here.
SPARKS:	Is that why you can't find your cigarette?
POOLE:	No, in terms of Mitchellism.
SPARKS:	That's okay, I'm good at organizing things.

POOLE: There you are!

SPARKS: That's a very oppressed-looking cigarette.

POOLE: Mitchellism isn't a political party. There aren't any card-carrying Mitchellists around. In fact, there really aren't all that many people involved in the whole thing.

SPARKS: Are you saying it's some kind of hoax? But what about this newsletter? Why would my boyfriend bring it to YCL headquarters?

POOLE: How would I know? Some of us joined the Party. They thought we ought to use science fiction as a political recruiting device.

SPARKS: Well, it worked for me, only in reverse. (angry) What a sap I am!

POOLE: Don't feel so bad. Most of us agree with what Mitch is saying, but we have very different views on how practical his program is. The whole thing is pretty informal.

SPARKS: You mean imaginary?

POOLE: Well, I wouldn't go as far as that. But admittedly... at this point... membership in the Mitchellist move-ment will only gain you entry into (with mock grandness) *the Invisible City of Futuria!*

SPARKS: So it's more of a state of mind? (laughs wearily) A streamlined church with fins?

POOLE: (a smile in his voice) Yeah, something like that.

SPARKS: So you're telling me that this trip out here may have been a waste of time.

POOLE: I suppose that depends on how much you value the imagination.

SPARKS: If you can find me another cigarette, the afternoon won't have been a complete waste.

POOLE: Sorry...

SOUND:	<u>POOLE STRIKES A MATCH AND INHALES ON HIS CIGARETTE.</u>
POOLE:	...this is my last one.
SPARKS:	That's okay.
POOLE:	Hey! (laughs in surprise) Let go of my wrist!
SOUND:	<u>SPARKS TAKES A LONG DRAG OFF POOLE'S CIGARETTE.</u>
SPARKS:	Sharing is what communism is all about.

Scene Nine

The basement meeting room of the Queens district of the Young Communist League Headquarters. Three days later.

ISAACS: (whispers) We shouldn't be here, we could get into trouble.

MITCHELL: (tired) W-what was that?

ISAACS: Well, I mean the people who work here, they're communists, aren't they?

MITCHELL: (patiently) That's right, Sheldon. That's why it says Young Communist League on the front door.

ISAACS: But everybody knows that communists are a bunch of subversives.

MITCHELL: Sheldon, please... (sighs)

CLYDE: Why don't we begin? That way we can get finished that much quicker and go home sooner.

MITCHELL: We can't start until David gets here.

SOUND: DOOR OPENS, TWO SETS OF FOOTSTEPS APPROACH.

CLYDE: Hi, David.

POOLE: Sorry we're late.

MITCHELL: No problem, we were about to start Sheldon's political education. Thank you for sparing us that.

POOLE: Gentlemen, I'd like to introduce you to Miss Ray Ann Sparks. Ray is a junior cell leader in the League in the Queens area. She's also become very interested in Gerald's recent editorials in the Bulletin.

MITCHELL: So I gathered.

POOLE: Ray has a proposition to put to the group.

SPARKS: (with confidence) Comrades, it's an honour to meet you...

ISAACS: (giggles)

DENSEN: Nice to meet you... (trails off)

SPARKS: Excuse me, is there something wrong?

CLYDE: You'll have to excuse Mr. Densen and Sheldon. We think it's a Pavlovian Response. Every time they're exposed to any form of female stimulus they react with an infantile response.

DENSEN: (angry) Oh, yeah! Well, what do you know, anyway?

CLYDE: Stunning wit there, Dennie.

DENSEN: (mutters) Moron.

SPARKS: Perhaps this is a bad time?

CLYDE: Don't worry, just go ahead. These two have very limited memory capacities. They'll join into the conversation once they forget what we were just talking about.

SPARKS: Well... as David was saying, I read Gerald Mitchell's articles and I think they are really interesting, they sum up what's truly exciting about science fiction.

MITCHELL: Thank you.

SPARKS: Gerald has told me about your writer's collective and a few of us in the Party think you have a real contribution to make to the evolution of World Socialism.

DENSEN: (timidly) What's a collective?

ISAACS: I think it's communist for club.

CLYDE: So why do you want to see us? You think we might like to use your meeting space?

SPARKS: (smile in her voice) We had something more ambitious in mind. The YCL is interested in financing a new science fiction magazine. The circulation would be limited at first, but all of you would be part of the joint editorial committee...

ISAACS: I'm not so good on committees.

SPARKS: ...and obviously you would be the main contributors. At least until you built up a supply of literary workers.

MITCHELL: Thanks but no thanks. I can't see getting involved in another fanzine right now.

POOLE: This won't be another fanzine.

SPARKS: It won't be *LIFE* or *LOOK* but it will be a good-looking publication. Reasonable paper stock, nice typeface and even colour covers. We want this to be something young people will take seriously.

ISAACS: (suspicious) So, what's in it for you?

SPARKS: We all agree that science fiction is the pathway into the minds and hearts of American young people. Your role will be to turn these reading hearts down proper progressive routes.

DENSEN: What does that mean?

CLYDE: They want a political editorial policy.

ISAACS: (horrified) They want us to be commie stooges!

DENSEN: (delighted) Hey, neat!

POOLE: Is that a problem, guys? Sheldon, you have to know that some of us are already members of the Party: Me, Gerald, Bob...

CLYDE: Am I a communist?

ISAACS: How can you not know that?!

CLYDE: It must have slipped my mind. Anyway, my politics may have been keeping me out of print, so it would be nice if they got me published for once.

SOUND: <u>ISAACS VIOLENTLY PUSHING BACK HIS CHAIR AS HE RISES TO HIS FEET.</u>

ISAACS: (furious) Well, I'm not going to do it! No one's going to make into some stinking red!

SOUND: <u>FOOTSTEPS AS CLYDE FOLLOWS ISAACS.</u>

CLYDE: But Sheldon, this is my big chance. Now I can finally get all your great Alexander Steel stories in print.

SOUND: <u>FOOTSTEPS STOP.</u>

ISAACS: Maybe you're right, Bob. I owe it to our professional friendship. (pause) Besides, it's probably my patriotic duty to fight fascism.

CLYDE: So, come on back to the group.

SOUND: <u>FOOTSTEPS LEADING BACK TO THE CHAIRS.</u>

ISAACS: Okay.

SOUND: <u>CLYDE AND ISAACS SIT DOWN.</u>

SPARKS: So do we have an agreement?

MITCHELL/CLYDE/ISAACS/DENSEN: (sort of in unison) Yes, yeah, sure.

SPARKS: Then I propose that the highlight of the upcoming First World Science Fiction Convention be a public statement of the Mitchellist Manifesto—that will conclude with the announcement of a new magazine dedicated to progressive science fiction!

CLYDE: (VO, mature) Our vague, New York lefty inclinations had suddenly been roused into revolutionary zeal. And while we were planning the magazine, some of us came up with some pretty interesting names for it: *Tales of Dialectic Hyper-Materialism* was one. *Means of Production Wonder Stories* was another.

SOUND: <u>NON-TIME/NON-SPACE   OSCILLATING SOUND.</u>

CLYDE: (VO-cont'd) To my surprise, it was Sheldon and Denson who thought of the best title:

ISAACS: (distant, very excited) *Amazing Struggles!*

CLYDE: (VO) I still like that one. Mitchell was the one who really got caught up in all the excitement. At first, all he wanted to do was spew some venom and embarrass Stewart D. McReady. And now he was being set up as a technocratic socialist saviour, a young spokesman for the next American Revolution. (pause) Kind of a risky situation to find yourself in.

Scene Ten

McReady's office. The next day.

McREADY: Where was I?

WILLIAMS: (controlling her irritation) "Dear Sheldon".

McREADY: Of course. Dear Sheldon. I'm a little pressed for time so I regret to inform you that this will be a very brief letter. I also regret to say that I am unable to accept your latest submission... what was it, again?

WILLIAMS: "Outraged Virtue on Ganymede".

McREADY: Right. "Outraged Virtue on Ganymede" for publication in its present form. (clears his throat) But take heart, lad. You are beginning to show promise as a writer and there may be the off chance that we can salvage this one. Why don't you drop by sometime and we can talk about it... (fades)

Scene Eleven

McReady's office, two days later, it feels like two seconds later.

SOUND:

ISAACS: Hello? Mr. McReady?

McREADY: (surprised) Who?

ISAACS: I'm Sheldon Isaacs.

McREADY: Uhm, how...?

ISAACS: Sorry, I guess your secretary hasn't arrived yet.

McREADY: (now annoyed) What are you doing here?

ISAACS: I just received your letter. About my last submission, "Outraged Virtue—"

McREADY: (now friendly) "—on Ganymede"! Oh, yes. You must be Isaac Sheldon.

ISAACS: Sheldon Isaacs, sir.

WILLIAMS: (angry) Young man! You can't just charge into Mr. McReady's office!

McREADY: Could you excuse us? I believe I have an unscheduled editorial conference coming up.

WILLIAMS: Very well, Mr. McReady.

SOUND: DOOR SHUTS SHARPLY.

McREADY: Sheldon, my boy. Have a seat.

ISAACS: (in awe) Thank you, sir.

SOUND: FILE CABINET OPENS. SHUFFLING OF FILE

<table>
<tr><td></td><td><u>FOLDERS.</u></td></tr>
<tr><td>McREADY:</td><td>Now, where did I put that thing? Aha! Here it is. Your manuscript.</td></tr>
<tr><td><u>SOUND:</u></td><td><u>CREAKING OF WOOD AND METAL SPRINGS AS MCREADY SITS DOWN BEHIND HIS DESK.</u></td></tr>
<tr><td>McREADY:</td><td>Interesting work. Very interesting work, indeed.</td></tr>
<tr><td>ISAACS:</td><td>Thank you, sir.</td></tr>
<tr><td>McREADY:</td><td>Sheldon, the reason I asked you here is because I truly feel a strong sense of obligation to the future of science fiction. I feel that it's important to speak with young writers, guide them, channel them, in the right direction.</td></tr>
<tr><td>ISAACS:</td><td>(completely sincere) That's very noble of you, sir.</td></tr>
<tr><td>McREADY:</td><td>Now, in your case, I do see some real problems with this story...</td></tr>
<tr><td>ISAACS:</td><td>(upset) Oh, no!</td></tr>
<tr><td>McREADY:</td><td>...but there's still some real potential here. I seem to remember that this character of yours Horatio Steel—</td></tr>
<tr><td>ISAACS:</td><td>Alexander Steel.</td></tr>
<tr><td>McREADY:</td><td>Quite right. This isn't the first story you've sent me with him in it. Is it?</td></tr>
<tr><td>ISAACS:</td><td>(proud) So far, I've written twenty-two Alexander Steel stories. And I always send them in to you first.</td></tr>
<tr><td>McREADY:</td><td>Sheldon, I can't tell you how much I appreciate that.</td></tr>
<tr><td>ISAACS:</td><td>I thought you might feel that way!</td></tr>
<tr><td>McREADY:</td><td>Have any of these stories been published yet? I don't want my fellow editors to think that I'm poaching their talent.</td></tr>
<tr><td>ISAACS:</td><td>Well, nobody's paid me anything for them. My club newsletter has printed a few.</td></tr>
</table>

McREADY: Really?

ISAACS: (earnest) But only the really bad ones!

McREADY: (trying to sound off-hand) What kind of club is that?

ISAACS: The Fabulists. (laughs inanely) But I'm just a part-time member. I'm not a Red or anything. I just like to use the crokinole table.

McREADY: I understand, Sheldon. (a little pompous) True art is always above politics.

ISAACS: (serious) That's what I'm always telling them.

McREADY: Anyway, back to the manuscript. There are one or two spots where I need a little clarification.

ISAACS: Really, Mr. McReady? But I wrote it all down.

McREADY: Do you mind if I make a few notes while we talk?

SOUND: <u>RUSTLING OF PAPER.</u>

McREADY: Now, over here on page nine, you have the Chief of the Interplanetary Police Force chuckle happily as he orders a squadron of his rocketship crewmen to an almost certain death.

ISAACS: That's right!

McREADY: But in the rest of the story, the Chief is supposed to be a sympathetic character.

ISAACS: (enthusiastic) Oh, yes. Chief Korgle-Xon is a lovable curmudgeon. No matter what, he's always laughing and cheerful.

McREADY: Let's not worry about that right now.

SOUND: <u>FAINT SCRATCHING OF PEN ON PAPER.</u>

McREADY: It may be that characterization isn't one of your strong points.

ISAACS: But I thought he was a good character.

SOUND: <u>PEN MAKING A BIG 'X' ON A SHEET OF</u>

	<u>PAPER.</u>
McREADY:	Here's a bold thought, Sheldon: Why not get rid of Chief Korgle-Xon altogether?
ISAACS:	(hesitant) Well, I don't know, sir...
McREADY:	That way the story would be much more scientific.
ISAACS:	(now happy) Oh, okay!
SOUND:	<u>MORE RUSTLING OF PAPER.</u>
McREADY:	Now, later in the story, you have the Police Force using two rocketships to send Steel and Officer Gretchen O'Molly to Ganymede. There's a tiny logical problem here; even if we assume that anti-gravity fields and repulsor rays are commonplace by the year 1987, sending two spaceships to the same moon must be a pretty expensive proposition. Why don't they use the same ship?
ISAACS:	(horrified) All the way through the solar system? Alone? Together?! I'm sorry, Mr. McReady, but my career as a serious author would be over quick as a wink if my mother ever caught me writing smut!
McREADY:	(sighs) Okay, let's leave that one.
SOUND:	<u>MCREADY PUSHES A STACK OF PAPERS ACROSS THE DESK.</u>
McREADY:	Here is your manuscript back with my editorial comments.
ISAACS:	Gosh, Mr. McReady, that's a lot of comments.
McREADY:	What I want you to do is work on these comments and after that I *think* we *might* have a printable story here.
ISAACS:	(excited) Really?! Yes, sir!
SOUND:	<u>ISAACS SCOOPS UP THE PAPERS AND HEADS TOWARD THE DOOR.</u>
ISAACS:	I'll send back the changes, tomorrow!

SOUND:	DOOR CLOSES.
McREADY:	(muttering) Two rocketships, jeez.
SOUND:	DOOR SWINGS BACK OPEN.
ISAACS:	(loudly) Mr. McReady!
McREADY:	(startled) What?!
ISAACS:	We have a terrible problem! I just remembered, I can't let you have my story!
McREADY:	How's that?
ISAACS:	Somebody else wants to publish it, I forgot that I'd sent you a copy. I guess I sort of assumed that you'd reject it.
McREADY:	(slightly incredulous) Who would want to publish it?
ISAACS:	It's a new one, it doesn't have a name yet. My friends in the club are going to publish it.
McREADY:	Gosh, Sheldon, that's a real shame. I really wanted to work on that story with you. Is there somebody at your club I could talk to?
ISAACS:	Maybe Dave, he's friends with the publisher.
McREADY:	Dave who?

Scene Twelve

Poole's bachelor apartment. Three days later, late morning.

SOUND:	<u>ENVELOPE BEING OPENED. LETTER UNFOLDING. BAND PLAYING "STARDUST" ON THE RADIO.</u>
POOLE:	Let's see what abuse will emerge from fortress *Tremendous*.
McREADY:	(VO) Poole, I dearly hope you weren't too disappointed about the last rejection letter.
POOLE:	Oh yeah, it was great.
McREADY:	(VO) I trust you will be somewhat happier with the following proposal: science fiction is a creative form with an obligation to its own future. To be brief: I need an assistant and I hear that you've got the potential for the job. (voice cracks a little) So, what do you think?
POOLE:	(stunned, mutters) Wow! Karl Marx on a rubber crutch...
SOUND:	<u>RUSTLING OF PAPER AS POOLE LOOKS AT BOTH SIDES OF THE LETTER AND CHECKS THE ENVELOPE FOR MORE CONTENTS.</u>
POOLE:	This looks for real, but if this letter is from McReady, where's the other 49 pages?
SPARKS:	(distant, the bathroom) Dave?
CLYDE:	(VO, mature) So there they are, my friend David Poole and the idealist Ray Ann Sparks, alone together in his apartment. What could they be up to? Probably some political, professional thing...

SPARKS: Are you dressed yet?

CLYDE: (VO) Hell's bells!

POOLE: Naw, I'm still lying in.

CLYDE: (VO) This just isn't fair. Not only has Dave got a relationship with the only fertile woman I knew back then, now he's going to become a pro. Why did McReady go to Dave? Why not somebody better qualified? Or why not me?

SOUND: <u>SPRINGS CREAK AS SPARKS JUMPS INTO THE BED.</u>

SPARKS: What are you reading?

POOLE: Just a letter. You were in the can so long I was getting bored.

CLYDE: (VO) Poole, you are such a pig.

SPARKS: Who's it from?

CLYDE: (VO) Another pig.

SOUND: <u>POOLE DEFTLY FOLDS UP THE LETTER AND RETURNS IT TO THE ENVELOPE.</u>

POOLE: It's just another letter from McReady, saying the usual reactionary things.

CLYDE: (VO) You sneaky stack of scum!

SPARKS: (laughs) I thought you said you needed both hands to lift one of his letters.

POOLE: Maybe he's getting some editorial assistance.

CLYDE: (VO) You liar!

SOUND: <u>BEDSPRINGS AND RUSTLING OF SHEETS AS SPARKS SNUGGLES UP TO POOLE.</u>

SPARKS: I don't want to sound too bourgeois, but I really don't do this sort of thing.

POOLE: What sort of thing?

SPARKS: Invite myself into young men's beds.

POOLE: (mock surprise) Really? I thought sharing was what communism was all about.

SPARKS: Oh, very witty.

CLYDE: (VO) *Poole, you son of a—*

SPARKS: (sighs happily) I'm really excited about the convention. I had to work really hard to convince the League office to take you guys seriously. But it's all going to happen. After Mitchell's speech, things are really going to change.

POOLE: (a little distant) That's what science fiction is all about... change.

CLYDE: (VO, bitter) Oh, yeah. Things were going to change all right.

Scene Thirteen

The Hotel Metropolis. Opening day of the First World Science Fiction Convention, 1937.

MUSIC: <u>ARTHUR BLISS' MARCH FROM THE SCORE OF THE H.G. WELLS FILM "THINGS TO COME".</u>

FAN #1: I like your costume! I like your costume!

FAN #2: Thanks, yours too. So what did you say to him?

FAN #1: FIAWOL, FIAWOL! But ever since they wouldn't print him in the last lettercol, he says all he wants to do is GAFIA.

FAN #2: Aw, he's just looking for some egoboo. He thinks we'll miss him... (fades out)

FAN #3: (fades in) ...it's going to be fantastic! It'll be the first all-fan community.

FAN #4: Where's it going to be?

FAN #3: New Mexico. We're all going to pitch in and buy some vacant ranch land. Cosmic Village!

FAN #4: I like the drawings.

FAN #3: We'll build streamlined cabins, learn all about science and technical stuff, maybe even do some rocket experiments.

FAN #4: New Mexico? I hope you really have a water supply there. I think that lake on the map is actually twonks disease from your gestetner... (fades out)

ZUCKERMAN: (fades in, laughing) Run! Run! It's Roscoe the Invisible Beaver God! (fades out)

CLYDE: (VO, mature) I was never sure why we called them

world science fiction conventions. Back in 1937, it was very unlikely that anybody further than fifty miles out of town could make it here. Pretty small world if you ask me. Let's not even talk about the universe.

SOUND: <u>EXCITED VOICES OF FANS TALKING IN THE LOBBY.</u>

CLYDE: (VO) I eventually learned that the primary function of these events is to validate the personal fantasies of some pretty alienated people. If you happened to be a strange individual, living in your own little science fiction universe, then it's reassuring to discover some other individual doing the same sort of thing.

SOUND: <u>ANGRY SHOUTING IN THE DISTANCE.</u>

CLYDE: (VO) Of course, there can be some complications...

ISAACS: (fades in) That's the dumbest thing I ever heard!

DENSEN: Don't be such a crybaby.

ISAACS: Your costume is all wrong! Robert, you know! What colour are Alexander Steel's boots?

CLYDE: (as a youth) Gosh. Hmmm. Let me think about that for a moment, Sheldon.

ISAACS: (very angry) Well, I know! His boots are *black*! "Black as shimmering cylinders of oil-slick obsidian floating in the nebula-filled sky." I know that because I wrote it!

CLYDE: I kind of figured you did, Sheldon.

ISAACS: So his boots are not brown!

DENSEN: No way am I painting my dad's boots black.

ISAACS: (furious) I am Alexander Steel! You are supposed to be his evil-energy duplicate! How can an evil-energy duplicate have *brown boots*?!

CLYDE: Take it easy, Sheldon.

DENSEN: Yeah. You really have to get more mature, or you're in danger of evolving into a permanent dork.

ISAACS: (exasperated) Oh! Oh! *Oh! Rats!* You've invalidated the whole concept!

<u>SOUND:</u>   <u>ISAACS STOMPING OFF.</u>

DENSEN: (slowly fading) Hey, Sheldon? Couldn't a frequency flux in the duplicator field create a mild colour distortion?

ISAACS: (shouting, in the distance) *Shut! The! Heck! Up!*

CLYDE: (VO) Thus endeth one of science fiction's more profound philosophical discussions. These conventions had another important function: they were places where aspiring writers might happen to meet some professionals and make some contacts. And at this convention, McReady, Cross and Evanston had agreed to attend. As well as my Fabulist friends... (blows his nose, then...)

Normally, I'd be networking my brains out, but today... today, I was eagerly awaiting the dawn of a new age in progressive science fiction. (Blows his nose again).

Even though I wasn't feeling very well.

FREEDMAN: Bob! Where the hell have you been?

POOLE/WEISS: (ad lib) Yeah, where have you been?

CLYDE: (as a youth, sniffs) Sick. In New Jersey. (blows his nose) I had to go visit my aunt and I got this damn cold.

POOLE: So you haven't heard anything about the convention?

WEISS: Nobody's talked to you?

CLYDE: (sniffs) Sorry, I was sick. I really ought to be in bed, but I'm not going to miss Mitch's speech. It's going to be a joy to watch McReady squirm.

POOLE: Bob, we have to talk.

Scene Fourteen

The action alternates between two meeting rooms at the First World Science Fiction Convention. One hour later.

MITCHELL: (in quavering and unnatural public speaking voice) How tired we are of this brutal world, this criminally stupid system that forces us to surrender our better nature, our curiosity, our compassion—just to eke out a few pennies in a violent, cruel and soul-deadening struggle for survival...

SOUND: MITCHELL'S VOICE ECHOES IN A LARGELY EMPTY ROOM. WE HEAR A FEW ISOLATED COUGHS FADE OVER TO THE SOUND OF A MUCH MORE CROWDED SPACE, LOTS OF EXCITED WHISPERING AMONG THE AUDIENCE.

McREADY: (through P.A. system) America is the wave of the future, its heady combination of free enterprise and individualism will make us leaders in science and technology—well into the next century—and science fiction is America's literature. It is the genre that drives our upward spiral of progress that is our Nation, a pathway that will take us to very stars!

SOUND: ENTHUSIASTIC CLAPPING AND A FEW WHISTLES.

MITCHELL: I offer you a new vision of science fiction, a combination of social speculation and Marxism. My comrades in this creative struggle have honoured me by naming this new literature for the workers of the future as *Mitchellism*.

SOUND: MITCHELL PAUSES AND CLEARS HIS THROAT. DEAD SILENCE FROM THE

	<u>AUDIENCE.</u>
MITCHELL:	Mitchellism is the philosophy that states that followers of science fiction should actively agitate and strive for the realization of a scientific state of world socialism and universal social justice. This goal must be the driving force behind all our actions as artists and citizens of this promised future state!
<u>SOUND:</u>	<u>BACK TO THE CROWDED ROOM.</u>
CROSS:	(through P.A. system) Scientifiction reveals a range of internal mental states and conceptual constructs. Many of these psycho-cerebral configurations are infinitely more stimulating than real-world events. This speculative datum therefore offers a feasible alternative to physical actions and poses new options for inner individual development.
<u>SOUND:</u>	<u>POLITE APPLAUSE.</u>
MITCHELL:	Mitchellism asserts that science fiction is a force—that acts through the medium of imaginative stories—on the hearts and minds of the youth of the world. Progressive science fiction unerringly advocates the necessity for equality and socialism in a unified world-nation.
EVANSTON:	But we have to be real careful that we don't get too optimistic with all our dreams for the future. There are a lot of secret agencies in the world: big business, big government, the reds, even people close to F.D.R. These "intellectuals" would like to keep us under their heel. How many of you know that our own Navy has designed a flying submarine? Or how Ford and GM are keeping their plans for cheap water-powered engines a secret? What about those cheap inflatable houses we could each buy for just five dollars? You don't know because the unions and the governments want to hang on to the status quo. Someday us little guys are going to take these big guys on.

SOUND:	<u>MORE ACTIVE APPLAUSE.</u>
MITCHELL:	(on the verge of tears) ...and to reach these vital objectives... the informed predictions of science fiction... should focus us on... the triumphant... values of the Communist... International... aw, the hell with it!
SOUND:	<u>MITCHELL STORMS OFF STAGE. HIS FOOTSTEPS ECHO IN A NEAR-EMPTY ROOM.</u>
FAN #1:	Are you okay? You look like you have a headache.
SPARKS:	(distracted) Yes, er, no, no, I'm fine.
FAN #1:	Pretty wacky guy, huh?
SPARKS:	(explodes) *Oh, for God's sake! What kind of a bunch of morons are you people?!!*
SOUND:	<u>NOW SPARKS STORMS OUT OF THE ROOM. APPLAUSE IN THE OTHER ROOM RISES.</u>
POOLE:	Mr. McReady?
McREADY:	Yes, young man?
POOLE:	I'm Dave Poole. We spoke on the phone the day before yesterday.
McREADY:	Poole? (happily) Oh yes, Mr. Poole!
POOLE:	I'm still very interested in your offer and I thought you might like to meet some of my associates. This is Jack Weiss and Robert Clyde.
McREADY:	More budding writers, wonderful! (fades)

Scene Fifteen

	A lobby in the convention hotel. About half an hour later.
CLYDE:	(blows his nose, then...) Oof! Hey, watch—Oh, sorry, Ray Ann.
SPARKS:	(still angry) Yeah, I'll bet.
CLYDE:	Is something wrong?
SPARKS:	*Wrong!?* I just witnessed the greatest set-back in the history of socialism! What member of the Klan schedules the programming at this goddamned worthless convention? And where the hell were you?! I thought you were supposed to be his friends!
CLYDE:	You mean I missed Gerald's speech? (blows his nose) Damn! Ray Ann, I've been sick. I dragged myself out of bed for it but I guess I messed up on the time.
SPARKS:	Oh... (calmer) Sorry, Bob... I didn't know you were sick.
CLYDE:	(VO, mature) As with many things in life, there's a degree of ambiguity here. I did actually show up to see my friend speak and support the cause, even though it was pretty much a lost one. But now with Poole as assistant editor of *Tremendous Stories*, we had our collective foot in the door. And if I applied a bit of guile myself, I would get to make friends with Ray Ann.
CLYDE:	(in youthful voice) Why don't we get some coffee somewhere and talk about it?
CLYDE:	(VO, mature) So the convention was about as suc-

cessful for me as it could get. There was only one casualty that day in 1937. Gerald Mitchell was the only one of us who did not become one of Stewart D. McReady's new stable of writers. In fact, Mitchell and Mitchellism disappeared from science fiction fandom forever.

Scene Sixteen

The offices of *Tremendous Stories*. Autumn 1943.

<table>
<tr><td>SOUND:</td><td>MONTAGE OF RADIO CLIPS FROM THE LATE 1930S AND EARLY 1940S. MUST INCLUDE THE THEME TO ORSON WELLES AND THE MERCURY THEATRE ON THE AIR (TCHAI-KOVSKY'S *"PIANO CONCERTO NO. 1"*); WELLES' NARRATION AT THE END OF THE BROADCAST; ROOSEVELT'S DECLARATION OF WAR IN 1941; FADING INTO COPLAND'S *"FANFARE TO THE COMMON MAN"*.</td></tr>
<tr><td>CLYDE:</td><td>(VO, mature) Let's head to the year 1943 with some suitable footnotes to this part of our story. By that time I was hauling a bazooka somewhere on my way to Berlin. I really did get to fight fascism, but not in exactly the way I thought.</td></tr>
<tr><td>SOUND:</td><td>EXPLOSIONS, RUMBLING OF TANKS IN THE DISTANCE.</td></tr>
<tr><td>CLYDE:</td><td>(VO, mature) Camp Fantastic and the Fabulists are pre-war memories now. But Poole kept his word to all of us—we had all been drafted into the pages of *Tremendous Stories*.</td></tr>
<tr><td>SOUND:</td><td>DISTANT EXPLOSIONS GIVE WAY TO THE SOUND OF TYPING, WITH OCCASIONAL SNEEZES AND COUGHS FROM STEWART D. MCREADY.</td></tr>
<tr><td>POOLE:</td><td>Mr. McReady?</td></tr>
<tr><td>McREADY:</td><td>(very congested) What is it, Poole?</td></tr>
<tr><td>POOLE:</td><td>My goodness, you're really suffering, aren't you?</td></tr>
<tr><td>McREADY:</td><td>It's my allergies acting up again.</td></tr>
</table>

POOLE: It might get better if you didn't smoke quite so much.

McREADY: (irritated) Was there something related to your job that you wanted to talk to me about, Poole?

POOLE: Yes. I need to talk to you about Sheldon's latest story.

McREADY: Oh, yes.

POOLE: He's written in a conveyor belt system that spans the Atlantic Ocean—he's got the engineering society calling them "super rubbers".

McREADY: (amused) Pah!

POOLE: (amused) I think we need to use a less suggestive term here.

McREADY: Yes, I can see that. Let's call them "flexible titano-syntha-transports".

POOLE: That sounds good, Mr. McReady.

WILLIAMS: (in other room, very upset) Oh dear! *Mr. McReady!*

SOUND: <u>DOOR LOUDLY SWINGS OPEN. TWO SETS OF HEAVY FOOTSTEPS STOMP INTO THE OFFICE.</u>

WEBB: You S.D. McReady? Editor of *Tremendous Stories of Super Science*?

McREADY: Er—yes. What's the meaning of all this?

WEBB: We're federal agents. This is our warrant. We have orders to seize all files and documents on the premises.

SOUND: <u>FILING CABINETS ROLL OPEN. MASSES OF PAPERS BEING DROPPED INTO BOXES.</u>

WEBB: You there! Drop those files!

POOLE: Hope you don't mind cleaning up. Why are you doing this?

WEBB: National security.

SOUND: DOCUMENT BOXES BEING LOADED ONTO DOLLIES.

JOHNSON: Yeah, don't you know there's a war going on?

McREADY: But, sir—(sneezes)—we're a patriotic, law-abiding magazine. You can't possibly be angry about some silly editorials we printed over five years ago—(sneezes several times)—many engineers, service men and government scientists read our magazine on a regular basis.

WEBB: In the January 1943 issue of *Tremendous Stories*, did you not print a story titled "The Mightiest Monster-Weapon" where a race of alien beings was destroyed by a weapon powered by a force called "atomic fission"?

McREADY: Ah... (sniffs and sneezes)

POOLE: Yes, we did. Is that a problem?

JOHNSON: Could be, Adolph, or is that Tojo?!

WEBB: (pointedly at Johnson) We cannot answer your question on the grounds that it may undermine military research integrity.

McREADY: Oh, god! (sneezes and wheezes) *God!*

WEBB: Don't take it so hard, fats. No need to cry.

POOLE: It's not that, he's allergic to your carnation.

JOHNSON: I'll get this stuff down to the van.

WEBB: Right. Now, Mr. McReady. Your files will be returned following the successful conclusion of this investigation. Provided some tribunal doesn't find you guilty of treason.

McREADY: (in despair) Oh, god!

SOUND: PACKING OF FILING CABINETS AND WHEELING DOLLIES FADE.

Scene Seventeen

<table>
<tr><td></td><td>D.H. Evanston's apartment, later the same evening.</td></tr>
<tr><td>SOUND:</td><td><u>TRAFFIC SOUNDS IN THE DISTANCE. MAHLER'S RESURRECTION SYMPHONY PLAYS ON THE RADIO.</u></td></tr>
<tr><td>CROSS:</td><td>I am undergoing a subjective state of astonishment. Never before have I assimilated such intense concepts and sensations. What you have communicated has shattered my preconceptions while expanding my perceptual field.</td></tr>
<tr><td>EVANSTON:</td><td>The manuscript is incredible, isn't it? All of it based on techniques I learned from the transcendental contortionists of Istanbul.</td></tr>
<tr><td>CROSS:</td><td>Incredible. Yes, that may be an appropriate description of my emotional response.</td></tr>
<tr><td>EVANSTON:</td><td>Here, relax, have another drink.</td></tr>
<tr><td>SOUND:</td><td><u>WINE POURED INTO A GLASS.</u></td></tr>
<tr><td>EVANSTON:</td><td>We can really knock some heads around with this stuff—we're right on the cutting edge, you and I.</td></tr>
<tr><td>CLYDE:</td><td>(VO, mature) Patience, dear listeners. The meaning of that exchange will become clear later. Let's move ahead just about two years, where we'll have bigger fish... bigger cities... to fry.</td></tr>
<tr><td>SOUND:</td><td><u>DRONE OF BOMBER AIRCRAFT ENGINES.</u></td></tr>
<tr><td>CLYDE:</td><td>(VO, mature) So when did it all change for us? When did the Fabulists truly grow up? When did science fiction lose its virginity?</td></tr>
<tr><td>NAVIGATOR:</td><td>(on speaker) We're over the target...</td></tr>
</table>

PILOT: (on speaker) Bombardier! Release the payload!

BOMBARDIER: (on speaker) Payload away!

SOUND: <u>WHISTLE OF BOMB FALLING TO EARTH.</u>

CLYDE: (VO, mature) It was at 9:03 a.m., local time...

SOUND: <u>A SHOCKING "CRACK!" AND LOW ROAR THAT BUILDS AND BUILDS.</u>

CLYDE: (VO, mature) ...Monday, August 6, 1945. Hiroshi-ma.

SOUND: <u>ROAR OF THE ATOMIC EXPLOSION SLOWLY FADES.</u>

**End of
Amazing Struggles**

art by Emily O'Brien

Astonishing Failures

Play Two:
Astonishing Failures

Characters – In Order of Appearance

JAY E. CROSS	An accomplished science fiction writer and self-educated philosopher and commentator. A proponent of Mentotechnics.
LAUXEN BIRNETTE	A female character from Jay E. Cross's novel *The Mind Manipulators*.
VENUSIAN PREMIER	The villain from the same novel.
JONZZ STOV	The hero from the same novel.
D.H. EVANSTON	Another popular science fiction writer, an associate of Cross' and founder of the Temple of Mentotechnics.
ASSISTANT DIRECTOR	Of the television program *Alexander Steel and the Solar Police Force*.
STAGE HAND	From the same television show.
TV NARRATOR	From the same television show.
SOLAR POLICEMAN ALEXANDER STEEL	Hero of the television series. Created by Bob Clyde and Sheldon Isaacs.
BOB CLYDE	Our protagonist and narrator. Now a television writer who occasionally publishes stories in *Tremendous Stories* and other science fiction magazines.
STEWART D. McREADY	Still editor of *Tremendous Stories*. A key public proponent of Mentotechics.

PAM McREADY	Stewart McReady's wife.
BARBARA ISAACS	The young and patient wife of Sheldon Isaacs.
SHELDON ISAACS	Bob Clyde's sometime collaborator and driven writer of science fiction. By day he is a teacher of industrial food chemo-technology at Newark Polytechnic.
DEAN OF INSTRUCTION	At Newark Polytechnic. Sheldon Isaacs' boss.
DAVID POOLE	Assistant editor at *Tremendous Stories*. The actual source of good taste and sound judgment at the magazine.
RAY ANN SPARKS	A science fiction writer. Married to Bob Clyde.
SF WRITERS #1, #2, #3, #4, #5	Can be voices of fans and other writers from Amazing Struggles and elsewhere in Astonishing Failures. Will describe scenarios from their stories.
RADIO NEWSREADER	In the media style of the 1950s.
BAND MEMBERS	(various)
MADELEINE & SHEILA	Housewives.
ROGER & McALISTER	A teenage boy and his father.
STAN & MARIE	Two middle-aged married people (but not to each other).
ROLF DENSEN	Now an occasionally successful science fiction writer.
ROD SERLING	The famous television writer and creator of *The Twilight Zone* at an early point in his career.
RADIO INTERVIEWER	The host of the late night talk show *Dark Words*. A 1950s version of Larry King.
DR. ROLAND PAIGE	A guest on *Dark Words*. An official

	representative of the Organization of Psycho-Medical Practitioners.
MISS MAUBAUM	D.H. Evanston's secretary.
JACK WEBB	An FBI agent.
BEN JOHNSON	Another FBI agent.

Scene One

The science fiction universe of J.E. Cross, as written in 1949-50.

SOUND AND MUSIC: CRASH OF THUNDER, A CLASH OF CYMBALS AND THE GRATING HOWL OF PRE-SYNTHESIZER ELECTRONIC MUSIC. SLOWLY THE COSMIC STORM SUBSIDES. THE SOUND OF ULTRA-COOL AND SINISTER JAZZ MUSIC RISES.

CROSS: (VO with sound of typing in the background.) ...the beautiful mento-technical assistant, Lauxen Birnette, sensed that she was in great peril... Primarily because of the unbreakable plasti-steel cords that strapped her helplessly onto the otherwise quite comfortable sedan chair in this 28th century luxury hotel.

SOUND: SOFT METALLIC HUM. HEAVY FOOTSTEPS.

CROSS: (VO, cont'd) Then the Venusian Premier entered. He leered at her, and Lauxen Birnette allowed herself the emotional response of loathing.

LAUXEN: Let me go!

SOUND: SOFT THEREMIN-LIKE SOUND WAVES.

PREMIER: It's no use, little suckling, my animal charisma protects me from your pitiful telepathic machinations.

CROSS: (VO, with typing) Lauxen then realized that this foul, power-seeking individual was correct, her strongest mental commands were ineffective...

LAUXEN: (gasps)

CROSS: (VO, with typing) The room swam with metaphoric panic as Lauxen realized that the Premier of Venus was right. Within her own mind, she found that she was unable to carry out even the most basic quadratic factorials and hyper-logic exercises...

SOUND: <u>HEAVY FORM OF THE PREMIER SITS ON THE CUSHIONS OF THE CHAIR. SUGGESTIVE RUSTLE OF SILK AND LACE.</u>

PREMIER: In fact, you'll soon discover that my enhanced personal charisma will exert its influence over you.

LAUXEN: Mr. Premier, you disgust me!

PREMIER: (laughs) An impressive show of virtue, my soft lump. You have defended your moral integrity even after treatment from my persuader-beam.

SOUND: <u>MORE SILK BEING MOVED AROUND.</u>

PREMIER: (grunts happily) But I'm sure we'll still manage somehow...

CROSS: (VO, with typing) In spite of his hateful bodily emanations, Lauxen could feel her resolve slipping. With horror she concluded that she would soon be under the complete psycho-physiological domination of the Venusian dictator...

PREMIER: I suppose I should be insulted by your resistance. Most women don't need the prod of electro-lobotomy to give themselves to the most powerful man in the solar system.

SOUND: <u>THE PREMIER GIVES A ROUGH KISS AND THEN THROWS HER HEAD BACK.</u>

LAUXEN: (in pain) *Oh!*

PREMIER: But never mind. Soon you will be my mistress

and then you will willingly reveal all you know of those foolish freedom-loving scientists.

LAUXEN: *Blah! Yuck!* You may gain access to my physical orifices, but I'll tell you nothing! You monstrous embodiment of entrenched vested interests and *lustful self-indulgence, you!*

SOUND: THE PREMIER PLANTS ANOTHER LONG HARD KISS SOMEWHERE ON LAUXEN.

PREMIER: That's me, all right.

SOUND: MUFFLED BLAST, GREAT CRASH AS THE HOTEL DOORS FALL TO THE FLOOR. A PAIR OF METAL-HEELED BOOTS STRIDES INTO THE ROOM.

LAUXEN: (gasping with relief) *Oh, Jonzz! Praise the Lords of Logic!*

SOUND: RISING HUM OF A STRANGE DEVICE.

JONZZ: You there, dictator! Cease that sexual aggression!

PREMIER: *Jonzz Stov!* It can't be! I saw you die in the plasma pits of Luna! (yells) Guards! Guards! Needle-beam this intruder to death!

JONZZ: Don't bother crying out for help, Mr. Premier. It will be some time before your lackeys recover from my mind-blast!

SOUND: ANOTHER RISING HUM OF ANOTHER STRANGE DEVICE.

PREMIER: I won't need those stooges to atomize you, you naive fool! You'll soon appreciate the destructive power of my neutrino blaster!

JONZZ: I doubt that...

SOUND: JONZZ'S HUM GETS EVEN LOUDER AS HE TWISTS A DIAL ON HIS DEVICE.

CROSS: (VO, with typing) ...Jonzz Stov turned his

	cerebro-amplifier to its lowest setting...
JONZZ:	I want you to know that only you are responsible for the following events, Mr. Premier.
SOUND:	WILD ELECTRONIC WHISTLING SOUNDS, CRACKLES OF STATIC.
CROSS:	(VO, with typing) ...the tiny mechanism emitted a selective particle field which located the Premier's nervous system and randomized all information passing through the Venusian dictator's brain...
SOUND:	THE PREMIER DROPS HIS BLASTER AND CRASHES TO THE FLOOR.
PREMIER:	*Nigh!*
LAUXEN:	Oh, Jonzz! You've saved me!
CROSS:	(VO, with typing) Jonzz Stov recalled the Premier's plan to violate his beloved's moral and physical integrity. He turned the cerebro-amplifier up to its second level...
SOUND:	JONZZ'S DEVICE WHISTLES WITH A SHRILL BUZZING.
CROSS:	(VO, with typing) The instrument's beam now accelerated all the electro-chemical reactions in the Premier's neural network, causing all his nerve cells to fire at once and evaporating the fluids at the axial junctions...
SOUND:	THUDS AND BUMPS AS THE PREMIER JERKS AND FLOPS AROUND ON THE FLOOR.
PREMIER:	*Nigh! Nigh! Yeeeooow! Yeeeeeeooooooow! Ying! Piddle! Pong! Pi! Po!*
SOUND:	JONZZ TURNS THE OFF SWITCH ON HIS DEVICE. THE BUZZING STOPS.
PREMIER:	(gasping heavily) Oh, god, it's stopped! T-thank you...

CROSS: (VO, typing) Then Jonzz remembered the Premier's huge... conspiracy against scientific and social progress, and how his elite corps of secret police and political strongmen had machinated to suppress the healthy propagation of mento-technology.

SOUND: JONZZ RE-ACTIVATES HIS DEVICE; IT PROJECTS A HIGH-PITCHED ELECTRONIC SCREAM.

CROSS: (VO, with typing) ...He turned the cerebro-amplifier to its highest setting—which would initiate the instantaneous explosion of all brain matter in the victim...

PREMIER: *Ouch! Man, this really hurts!*

SOUND: THE PREMIER CRASHES BACK TO THE FLOOR.

Scene Two

The New York City office of J.E. Cross and Donald H. Evanston. March 1950.

<u>SOUND:</u>	<u>RAPID-FIRE TYPING BY CROSS. HE SUDDENLY STOPS.</u>
CROSS:	Have you identified any difficulties with the narrative?
EVANSTON:	No, no, chummie, it's great stuff. Ripping tale. I particularly like the part where you blow up the Premier's brain.
CROSS:	Thank you, Donald.
<u>SOUND:</u>	<u>CROSS RESUMES TYPING.</u>
EVANSTON:	Keep up the good work, Jay. You have to finish the trilogy by the end of the week.
<u>SOUND:</u>	<u>TYPING FADES.</u>
CLYDE:	(VO) A few years have elapsed since we last talked. To be more precise, it is early 1950. The Fabulists as an organized group of deluded adolescents have broken up. We are now a diffuse group of deluded adults. Accordingly, most of us... take me for example...

Scene Three

Saturday Morning, March 1950. Studio C, WBS TV, New York City.

<table>
<tr><td>SOUND:</td><td><u>MASSIVE TV CAMERAS ROLLING AROUND ON A TILED FLOOR. HURRIED FOOTSTEPS.</u></td></tr>
</table>

ASSISTANT DIRECTOR: (sarcastic) Hiya, Bob! Nice of you to join us.

CLYDE: Sorry I'm late, re-writes.

ASSISTANT DIRECTOR: Okay, set crew, the lights are looking good.

STAGEHAND: Close the set!

ASSISTANT DIRECTOR: (voice echoes through the studio speakers) Quiet, everyone! Sound, please! In five seconds, we're live. Five... four... three... two... one...

SOUND: <u>SOMEONE HITS A LARGE ELECTRICAL SWITCH. CHEEZY RECORDED MUSIC BOOMS OUT.</u>

TV NARRATOR: (miked) Yes, boys and girls, it's *Alexander Steel and the Solar Police Force*! Back again for this week's instalment of rocket-racketing exploits! Today's adventure is brought to you by Bof-foMug—the healthful barley and oat-flavoured breakfast drink that's delicious, nutritious and power-packed!

SOUND: <u>BAD EFFECT OF A ROCKET ENGINE FIRING.</u>

TV NARRATOR: As you may recall from last week's episode, Alexander Steel had been ordered by the Robot Brain to infiltrate the caves of Io to stop the traitorous alien mutants who were plotting to overthrow the Interplanetary Republic...

STEEL: *Get back, you inhuman slavering hordes!*

SOUND: <u>CHEAP "DRAMATIC" MUSIC RISES THEN FADES.</u>

CLYDE: (VO) Well, I warned you. We grew up. And we had to make some of the tiresome and unpleasant decisions grown-up type people have to make sometimes. I got a job as a publicist for an outfit who were pushing ads for this new fad called "television". An interesting medium, which my science fiction colleagues and I occasionally referred to as "visi-screens" or "radio-scopes". I figured none of this would last but it might be fun for a little while.

There is a rough justice to the universe. After an adolescence spent humiliating my devoted chum and collaborator Sheldon Isaacs, here I was, working every night churning out the same horrible stories we used to write in his mother's kitchen.

This should give you some idea how good I was at predicting future trends. So perhaps as advance punishment for a wasted old age, I got a job during television's so-called "golden age". Of course, as the co-creator of this old pulp favourite, I'm sure I had a little bit of inside track.

There is a rough justice to the universe. After an adolescence spent humiliating my devoted chum and collaborator Sheldon Isaacs, here I was, working every night churning out the same horrible stories we used to write in his mother's kitchen.

Scene Four

New York City, the McReady Kitchen. Sunday morning, March 1950.

<table>
<tr><td><u>SOUND:</u></td><td><u>BIRDS CHIRPING. TRAFFIC IN THE DISTANCE.</u></td></tr>
<tr><td>CLYDE:</td><td>(VO) To be truthful, my colleague Sheldon Isaacs was slowly developing a measure of fame. He had continued to supply our mutual associate Stewart D. McReady with stories, and ultimately replaced Evanston as the most frequently published writer in Tremendous Stories of Super Science. And speaking of McReady...</td></tr>
<tr><td>McREADY:</td><td>(mutters) Mornings...</td></tr>
<tr><td><u>SOUND:</u></td><td><u>HE POURS HIMSELF A CUP OF COFFEE AND SITS DOWN AT THE TABLE.</u></td></tr>
<tr><td>McREADY:</td><td>...we must develop a cure for them.</td></tr>
<tr><td>CLYDE:</td><td>(VO) Some people just seem to stay in your life. Like an annoying song from a TV ad. McReady was like that. He and Poole were still editing Tremendous. Dave was still keeping his word and keeping most of the ex-Fabulists in print. And the word was that Dave was the only thing keeping the magazine together.</td></tr>
<tr><td>PAM McREADY:</td><td>(distant, calls) Stewart! I'm in the garden!</td></tr>
<tr><td>McREADY:</td><td>(softly) Hell's bells. (calls) Wonderful, dear!</td></tr>
<tr><td>CLYDE:</td><td>(VO) The word was also that McReady was starting to get involved in some very strange stuff. I sometimes wondered if he was living proof that some people shouldn't stay in the</td></tr>
</table>

same job too long.

SOUND:	DOOR SWINGS OPEN LOUDLY. PAM MCREADY MARCHES INTO THE KITCHEN.
McREADY:	My goodness! Look at all those flowers.
PAM:	One from every variety in the garden.
SOUND:	RUSTLE AND THUMPING AS PAM MCREADY PUTS THE FLOWERS INTO VASES AND SETS THEM ON THE TABLE.
PAM:	It's all set. Now, are you ready?
McREADY:	I don't know about this, dear. If this doesn't work I'm gonna suffer all day.
PAM:	(irritated) Stewart, I do not want to hear this. After all your talk, you aren't even going to try?
McREADY:	(whining) Aw, Pamela...
PAM:	(sternly) We did the mental exercises last night, didn't we?
McREADY:	Yes, we did, dear.
PAM:	So, do you believe what those two have been telling you? Do you believe what you've been telling me?
McREADY:	(steeling himself) Yes. Yes, I do believe.
PAM:	Well, then.
SOUND:	MCREADY GETS OUT OF HIS CHAIR.
PAM:	Inhale.
McREADY:	(sniffs a little)
PAM:	(irritated) Come on! Get your nose in those petals!
McREADY:	(sniffs loudly)
PAM:	Any reaction?

McREADY: (breathes loudly through his nostrils) Hmmmm. No... nothing.

PAM: Try some of the other flowers.

McREADY: (sniffs loudly)

PAM: Inhale! Inhale! Inhale!

McREADY: (sucks air repeatedly through his nose, then stops and breathes freely through his nose)

PAM: (expectant) Well, well?

McREADY: Nothing. Absolutely no reaction. (now very excited, very happy) The exercises work! *My allergies are cured!*

PAM: (jubilant) Really?!

McREADY: (very emotional) Pamela! Do you know what this means? Evanston and Cross are right, Mentotechnics works. *The future is now!*

Scene Five

New York City, the kitchen of the Clyde apartment. The same Sunday morning.

SOUND:	<u>DOOR OPENS, CLYDE TIP TOES IN AND PUTS HIS BRIEFCASE DOWN.</u>
CLYDE:	(calling softly) Sweetheart?
SOUND:	<u>CLYDE OPENS PERCOLATOR.</u>
CLYDE:	There's no coffee left, darling!
SOUND:	<u>CLYDE OPENS THE REFRIGERATOR. HE TAKES A LONG DRINK FROM A BOTTLE OF MILK.</u>
CLYDE:	Honey! I'm home!
SOUND:	<u>CLYDE DROPS INTO A CHAIR AT THE KITCHEN TABLE.</u>
CLYDE:	*Sweeeetiee! Wake up, dearest!* You can't sleep another day away!
SOUND:	<u>HE TAKES ANOTHER LONG SWIG FROM THE MILK BOTTLE.</u>
CLYDE:	I sure could use some sleep myself, sweetheart. We had another all-night re-write session. Who'd'a thought kiddie show scripts could get so complicated? It took four hours to figure out a believable reason for our protagonist to stop blowing up Jupiter long enough to "relax with a steaming healthful serving of BoffoMug—the breakfast snack of kids, champs and space heroes!" (chuckles)
	Pretty good copy, huh? So, honey, do you want to get up and grab some grub? (pause) What's this?

SOUND:	HE PICKS UP A NOTE ON THE KITCHEN TABLE.
CLYDE:	(reads aloud) "Dear Robert, I've stopped over to Vonda's for a short visit. I think there's some milk left in the fridge. Help yourself..."
SOUND:	THE TELEPHONE BESIDE THE REFRIGERATOR RINGS. CLYDE GETS UP AND ANSWERS IT.
CLYDE:	Hello, Clyde residence. Oh, Vonda! Can I speak to Ra—? Oh, I see. (pause, then speaks a little stiffly) No, no, as you can gather, she's not in right now. (tone of forced joviality) Well, we're a little low on provisions, so I suspect that being the good soldier she is, she's out replenishing our stocks. (listens for a moment) Yes, even on a Sunday. Of course, I'll have her call you right away. Bye-bye.
SOUND:	CLYDE HANGS THE PHONE UP HARD.
CLYDE:	(angry) *Ray!* Where the hell are you? (sighs)
SOUND:	MOMENT OF SILENCE.
CLYDE:	(VO) Aw, what the hell. This is what happens when you clock in too much overtime. But the approaching disintegration of my first marriage was pretty upsetting. At the time I believed that marriage was a solution, a joyous completion, a spiritual, intellectual and physical communion. Only there seemed to be a widening gap between my expectations and the reality. If I really could jump back and forth in time like this, I would reach back to my young self, tell myself to hire a good lawyer and take a hard look—
SOUND:	THE TELEPHONE RINGS AGAIN. CLYDE ANXIOUSLY SNAPS UP THE RECEIVER.
CLYDE:	(a little frantic) *Hello?! Ray?* Oh... (pause) ...oh. Sorry, ma'am. You're calling for Mr. Zeigler. No, you're not interrupting anything, I was just

waiting for another call. (listens, then sounds re-lieved) Well, I'm glad he was happy with the last submission.

SOUND:	CLYDE OPENS HIS BRIEFCASE.

CLYDE: The final chapters? Well, I'm not exactly sure. I've been very busy with my work at the studio lately, and I'm currently collaborating on my latest novella with Mr. Isaacs...

SOUND: SOUND OF TYPING RISES.

CLYDE: ...but I'm sure I can get to them this morning.

Scene Six

Newark, New Jersey. The world of Sheldon Isaacs: the action starts at the Isaacs household and moves to his classroom at Newark Polytechnical Institute. All of this occurs on the following Monday morning.

SOUND: THE TYPING IS NOW VERY NEAR AND VERY FAST. THIS IS HOW SHELDON ISAACS TYPES.

BARBARA ISAACS: Sheldon! Sheldon Isaacs!

SOUND: ISAACS CONTINUES TYPING WITH NO CHANGE IN SPEED AT THE SOUND OF HIS WIFE'S VOICE.

BARBARA: (now very close) Sheldon, have you been listening?

SOUND: BARBARA ABRUPTLY PULLS THE PAPER OUT OF THE TYPEWRITER ROLL. ISAACS CONTINUES TYPING.

ISAACS: Hey! Where did my paper g—? (pause—now in a soft voice) I beg your pardon, Barbara? Am I supposed to be doing something right now?

BARBARA: Oh, Sheldon! I told you not to forget to pick up some more cough medicine for Aaron, and that we have a parent-teacher interview with Beth's math instructor tomorrow night.

ISAACS: (still mild but now a little defensive) I heard you. I knew that.

BARBARA: And did you remember that you were supposed to drive the twins to their bubbie's this morning?

ISAACS: (embarrassed) Well...

BARBARA: (exasperated) Well, never mind, I'll do it my-self! Again.

SOUND: BARBARA WALKS OUT OF THE ROOM AND CLOSES THE DOOR BEHIND HER, QUITE LOUDLY. THERE IS A PAUSE. ISAACS THEN FEEDS ANOTHER SHEET OF PAPER INTO HIS MACHINE AND RESUMES TYPING.

BARBARA: (in the distance, through the door—yells) Shel-don!

ISAACS: (calls back) Yes, Barbara?

BARBARA: (still yelling) *Work! It's time for you to go to work!*

SOUND: STUDENTS WHISPERING AMONG THEM-SELVES IN A LARGE CLASSROOM.

ISAACS: So, let's see if any of you are ready to graduate from this introduction to industrial food chemo-technology...

SOUND: HARD CRUNCHES AND SWOOSHES AS ISAACS WRITES ON THE BLACKBOARD.

ISAACS: Can anyone here tell us what I've just shown you?

SOUND: TOTAL SILENCE. FINALLY SOMEONE AT THE BACK OF THE ROOM TRIES TO SUPPRESS A COUGH.

ISAACS: All right, I will tell you. This is the chemical process that allows us to extend the shelf life of doughnuts and pies by an extra six to eight weeks. So once again, we see how economics and industry contribute to the profitability of modern consumer services and food sciences. Or to put it another way...

SOUND: MORE DRY HARD IMPACTS AND SOFT

	SCRAPES AS ISAACS WRITES WITH HIS CHALK.
ISAACS:	"E + I = x\$ - CS/FS". Let me explain this formula further: Here then, mass production of bakery consumables allows us to create far more product than we could before—and through the power of chemical preservatives we extend product durability. Let's look at another core principle in industrial food technology...
SOUND:	MORE CHALK WRITING.
ISAACS:	"xCP ^ xPD+".
SOUND:	PUTS THE CHALK DOWN AND DUSTS OFF HIS HANDS.
ISAACS:	(very solemn) Greater productivity. Greater availability. Greater profit. We live in great times, ladies and gentlemen.
SOUND:	THE CLASS BELL RINGS. THE STUDENTS BREATHE WITH RELIEF AND LEAVE THEIR DESKS.
ISAACS:	(calls out) Don't forget, read Swanson chapter six: "The Evolution of Plastic Wrap Packaging" and Lee's paper on frosted icing sculpture forms. There may be a quiz next week!
SOUND:	THE RUMBLE OF DEPARTING STUDENTS SUBSIDES. ISAACS SITS, RE-LOADS HIS TYPEWRITER AND RESUMES TYPING. DOOR OF ISAACS' OFFICE OPENS AND THE DEAN STEPS IN.
DEAN:	Dr. Isaacs, a word in your shell-like ear.
SOUND:	ISAACS CARRIES ON TYPING AS THEY SPEAK.
ISAACS:	Yes, Dean? How can I help you in your important duties, sir?
DEAN:	I've been getting a few comments about your

classes, Isaacs. Concerned comments. (clears his throat) From what I hear, you have a rather unique approach: Jelly doughnuts mass production as a brave new technology for feeding the world's hungry? Artificial preservatives as a vital tool for feeding space travellers on their way to the distant planets?

ISAACS: Yes, that's some of the more advanced levels of discussion, reserved only once we've covered the basics of the day's curriculum.

DEAN: Still, I really think you ought to tone down your lectures to more closely suit the image of the Newark Polytechnical Institute. (laughs feebly) After all, our student body isn't heading for MIT or Cal Tech, are they? Waiters and bakers can't work if they've been blinded with too much science, can they?

SOUND: <u>ISAACS SUDDENLY STOPS TYPING.</u>

ISAACS: (he speaks clearly and with great sincerity) I want to thank you, *very deeply*, for those completely candid and tremendously valuable comments, Dean. I'm truly touched that you would take time from your demanding schedule to speak to me personally. And all I can say is that I truly believe that as the mentors of tomorrow's service technicians, we are at the cutting edge of scientific progress! I humbly, *humbly* apologize if my zeal and enthusiasm for the grand mission, and your profound vision for the Newark Polytechnic, has in any way caused these fine young people any personal anguish, or given you any personal or professional setbacks.

SOUND: <u>(OR LACK OF IT) A LONG SILENCE AS THE DEAN TRIES TO ABSORB ISAACS' STATEMENT.</u>

DEAN: Well... I appreciate all that, Isaacs... I think.

<u>SOUND:</u>	<u>DEAN OPENS THE DOOR.</u>
DEAN:	So... keep up the good work... and maybe we can talk about all of this later on... when it's convenient...
ISAACS:	(earnestly) *Absolutely*, sir. Please come and see me anytime!
<u>SOUND:</u>	<u>DEAN WALKS OUT, SHUTS THE DOOR BEHIND HIM. ISAACS RESUMES TYPING. AFTER A FEW SECONDS WE ALSO HEAR THE DISTANT SOUNDS OF CHILDREN WHINING AND COUGHING.</u>
BARBARA:	*Sheldon!* Stop typing! We are *trying* to sleep!
ISAACS:	Coming, Barbara...
<u>SOUND:</u>	<u>HE PULLS THE LAST SHEET OF PAPER FROM THE TYPEWRITER.</u>
ISAACS:	...just as soon as I get this story ready to send to Mr. McReady.
BARBARA:	Great, great. I'm sure he won't sleep until he gets it.

Scene Seven

The editorial offices of *Tremendous Stories of Super Science*. 6:05 p.m. The next day.

SOUND: POOLE ROLLS A FILING CABINET SHUT WITH A SHARP BANG.

POOLE: (attempting enthusiasm) Well, it looks like March will be a bumper month for *Tremendous*. I've got the new novella from Denson, the one you were so anxious to see? Then Clyde's managed to turn in this nice short, short...

McREADY: (distant) Clyde? He still around? I thought he'd gone into radio.

POOLE: Television. But he's working hard to keep his hand in the magazines.

SOUND: POOLE SHUFFLING PAPERS AROUND ON HIS DESK.

POOLE: And there's another story from that new author Magnus O'Toole...

McREADY: Who the hell is that?

POOLE: Pen name for Ray Ann Sparks. (pauses) That's Clyde's wife.

McREADY: I want you to watch that. I don't want to see the spectre of nepotism wrapping its oily tendrils around the pages of *Tremendous Stories*.

POOLE: (sighs) Yes, I'll take all appropriate precautions.

SOUND: POOLE PUTS THE PAPERS INTO HIS DESK AND LOCKS IT.

POOLE: The art department says that Stephen sent in a

magnificent set of line drawings for most of the stuff you approved last week. And of course there's the serial novel. I really think that Cross' latest chapter is incredibly long...

McREADY: (annoyed) And it's going to stay that way! David, I'm over-ruling all your so-called edits on the manuscript. I really don't understand why you refuse to appreciate that man's genius!

POOLE: (his sarcasm would be apparent to all but McReady) Yes, I must be wracked with professional jealousy.

SOUND: <u>POOLE PUSHES HIMSELF AWAY FROM HIS DESK. HIS CHAIR ROLLS BACK WITH JUST A LITTLE TOO MUCH FORCE.</u>

POOLE: And don't forget, we still have instalment seventeen of Isaacs' *Macrocosmic Voyagers*.

McREADY: (irritated) You mean it hasn't finished *yet*?

POOLE: Judging from our mail and the fanzines, it's still pretty popular. Actually, I think it's kind of fun, and we can always depend on him.

McREADY: Like growths on a toad.

POOLE: Anyway, I've gone over the manuscripts again...

McREADY: (temper rising) And?

POOLE: ...and I just can't see a good place for the new articles. Especially if you won't let me cut down Cross. We're booked solid through the summer, let alone the March or April issues. Besides, I've got most of the layouts already done...

McREADY: (struggles to stay calm) David. David. David. The articles are going in. Either in the March or April issues. Drop half the lithos and scratch the woman's story. That ought to free up some space.

POOLE: (a little desperate) But I've already sent acceptance letters and cheques. They're expecting to see the stories in print, the illustrations are already paid for.

SOUND:	MCREADY CLICKS HIS CIGARETTE LIGHTER AND INHALES.
McREADY:	This is a senior editorial decision, my boy. These may be the most important written communications of the century. I'm not going to let your minor commitments and little concerns get in the way of this Mission of Science.
POOLE:	(now openly upset) *Minor concerns?!* What the *hell* am I supposed to tell our writers? We're not the only game in town these days!
McREADY:	We tell them the truth. There's been a change in the editorial philosophy of *Tremendous Stories*, and we may accidentally skin a few noses as we move along the upward spiral of progress.
POOLE:	(evenly) Well, in that case...
SOUND:	POOLE UNLOCKS HIS DESK AND REMOVES AN ENVELOPE FROM THE DRAWER.
POOLE:	I had the following change in *personal* policy prepared for this eventuality.
SOUND:	THROWS THE ENVELOPE ON MCREADY'S DESK.
POOLE:	This is my resignation.
SOUND:	POOLE OPENS THE DOOR.
POOLE:	But I'm sure with your newly advanced mental powers, you can run this place on your own now.
SOUND:	THE DOOR SHUTS. SILENCE.
McREADY:	(sad, surprised) David...

Scene Eight

A hotel room. A few hours later, the same evening.

SOUND: <u>MUSIC ON THE RADIO, *"STORMY WEATHER"* OR SOMETHING SIMILAR.</u>

POOLE: It was inevitable. Like the unstoppable force colliding with the immovable object. But we've worked together to build the reputation of that magazine for over ten years! I'm going to go ahead and get comfortable, okay?

SOUND: <u>POOLE OPENS A CLOSET DOOR, RUSTLING OF CLOTHES.</u>

POOLE: And now that sociopath is going to annihilate it all with those damned articles.

FEMALE VOICE: (hard to make out from behind the bathroom door) Couldn't you have found some way to stop him?

SOUND: <u>BEDSPRINGS CREAK AS POOLE SETTLES IN.</u>

POOLE: Nope. The editorial autonomy I carved out from the publishers has turned out to be a two-edged sword. For years Steadman has let us print what we want, but now the old fart refuses to get involved.

                  (now angry) *Mentotechnics!* Damn that Evanston, they're all *obsessed!*

FEMALE VOICE: (still in bathroom) So what are you going to do now?

POOLE: I've set up a few possibilities. Yellow Tag Books is planning to start up a series of paperback anthologies and I might pick up some reader fees there.

(stretches and yawns) Then I got a call from Zeigler's office, wondering if I could come down and see them about their magazine. God knows, I might do something really outrageous and actually try and write something.

FEMALE VOICE: (emerges from the bathroom and is revealed to be Ray Ann Sparks) Well, I wish you better luck than I had. That moron's trashing my story.

POOLE: (surprised, happy) Hey! What happened to your clothes?

SPARKS: (laughs) Well...

POOLE: Never mind, I'm glad you're here.

SOUND: <u>MORE BEDSPRINGS AS SPARKS SETTLES IN BESIDE POOLE. THEY KISS FOR A LONG TIME.</u>

POOLE: (sighs, not completely happily) Ray, how do you manage it? Doesn't he wonder where you are?

SOUND: <u>THEY KISS AGAIN.</u>

SPARKS: How can I stay away? The rejected artist needs solace. Besides, we're sort of like the unstoppable force and the immovable object.

POOLE: (laughing) Immovable? Don't you mean rigid?

SPARKS: I certainly hope so... (fades)

CLYDE: (VO) By this time I was pretty sure that something was very seriously wrong, and I suppose if I had any brains I would have figured out that she was seeing someone else and might even have been able to work out who she was seeing. (sighs) But alien invasions and exploding solar systems are a lot easier to face than admitting that the one you love thinks you're less interesting than Martian pond-scum.

Scene Nine

The homes of several science fiction writers, including Clyde's apartment. The same evening.

CLYDE: (VO) I guess if I had the righteous determination of a domestic Alexander Steel, I might have tracked down my wife. Then with alarming virility I might have wrested her from the insidious clutches of the evil lecherous assistant editor from the Seventh Dimension. I guess I could have, I mean some marriages do manage to survive the occasional affair, don't they?

SOUND: <u>CLYDE LOADS A SHEET OF PAPER INTO HIS TYPEWRITER.</u>

CLYDE: (VO) Yeah, I suppose I could have found her and brought her home.

SOUND: <u>STARTS TYPING.</u>

CLYDE: (VO) But I had something else to do, something more important, and I needed peace and quiet in the apartment.

SOUND: <u>HIS TYPING CONTINUES, JOINED BY OTHER WRITERS ALL TYPING ON THEIR MACHINES. THE MASS OF UNCOORDINATED CLICKS ECHOES.</u>

WRITER #1: This is the story of an old man, whose job becomes obsolete because of automation. His family wants to move to Mars, but they can't afford it.

NEWSREADER: Engineers switched on Univac, the world's most powerful calculating machine!

WRITER #1: Then they offer to reprocess his brain as a com-

	ponent in their master computer.
SOUND:	THE TYPING CONTINUES.
WRITER #2:	In this story they keep sending this soldier into battle and he keeps getting killed.
NEWSREADER:	The United Nations announced no intention of scaling back the police action in Korea, in spite of heavier than anticipated casualties.
WRITER #2:	But they foul up the paperwork, and they won't let him stay dead.
SOUND:	THE TYPING CONTINUES.
WRITER #3:	In the future, everybody has to buy things and take dope.
NEWSREADER:	Economists warn that we may be heading for another recession...
WRITER #3:	The less you work, the more you have to consume.
SOUND:	THE TYPING CONTINUES.
WRITER #4:	In my future, business and the churches have seized power.
NEWSREADER:	Investigations into stolen H-Bomb secrets continue...
WRITER #4:	They use special effects to regularly fake miracles.
SOUND:	THE TYPING CONTINUES.
WRITER #5:	In my future, the devil declares war on humanity, and sends in an invasion force to Washington.
NEWSREADER:	The Senate Committee Hearings into un-American Activities is set to begin tomorrow.
SOUND:	THE TYPING CONTINUES BUT GRADUALLY FADES INTO JUST ONE SOLITARY TYPIST—CLYDE.

CLYDE: In my future, television is used to fake the colonization of the planets, so people don't worry about the destruction of the Earth's natural resources.

NEWSREADER: The use of atomic weapons and radioactive waste on North Korean troops was a subject of discussion in Congress today...

SOUND: <u>CLYDE STOPS TYPING AND REMOVES THE PAGE FROM THE TYPEWRITER.</u>

CLYDE: (VO) Maybe I could have found her and made her come back. But I had to write, and this was my *best* work. Somehow I knew that I could never again write as well as I did in the darkness of that awful decade.

SOUND: <u>LOW RUMBLE OF ALL THE OTHER TYPEWRITERS HAMMERING AWAY IN THE DISTANCE.</u>

CLYDE: For many of us, it was our best work. It was in those black nights that we found our voices.

SOUND: <u>MANY FARAWAY TYPEWRITERS...</u>

Scene Ten

A musical interpretation of the editorial pages of the April 1950 issue of *Tremendous Stories of Super Science.*

CLYDE: Thank you, thank you, ladies and gents, aliens and alienated. Welcome to this astonishing cabaret re-creation of the editorial pages of the April 1950 issue of *Tremendous Stories.* This the one you've heard about! It's not a hoax, not an imaginary tale! No, no! In this very issue you will see writers and editors of science fiction claim that they have uncovered the cure to all human suffering!

THE BAND: (a little stoned) Yeah! All right!

CLYDE: And here they are, to sing a medley of their *hits*, those modern-day alchemists of popular culture... *The Mentotechnic Magic Guys!*

SOUND: BRIEF HOWL OF THE P.A. SYSTEM.

McREADY: Dear Readers: I am pleased to announce in the pages of this magazine a discovery which may be equated with the harnessing of electricity and invention of the printing press. What you are about to read may be the most important article ever printed in *Tremendous Stories.* It is a paper on the most important topic imaginable: the care and operation of the human mind!

CROSS: This is not psychoanalysis or psychology, which

are not true sciences because they have no basis in engineering or the hard sciences. Nor is this paper on the disciplines of theosophy, general semantics or dianetics.

EVANSTON: A proclamation to the American Public and the Free World: it is my solemn duty to declare the culmination of my decades of personal scientific research and announce my invention: *Mentotechnics.* Mentotechnics is a science, which describes and controls the structures and mechanisms of the thinking brain. The power of Mentotechnics promises greater intellectual ability, improved mental and physical health, and enhanced social relationships and popularity.

MUSIC: <u>THE OPENING FANFARE OF A BIG BAND ORCHESTRA.</u>

EVANSTON: (voice assumes a musical tempo) AAAAnnnndddd... like all major scientific discoveries, the principles underlying Mentotechnics are simple and readily understood:

MUSIC: <u>THE BAND BEGINS TO PLAY.</u>

CROSS & MCREADY: (singing in unison)
Listen to me, honey dear
Something's wrong with you I fear
It's getting harder to please you
Harder and harder each year.

EVANSTON: (now in normal speaking voice) The power of the mind, focused and enhanced by Mentotechnic treatment, proves that the mind controls the body and in turn—all matter in the universe. The power of the mentotechnically-trained mind can easily cure ailments such as migraines, allergies and high blood pressure. All psychosomatic ills can be banished and I have personally recorded increases in intelligence quotient scores of over 65 points in some test subjects.

CROSS & MCREADY: (singing in unison)
> *I don't want to make you blue*
> *But you need a talking to*
> *Like a lot of people I know*
> *Here's what's wrong with you:*
> *After you get what you want, you don't want it*
> *If I gave you the moon, you'd grow tired of it*
> *soon!*

EVANSTON: I have defined Mentotechnics as thought technology because, as with engineering and the so-called "hard" sciences, Mentotechnics is an undertaking which yields concrete and measurable results. Mentotechnics offers real and accessible answers to the urgent personal and social problems of our times.

CROSS & MCREADY: (singing in unison)
> *You're like a baby*
> *You want what you want when you want it*
> *But after you are presented*
> *With what you want, you're discontented.*

EVANSTON: Mentotechnics is an exact science which can be applied by any intelligent layman. We no longer have to rely on unsympathetic or foreign specialists for our mental health and personal reconstruction.

CROSS & MCREADY: (singing in unison)
> *You're always wishing and wanting for something*
> *When you get what you want*
> *You don't want what you get!*

EVANSTON: With the exercises presented in this article and my upcoming book on Mentotechnics, the doctor, cleric, executive or the concerned family member can invariably cure all emotional disorders and intellectual inhibitions. Properly applied, my treatment will produce the optimum personality with higher levels of intelligence and creativity after just 72 hours of treatment!

	No relapse from a Mentotechnic cure is possible.
MUSIC:	<u>THE BAND APPROACHES THE FINALE.</u>

EVANSTON, CROSS & MCREADY: (singing in unison)
> *And tho' I sit upon your knee*
> *You'll grow tired of me*
> *'Cause after you get what you want*
> *You don't want what you wanted at all!*

<u>MUSIC AND SOUND: FLOURISH OF BAND MUSIC. ENTHUSI-ASTIC APPLAUSE.</u>

CLYDE: (VO) A few friendly words of explanation: Evanston cooked up this do-it-yourself psycho-therapy called Mentotechnics. The therapy was just weird enough for Cross to buy into it. Then Evanston used simple hypnosis to cure McReady's chronic allergies. So with the two most powerful voices in science fiction on his side, Evanston was able to use the pages of America's most popular science fiction magazine as the springboard for his product.

<u>SOUND: A FEW INDIVIDUALS IN THE AUDIENCE, STILL APPLAUDING.</u>

CLYDE: (VO) But do you want to know the wildest thing? When Mentotechnics came out as a book with introductions by McReady and Cross, not only was it the fattest book of 1950, it became a runaway bestseller and started a nation-wide shrink-your-own-brain fad!

<u>MUSIC: ANOTHER STING OF MUSIC FROM THE BAND AS THEY GET READY TO PLAY ANOTHER NUMBER.</u>

CLYDE: (in M.C. mode) But that's just one more of those wacky things all you crazy people get up to! Don't ever change, you nutty kooks, you!

<u>MUSIC: (FADES.)</u>

Scene Eleven

The action alternates between a lecture hall in Dayton Ohio and the Clyde bedroom. An evening in early June 1950.

<table>
<tr><td><u>SOUND:</u></td><td><u>BRISK, POLITE CLAPPING.</u></td></tr>
</table>

SOUND: <u>BRISK, POLITE CLAPPING.</u>

EVANSTON: (echoes at first) Thank you for that kind and enthusiastic introduction, Mrs. Pugh. Not since my initiation into the harvest cults of southeastern Australia have I met with such a motivated, and I must say, attractive, group. Now, as Mrs. Pugh mentioned, I am Donald H. Evanston, author of the critically-acclaimed and best-selling book *Mentotechnics: Contemporary Thought Technology for Personal Reconstruction.*

(Clears his throat) At the request of the organizing committee of the Dayton Women's Self-Improvement and Home Gardening Association, I will skip my usual description of how my ground-breaking theories were the result of decades of personal sacrifice and systematic psychological research around the world. Instead, I will discuss how the principles of Mentotechnics can be utilized to help all of you make a greater contribution to American society—by becoming more efficient and content housewives. I will also talk about something you might find even more interesting...

(Now a little lewd) ...how Mentotechnics can provide the avenue to enhanced and more satisfying *marital relations.*

CLYDE: (a bit sad) What are you thinking?

SPARKS: Nothing. You always think I'm thinking something. I'm just reading.

EVANSTON: Most experts agree that the root cause of all marital problems is a general failure in interpersonal communication technique.

SPARKS: (yawns and stretches)

CLYDE: It's all right, really. I understand. I guess it's just one of those things.

SPARKS: (absently) What's all right? What do you understand?

CLYDE: (embarrassed) Well, that you can't, you know...

SPARKS: (matter-of-factly) Then you really don't understand. If you must, you can go ahead if you really want to.

CLYDE: (shocked) What do you mean?!

EVANSTON: This general breakdown in empathetic and informational exchange can be re-established through a regime of Mentotechnic treatment.

First, the couple must carry out the exercises I describe in chapters seven and twelve in my best-selling book. Through this range of thought technology training, the married couple will attain a state of emotional competence—whereupon it is relatively simple to enact my three laws of marital harmony and co-habitational bliss.

Number One: establish a climate of universal respect and total honesty...

CLYDE: (upset) I don't think I do understand.

SPARKS: What I'm saying is that maybe you think about going somewhere else for sex.

CLYDE: I don't want to understand this!

SPARKS: (still matter-of-factly) I suppose if I were a better wife I'd find a nicer way to accommodate you, but I really can't be bothered anymore.

EVANSTON: Once the couple have generated a climate of general well-being and happiness, mental auras will be in place to establish in-depth, long-term psychosexual meta-communication.

We are then ready to apply Marital Harmonics Law Number Two: always think positive thoughts and don't forget to telepathically share vibrational optimism.

CLYDE: *What the hell are you talking about!?*

SPARKS: Don't tell me you haven't noticed just a little, well maybe a complete, lack of response cn my part? Aren't you just a teensy-weensy bit sick of the pathetic ritual we call love-making?

CLYDE: *I can't believe I'm hearing this!*

SPARKS: And I can't believe that you enjoy sex with me anymore. God knows, I don't think I ever liked it with you.

                Do you think maybe you're a latent homosexual? Maybe you don't know the difference between good and bad sex with a woman.

EVANSTON: Marriage is darned hard work.

                Rule Three: after sharing in connubial bliss and mental harmony, the couple must institute a rigorous program of Mentotechnic discipline. This should include abstaining from any verbal utterances during the act of conception, conducting algebraic or sports trivia computations as the man enters a state of expressive physical excitement, and...

                (lascivious tone returns) ...encouraging the female partner by judiciously donning fantasy garments and playfully applying bondage instruments prior to the act of intercourse.

CLYDE: (furious) *I'm not queer!*

SPARKS: Okay, okay. I'm sorry. Of course you're not a homosexual, you're just too dumb to know what's going on in your own marriage.

CLYDE: *What?!*

SOUND: <u>SPARKS GETS OFF THE BED AND OPENS THE CLOSET DOOR.</u>

SPARKS: Robert, just how obvious do I have to be about this?

SOUND: <u>HANGERS RATTLE AND CLOTHES RUSTLE AS SPARKS DRESSES.</u>

CLYDE: Obvious about what? *You don't make any sense!*

SPARKS: I'm not very happy. Actually, incredibly, close to suicide, miserable.

CLYDE: But honey, we can work it out. We love each other...

SPARKS: No, we can't and no, we don't. Intellectually, I can remember why we got married. But you're never around anymore and there's nothing between us anymore.

              And I don't think you're going to ever write your way out of television, either.

CLYDE: (taken aback—suddenly a little calmer) Hey, my writing's good. And in time we...

SPARKS: There is no time, *Robert.* Not in the whole infinity of time and space.

SOUND: <u>SHE OPENS THE DOOR.</u>

SPARKS: I thought I wouldn't be able to say this, but actually it's going to make it easier: I've been seeing someone for the last six months. Right now I can't tell which is worse, the guilt or my irritation at you for not catching on.

SOUND: <u>DOOR CLOSES.</u>

CLYDE: But, but, Ray... why? (sobs) *Who?*

EVANSTON: Of course, if the therapeutic program I have recommended in this talk proves to be ineffective, another range of more advanced and potent treatments will be included in my upcoming work *Mentotechnics Plus: Integrating Your Family and Your Nervous System.*

CLYDE: (VO) I hate to admit it but Ray was right about a few things; I wasn't gay, but I sure was stupid, or at least stubborn. Right up to the last moment I wouldn't let myself believe any of it was happening.

But do you know what *really* hurt? When she said I couldn't *write!*

Scene Twelve

The action alternates between a series of homes, a hotel room and the editorial office of *Tremendous Stories*. July–September 1950.

CLYDE: (VO) Some Freudian rake once said that the super-ego was the only component of the human personality that is soluble in alcohol. Maybe something like that was the problem with me and Ray Ann, our marriage was career soluble.

SOUND: HE TAPS AT HIS TYPEWRITER.

CLYDE: But then again, maybe not. But I was sure about one thing; I was in a really crummy mood for most of 1950. It felt like my life had been sucked into a black hole, and I don't think the damned things had been discovered yet.

But even though I wasn't paying attention, big things were afoot. Millions were buying Evanston's book and buying into his therapy. This was unfortunate, as it suggested to D.H. that he knew what he was talking about.

Thanks to Mentotechnics, thousands were busy trying to purge their psyches of all weaknesses and inhibitions and transform themselves into perfect thinking machines—upwardly mobile missiles of professional achievement and material success.

SOUND: HE PULLS A SHEET OF PAPER OUT OF HIS TYPEWRITER.

CLYDE: (VO) Yeah, it was great.

SOUND: MARTINI GLASSES BEING FILLED.

MADELEINE: Is that it?

SOUND:	<u>HER FRIEND SHEILA STARTS UNPACKING THE CONTENTS OF A BOX. RUSTLE OF PACKING PAPER AND TINKLE OF GLASS AND WIRES.</u>
SHEILA:	Sure is. Phil cannibalized the hi-fi last night for parts.
MADELEINE:	Really?
SHEILA:	(laughs) With a little persuasion. Now put this on.
MADELEINE:	Oh, gawd, Sheila! I'm not going to put this thing on my new hair.
SOUND:	<u>SHEILA ADJUSTS A DIAL. THERE IS A BRIEF WAIL OF ELECTRONIC FEEDBACK.</u>
SHEILA:	You don't have to, Maddie. Just put one of the earpieces next to your head and talk into the microphone.
MADELEINE:	Okay...
SHEILA:	(excited) Ready, Maddie? Okay, why don't you start by describing in detail all your feelings about your mother?
SOUND:	<u>ELECTRONIC WAIL AND THE CLICKING OF SOMETHING THAT SOUNDS A LOT LIKE A LIE DETECTOR.</u>
ROGER:	(whines) Dad! This is real dumb! I thought you said it was gonna be electric!
McALISTER:	Settle down, lad. The book says that under some circumstances this low-cost alternative will be effective.
ROGER:	But, Dad! This is a tin-can telephone!
McALISTER:	(sternly) Roger, your mother and I are not made of money. Now put the *aural receptor-link* in place.
ROGER:	I still think this is dumb.
McALISTER:	That's not important, Roger. (echoes into the tin

can receiver). Now Roger, we will begin by treating your pathological refusal to factor quadratic equations. (fades)

SOUND: <u>DOOR OPENS. FOOTSTEPS ON CARPET. DOOR CLOSES AGAIN.</u>

STAN: This is the place!

MARIE: Stan, you sound like Brigham Young. It's only a hotel room.

SOUND: <u>STAN DEPOSITS A BOX ON A DESK. STAN AND MARIE SIT DOWN.</u>

STAN: For $15 a night, there isn't any *only* about it, Marie.

SOUND: <u>STAN OPENS THE BOX. RUSTLE OF PACKING MATERIAL.</u>

STAN: But there may be some Mormon blood in my background, anyway.

MARIE: (under her breath) That might explain one or two things.

SOUND: <u>CLICKS AND SNAPS AS STAN ASSEMBLES AN ELECTRICAL ASSEMBLAGE.</u>

STAN: Presto! The advanced Q-Wave Cerebro-Helmet as described by Donald H. Evanston. Do you want to go first?

MARIE: Why don't you? I think you're the one who wants to expand his mind tonight.

STAN: Okay. Take the microphone... (pause) Is something wrong?

MARIE: I don't know, there's something familiar about that get-up that reminds me of something I think I read in *Amazing Stories* years ago... some kind of electro-hypno-scope. Can't remember, really.

SOUND: <u>ELECTRONIC WAIL AND HOWL. FADES TO SOUND OF WRITER DENSON OPENING A THICK ENVELOPE.</u>

McREADY: (VO in dictation voice) Dennie, my boy: Please find enclosed a copy of your last story which I have revised somewhat. You might want to see this, although I have already sent it down to layout...

DENSON: (outraged) *What?!*

McREADY: (VO) ...I know this is a tad irregular, but I bought your story just before we underwent a major change in editorial policy at *Tremendous*. Rather than set you off floundering on vast new philosophical seas, I have taken the liberty of re-writing and re-casting your manuscript to bring it more in line with our current direction...

DENSON: I've been writing for him for years, what's the problem?!

SOUND: <u>DENSON PAGING THROUGH THE MARKED-UP MANUSCRIPT.</u>

McREADY: (VO) ...For example I've changed the occupation of your character from a returning space-war veteran to that of a rising young psycho-engineer. I've also moved the setting from a post-nuclear holocaust Earth to a prosperous corporate colony on the Moon...

SOUND: <u>DENSON THROWS THE MANUSCRIPT AGAINST THE WALL.</u>

DENSON: (enraged) *You egotistical bastard!*

McREADY: (VO) ...also please note that I have completely re-cast your female lead character. She's far too dominant in your first version. Biologists have long since established that the females of all mammalian species are more passive and receptive than the male. Please avoid undermining the basic credibility of your stories by violating known scientific facts...

DENSON: (screaming) *I will never write for you again!*

McREADY: (VO) ...If you wish to have your future submissions less rigorously edited, I recommend you review some of Evanston's recent articles on Mentotechnics, or even some of Cross' recent novel serials for ideas for possible themes and storylines.

DENSON: (still screaming) *Zeigler! Where the hell is Zeigler's phone number?!*

SOUND: <u>ELECTRONIC HOWL RISES.</u>

SHEILA: So what happened after the train came out of the tunnel?

MADELEINE: Well, it was the strangest thing. I was suddenly falling and falling, and then there was my father! Only, well... (her voice lowers with embarrassment.) ...he wasn't wearing any... any clothes.

SOUND: <u>THE MECHANISM INSIDE THE METAL BOX EMITS A LOW BUT INSISTENT TICKING.</u>

SHEILA: (interested) And then what happened?

MADELEINE: (cheering up) Then, suddenly, we were laughing and riding together on a big white horse. We were riding along the sea shore beside the crashing waves. Then I woke up. Junior had crawled into bed with us and had stolen all the covers.

SHEILA: What do you think that this dream meant? I mean, er, let me check my copy of *Mentotechnics*... (reading from the page) "please compute the emotional values of these non-rational, sub-intellectual manifestations."

MADELEINE: (confused) Well, I think...

SOUND: <u>CLICKING MECHANISM.</u>

MADELEINE: We're supposed to be completely honest when we do this, aren't we, Sheila?

SHEILA: That's what the book says.

MADELEINE: Then, to tell the absolute truth, I think my dream is saying that my mother is jealous of me.

	(Both women laugh)
McREADY:	(in dictation voice, echoes) Dear Sheldon: My boy... (he chuckles) ...I think you might enjoy the learning experience I'm providing in this letter.
SOUND:	<u>BIRDS CHIRPING, EARLY MORNING TRAFFIC OUTSIDE THE ISAACS' KITCHEN.</u>
BARBARA:	Is that a letter from Mr. McReady, Sheldon? What's the matter?
ISAACS:	It's my manuscript. He returned it.
BARBARA:	Really? He hasn't sent you a rejection in years.
SOUND:	<u>ISAACS STARTS PAGING THROUGH THE MANUSCRIPT.</u>
McREADY:	(echoes) We both know how much difficulty you have in developing balanced characters. Well, while Pam and I were undergoing our evening therapy session, it suddenly came to me—you're suffering from chronic psycho-sexual blockage.
ISAACS:	(gasps)
BARBARA:	What's the matter, Sheldon? Is it really a rejection?
ISAACS:	(tense) I don't know yet.
McREADY:	(echoes) You probably witnessed some parental physical indiscretion when you were an infant, or possibly you were the victim of incompetent breastfeeding.
ISAACS:	(horrified) *Argh!*
McREADY:	Not to worry, my hard-working Hebrew friend. The sure cure is what Evanston and I would call a "mentotechnic confessional"—where those things you find the most uncomfortable are publicly associated with you. So as a personal favour to you, I have re-written your latest story with a somewhat sexier theme.
ISAACS:	(shocked) *What?!*

BARBARA: Sheldon? Are you all right? What's happened?

McREADY: (echoes) Please note that I have re-written the character of the wife of the President of the World Scientists Association to be something of an adulterous nymphomaniac with incestuous designs on her son...

ISAACS: (shocked and horrified) *Oh, my god!*

BARBARA: (concerned) Sheldon?

McREADY: (echoes) Also, to pick things up a little I've added a harem scene where our hero must repeatedly prove his sexual mettle with several dozen wanton alien women before he is given access to planetary master-control.

ISAACS: *Oh, this is terrible! This can't be happening to me!*

McREADY: I'm particularly proud of some of the descriptive passages in the harem and the wife's bedroom. I know your prose style so well that most readers will swear you wrote them yourself.

ISAACS: (in tears) *How could he do this to me?! What is Mother going to think?*

BARBARA: (a little confused) Well... we just won't tell her whatever's in that letter. Okay, honey?

McREADY: I'm so enthusiastic about your new image that I've already commissioned the illustrations. I'm going to carry the erotic theme into the graphics. I think I'm going to use one as the cover for the September issue.

ISAACS: (sniffs) It's that darned "mental" book. Cross and Evanston have done something to him. Oh, Barbie, what am I gonna do? I'll have to quit... I can't let people think I write that kind of pornography!

BARBARA: Why don't you just quit writing for McReady? Why don't you answer that letter from Mr. Zeigler?

SOUND: CLICKING OF A Q-WAVE DEVICE.

McALISTER: Now that you have completed the mental exercises you are entering a state of deep relaxation...

ROGER: Dad, this isn't working.

McALISTER: (stern, into the tin can telephone receiver) As your father, I am instructing you to completely relax *this very instant*, young man!

ROGER: (quiet but defiant) Yes, sir.

McALISTER: Roger, I want you to shift your consciousness from present-time to past-time.

ROGER: (mutters) Yeah, right.

McALISTER: Now, I want you to remember the first time you wilfully defied my perfectly reasonable parental requests. Tell me about the first time you decided to become an obstinate and disobedient boy.

ROGER: (whining softly) But, Dad...

McALISTER: More defiance, young man? You've always been disobedient! That's why you *refuse* to understand algebra!

ROGER: But, Dad...

McALISTER: (now raving) Even when you were two weeks old you were disobedient! A regular neonatal schemer! Stealing your mother's affections, constantly drawing her attention to you through your infantile mischievous behaviour!

ROGER: (close to tears) ...I don't understand, Dad.

McALISTER: And your stubborn refusal to excel academically is just another ploy to drive your mother away from me!

ROGER: *What do you want me to do?*

McALISTER: (still raving) You think that you can live like some kind of uncooperative, lazy indigent, with your mother always there to look after you. Keeping her away from me...

ROGER: (recovering, testy) Is there *anything* you want me to do?

McALISTER: (still raving) ...always disobeying me, always getting in the way...

SOUND: ROGER STANDS UP AND KNOCKS OVER THE Q-WAVE DEVICE.

ROGER: (screaming into the other tin can) *The hell with you, Dad!*

SOUND: ROGER STORMS OUT OF THE ROOM. DOOR SLAMS. HUMS AND CLICKS OF ANOTHER DEVICE RISES.

STAN: Is something the matter? Let's keep going.

MARIE: Stan, you look ridiculous. I think it's time we got honest with ourselves and you took off that stupid headgear.

STAN: (awkward) Uh, okay.

SOUND: CLUNKS OF METAL AND GLASS AS HE PULLS OFF THE HEADSET.

STAN: What did you have in mind?

MARIE: What did *we* have in mind? Why do you think we rented a hotel room for this session?

STAN: To carry out mentotechnic practice "away from the prying eyes and skepticism of uninformed family and friends"?

MARIE: (sighs) No, we rented a hotel room to get away from our respective spouses.

STAN: And that, too.

MARIE: So that we could start that affair that we've been thinking about. Now get your clothes off and get into bed.

SOUND: KNOCKING ON A DOOR.

McREADY: (absently) Come in.

CROSS: McReady? As we agreed, I am personally delivering the latest instalment of my novel.

SOUND: <u>HOLLOW THUD AS CROSS DEPOSITS A LARGE ROLL OF NEWSPRINT ON MCREADY'S DESK.</u>

McREADY: What's this?

CROSS: To save time I have been typing directly onto rolls of newsprint.

McREADY: Wonderful, great, couldn't you have cut it into pages first?

SOUND: <u>CROSS TAKES A SEAT.</u>

CROSS: To confirm our communication of yesterday, this chapter is a fictional demonstration of mentotechnic training principle no. 87: "the real-world power of affirmative thought conceptualization". The story climax occurs when the protagonist develops a mind-activated time-distortion probe designed to obliterate the race of libidinally-motivated lust-beasts.

SOUND: <u>MCREADY UNRAVELLING MORE AND MORE OF THE ROLL AS HE READS FROM THE MANUSCRIPT.</u>

McREADY: (absently) Wonderful, great, terrific. Next time don't forget to cut the story into pages.

CROSS: McReady, please confirm that you understand.

McREADY: (surprised) What? Sorry, old boy. You've talked to Evanston about this instalment? He's happy with it?

CROSS: Affirmative. The lust-beasts were his suggestion.

McREADY: Well, that sounds likely.

SOUND: <u>MCREADY PUTS THE ROLL BACK ON HIS DESK.</u>

McREADY: I'm sure it's fine, Jay. Mention to Evanston that I'd

	like the next instalment in pages.
CROSS:	I will convey that information.
McREADY:	Wonderful, great.
CROSS:	McReady, I sense emotional agitation emanating from your position in space. Are you able to elaborate on your potentially dysfunctional condition?
SOUND:	MCREADY LEANS BACK IN HIS CHAIR.
McREADY:	(sighs) Nothing serious, Jay. There's just a few bugs in our program at my end. I've heard from Denson, Clyde and now Isaacs. None of them will accept our re-writes. They're all jumping ship from *Tremendous.*
CROSS:	Did they elaborate on their motivations?
McREADY:	None of them will go along with the new editorial policy. Aside from you, I can only get unknowns to write Mentotechnic fiction.
CROSS:	Do these developments present a major problem?
McREADY:	I'm not sure. I've got a huge supply of young hopefuls, all of them eager to write to our specifications.
CROSS:	I still sense your distressed vibrations.
McREADY:	Maybe I'm just upset about how my former regulars reacted to my re-writes. I worked *hard* to make those manuscripts into important stories. And I thought those bastards were my friends.
CROSS:	Such an emotional response is understandable with any major informational change. Have magazine sales been affected?
McREADY:	So far, so good. Magazine sales seem to have peaked on Evanston's articles but Thoreau House's distribution people say the book is still selling well.
CROSS:	I will also convey this information to Evanston. Are you certain those are the only problems?

McREADY: Some of my own "emotional responses", I suppose. I worked for years with those writers; sharing ideas, giving them support, adding some meaning and context to the science fiction in *Tremendous Stories*. And all that effort, all that experience and creativity is out the door. I'll miss their work. (pause) I just hope our readers don't.

SOUND: <u>MCREADY SUDDENLY SNEEZES VERY LOUDLY, SEVERAL TIMES.</u>

McREADY: (with surprise and shock) *Oh, my God!*

CROSS: (concerned) You just displayed an allergic reaction.

McREADY: (sniffing, dismayed) *That shouldn't have happened!*

Scene Thirteen

A Lexington Avenue bar in downtown New York City. 9:45 p.m. July 1950. A few days after Cross' conversation with McReady.

SOUND: LOUNGE PIANO, TINKLING OF GLASSES, LOW MURMURING OF PATRONS.

SERLING: So what exactly are you trying to tell me? That the ending's weak?

CLYDE: (carefully) No, no. I'm sure this is perfectly acceptable as a radio or television script; the last prediction of the dead scientist's computer is the date of the end of the world, correct?

SERLING: Yeah, the next morning. I thought it was kind of clever.

CLYDE: Surprise endings are really tricky. You're telegraphing it here on page three, when his widow is talking about his research.

SERLING: Telegraphing? But how else is the reader supposed to know what the computer does?

CLYDE: Exposition is always a big problem in science fiction stories. You have to explain everything without being too obvious. But the way you've set up this whole scene will give the ending away to anyone who's familiar with the genre.

SERLING: So, is that it?

CLYDE: (sheepish) Nope. I'm really sorry but there's a few more basic things you ought to think about.

SERLING: Like what?

CLYDE: Like whether the story's worth writing in the

first place. I mean you have to consider why the story is a science fiction story, and what will make it a good science fiction story.

SERLING: So what kind of artistic criteria are we talking about here? Good characterization? A profound theme? Social commentary?

CLYDE: None of that, all of it. It's a gut feeling, the sort of thing you can only develop if you've been struggling to write these things for years. The whole premise for your script, it's just not original enough...

SERLING: What?!

CLYDE: ...to be successful as an exercise in science fiction. You will have to come up with some new variation on the ultimate computer and end-of-the-world themes for this script to work.

SERLING: (irritated) That's it? I have to come up with some "gimmick-of-the-week" to be a good science fiction writer? I can't believe that, that's not why I admire you guys!

CLYDE: (amused) Really? So what do you admire about us?

SERLING: There's a hell of a lot more in what I see in *Galaxy* and *Astounding* than stories based on some new wrinkle—there's some important commentary in those stories! Now, in my script I was trying to talk about fatalism and the dangers of believing too much in science. I may have a ways to go, but you can't tell me that all that's needed is a new and better cute idea.

CLYDE: I guess the secret's out, Rod. A lot of what we do write is more about 1950 than 2150...

SERLING: (now excited) Yes! But set on another planet! To protect the innocent and confuse the hell out of the guilty. That's what I find so appealing about science fiction; it's easier to write about

McCarthy or Uncle Joe if you re-baptize them as Xenotar and Klizdon, switch the A-Bomb for death rays, and put 'em all in the Andromeda Galaxy.

<u>SOUND:</u>	<u>CLYDE FINISHES TAKING A LONG DRINK.</u>

CLYDE: Send Stalin and McCarthy to another galaxy? Excellent idea. But you've got it, friend. That's why some of us are writing science fiction.

SERLING: The genre lets us write about big issues with no censorship or political backlash. It's a free rein for relevant drama... *Which is why it has to happen on television!*

CLYDE: Social commentary on *The Adventures of Alexander Steel and the Solar Patrol*? Now, that would stretch the boundaries of the imagination, unless you grew up with me and my friends.

SERLING: What's that supposed to mean?

CLYDE: Never mind. Anyway, the situation in the genre isn't that clear cut.

SERLING: Okay, now what is *that* supposed to mean?

CLYDE: Ask Kurt Vonnegut. Weird guy, can be an interesting writer. Used to work as a publicist for G.E. He was right when he pegged most SF writers as a pack of incestuous "joiners". We fight too much and we forgive too much among ourselves, and if you're from outside the clique it don't matter how good you are. To some people, if they didn't see you at the 1937 World Science Fiction Convention—you just don't exist.

SERLING: I can't believe that. If you've written something strong enough, people will respond no matter who you are.

CLYDE: And not everybody in the field has the same

values. At first I thought television was the per-fect medium for a science fiction writer: sound, vision, advanced technology bringing stories to the masses! But no. Most of my associates haven't even seen a TV set, let alone considered its impact on society.

Hell, some of my best friends even won't fly in an airplane or drive a car. Science fiction writers are still producing some of the most hackneyed and formula-driven stories in the English language. All these alleged visionaries can only think of the future in terms of "radio-scopes" and "visi-screens"!

SOUND: <u>SOMEONE IN THE BAR TURNS ON A RADIO AND TUNES IT TO A STATION PLAYING THE CLOSE OF A RACHMAN-INOFF PIANO CONCERTO.</u>

SERLING: Maybe there's some truth to what you're saying. But I still think my idea is a good one. An an-thology series dedicated to high-quality science fiction stories would be a television landmark.

CLYDE: Maybe, maybe. But don't expect any of my asso-ciates to thank you for it.

RADIO ANNOUNCER: (distant) ...and it's coming up on 10:00 and stay tuned for "Dark Words" with...

CLYDE: Look, Rod, I'm really sorry. I'm just going through this separation thing and my attitude about life and art hasn't been very exemplary lately.

SERLING: I'm sorry to hear that. I hope I wasn't bothering you with all these ambitions from the under-belly of Ohio.

CLYDE: Not at all. Reading your script was the most fun I have had all week. You make me want to dump that damned serial and try to write some-thing worthwhile.

SERLING: Thanks.

CLYDE: I'm only coming down on you so hard because the story is worth the re-write. Failing that, I think you have to keep working on that thing about the boxer. That's not my area of expertise, but I think it has real potential.

SERLING: Well... Thanks.

SOUND: THE YOUNG WRITER RISES FROM HIS CHAIR.

SERLING: I have a train to catch, but you certainly have given me a lot to think about on the trip.

CLYDE: Good luck to you. We should keep in touch, I'd be interested to see if your anthology idea ever works out.

SERLING: It's one of my longer-term goals, but I'll be sure to let you know how it works.

SOUND: FOOTSTEPS AS ROD SERLINGS LEAVES. AMBIENT NOISE OF THE BAR, THE VOLUME OF THE RADIO RISES.

RADIO INTERVIEWER: (on speaker) And good evening, listeners! Welcome to "Dark Words!" The interview program for late-night thinkers. Tonight, we have in our studios Roland Paige, noted psychoanalyst and an outspoken critic of Mentotechnics—the fad that's sweeping the United States.

PAIGE: (also on speaker) Good evening...

RADIO INTERVIEWER: Dr. Paige is here to provide a different perspective on some of the things Donald H. Evanston said when he was here on "Dark Talk" last week.

PAIGE: Yes, that is correct. I am here as a representative of the Organization of Psycho-Medical Practitioners.

RADIO INTERVIEWER: Now, Dr. Paige, you've been quoted as

calling Mr. Evanston a "delusional hysteric" and stating that Mentotechnics is "a body of hazardous lies which could lead millions to at best foolishness and at worst, psychosis." Is that quote correct?

PAIGE: I made those remarks at the annual conference of the American Psychological Society last month. But perhaps your listeners may want to evaluate Mentotechnics, not just on my word, but on its own terms. Where are the thousands of people supposedly cured by Evanston's treatment? Has even one person become healthier through Mentotechnics? Has anyone's intelligence quotient been raised a single point through the exercises he describes in his book?

CLYDE: (softly) It's all coming home to roost, McReady.

Scene Fourteen

The Boardroom of the Mentotechnic Educational Institute on the 17th floor of a Manhattan office building. Late afternoon, October 1950.

SOUND: <u>BIG SET OF DOORS SWING OPEN. LOUD, CONFIDENT FOOTSTEPS.</u>

EVANSTON: Mac! Jay! *Great* to see you both here!

SOUND: <u>FOOTSTEPS STOP AS EVANSTON DROPS INTO BIG PADDED CHAIR.</u>

EVANSTON: Hope I didn't keep you waiting too long. (pause) Let's get started, shall we?

CROSS: Shall we not wait for the secretary to arrive, and record all points of discussion and policy decisions?

EVANSTON: (laughing) Naw. Pioneers in science and commerce such as ourselves shouldn't be bound by bureaucratic convention!

McREADY: Donald...

EVANSTON: (laughing) But if you insist...

SOUND: <u>HE LOUDLY SLAPS THE TABLETOP WITH HIS OPEN PALM.</u>

EVANSTON: I hereby declare the monthly meeting of the Board of Directors for the Mentotechnic Educational Institute to be in session!

McREADY: (irritated) Well, I'm glad you're so happy.

CROSS: I am also compelled to query the reasons for your apparently positive frame of mind.

EVANSTON: Oh, I admit we seem to have a few short-term expansion problems...

McREADY: (upset) A few problems? Have you read the papers lately? We're getting creamed in the press! Christ, even the fanzines are making fun of your last lecture.

CROSS: I must substantiate Stewart's concern: August sales of the Mentotechnics book have dropped to less than 0.6% of the sales for June and July. Extrapolating this trend, we can estimate that less than 250 books have been sold so far in this month.

EVANSTON: You're right, I suppose the demonstration could have gone a little better...

McREADY: (very angry) *A little better?!* Not only did you fail to prove that you had doubled the boy's I.Q., the kid collapsed on stage!

EVANSTON: It was a technical problem. Besides, there's no such thing as bad publicity, right?

McREADY: *No such thing as bad publicity?!* Are you insane?! We've been condemned by the AMA, ridiculed by the American Psychological Society, and attacked by the National Mental Health Association! We may get subpoenaed by the Food and Drug Administration, for God's sake!

EVANSTON: Oh, stop worrying, all that's in the past. I've got three new books on the stands this month.

CROSS: Cumulative sales for all three of the new publications total less than 25% of the initial sales of the original Mentotechnics book.

McREADY: We really don't want to mess with the feds, Don. I know.

CROSS: If current sales continue at present levels, the new books will not achieve best-seller status until the year 2362.

EVANSTON: (still cheerful) Okay, okay, you got me, guys! I admit it. We have a couple of fairly serious P.R. and cash flow problems. But I've got a solution for our present difficulties.

McREADY: (disbelieving) Like what?

CROSS: Please elucidate.

EVANSTON: Of course.

SOUND: <u>EVANSTON PULLS A CORD. THERE IS A "SWISH" AS A LARGE SET OF CURTAINS PART.</u>

EVANSTON: Explorers of the mind, witness the future!

McREADY: What the hell is going on here? We didn't authorize anything like this!

CROSS: I am experiencing momentary disorientation. Why are we looking at a wall of multi-coloured parcels?

EVANSTON: Please, please, my friends. It is the blood of generations of entrepreneurial geniuses and the robber barons of the Evanston lineage that speak to you now.

McREADY: Oh, my god...

EVANSTON: Now, gentlemen, what are the two main causes of the Institute's problems? One: *diffusion of profit.* People are interested in Mentotechnics so they go out and buy the book. Once! Or worse, they borrow the book from a library or they may hear about Mentotechics from a friend or family member. 1.3 million people may have bought the book, but uncounted millions more are out there practising the therapy—and we see no money from this aside from book sales and lecture fees. The result? We get paid a little for sowing the seed, but we get nothing of the bounteous harvest! So gents, how do we make a buck from all those people who are out there, chomping at the bit to discover their new minds, and *making* all that *homemade* therapy equipment?

McREADY: Well, I...

EVANSTON: Problem number two: *consumer dissatisfaction.* Okay, I admit the following scenario can happen: people buy the book, do what they think it says, and then they find that they aren't any smarter, richer or more popular. Erroneously they conclude that Mentotechnics doesn't work—so they start spreading vicious rumours to their friends and family, and believe me, that kind of word-of-mouth is really bad for business.

McREADY: (angry) Well, some of that has certainly been coming around to me.

EVANSTON: Isn't it terrible how these things can get started? But don't despair, I have the answer to both our problems: *Merchandising!*

McREADY: (sarcastic) Now, why didn't I think about that?

EVANSTON: We tell people that the therapy didn't work for them because they neglected to purchase a number of useful products which are invaluable aids to attaining Mentotechnics self-improvement objectives. And, here's the kicker: all the profits from the products we produce and promote will go directly to the Institute! Of course some of these funds will be used to reward the considerable efforts of its hard-working Board of Directors.

McREADY: (disgusted) What's next, man? We start selling door to door?

CROSS: Would not retail services of this scope require a fundamental re-direction of the Institute's philosophy and mandate?

EVANSTON: Why don't I tell you about some of the products?

SOUND: <u>CARDBOARD BOX IS OPENED, PACKING MATERIAL FALLS OUT.</u>

EVANSTON: The Evanstonian Cerebroscope Commercial Mk. One. This is a device tailor-made to augment the effectiveness of advanced Mentotechnic treatment. It operates on two penlight batteries and retails for a very reasonable $388.99.

McREADY: (sarcastic) Oh, *very* reasonable.

SOUND: TINKLE OF EVANSTON SHAKING A BOTTLE OF PILLS.

EVANSTON: Well, here's something a little less expensive. Technol-M. A revolutionary medicinal additive and mineral compound which promotes regularity and harnesses ambient mental energies. Technol-M is reported to counteract the effects of toxic chemicals and radiation and promote the healing of decayed nerve endings.

CROSS: But what possible combination... of chemical components could... have... these... properties?

McREADY: And where the hell do you get that crap?!

EVANSTON: And this is an important educational tool for people who may be a little queasy about taking medication on a regular basis: *Sonic-Self-Improvement with Donald H. Evanston*, a series of readings and exercises recorded by myself for posterity and convenient use on this set of 14 78rpm records. The set will go for 200 bucks but with regular inventory discount sales for $99.99.

McREADY: Oh yes, a bargain at twice the price.

EVANSTON: So, my friends and partners, whaddya think?

CROSS: (voice cracks with suppressed emotion) I... I... I... cannot condone any of your intentions. Your proposal represents a complete deviation from the overall purpose of Institute research, which is to discover unknown and untapped resources and potentials of the mind.

(on the verge of tears) You want to compromise the integrity of the Mentotechnics Movement. I simply do not believe the Institute to be a commercial entity!

EVANSTON: (impatient) Yeah, yeah. We can still do some re-

	search, but we'll fund that work from the profits we get from product sales.
McREADY:	Donald, you're on damned dangerous ground here. Anything that looks like a drug or therapeutic equipment will have to be approved by the government as safe and bona fide medical products. Everything here will have to be tested and certified by the Food and Drug Administration. I'll bet you haven't thought about that, have you?
SOUND:	<u>MCREADY PICKS UP ANOTHER PILL BOTTLE AND POURS ITS CONTENTS OUT ON THE BOARDROOM TABLE.</u>
McREADY:	Technol-M! Good God! Why the hell don't you set up a concession for pushing hair restorer or Spanish Fly? The only way you can sell this legally is if they agree to classify it as hobby equipment or religious artifacts.
EVANSTON:	Very interesting thought, Stu!
McREADY:	I didn't get into this because I wanted a career as a carny huckster! But that's what you're proposing we do! I support Mentotechnics because I believe that it's a practical way for the average man to improve his life! I helped you because I thought we would stimulate new ideas and challenge some assumptions!
CROSS:	I intuitively sense that both McReady and I are in agreement. Donald, as your Board members we cannot concur with your proposals, and as we constitute the majority of the Board of the Mentotechnics Institute...
McREADY:	...we are terminating this little venture of yours, Don.
SOUND:	<u>HE PULLS THE CURTAIN BACK OVER THE DISPLAY CASE, THEN SNEEZES.</u>
McREADY:	Maybe we'll just have to scale down the Institute's operations. For a start we can move somewhere

	where we can afford the rent.
SOUND:	SNEEZES LOUDLY INTO A HANDKERCHIEF.
McREADY:	Maybe we can invite some outside researchers and shrinks to comment on the work we've done so far...
SOUND:	HE SNEEZES AGAIN.
McREADY:	...stop putting all the pressure on Don's books and lectures for income.
SOUND:	HE SNEEZES AGAIN.
EVANSTON:	(quietly) What's with all this sneezing?
McREADY:	(sniffs) Last of the summer allergies, I guess.
CROSS:	Stewart has experienced a minor relapse. I have been helping him with remedial treatment sessions.
EVANSTON:	(with exaggerated surprise and dismay) *You* are helping him?! I completely cured all his allergies. There shouldn't be any relapses. (enraged) *Well, I know what this means!*
SOUND:	EVANSTON PULLS OPEN A DRAWER AND STARTS RIFLING THROUGH PAPERS.
McREADY:	Don, what's the big deal...?
EVANSTON:	(intense) Just a minute, *just one damn minute!*
SOUND:	RIFLING OF PAPERS STOPS.
EVANSTON:	Aha! Here it is, the charter document for the Mentotechnics Institute! (He reads from the page in a loud voice) "...the reasons for dismissal from the Board of the Institute include:

1) Failure to adhere to the theory and practice of Mentotechnics as described in the works of Donald H. Evanston, or; 2) If said Board member or members are found to be acting against the best interests of Mentotechnics...

...as determined by Donald H. Evanston!"

McREADY:	What are you getting at, Don?
EVANSTON:	(furious) You bloody bastards should have looked at the fine print. It says what I say goes, and I say, *you go! Get the hell out of here, you traitors!*
McREADY:	Come on, Jay. We don't need to suffer this fool gladly.
SOUND:	<u>THE TWO MEN RISE FROM THEIR SEATS AND WALK TOWARDS THE DOOR.</u>
CROSS:	(sad) Goodbye, Donald.
SOUND:	<u>THE BIG DOORS CLOSE.</u>
EVANSTON:	(mutters) Traitors.

Scene Fifteen

The action moves between the Clyde apartment and the Isaacs household. February 1951.

SOUND: <u>DOORS ON A MOVING VAN SLIDING SHUT. DIESEL ENGINE STARTS, THE VAN DRIVES OFF.</u>

CLYDE: (VO) I am, once again, a single man. The flight into Reno suggested a new theory of life to me: aviation existentialism. Life is a series of very long runways, short mad flights, and desperate landings on new runways. You roll along the latest runway thinking this must be your situation in life, but just when you get used to things, you're at the end of this runway and you have to take off again. Then you land and you think, for sure, this is where you're meant to end up, until... (he shrugs) ...well, you can guess how this continues.

Anyway I am now about to make my first big takeoff in life. I seem to be getting over the divorce pretty easily, and I think I've grown up some, which can only be an improvement.

SOUND: <u>CLYDE PICKS UP THE TELEPHONE AND STARTS TO DIAL A TELEPHONE NUMBER.</u>

CLYDE: (VO) Of course, I wasn't tough or smart enough to get Ray to tell me who her lover was, which is why we had to go out to Reno in the first place. There is definitely such a thing as being too nice.

SOUND: <u>LINE AT THE OTHER END RINGS.</u>

CLYDE: (VO) I had other things to attend to; and with

	any big change, there are often a number of loose ends which have to be tied off.
<u>SOUND:</u>	<u>CLICKS AS SOMEONE PICKS UP THE RECEIVER.</u>
BARBARA ISAACS:	(over receiver) Hello? This is the Isaacs household.
CLYDE:	Hello? Barbara? This is Bob Clyde.
BARBARA:	(friendly) Oh, hello, Bob. How are you doing?
CLYDE:	Oh, fine.
BARBARA:	Are you sure? If there's anything Sheldon and I can do, you be sure to let us know.
CLYDE:	That's very kind of you, but really, I'm fine. Listen, Barbara, can I speak to Sheldon for a moment? It's a business matter.
BARBARA:	Why sure, Bob.
ISAACS:	(grave) Robert? This is Sheldon. You aren't contemplating suicide or anything, are you?
CLYDE:	(amused) No, no. But thank you for asking, Sheldon.
ISAACS:	Well, thank god for that.
CLYDE:	Listen, Sheldon, the moving van has just left and I thought I'd let you and Barb know that I'm going to be changing my address shortly...
ISAACS:	Excellent idea, Robert. Change the locale, get a fresh start, obliterate any trace of that she-devil...
CLYDE:	...to Hollywood.
ISAACS:	(horrified) Good grief, *California*! Whatever for, man!?
CLYDE:	Well, Allied Artists needs somebody to do some script doctoring on a couple of SF projects. There's a chance that I could be working on

	some Finney and Ehrlich treatments.
ISAACS:	But Los Angeles. It's human life without civilization. It's so vapid, the driving is loose, and the people are so promiscuous.
CLYDE:	Actually, I was kind of counting on all of that, Sheldon.
ISAACS:	But what about the television series? How can you keep working on *Alexander Steel* from Los Angeles? You can't abandon our creative offspring, can you?
CLYDE:	Sheldon, they won't have any trouble replacing me. All they need is someone who can write and watch at the same time. Anyway, to be perfectly honest, Sheldon, I think the character is starting to run out of gas. I would be very surprised if the sponsor picks up the series for another year.
ISAACS:	(shocked) Really?! Well, I hope you're wrong, because I'm halfway through the second trilogy and we're going to need a new magazine to carry it.
CLYDE:	I didn't know you'd done so much work on the latest book. (Pause.) Look, Sheldon, I really think that you should finish any new Steel books on your own. I think you're the one who's the most committed to the character.
ISAACS:	Goodness, Bob! Do you really mean it? That's tremendously generous of you.
CLYDE:	(VO) More generous than I knew. As we will discover later on, this was the most expensive phone call of my life.
CLYDE:	Forget it, Sheldon. Look at it as compensation for all the rotten things I did to you when we were kids.
ISAACS:	(solemn) I shall try to live up to this responsib-

ility, Robert. I hope you'll be proud of the many new adventures of *Alexander Steel and the Solar Police.*

CLYDE:

Oh, I'm sure. Look, Sheldon, I have to get uptown to see some people this afternoon before I catch the train. You take care and I'll drop you and the family a postcard once I get settled in. Bye!

ISAACS:

I shall miss you, Robert. Don't pick up too many bad habits.

SOUND:

THEY HANG UP.

Scene Sixteen

The action moves between one of the editorial offices of Rake Publications and the Head Office of the Mentotechnics Therapy Institute. About two hours after the last scene.

CLYDE: (VO) Now I only had one more thing to settle. Hopefully, I was going to reap a measure of satisfaction for all those months of grief.

SOUND: MORE TYPING.

EVANSTON: (reads out loud as he types) *Mentotechnics Newsletter*, Number 162, Volume 30. "Truth and Survival", an editorial for loyal and honest Mentotechnic practitioners. Beware, my faithful students, you may be surrounded by traitorous, lying monsters who seek only to bring about your ruin. Even those you trust the most may be plotting against you and only too late will their true loathsome natures be revealed...

SOUND: SOMEONE SCREAMS. DOOR OPENS. SOMEONE RUNS INTO EVANSTON'S OFFICE.

MISS MAUBAUM: (near hysterical) Mr. Evanston! Mr. Evanston! Help! Help! They've got guns! They've got guns!

SOUND: MORE TYPING. SOMEONE KNOCKS AT THE DOOR.

POOLE: Come in.

SOUND: CLYDE OPENS THE DOOR AND WALKS IN.

CLYDE: (coolly) I wondered if I'd find *you* here.

POOLE: (very startled) *Bob Clyde! Good God, it's you!*

SOUND: <u>CLYDE SITS DOWN IN FRONT OF POOLE.</u>

CLYDE: (still cool) Yes, it is indeed, me.

MISS MAUBAUM: *Guns!*

EVANSTON: What are you talking about, young lady?!

CLYDE: Out of everybody I knew, I really didn't think it would be you.

POOLE: (very nervous) M-me?

CLYDE: I guess we have a few things to talk about, don't we?

POOLE: Look, Bob. I-I don't know what-what you may have been told, but-but-but, the world is a really, *really* crazy place sometimes and, and, and...

SOUND: <u>THUNDERING FOOTSTEPS AS FEDERAL AGENTS MARCH INTO EVANSTON'S OFFICE.</u>

WEBB: Are you Donald Harlan Evanston?

EVANSTON: (defiant) Yes, I am. What is the meaning of this outrage?

WEBB: We're federal marshals authorized by the U.S. Department of Justice. We have a warrant for your arrest and the seizure of all contents of these premises.

EVANSTON: (his resolve slipping a little) Uh, on what charge, officer?

SOUND: <u>FILING CABINETS OPENING. FILES BEING STUFFED INTO BOXES.</u>

WEBB: (reading off a document) Practising medicine without a license, distributing unauthorized medicinal substances without FDA approval, suspected transport of unregistered drugs and consumables across state lines, fraud, theft, income tax evasion, and *generally raising the level of bullshit in America past acceptable levels!*

CLYDE: Dave, how badly did you guys edit my manuscript?

POOLE: (now confused) *Your manuscript?*

CLYDE: Yeah, my new novel. What the hell did you think I was talking about? Your boss Zeigler asked me to stop by and talk about it before I left town. I was just surprised to see you cross over to the competition so fast.

POOLE: You have a novel with us?

SOUND: POOLE PULLS OPEN A FILING CABINET. SHUFFLING OF FILE FOLDERS.

POOLE: (relieved) Oh, yes, yes, of course.

EVANSTON: (outraged) Stop! You can't do this! This is an affront against Science! It's a crime against *Freedom*!

SOUND: GRUNTING AS AGENT WEBB GRABS EVANSTON BY THE LAPELS AND HAULS HIM OUT FROM BEHIND HIS DESK.

WEBB: Agent Phelps, this suspected felon has been witnessed obstructing duly empowered federal marshals in the execution of their duty. So, cuff the jerk!

SOUND: PHELPS DROPS A BOX. WE HEAR THE CONTENTS CRUNCH AND TINKLE INSIDE. HE ROUGHLY SLAPS THE CUFFS AROUND EVANSTON'S WRISTS.

EVANSTON: (blubbering) You can't do this to me! I'm a respected writer, therapeutic commentator and scientific researcher...

WEBB: (with contempt) Get him outta here! And cuff

	his girlfriend, too!
MISS MAUBAUM:	(wailing) *Oh, no!*
JOHNSON:	They say they can't find the keys to the filing cabinets in the other offices, sir.
WEBB:	Boys, the IRS is gonna wanna see those files ASAP.
JOHNSON:	So you're ordering us to...?
WEBB:	Yeah, use the sledgehammers.
SOUND:	<u>LOUD SMASHING AND VIOLENT RENDING OF METAL AS THE AGENTS DESTROY THE FILING CABINETS WITH SLEDGEHAMMERS. FADES.</u>
POOLE:	Sorry if I seem a little slow on the uptake here, I'm still just getting settled and Zeigler hasn't briefed me on everything.
CLYDE:	So what is the mysterious Mr. Zeigler like? He's a bit of an enigma to most of us.
SOUND:	<u>POOLE DROPS A HEAVY BINDER FROM THE FILING CABINET ONTO HIS DESK TOP.</u>
POOLE:	He's a *lot* of an enigma to me. I still haven't met the man.
SOUND:	<u>FLIPPING OF PAGES AS POOLE LOOKS THROUGH THE BINDER.</u>
POOLE:	He lives somewhere out in New Hampshire, never leaves his home. I maintain the New York office, and we communicate by telephone.
CLYDE:	How bizarre.
POOLE:	Yes, well, let's just consider the line of work we're in, Bob. Okay, well, I've got your manuscript. Zeigler just sent it in yesterday, so I haven't had a chance to see what he wants to do with it...

<u>SOUND:</u>	<u>POOLE OPENS AN ENVELOPE.</u>
POOLE:	Humph. This is quite an honour, Bob. Zeigler's telling me that he has already done all the edits, *personally*... well... and according to this he's only making some minor edits. He's divided chapter four into two separate chapters, at the rocket escape sequence, cut a little exposition from chapter two, and he wants to change the title of the novel from *The Exploitation Syndrome* to *Galaxy of Madness*.
CLYDE:	(a little surprised) He liked it that much?
POOLE:	Compared to what McReady's been doing to his people, I'd say you got off easy with this guy.
CLYDE:	But *Galaxy of Madness*? I don't know, Dave.
POOLE:	Bob, we have to be flexible here. Hell, the story's the same, right? Science fiction paperbacks are a new beast. Nobody's sure about the market, so we have to do everything we can to build sales.
CLYDE:	So there's going to be some cleavage on the cover, is there?
POOLE:	I've seen the cover illustrations for the whole line of paperbacks. None of them have any relationship to the story inside and every one of them... (laughs sadly) ...have big, really big ones in the foreground. Personally, I don't think low-cut spacesuits are possible, but this seems to be one point on which the readership is willing to suspend its usual insistence on scientific feasibility.
CLYDE:	Okay, okay. Since the damned book is probably going to sink to the Earth's core without a trace, the title and cover will probably be the least of its problems.
<u>SOUND:</u>	<u>THE MYSTERIOUS SONIC WAVES OF NARRATIVE NON-TIME RISE.</u>

CLYDE: (VO) Again I am mistaken. This time, happily so. In its first printing, *Galaxy of Madness* was by no means a runaway bestseller, but it got good reviews and developed a loyal readership. Over the next thirty years, the book stayed in print, and gradually attracted several million readers.

SOUND: <u>THE ELECTRONIC TONES GIVE WAY TO SERENE ORCHESTRAL MUSIC.</u>

CLYDE: Some of what we wrote in those dark nights was commentary... cries of protest from a trivial place. We were safe because we were so crazy. But what we didn't know was that we were also writing the "classics" of science fiction. We were directing the hearts and minds of the next generation—directing them in ways none of us could predict.

EVANSTON: (screaming in the distance) *No! No! I won't let you do this!*

**End of
Astonishing Failures**

art by Emily O'Brien

Disappointing Success

Play Three:
Disappointing Success

Characters – In Order of Appearance

HAYDEN MacARNOLD	Author of the 1960s cult science fiction classic *The Martian Messiah*.
SPARKY	A female character from *The Martian Messiah*.
BAMBI	Another female character from *The Martian Messiah*.
ELIJAH Q. WITTENTHORPE	An old, world-weary man, the mentor figure from *The Martian Messiah*.
PHILLY	Yet another female character from *The Martian Messiah*.
GEORGE WASHINGTON LISZT	The hero of *The Martian Messiah*. An orphaned human raised by (of course) aliens.
UN SPACE POLICE CAPTAIN	Minor character from *The Martian Messiah*.
D.H. EVANSTON	The now ultra-wealthy reclusive leader of the Temple of Mentotechnics.
SEEKERS #1, #2 AND #3	Trainees in a Mentotechnics program.
ROLF DENSEN	Still a moderately successful science fiction writer of modest reputation. Not much wiser, just older.
BOB CLYDE	Our protagonist and sometimes

	narrator. Now head writer of *Space Spanners*, a network television series struggling through its second season.
RAY ANN SPARKS	Leading edge, but not particularly financially successful, science fiction writer, editor and anthologist. Married to David Poole.
DAVID POOLE	Works as Sparks's assistant editor and husband.
DR. SHELDON ISAACS	Now a well-known media commentator, science pundit/ popularizer and author of a vast amount of science fiction.
STEWART D. McREADY	Still editor of *Tremendous Stories*. Both the magazine and the man have seen better days.
JAY E. CROSS	Has retired from writing science fiction. His work still has a dedicated if not somewhat strange following.
STANLEY THOMPSON	Member of the Ontario Provincial Parliament for the Riding of North Bay, North. Chair of the Provincial Inquiry into the activities of the Temple of Mentotechnics.
RUBIN WEISS	Member of Provincial Parliament for Central Toronto. Also a part of the Provincial Inquiry.
DR. GLORIA McPHERSON	Member of Provincial Parliament for Hamilton West. Also a part of the Provincial Inquiry.
HARLAN DIAMOND	Lawyer from the firm of Gordon, Nolan, Diamond and Wylie. Represents the Toronto branch of the Temple of Mentotechnics.
COMMANDER HUGHES/KYLE	Fictional leader of the starship "Astral Arrow" on the TV series *Space Spanners*. Played by actor

	Kirkman Kyle.
LT. ZAGAR/SHECKLEY	Fictional second-in-command for the starship "Astral Arrow". Played by actor Leo Sheckley.
DR. STURGEON/CLARK	Medical officer onboard the "Astral Arrow". Played by actor Sybil Clark.
MICHELLE JOQUIN	Assistant director for the series *Space Spanners*.
FRANCIS FREEDMAN	A moderately successful science fiction writer. Rolf Densen's slightly smarter friend.
MR. MARTIN	A worker in an Ontario manufacturing plant. Witness at the Mentotechnics hearings.
MRS. MARTIN	Also a witness at the hearings.
MASTER COMPUTER	A machine intelligence from an episode of *Space Spanners*.
HEATHER ATKINSON	Graduate student and assistant to Sheldon Isaacs, soon to be his lover.
ANGELICA MEYER	20-year-old former member of the Temple of Mentotechnics. A witness at the hearings.
ELDER #1 AND #2	Some villains from an episode of *Space Spanners*.
STAGE HAND	Part of the crew on the *Space Spanners* set.
DR. SUSAN LAMBERT	Associate professor of social psychology at McMaster University.
PAGE	Young intern at the hearings.
QUEEN DORXINDRA/LEA	Guest love interest from an episode of *Space Spanners*. Played by actress Christina Lea.
LARRY HOLMES	Executive producer of *Space Spanners*. Christina Lea's uncle.

STUDIO TECHNICIAN   Part of the crew on the set of *Space Spanners*.

HIPPIE FREAK   Apparently an eccentric science fiction fan and aspiring writer.

Scene One

A scene from *The Martian Messiah*, a 1960s cult science fiction novel written by Hayden Mac-Arnold. The events take place aboard the orbital space platform "Zarathustra Love-Nest" during the fictional year of 2064.

SOUND: HIGH PITCHED HUM OF A LARGE "VISI-POD".

SPARKY: Oh, look! An incoming transmission!

SOUND: TYPING IN THE BACKGROUND.

MacARNOLD: (VO) *The Martian Messiah*. A novel by Hayden MacArnold. Chapter One, paragraph one: George Washington Liszt was a human being who was born on one of the moons of Mars. Aliens gave him superpowers which enabled him to save the world. But Liszt was an innocent, and people were either too stupid or self-centred to listen to him. He became fabulously rich anyway and tried to set up his own country in orbital space—away from the restrictions of a mediocre global society. But Vested Interests in Big Business and Big Government were jealous of his advanced intelligence and the fact that he was really good in bed. There was going to be trouble...

SOUND: HEAVY FEMININE BREATHING, RUSTL-ING OF SHEETS.

BAMBI: Oh, Mr. Wittenthorpe, this is a big bed, nobody will mind if we want get friendly...

WITTENTHORPE: Stop that! You know I'm too old and impotent for that sort of thing!

SOUND:	<u>MORE RUSTLING OF SHEETS.</u>
PHILLY:	(sighs) Elijah, why fight it? Don't you know how much we want to share essence with you?
WITTENTHORPE:	(panicking) But I can't! I'm a tired, feeble old man! You girls know that I love you very deeply, but I just can't!
BAMBI:	Why are you denying yourself, Elijah? Why are you denying us your essence?
WITTENTHORPE:	(now desperate, to Liszt) For god's sake, G.W.! Use your advanced mental abilities to explain to these young hussies that I'm old enough to be their grandfather!
SOUND:	<u>CLICKS AND WHIRS AS LIZST ADJUSTS THE SIGNAL ON THE VISI-POD.</u>
SPARKY:	Yummmmm!
LISZT:	Hello, Miss Sparky, is that your tongue in my ear?
SPARKY:	*Yummmmm!*
LISZT:	(calmly, to Wittenthorpe) Why are you denying yourself, my Earth-mentor? The rest of us have exchanged our spiritual fluids. And your physical essence would add vitality to our new socio-sexual community—if only you could overcome these irrational inhibitions.
PHILLY:	(giggling) There, you see?
SOUND:	<u>BAMBI PLANTS A LONG, WET KISS ON WITTENTHORPE.</u>
BAMBI:	Now, share your manly bodily essence with us, you sexy old coot!
SOUND:	<u>LOUD SIREN FROM THE VISI-POD SPEAKER.</u>
SPACE POLICE CAPTAIN:	(on visi-pod speaker) Attention, orbital platform "Zarathustra Love-Nest"! Attention!

This is the Aerospace Tactical Division of the Global Police Force!

WITTENTHORPE: (angry) Damn! It's the U.N. Space Authority; we must have lost the appeal in the World Court.

SPACE POLICE CAPTAIN: (on visi-pod speaker) To occupants of orbital platform: prepare to be boarded!

BAMBI: (wailing) Oh, Elijah! What are we gonna do?!

WITTENTHORPE: (sadly) I don't know, princess. It looks like our little beacon of freedom is going to be snuffed out. And just when I thought I might be able to share my manly essence with you.

LISZT: Be not afraid, my mentor and friends! Our community will not die at the hands of small-sexed, small-brained weaklings!

SOUND: CRACKLING RISES AS LISZT MARSHALS HIS TELEKINETIC ABILITIES.

LISZT: It is time for me to exercise the ultimate powers bestowed upon me by the Elders of Phobos.

SPACE POLICE CAPTAIN: (on visi-pod speaker) You have been found guilty of illegal possession of Planet Earth technologies and crimes against egalitarian resource-sharing. You are ordered to clear all airlock shields and prepare for docking with our tactical squadron. Repeat... prepare to be—

SOUND: MASSIVE EXPLOSION IN THE DISTANCE AS THE PERCUSSION ROCKS THROUGH THE HULL OF THE ORBITAL PLATFORM.

WITTENTHORPE: (in awe) The Government spaceships, G.W.! You destroyed them!

LISZT: I de-integrated their material forms. It was a kindness; they were out of sync with the harmonic structure of the cosmos.

WITTENTHORPE: It doesn't make any difference, son. Now they'll just nuke us out of the sky.

LISZT: (sighs) Earth-mentor, how can a man of your wisdom still be such a weak and frightened creature?

SOUND: <u>AGAIN THE CRACKLE OF LISZT'S TELE-KINETIC POWERS.</u>

LISZT: I see that I must act to re-establish the natural hierarchy of the Elders.

SOUND: <u>SERIES OF VERY DISTANT EXPLOSIONS.</u>

BAMBI: Wow! Look at all the pretty flashes!

SPARKY: Uh, Georgie? Um, what are you doing to the planet?

LISZT: I am de-integrating the molecular form of all Earth cities with Space Authority missile silos and beam projectors.

WITTENTHORPE: (horrified) Do you know what you've just done?! You've just vaporized billions of innocent people!

SOUND: <u>RUSTLE OF SHEETS AS LISZT SETTLES BACK INTO BED.</u>

LISZT: (very calm) An acceptable cost in my estimation. I suppose it was naive of me to think we could have negotiated with beings of such inflexible values... I should have de-integrated them at the outset.

WITTENTHORPE: (close to tears) But this isn't what I meant by true freedom! *You don't have the freedom to do this!*

LISZT: (innocently) Why not?

WITTENTHORPE: (sobs) N-no one...

LISZT: Worry not, my Earth-mentor. Soon you will understand and forgive me. After all, these are your lessons too.

Scene Two

The basement of an office building somewhere in downtown Toronto. Spring 1967.

SOUND: <u>BIG CLICK OF SOMEONE TURNING ON A VERY BIG AND OLD-FASHIONED REEL-TO-REEL TAPE RECORDER. HISS OF STATIC AND THE TAPE ROLLS THROUGH THE PLAYER HEADS.</u>

EVANSTON: (on tape recorder speaker—he speaks slowly, with condescension) Hello, students. I'm taking time away from my busy research schedule at High Command to give you lecture number two in this advanced orientation to Mentotechnical Epistemology. Is everyone ready?

SEEKERS #1, 2, & 3: (not quite in unison) Yes.

EVANSTON: Do you have your pencil and paper ready?

SEEKERS #1, 2. & 3: (not quite in unison) Yes.

EVANSTON: Very good. It is very important that you take down, review and analyze every word of what I am about to say.

SEEKERS #1, 2. & 3: (not quite in unison) Yes.

EVANSTON: Now, the last time, we discussed how my original vision of Mentotechnics was perverted and sabotaged by traitorous evil agents of the United States government who were, of course, deeply jealous of my discoveries and my genius. But it was these very attacks on Mentotechnics which led to the next great step in therapeutic evolution. Mentotechnics was correct... but it needed to go further.

SEEKER #1:   (mutters to herself as she writes) "...needed to go further..."

EVANSTON: In its present form, Mentotechnics is a spiritual revolution which promises the fundamental transformation of man into his ultimate, self-actualized form.

SEEKER #2:   (mutters to himself as he writes) "...ultimate... self-what-cha-ma-call-it form..."

EVANSTON: Now, the new Faith of Mental Technology is more than science—it is more properly a form of religious education which if properly applied brings about personal salvation and world-wide happiness. And you, my friends, are undertaking the first steps to becoming an important part of this movement which will transform us all. First, we must review the basic principles of Mentotechnics...

SEEKER #3:   (mutters to himself) Not more review.

Scene Three

A lounge at the Erewhon Inn, a rustic hotel near Madison, Wisconsin. Spring 1967.

DENSON: (whispers) Uh, Bob! Vengeful apparition at three o'clock!

CLYDE: (also whispers) Hell's bells! You didn't tell me Ray Ann would be here!

DENSON: I didn't—

SPARKS: (rants) Bob Clyde, you S.O.B.! You TV sellout! How dare you criticize David's work?!

POOLE: Ray, let's not make a—

SPARKS: Shut up!

ISAACS: (pompous) Why if it isn't the illustrious and outspoken, Miss—

SPARKS: You really shut up!

ISAACS: (offended) Well!

SPARKS: (rants) None of you would appreciate the revolutionary nature of real literature if it came over, burned down your house and cut off your—

POOLE: (a little desperate) *Ray...*

CLYDE: (angry) You idiot snob. You and your man set yourselves up as the royal family of Nowheresville and then get PO'd because we happen to miss the turn-off! It's not my fault that nobody cared about a stupid piece of instant obscurity magazine called *Unwanted Worlds of Science Fiction.*

SPARKS: (now yelling) *Unexpected Worlds!* It was called

Unexpected Worlds of Science Fiction!

POOLE: We changed the name anyway, Robert. It's now called *Quank!* With an exclamation mark.

DENSEN: (confused) What's that? You say you're now printing wank?

SPARKS: (screaming) *QUANK!* The magazine is called *Quank! Quank! Quank!*

CLYDE: Well, it reads like—

SPARKS: (screams) *You f—*

CROSS: (interrupts, very calm) I commend both of you on your artistic dedication.

McREADY: (amused) Hello, gentlemen and "lady".

SPARKS: (startled) Uh, hi. What do you mean, Cross?

CROSS: I gather that you are externalizing your past hostilities in order to purge yourself of latent unresolved tensions which could hinder future creative expression.

CLYDE: Um... yeah... I guess...

SPARKS: (now calm) Yes, yes of course, that's what we're doing. We're researching a psychodrama scene in my new novel.

CLYDE: So what brings you to the wilds of Wisconsin?

McREADY: Sheldon issued an open invitation to attend this little writers' retreat of yours...

ISAACS: Indeed, I did.

POOLE: (a little bitter) But we heard you weren't coming.

CROSS: We reconsidered. This juncture in space and time appears to be a very opportune period to spend in relative isolation with you.

SOUND: DISTANT THROB OF DOZENS OF PROPELLOR-DRIVEN ENGINES IN THE DISTANCE.

Scene Four

A hearing room in the Ontario Provincial Parliamentary Building in Toronto, Canada. The same day in 1967.

SOUND: <u>CROWD OF PEOPLE IN THE GALLERY TALKING SOFTLY TO EACH OTHER. HEAVY WOODEN DOOR SWINGS OPEN. THREE SETS OF FOOTSTEPS MARCH ACROSS THE ROOM. THE CROWD GROWS QUIET AS THE MEMBERS OF PROVINCIAL PARLIAMENT (MPPS) TAKE THEIR SEATS AT THE FRONT OF THE HEARING ROOM.</u>

THOMPSON: (whispers) Shall we?

WEISS: (whispers) I think so.

SOUND: <u>THOMPSON BANGS THE GAVEL LOUDLY ON THE TABLE.</u>

THOMPSON: On the recommendation of my fellow honourable members, I declare this Provincial Parliamentary Inquiry to be in session. This is the beginning of our fourth week of hearings and interviews regarding the nature of the activities of the Temple of Mental Technology in the Province of Ontario.

SOUND: <u>PAINFUL SCREECH OF SOMEONE TURNING ON THE PUBLIC ADDRESS SYSTEM.</u>

THOMPSON: (now miked) Ow! Thank you. Now, I've advised that some members of the foreign press, the Buffalo News, I believe, are attending these hearings for the first time. So, I've been asked to re-introduce the members of this committee. So, I am Stanley Thompson, member for North Bay, North, to my left is...

McPHERSON: Gloria McPherson, member for Hamilton West. I'm also a medical doctor.

WEISS: Rubin Weiss, member for central Toronto.

THOMPSON: Thank you. I think we can move right into today's proceedings. Will the honourable member from Hamilton West remind this committee and all present of who we are interviewing this morning?

SOUND: <u>SHUFFLING OF PAPER.</u>

McPHERSON: We will be hearing from Mr. Harlan Diamond of the firm of Gordon, Nolan, Diamond and Wylie... and attorney representing the Toronto branch of Mentotechnics Inc. and the Temple of Mental Technology.

THOMPSON: Send the gentlemen in.

SOUND: <u>FOOTSTEPS APPROACH FROM THE BACK OF THE ROOM. DIAMOND TAKES A SEAT.</u>

THOMPSON: Good morning, Mr. Diamond. What is it you wish to tell this Commission?

SOUND: <u>DIAMOND OPENS HIS BRIEFCASE. FLIPPING OF PAGES IN A NOTEPAD.</u>

DIAMOND: I will speak on the behalf of the Toronto Temple and Mr. Evanston personally. (assumes a formal tone as he reads from his notes) I have been instructed to convey Donald H. Evanston's deepest and most sincere regrets that he is unable to comply with this highly esteemed Commission's request to appear personally to answer your questions... at this time.

McPHERSON: (a little annoyed) Did Mr. Evanston give any indication at what point in time he might be able to free up his busy schedule and come up and see us?

DIAMOND: I have no knowledge of Mr. Evanston's future travel plans.

McPHERSON: (now very annoyed) So much for Evanston's deepest and sincerest regrets.

WEISS: So, you have no idea whether Mr. Evanston will ever speak to this Commission?

DIAMOND: I have no information at this time.

SOUND: ANOTHER SET OF FOOTSTEPS.

PAGE: (whispers) Excuse me... excuse me...

SOUND: MUFFLED THUDS AS VERY THICK LEGAL DOCUMENTS ARE DEPOSITED IN FRONT OF EACH MPP.

THOMPSON: (also annoyed) Oh, no! Not this thing again!

DIAMOND: I was asked by Mr. Evanston's associates to refer to the written response provided by legal counsel in the United States to similar questions posed by the American Food and Drug Association, the Federal Department of Justice, and the IRS.

WEISS: Which you know is in excess of 2,500 pages in length.

DIAMOND: Mr. Evanston felt that a thorough and most detailed account would be the most use to the American government.

WEISS: But I'm sure they were able to contain their gratitude.

DIAMOND: With sincere respect, we suggest that Mr. Evanston's written answers will address many apparent controversies and unfounded areas of concern... from the Temple's point of view.

SOUND: FLIPPING OF PAGES.

THOMPSON: (sighs) Lord, preserve us...

McPHERSON: Mr. Diamond, we spent most of the last two weeks with this document. It has some wonderful passages... on page 153 it says that there is a worldwide conspiracy against the Mentotechnics organization coordinated by the FBI, the CIA, the KGB,

	as well as MI5 and the RCMP.
WEISS:	It also alleges that mental health and medical professional organizations in most developed countries are participants in this conspiracy.
DIAMOND:	But Mr. Evanston also states on the next page that many elected officials, such as your honourable selves, are either hostile to, or ignorant of, these illegal covert activities against the Temple.
McPHERSON:	(sarcastic) That's very nice of him. So, I guess as an elected official and a medical doctor, I'm plotting against myself, eh?
DIAMOND:	I really can't say, ma'am. Perhaps in the new appendix...
WEISS:	Yes, the appendix, it's very insightful. On page 87, Evanston recommends that the Ontario Parliament should terminate this inquiry, as well as all other provincial government activities, to establish an all-party lobby...
SOUND:	<u>THE OTHER TWO MPPS QUICKLY TURN TO PAGE 87.</u>
McPHERSON:	(reading in disbelief) ...to require the American government to develop a manned space probe to Saturn.
DIAMOND:	(coughs)
THOMPSON:	Do you have something you wish to say, Mr. Diamond?
DIAMOND:	Ah, yes. Mr. Evanston's research indicates that the planet Saturn emits a continual, non-stable band of vibrational radiations.
SOUND:	<u>PAPER SHUFFLING AS DIAMOND CHECKS HIS NOTES.</u>
DIAMOND:	These, uh, strange and powerful emanations, Mr. Evanston theorizes, are a source of genetic trauma to the human race... (his voice drops as his embar-

rassment grows) ...throughout its entire evolution...

THOMPSON: (irritated) As an attorney, how do you feel about that? Does it bother you to give statements like these to a Parliamentary Commission?

WEISS: (softly) Steady on, Stan...

DIAMOND: I'm neither an astronomer or a theologian, so it would be improper for me to comment on these matters personally, Mr. Chairman. I am only passing on information as directed by my client.

McPHERSON: Fine, then let's just deal with this example of what Mentotechnics teaches. Now, Mr. Diamond, Saturn's rather large, isn't it?

DIAMOND: I've been told it is, ma'am.

McPHERSON: Well, if they taught any science at law school you'd know that it is at least several thousand times larger than our Earth. Saturn is also rather far away, isn't it?

DIAMOND: So I understand.

McPHERSON: So even if we get out to Saturn, what exactly does Mr. Evanston propose we do with this offensive planetary body? Tow it out of the solar system?

DIAMOND: I believe Mr. Evanston recommends—

SOUND: <u>MCPHERSON SLAMS THE DOCUMENT SHUT.</u>

McPHERSON: (very angry) Why even try to answer, Mr. Diamond? This submission is more of the same pseudo-scientific claptrap designed to mock the "duly elected officials" you and Mr. Evanston say you have so much respect for!

DIAMOND: (also getting angry) Dr. McPherson, I'm sure my client would have some questions about your motives—

SOUND: <u>THOMPSON BANGS HIS GAVEL.</u>

THOMPSON: Order, please. Outbursts like this will not advance the work of this Commission.

McPHERSON: Oh, Stan, come on!

THOMPSON: Further discussion with Mr. Diamond will be pointless until we have further reviewed the written submission. Therefore I move that we review these statements in study session and pronounce our findings at a later public meeting.

WEISS: And if we have any questions to ask of Mr. Diamond, he can be recalled to this Commission at that time?

THOMPSON: Agreed.

McPHERSON: I don't agree. I think we should deal with this man while we have him right here.

THOMPSON: Your opinion is noted, Dr. McPherson. But I am the chair of this committee.

SOUND: THOMPSON BANGS THE GAVEL AGAIN.

CLYDE: (VO) What you just heard was part of a Canadian government commission established to investigate possible charges of fraud, kidnapping and abuses of human rights by Evanston's newest project... a church based on his therapy of Mentotechnics. I thought we'd heard the last of Evanston!

Welcome to the 1960s. We had all gotten quite a bit older, and foolishly assumed that we were now a least at little bit wiser. As SF writers, we were becoming a strange hybrid of half-guru and half-guinea pig. But we were getting reprinted pretty solidly through the fifties and sixties. A whole generation was picking up its values from us. And these new values were having some pretty unexpected and, if you'll forgive the expression, far-out, consequences.

Scene Five

Stage 17, Summit Studios, Burbank, California. A shoot for the TV series *Space Spanners* during the spring of 1967.

SOUND: <u>EERIE WINDS ON A BARREN ALIEN LANDSCAPE. THREE PAIRS OF BOOTS CRUNCH ACROSS THE DRY SOIL.</u>

COMMANDER HUGHES: (grimly) Okay, Zagar, you're the technical genius, where are they?

SOUND: <u>BEEPS AS ZAGAR STUDIES THE READINGS ON HIS BIO-SCANNER.</u>

ZAGAR: I cannot explain it, Commander. We have landed the excursion craft at the signal's point of origin. The Zephulons should be here waiting for us.

HUGHES: But as friends, or as attackers?

ZAGAR: I do not have sufficient information to answer that question, Commander.

STURGEON: They could be hurt, Commander! We've got to find them!

SOUND: <u>WHINE AS HUGHES DE-ACTIVATES THE SAFETY ON HIS PARTICLE-BEAM WEAPON.</u>

HUGHES: Keep those kindly impulses in check, Dr. Sturgeon! You never can tell what dangers you face when you're stuck beneath the surface of a moon with a band of renegade Zebublands!

SOUND: <u>HORRIBLE AND UNEARTHLY HOWL IN THE DISTANCE.</u>

STURGEON: (alarmed) That terrible sound! It's coming from that cave!

ALIENS: (distorted, echoes) Ah, Space Commander Hughes, you have fallen into our trap!

ZAGAR: It's the Zephulons, Commander!

HUGHES: I know Bephazond threats when I hear them, mister! Fall back behind me!

ALIENS: *Die, humanoid scum!*

SOUND: <u>SCREAM OF PROTONIC EMISSIONS AS HUGHES FIRES HIS WEAPON.</u>

HUGHES: Get back, you inhuman, slavering, *Nonoblobs*!

ASSISTANT DIRECTOR (MICHELLE JOQUIN): (on megaphone) Cut!

KYLE (AKA HUGHES): (out of character) Now what's the problem? I was just getting into the scene!

SHECKLEY (AKA ZAGAR): Yeah, I saw your face move... twice.

CLARK (AKA STURGEON): (whining) Damn it, we are never gonna get through this shoot!

JOQUIN: Just be quiet, all of you. Let's just check our scripts, shall we? Kyle, you really have to remember the name of the alien race in this episode. You've said it differently, and wrong, all through the take.

KYLE: So, I'll dub it in later.

JOQUIN: Not a chance. We're almost at season's end and we have no more post-production budget. You have to say it right... on camera!

KYLE: I thought I was saying it right. The mutants are called Krepulongs, aren't they?

JOQUIN: No, they're Sephugonds.

CLARK: Are you sure? I thought they were Necrulands.

SHECKLEY:	Golly. I thought they were Zephulons.
JOQUIN:	Hmmm.
<u>SOUND:</u>	<u>JOQUIN FLIPS THROUGH HER COPY OF THE SCRIPT.</u>
JOQUIN:	(angry) Man! It's spelled four different ways in here! *Damn writers!* (yells) Sharon! Kim! Get the phone! We gotta call Clyde!

Scene Six

Clyde's room at the Erewhon Inn. A few moments later, in a different time zone.

SOUND: <u>SLOW, LABORIOUS TYPING. CRICKETS CHIRPING IN THE DISTANCE.</u>

CLYDE: (VO) Here we are back at the writer's retreat. You have just been watching them trying to film a scene from the classic TV series *Space Spanners*. When it was in production, I used to make an obscene amount of money as the story editor/head writer. (laughs) Which is why the last scene might have looked just a little bit familiar.

SOUND: <u>THE TELEPHONE RINGS. CLYDE ANSWERS.</u>

CLYDE: (in 1960s persona) Hello? (now irritated) Michelle, I thought this was supposed to be my vacation. (listens for a moment) I don't know the name of the aliens in episode #23. I wrote the damn script almost a year ago! (listens again, slightly pained) Okay, okay, okay. I remember now. The aliens are called Zephulons. Yeah, with a "zee". (now angry) Typos and spelling errors are not my responsibility! You know how hard it is to find a typist who can handle SF scripts. (sighs) Look, the simplest thing is to just change the name of the aliens. Re-name them something that Kyle can remember. You know, maybe they can come from the planet "Jones". (listens) We're too far into the shooting, huh?

SOUND: <u>CLYDE POURS HIMSELF SOMETHING.</u>

CLYDE: Okay, let's do this: don't have Kyle call the aliens by name. Yeah, and just edit out the lines he screwed up. Let the other cast members use the name. Yeah, things like: "Look, Commander, Zephulons!" or "Hey, jerk-face, watch out for those Zephulons!" You know, stuff like that.

SOUND: <u>CLYDE SIPS HIS DRINK.</u>

CLYDE: You think it'll work. Great, crazy man.

DENSEN AND FREEDMAN: (down the hall) Clyde, you thief! You fiend!

SOUND: <u>DRUNKEN FOOTSTEPS ENTER THE ROOM.</u>

CLYDE: What?

DENSEN: Episode #17 of Space Spanners was a direct steal from our story "Song of the Star-Woman" from the June 1958 issue of *Alternate Worlds.* You thief, you!

FREEDMAN: We've been trying to contact you for three months now! You bastard, you stole our art and now you won't even admit we exist!

CLYDE: (into the phone) Michelle, can you hang on just a minute? Situation here. (to the writers) Look guys, I know all about the problem. I've got one of the studio execs on the line from Los Angeles here and I'm trying to work something out.

FREEDMAN: (dubious) Oh, really?

CLYDE: (almost sounding sincere) Look, the whole studio is in shambles right now. Our co-star is almost a heroin addict and we had this... uh... earthquake... it completely destroyed all our files and we're almost a year behind in our correspondence.

DENSEN: (impressed) Heroin? An earthquake? Wow!

FREEDMAN: (still dubious) That's too bad. You'd really get

	some sympathy if you could find some way to pay us for the story rights.
CLYDE:	(into the phone) You still there? Just hang on. (addresses the writers) Look, the exec has just heard about this and she feels just terrible about the whole misunderstanding. It's just the sort of thing that a television professional absolutely dreads! I mean, it's more than our reputations are worth! In fact...
SOUND:	<u>PEN SCRATCHING ON A PIECE OF PAPER.</u>
CLYDE:	...she's just authorized me... to write you this personal check in the amount of fifty dollars to cover the initial option rights for your story, which may, or may not, have been used as resource material for episode #17.
SOUND:	<u>PAGE TORN OUT OF CHEQUE BOOK.</u>
DENSEN:	(impressed) Fifty dollars? Just like that? Wow!
FREEDMAN:	This is a start in the right direction, but I want you to understand that this is just a down payment. We expect to hear from your office, with contracts and the rest of the money... by next week.
CLYDE:	Absolutely, guys. See you at tomorrow's workshop.
SOUND:	<u>FOOTSTEPS, A LITTLE UNSTEADY, WALK OUT THE DOOR.</u>
CLYDE:	You still there? No, I'm not going to come back and help with the shoot. This is my vacation. If don't get started on the new novel, I will be forever trapped in the rotting body of a zombie Hollywood screenwriter. (He listens for a moment.) Of course, I'm joking. By the way, I'll be sending in an extra invoice for P.R. expenses when I do get back... and Michelle... we gotta tighten up the submission review procedure. Bye.

SOUND:	<u>HE HANGS UP THE PHONE.</u>
CLYDE:	(VO) I'm sorry you had to see that. But it happens in TV sometimes. To be completely honest, I don't remember if we ripped off their story or not. We might have stolen it... hell, I was so busy I didn't know where the ideas were coming from.
CLYDE:	(mutters) Oh, hell, this is crap!
SOUND:	<u>CLYDE TEARS A SHEET OF PAPER OUT OF HIS TYPEWRITER.</u>
CLYDE:	(VO) Fifty bucks was a pretty insulting amount even for a preliminary option. But it was obviously the most money Densen had seen for a while. Poor sod.
SOUND:	<u>CLYDE ROLLS ANOTHER SHEET INTO THE MACHINE.</u>
CLYDE:	(VO) But I've got problems of my own. I'm fighting for my creative soul! *Galaxy of Madness* has given me a modest reputation but nothing else's really happened since 1962. I'm making some good money in TV, but it feels like the artistic well is going dry. I'm at this retreat because I desperately need the inspiration.
SOUND:	<u>CLYDE TYPES FOR A WHILE. THE TYPEWRITER GIVES A TINY "PING!" CLYDE SLAMS THE RETURN LEVER AND CONTINUES TYPING.</u>

Scene Seven

The meeting room at the Ontario Provincial Parliament Buildings. Toronto, Canada. The next morning.

SOUND: <u>LOW ROAR OF THE CROWD. MICROPHONE HUMS AND SQUEAKS. THE MARTINS TAKE THEIR SEATS IN FRONT OF THE COMMISSION.</u>

WEISS: (miked) Mr. and Mrs. Martin. Thank you for coming all the way from Malton to answer our questions. We will try to get this over with as soon as possible.

MR. MARTIN: (meek) Thank you, sir.

WEISS: Now, can you confirm for us... just when did your son become involved with the Temple of Mentotechnics?

MRS. MARTIN: We first saw him with their literature about two years ago. He joined about three months after that.

McPHERSON: And do you have any idea why your son joined this group?

MRS. MARTIN: Patrick was a very intelligent and cheerful young man...

MR. MARTIN: Scored top marks all through high school.

MRS. MARTIN: But we never had a lot of money... since they shut down the AVRO plant... so Patrick couldn't go to college full-time.

MR. MARTIN: Pat was too proud to take out a student loan from the government... so he had to work at Dominion most days and go to the tech school at night. He was a smart boy, he was doing well...

MRS. MARTIN: But Patrick was so frustrated. He saw the other kids going off to the universities and got desperate to get ahead.

THOMPSON: How does all this relate to Mentotechnics?

MRS. MARTIN: Patrick thought he found an answer to his problem when he read their literature.

MR. MARTIN: The Mentotechnics people said they could increase your I.Q., make you work all night and learn in your sleep. Make you a hundred times smarter. They told Pat he could finish a college degree in four months.

McPHERSON: And so this literature from the Temple of Mentotechnics claimed that they could make your son a success?

MRS. MARTIN: Yes, but only if he would sign up for the courses at their Toronto offices.

WEISS: So he did end up paying some kind of tuition? Was the cost of these courses any less expensive than the fees for attending a college or university in Ontario?

MR. MARTIN: (disgusted, mutters) Expensive? *Heck!*

MRS. MARTIN: (whispers, shocked) *Andrew!* (to the Commission) We're not exactly sure. At first it seemed that the courses were very reasonably priced...

MR. MARTIN: (angry) He told me they were free.

MRS. MARTIN: ...but they kept making Patrick re-enrol every month as he moved through their diploma program.

MR. MARTIN: And as he moved up the course, the classes started getting pretty darned expensive.

SOUND: THOMPSON FLIPS TO THE MIDDLE OF A DOCUMENT.

THOMPSON: Now, it says in your written statement that neither one of you have ever attended any of the courses or meetings held at the Toronto Temple. How did you ever find out what your son was spending all that money on?

MRS. MARTIN: (embarrassed) Once I took a peek at one of their training manuals. It looked very complicated and very strange. Beyond me.

MR. MARTIN: (angry) It was darned silly. (now embarrassed) Sorry, your honours. But the books were full of nonsense! (to Mrs. Martin) Like that woodchuck thing.

McPHERSON: Woodchuck thing?

MRS. MARTIN: (hesitant, very embarrassed) When we... asked him... about it... he said... that it was an... exercise they gave him at the Temple.

MR. MARTIN: Pat said it was supposed to build confidence.

WEISS: What was this exercise?

MRS. MARTIN: Well... (awkward silence) Patrick showed us. He would walk right up to you... up to anybody. Then he'd put his face about two inches from the end of your nose... and then he'd say... he'd say... (her voice breaks down into sobs) ...how... how much... wood...

MR. MARTIN: He'd say: "How much wood could a woodchuck chuck..."

MRS. MARTIN: (wailing with grief) "...*if a woodchuck could chuck wood?!*"

MR. MARTIN: (heavy sigh) And he'd keep repeating himself, over and over again, with his face right in yours...

McPHERSON: ...until you completed the verse? (with sympathy) It must have been very difficult. Sometimes...

MR. MARTIN: Yes indeed, sometimes it was.

MRS. MARTIN: Yes. (blows her nose)

THOMPSON: I think we've heard all we need to.

WEISS: I have just one more question. Mr. Martin, why can't we speak directly to Patrick about his interest in Mentotechnics?

MR. MARTIN: We haven't heard from him in over six months. He disappeared after our bank manager caught him trying to forge our names for a loan of $30,000.

McPHERSON: (shocked) Why would he do such a thing?

MR. MARTIN: From what we can figure out, he was going to the Temple in Los Angeles for advanced training. And he needed the money for the tuition.

Scene Eight

Stage 17, Summit Studios, Hollywood. They are filming a scene in the Master Control Sanctum of the Planet Portox-12. The same day as the previous scene.

SOUND: <u>LOUD AND VERY DATED ELECTRONIC BEEPING. CLATTERING OF COMPUTER TAPES RATTLING THROUGH METAL CALCULATING PRESSES.</u>

MASTER COMPUTER: (booming machine monotone) Com-man-der Hugh-es. Yo-ur in-ter-fer-ence has dis-rupt-ed all plan-et-ary con-trol. The fu-ture of the en-tire Por-tox race is in dan-ger!

HUGHES: (affronted) Disrupted planetary control? You mean I've given the Portox people a taste of freedom!

MASTER COMPUTER: Our e-co-sys-tem is col-lap-sing! Bil-lions will die! You must be des-troy-ed for yo-ur cri-mes!

HUGHES: (angry) Oh, yeah, you big machine?! You think you're so intelligent? That you can control a whole planet? See if your logic circuits can handle this one...

ZAGAR: Commander, you must be careful...

HUGHES: (even more determined) ...how much wood could a woodchuck chuck... (he pauses for dramatic effect) ...*if a woodchuck could chuck wood!?*

SOUND: <u>ELECTRICAL SHORTS, TAPE REELS SPIN CRAZILY, SPRINGS AND WIRES SNAP.</u>

MASTER COMPUTER: (becoming hysterical) That is il-log-i-cal! I do not un-der-stand!

JOQUIN: (yells) Cut!

HUGHES/KYLE: Now what? We were really cooking here.

JOQUIN: Kyle, you're ad-libbing again! You can't wing it on another planet!

KYLE: Aw, the hell with the script. It's just a bunch of moral problems and numbers. Numbers are real boring.

JOQUIN: You are supposed to drive the Master Computer insane with logical problems and philosophical paradoxes. You need to say those numbers.

KYLE: Morals are boring too. It's all B.S. Only some kind of a sissy would say this crap.

JOQUIN: Or maybe the great space hero just has a bad case of math anxiety.

KYLE: And the hell with you too.

SOUND: <u>KYLE MARCHES OFF THE SET.</u>

KYLE: (calling) I'll be in my dressing room when you want to do the scene right!

JOQUIN: (fuming) That jerk...

ZAGAR/SHECKLEY: Sorry, I was trying to make the scene work.

JOQUIN: (yells) Bruce! Get Clyde on the line! We need another re-write!

Scene Nine

Clyde's rooms at the Erewhon Inn. That evening.

<table>
<tr><td>SOUND:</td><td><u>CLYDE POURS HIMSELF ANOTHER TUMBLER OF SOMETHING ALCOHOLIC. SPORADIC TYPING BEGINS.</u></td></tr>
<tr><td>CLYDE:</td><td>(VO) Let's set things up here. By now my old chum Sheldon is one of the Masters of Science Fiction. By 1967 there are 34 Alexander Steel books in print and Sheldon's managed to crank out another 70 books on his own. He's doing well... more than well... he's making that career jump that all science fiction writers dream of... he's writing colour bumph for the media.</td></tr>
<tr><td>SOUND:</td><td><u>TYPING GETS LOUDER, AS IF CLYDE WAS GETTING ANGRY ABOUT SOMETHING.</u></td></tr>
<tr><td>CLYDE:</td><td>No longer is he a depraved hack writer of depraved pulp fiction. No! No! Doctor Sheldon Isaacs is now a noted futurist and respected science commentator!</td></tr>
<tr><td>SOUND:</td><td><u>CLYDE STOPS TYPING AND TAKES A LONG DRINK. THERE IS A KNOCK AT THE DOOR.</u></td></tr>
<tr><td>ATKINSON:</td><td>Mr. Clyde?</td></tr>
<tr><td>CLYDE:</td><td>Yes? Can I help you?</td></tr>
<tr><td>ATKINSON:</td><td>I'm Heather Atkinson, Dr. Isaacs' personal assistant. We saw each other this afternoon, but we weren't formally introduced. He said I should meet him here...</td></tr>
<tr><td>CLYDE:</td><td>Well, I can't imagine how Dr. Isaacs forgot to mention that to me. But never mind, have a seat and we shall await the coming of the great man.</td></tr>
</table>

SOUND:	ATKINSON SITS DOWN. ANOTHER KNOCK AT THE DOOR.
ATKINSON:	Thank you.
CLYDE:	Come in, Sheldon!
SOUND:	DOOR OPENS.
ISAACS:	(jovial) Robert! I see you've met the ever-useful Miss A.
CLYDE:	Oh, yes.
ISAACS:	She's an absolute gem. B.A. in sociology from Vassar, M.Sc. in Theoretical Maths from MIT, and working on a PhD in Comparative Modern Literature at Harvard.
CLYDE:	Golly.
ISAACS:	She speaks three languages, does quadratic equations in her head, and types 95 words a minute. And she's read everything I've ever written. Even our early stuff.
CLYDE:	How wonderful for you, Miss Atkinson.
ATKINSON:	Dr. Isaacs' contribution to contemporary culture is the subject of my doctrinal dissertation. I find his ongoing inter-textual message, and the blending of C.P. Snow's model of separate scientific and aesthetic cultures with motifs from romantic adventure mythos, to be of particular importance.
CLYDE:	(quietly) Golly again.
ISAACS:	Since you said you wanted to talk a little business, I thought I'd ask Miss A. to come and take a few notes.
CLYDE:	Good idea.
SOUND:	ISAACS ALSO TAKES A SEAT.
ISAACS:	So what can I do for you, my old friend? I don't have much time. We have to get out to New York

first thing in the morning. I just got a call from ABC and they want me to tape some commentary for their Apollo 8 coverage.

CLYDE: I'll get right to the point then. I just heard from my agent that the first Steel trilogy went over the million sales mark with the fourteenth printing.

ISAACS: (impatient) I suppose that could be possible...

CLYDE: As you might remember, we are the co-authors of the early collections...

ISAACS: Well, I imagine that's *technically* correct.

CLYDE: (angry) We created Alexander Steel together! And I kept the damn character on TV back when nobody wanted to print him!

ISAACS: (also angry) I also seem to recall that you gave me all sale rights to the character once you decided that Steel was quote: "running out of steam", unquote. Given the fact that you have no legal or moral claim to the stories, what exactly is it you're proposing, Robert?

CLYDE: I don't agree about the moral claim, Sheldon, and I don't want anything unreasonable. I just want a share in the last printing of the first three books. And I want my name back on the cover of the next edition; this dedication to a "fellow adventurer" on the frontispiece is total B.S.

SOUND: <u>THINGS GET VERY QUIET. WE CAN ONLY HEAR THE FAINT SCRATCHING OF ATKINSON'S PEN ON HER NOTEPAD.</u>

ISAACS: What's this?

SOUND: <u>ISAACS PICKS UP CLYDE'S GLASS FROM THE DESKTOP.</u>

ISAACS: (sniffs)

CLYDE: Gin. An occasional hobby of mine.

ISAACS: Then, I can't agree to anything with you right now.

It would be unethical for me to negotiate any monetary arrangement with you after you've clearly been over-indulging in intoxicating substances.

SOUND:	ISAACS PUTS THE GLASS DOWN.

CLYDE: (outraged) *What?!* I'm not drunk!

ISAACS: I could be accused of taking advantage of you, or you might give away too much... out of some damned foolish emotional gesture!

CLYDE: (hurt) *Cripes, Sheldon!* Back then, you could barely pop zits without my help! At least half of the early stories are mine! Those are still the most popular books! *Are you saying I'm not even entitled to some credit?!*

ISAACS: (slowly exhales before he speaks) What I am saying, is that have your agent contact my lawyer... maybe they can work something out. (pause) And I don't want to hear from you ever again.

SOUND:	CLYDE POURS HIMSELF ANOTHER GIN.

CLYDE: You were always so sentimental, Sheldon.

ISAACS: You really should give up drinking. Do you know how many millions of brain cells just one ounce of alcohol destroys?

CLYDE: (takes a long drink, then sighs with contentment) I write for television. Destroying my brain cells is professional development.

ISAACS: Come along, Heather! There is much to be done, the hour is late, I have notes to dictate, (voice grows more distant as he walks down the hall) and I must telephone the ball-and-chain before we sleep!

ATKINSON: It was a pleasure to meet you, Mr. Clyde. At some point I would like to interview you.

CLYDE: Uh, why?

ATKINSON: In the introduction to my dissertation, I trace Dr.

	Isaacs' influence on minor literary figures such as yourself.
CLYDE:	(subdued irony) Yeah, sure. Call me anytime.
SOUND:	<u>DOOR CLOSES AS ATKINSON LEAVES.</u>
CLYDE:	(sighs) Sweet...
SOUND:	<u>THE TELEPHONE RINGS. CLYDE PICKS UP THE RECEIVER.</u>
CLYDE:	Hello? (annoyed) Michelle? Now what do you people want?
SOUND:	<u>AGITATED HUMAN NOISES ON THE OTHER END OF THE LINE.</u>
CLYDE:	He thinks the computer scene is too cerebral? With that kind of an attitude he'll be president of MGM soon.
SOUND:	<u>FAST UTTERINGS ON THE RECEIVER.</u>
CLYDE:	Yeah, yeah, okay, okay. I have the answer. Seriously. Here's what you do: give all of Kyle's lines to Sheckley. Yes, I'm aware that it's a crucial scene, I wrote it. Sheckley's pretty smart and his character is supposed to be a scientist anyway, right?
SOUND:	<u>MORE FAST UTTERINGS ON THE RECEIVER.</u>
CLYDE:	Look, the only reason Kyle always saves the universe is because he's listed first in the credits, right? Where's the starship captain at this point in the story? Well, after having been sexually assaulted by a platoon of Lust-Gorillas of Alpha Centauri, he's pretty tired.
SOUND:	<u>FAST UTTERINGS ON THE RECEIVER.</u>
CLYDE:	(laughs) Yes, I think we can assume that scenario is all off-camera backstory. But I knew you'd enjoy hearing it. Good night, Michelle.
SOUND:	<u>DIAL TONE. THEN CLYDE HANGS UP.</u>

Scene Ten

Ontario Provincial Parliament Building. The next morning.

SOUND: <u>CROWD SOUNDS, MUTTERING AND SHUFF-LING OF CHAIRS.</u>

THOMPSON: (miked) Miss Meyer, why don't you start by telling the Commission how you came to join the Temple of Mentotechnics?

MEYER: I joined because I thought I could help Donald H. Evanston save the world and bring unlimited joy to all living beings.

McPHERSON: And how did you acquire this commendable sense of mission, Miss Meyer?

MEYER: I met some of their representatives at a folk-rock concert. It was the Outstanding Acoustic Dream Quartet, I believe. It was kind of an awareness and consciousness development happening. People were trying to get in tune with themselves and develop a sense of caring and sharing.

WEISS: (skeptical) It sounds idyllic.

MEYER: I later learned that the Dream Quartet band is an official marketing division of the Temple.

WEISS: So after you met their representatives, you enrolled in one of their programs?

MEYER: Yes. And I did very well. I quickly reached the advanced levels of spiritual training at the Toronto Temple, and so I was transferred to the Cincinnati and then the Los Angeles Cathedrals. I received an excellent attitude evaluation and was eventually sent up to work at Airfleet.

THOMPSON: How's that? They sent you up to an airport?

McPHERSON: Minister, *Airfleet* is the name of the fleet of blimps Evanston owns.

MEYER: Excuse me ma'am, they aren't blimps. (proudly) Airfleet is the mobile main headquarters of the global Mentotechnics Movement. Airfleet is a squadron of five lighter-than-air-ships; reconstructed dirigibles modelled after the Royal Air Force's R-100 series—

WEISS: (a little annoyed) Thanks for straightening us out on the aviation details, Miss Meyer.

McPHERSON: Why was it so important for you to work at Airfleet?

MEYER: It was a great honour to be assigned to Airfleet duty. Evanston makes his home on the flagship, and the highest levels of Mentotechnic training are conducted there.

McPHERSON: And did you feel suitably honoured?

MEYER: (deflated) I suppose that depends on how you feel about cleaning chemical toilets.

SOUND: RUSTLING OF PAPER AS MCPHERSON CHECKS HER NOTES.

McPHERSON: If your written statement is accurate, you had a very taxing schedule while on Airfleet...

SOUND: NOW WEISS CHECKS HIS NOTES.

WEISS: ...you and the other new arrivals had to work 10-hour shifts; scrubbing the walk-ways and carrying out continual kitchen patrol.

THOMPSON: So Evanston ate a lot?

MEYER: And before bed we would spend six hours writing donation appeals for the Temple. (laughs) Every week we'd bundle up all the letters and drop them by parachute on top of one of the Temple's properties. It was a freaky scene.

WEISS: So you worked for 16 hours every day, then you'd do Mentotechnic training for another four hours. It doesn't take a rocket scientist to figure out that you were left with just four hours for things like eating, sleeping and bathing.

MEYER: It wasn't so bad. At five thousand feet, there isn't much else to do.

THOMPSON: I find that difficult to believe. How could you stand this treatment?

MEYER: Simple. (matter-of-factly) It was the greatest experience of my life. I was surrounded by dozens of intelligent, caring and committed people; together we were going to save the planet. And I was making incredible progress in my training.

McPHERSON: Progress?

MEYER: Yes. It felt like my senses were working on a whole new plane, like my intellect had expanded to incredible proportions. It was so... so... spiritual. (pause) I guess it would be difficult for most people to understand.

McPHERSON: That's why we're here, Miss Meyer. To understand.

THOMPSON: But if it was such a wonderful love-in, so darned up-lifting, why are you here?

MEYER: (sighs) It was an amazingly bad week. It was like karma. Suddenly, I had to pay for all the great stuff that happened before.

WEISS: (uncomprehending) Karma?

MEYER: We were floating over England and on the Monday morning I was transferred to Airfleet One.

WEISS: That's Evanston's ship?

MEYER: Yes.

WEISS: Did you meet the man?

MEYER: I never spoke to him. (coldly) I saw him.

McPHERSON: How is that distinction significant, Miss Meyer?

MEYER: When I saw Evanston, he was conducting Intermediary Level Discipline.

McPHERSON: And what does that mean?

SOUND: THE THROBBING HUM OF DIRIGIBLE ENGINES RISES. IN THE BACKGROUND, WE ALSO HEAR MENACING, EARLY PINK-FLOYD-LIKE MUSIC.

MEYER: Evanston gave up smoking a few years ago. Now, no one in the Organization is supposed to smoke. But on the Wednesday, one of the security officers found a new recruit lighting up. So the guy had to be punished.

SOUND: THE DRONE OF DIRIGIBLE ENGINES GROWS STEADILY IN HARMONY WITH THE MUSIC.

THOMPSON: And just how was he punished?

MEYER: (calm) They tied a rope around his ankle and threw him off the airship.

SOUND: THE MUSIC COMES TO A GRIM CLIMAX. WE HEAR A FAR-OFF, BARELY AUDIBLE, SCREAM OF UTTER TERROR.

THOMPSON: (horrified) Good grief! Was he killed?

MEYER: (still calm) Oh, no. They just swung him around for a while.

WEISS: And what was Evanston's role in all of this?

MEYER: He supervised the punishment. He told the security people to throw the guy over, how far to let the rope out, and how long to keep him out there.

SOUND: THE HUM OF THE ENGINES GRADUALLY FADES OUT.

WEISS: And they reeled this unfortunate person back into the ship?

MEYER: Oh... eventually.

WEISS: So it was after witnessing this blatant act of sadism that you decided to leave the Temple?

MEYER: No. I wasn't too happy about it, but my instructors explained the need for discipline... that Evanston was actually doing the recruit a favour. They said he really wanted to be punished, that this was a form of therapy.

WEISS: (exasperated) So what did make you quit?

MEYER: On Thursday afternoon they told me that I was going to be a server at High Table for Evanston's Sunday dinner. (a tone of disgust enters her voice) They gave me this... uniform... to wear. It was this leather bikini thing.

McPHERSON: And then you decided to quit?

MEYER: No. I told myself not to let middle-class values stand in the way of my spiritual advancement. I was going in for a special all-day training session the next day for my F.T.C...

McPHERSON: F.T.C.?

MEYER: Functional Telepath Certificate. It is a very advanced level of achievement in Mentotechnics.

WEISS: But you failed the course, and then you decided to leave?

MEYER: Not at all. I went into the session Friday morning and graduated with full F.T. Potentiality on the Saturday afternoon. (her voice grows more intense) When I left the training cabin I felt like I was levitating a foot off the deck; it seemed like my mind had infinite capabilities... like my perceptions were fantastically enhanced.

THOMPSON: Which only leads me back to my original question: if it was all so great, why are you speaking to this Commission today?

MEYER: (hesitant at first) Somebody took me to the recreation lounge to rest. And some idiot had left the TV on... and I saw... I saw...

THOMPSON: (very exasperated) What did you see!?

MEYER: (anguished) ...I saw these *things* coming out of the TV set!

McPHERSON: I beg your pardon?

MEYER: (voice cracks with fear) *Monsters! Mutants!* All the negative energies that Mentotechnics is supposed to protect us from! (now on the verge of tears) Sitting on that couch, it felt like all the evil in the universe was on that airship and... and... and *they were coming to get me!*

THOMPSON: Were you on drugs?

MEYER: *No!* I've never used drugs!

McPHERSON: Was it some kind of hallucination?

MEYER: (yells) *Of course it was a hallucination, you morons!*

SOUND: THOMPSON BANGS HIS GAVEL.

THOMPSON: (sharply) Miss Meyer!

MEYER: (struggles to catch her breath) I-I apologize, your honours. (now somewhat calmer) Yes, it was a very vivid and frightening hallucination. It was a very traumatic experience.

WEISS: Do you have any idea why you had that reaction?

MEYER: Extreme over-work. Intense physical and emotional stress. Plus the fact that the TV was tuned to the BBC. It was showing an English science fiction program, something called *Doctor Who*. When I finally calmed down I realized I was watching a bunch of actors walking around in papier-mache alien costumes.

McPHERSON: That's what drove you away from Mentotechnics?

MEYER: I never suspected that I could be so completely wrong about something. I was suddenly very aware that I was capable of being very confused about what was real and what wasn't. I had to re-think everything I'd experienced at the Temple.

McPHERSON: I think you made a very sensible conclusion. Thank you for helping us to understand.

SOUND: THOMPSON BANGS HIS GAVEL AGAIN.

THOMPSON: That will be all for now, Miss Meyer.

Scene Eleven

Stage 17, Summit Studios, Burbank, California. The action is set on a cheap re-creation of the Throne Room of the Capital of the Planet Portox. Afternoon, the same day of scene ten.

HUGHES: *Die! Die, you fiend!*

SOUND: <u>CRACKLING OF A DEADLY NEUTRINO WEAPON. ALIEN SCREAMS AND FALLS (SMOULDERING) TO THE GROUND.</u>

ELDER #1:   Please, Captain Hughes, have mercy upon us!

HUGHES: *Mercy?!* You take your solar system to the brink of atomic war with your telekenetic terrors, kidnap the female members of my crew, send your warrior mutants to kill me... and you dare to beg for mercy?

ELDER #1:   (sobs) W-we're sorry...

HUGHES: Why, I oughta vaporize you, with my neutrino gun!

JOQUIN: (on megaphone) Stick to the script, Kyle!

SOUND: <u>TAPED STRAINS OF AN ORCHESTRA GRADUALLY BUILD AS HUGHES SAYS HIS SPEECH.</u>

HUGHES: You aliens, living here on this alien planet, orbiting through a galaxy filled with alien suns, with your alien ways... everything about you is so... so... so *alien*!

ELDER #2:   But Commander Hughes, how could we do otherwise?

HUGHES: (sharply) Shut up! Everything about you, about your civilization is completely... *wrong*!

ELDER #1:   (gasp) Lords of the Galaxy! He's right!

HUGHES: You fail to recognize the sacred right of every individual to pursue their personal economic happiness in a democratic free-enterprise system based on self-respect and the values of fair play and open competition, where all men (and some women) are free to choose to live in a heterosexual monogamous man-wife relationship. (pauses briefly for breath)

Only when you surrender to the altar of individual choice, and convert to a monotheistic sect based on basic rights and truths... and only then... will your vile and degraded society crawl out of the sub-human barbaric totalitarian slime... and slowly progress towards the dignity and honour and goodness and incenses...

SOUND: <u>THE MUSIC REACHES A HEROIC CLIMAX.</u>

HUGHES: ...and neat stuff with 150 flavours of ice cream and cars with vinyl roofs...

JOQUIN: (on megaphone) Kyle!

HUGHES: (angry) Aw, the hell with all this talk!

SOUND: <u>SCUFFLING AS HUGHES/KYLE GRABS ELDER #2 AND STARTS TO PUNCH THE OTHER ACTOR.</u>

ELDER #2:   Ouch! Cut it out, you moron!

JOQUIN: (on megaphone) Cut! (off megaphone) Kyle! Have you completely lost your mind?!

STAGE HAND: Mr. Kyle, sir, don't you think we should at least try to do the scene as it was written?

ELDER #2:   (groans) That really hurt. My agent never said anything about getting punched in the kidneys.

KYLE/HUGHES: This is legitimate dramatic interpretation! The man's some kind of sissy alien, he deserves to be hurt!

JOQUIN: Anne! Gene! We gotta fix this scene! Call Clyde!

SOUND: <u>JOQUIN PUNCHES KYLE HARD IN THE STOMACH.</u>

KYLE: (winded) Hey, you punch pretty good for a girl...

JOQUIN: I don't know what the hell you're on, but smarten up. Some of us would like to finish this stupid episode!

Scene Twelve

Clyde's hotel room. A few moments later but in a different time zone.

CLYDE: (angry) He sticks to the script! I don't care if he's consumed with pent-up hostilities! I will not re-write the story to include an interstellar knife-fight!

SOUND: <u>VOICE AT THE OTHER END OF THE TELEPHONE.</u>

CLYDE: No! No way! No, I'm not married to the mono-logue, in fact I hate it! But you people are the ones who passed on the network's memo about putting in "patriotic story elements in a time of national uncertainty". Well, surprise, guys, I've cooperated with the Ministry of Truth, but I only do one draft for propaganda!

SOUND: <u>VOICE AT THE OTHER END OF THE TELEPHONE.</u>

CLYDE: (sarcastic) Fine, I'm glad you see it my way. (calmer) Maybe you can do the speech as a close shot and get everybody else off the set. (pause) Make him do the stupid speech! He is supposed to be an actor! Put the fear of God and the F.C.C. in him!

SOUND: <u>VOICE AT THE OTHER END OF THE TELEPHONE.</u>

CLYDE: Yeah, well, I'm sorry you're having to work late again. It's even later here in North Carolina. Bye.

SOUND: <u>HE HANGS UP.</u>

CLYDE: (heavy sigh)

<u>SOUND:</u>	<u>KNOCK AT THE DOOR.</u>
CLYDE:	It's open!
POOLE:	Hi, all is not groovy?
CLYDE:	Let's just say they know how to make the work day last.
POOLE:	Sorry to intrude, but do you think you could tune the sound level down a few decibels? Some of us are actually trying to do some writing here.
CLYDE:	Me too! But the fates are working against us!
<u>SOUND:</u>	<u>CLINK OF GLASSES.</u>
CLYDE:	So the best thing we can do at a time like this is drink.
<u>SOUND:</u>	<u>POOLE SITS DOWN ON A CHAIR.</u>
POOLE:	No thanks. I gave it up a while ago. But I'll be happy to watch you have one.
CLYDE:	My pleasure.
<u>SOUND:</u>	<u>CLYDE TAKES A LONG DRINK.</u>
POOLE:	Ray's still pretty shook up about that encounter session. You two have a lot of unfinished business.
CLYDE:	Really? I thought that professional jealousy had just driven her into an hysterical frenzy.
POOLE:	(calmly) Now that was a very cruel thing to say, Bob. True, but still very cruel.
CLYDE:	Things aren't working out for her?
POOLE:	The new magazine really isn't panning out. (sighs) Everybody says we need to see more serious writing in a science fiction magazine, but when it comes down to what people will actually buy... it's still big rockets, big guns and big chests in space.
<u>SOUND:</u>	<u>CLYDE POURS HIMSELF ANOTHER DRINK.</u>
CLYDE:	You don't need to tell me that our readership's get-

ting more conservative. And the critics seem to be the worst. Did you know some guy just reviewed *Galaxy of Madness* under the heading of "New Books in Print"? The book's almost 15 years old!

POOLE: Even so, you still may be at the cutting edge. At least in terms of audience. There's a huge fandom emerging around TV science fiction. Did you know that somebody's trying to organize a *Star Trek* convention next year?

CLYDE: No accounting for taste, I suppose. But whatever the reasons, Dave, I'm sorry *Alternate Worlds* folded around you. It was a good magazine.

POOLE: A.W. never survived the loss of its publisher and editor-in-chief. I'm a good word-technician, but I'm not much on creative vision.

CLYDE: Speaking of which, what was Zeigler really like, anyway? He's still a total mystery. You must have eventually met the guy after 20 years.

POOLE: (conspiratorial) You mean you want me to reveal the true identity of the invisible genius of Western science fiction?

CLYDE: Well, yes, of course.

POOLE: I will have a drink.

SOUND: <u>CLINK OF GLASSES. POOLE TAKES A DRINK.</u>

POOLE: Okay, I'll tell you. There was some legal action against us around '58. Trumped up plagiarism thing. I had to run some papers over for him to confirm and sign personally. I took the train, Zeigler used to live pretty close to here, did you know that? Anyway, I show up at his place, they show me in, and you'll never guess who I met.

CLYDE: (giggles) Jor-El? Roger Ramjet?

POOLE: Gerald Mitchell.

CLYDE: (shocked) *Mitchell?!* The Trotskyite from the '37

Worldcon?

POOLE: (sadly) He was blind. Crippled. Suffered from some kind of nervous trauma. Couldn't leave the house without totally freaking out... delayed stress syndrome.

CLYDE: What happened?

POOLE: After the Worldcon incident, he took a boat ride over to London. He bummed around for a while, I guess working with some socialist book club. Then during the Battle of Britain he tried to sign up with the RAF and fight the Nazi menace. They wouldn't take him on as a fighter pilot, but he did get assigned ambulance duty during the Blitz...

CLYDE: (dread creeps into his voice) I think I see where this is leading...

POOLE: And the Axis War Machine was so impressed with Mitchell's determination to fight tyranny, that they obligingly blew him up at the earliest opportunity.

CLYDE: I can't believe it! Why the hell didn't any of us hear from him? How could he stand working with us, after what we did to him?

POOLE: I asked him the same questions. At that point, I don't think he cared what any of us thought about him. Mitchell didn't stay in the SF business to make friends. He believed that science fiction was the most important form of literature in this century... "that the ideas in the genre were vital to education and social debate in a modern democracy".

CLYDE: You're kidding me, right?

POOLE: That's a direct quote. I think Mitchell was as idealistic on the day he died as he was that day in 1937. Maybe more so.

CLYDE: Maybe he had cause to be. You two were publishing the greatest SF magazine in history.

POOLE: Maybe, but it was a damned strange experience.

	Even after we met, he'd never mention the Fabulist days, or anyone from Camp Fantastic.
CLYDE:	But did he forgive you? Did he ever forgive us?
POOLE:	I don't think it ever occurred to him. He hired me because he knew I'd be useful in getting his magazine out. Full stop. As far as he was concerned, I didn't exist before March 1950.
SOUND:	BOTH MEN TAKE ANOTHER DRINK.
POOLE:	(sighs) Look, Bob, can you go easier on Ray Ann? We're breaking up and almost everything is getting to her these days.
CLYDE:	I'm sorry to hear that. Are you all right? I know how difficult it is to split up with Ray. Maybe we could start a club.
POOLE:	Really, there isn't anything funny about it. Ever since we got married, something went out of the relationship. The divorce really is for the best. (sighs) Still, after 30 years of sleeping together on a regular basis, living apart is going to be one hell of an adjustment. (long pause) Bob? Are you okay?
CLYDE:	(growing angry) Excuse me, did you just say *30 years*!? That would mean you two have been boffing each other since 1937. About the last time we saw Mitchell, in fact.
POOLE:	Uh, Bob, maybe you've had enough...
CLYDE:	Not only that, you said this was continuous boffing.
POOLE:	(quietly) Well, it's not really any of your business. Besides, I meant 15 years, not 30.
CLYDE:	No, you didn't and yes, it is my business. A precise word-technician such as yourself is not likely to make a slip like that. And if you were sleeping together, continuously, that would finally explain to me who her lover was... way back when it was my turn to be married to her!

POOLE: It's really not important, anymore.

CLYDE: Was this going on when she was married to Densen? Or Freedman!?

POOLE: She was never happy with them, they're like kids!

CLYDE: So, let's see... hmmm... after 17 years... am I still angry at the man who was my ex-wife's secret lover? I don't think it's sexual jealousy or anything... the sex wasn't that good... but the fact that you two were deceiving me all that time. And I did love her, in my own strange way.

POOLE: We have to be adults about this, Bob.

CLYDE: Yup! I was very hurt back then. And thinking about it, I'm still hurt now. You may be a good editor, Dave, but you're a spineless, loathsome excuse for a human being.

POOLE: (calm) I think you may be right.

SOUND: <u>CLYDE STANDS UP AND STARTS TO WALK, SOMEWHAT UNEVENLY, TOWARD THE DOOR.</u>

CLYDE: I believe I will go for a walk. I would greatly appreciate it if you could somehow arrange to leave the planet before I get back to my room.

POOLE: That would be difficult on such short notice. But I could leave the hotel tomorrow morning.

CLYDE: I suppose that will do for now. See what you can do about getting out of my life for the rest of the century, though.

SOUND: <u>CLYDE'S FOOTSTEPS SHUFFLING DOWN THE HALL.</u>

Scene Thirteen

The meeting room in the Ontario Provincial Parliament Building. Earlier that day.

SOUND: <u>LOW ROAR OF THE CROWD.</u>

WEISS: Dr. Lambert, our understanding is that this report was produced as part of your research in social psychology.

LAMBERT: That's correct, I am an associate professor at McMaster University.

McPHERSON: And for the last five years you have been conducting a study of so-called "minority religions" in Canada and the United States?

LAMBERT: As well as groups I refer to loosely as "therapy cults". I've been an active investigator in this field since 1955. I worked with Festinger and the original Princeton flying saucer sect research group...

THOMPSON: Well, that's just dandy. But what do you know about Mentotechnics and what this Evanston person has to do with the people of this Province?

LAMBERT: Well, I...

THOMPSON: I don't mind telling you, Dr. Lambert, just how frustrating this inquiry has been for all of us. How difficult it is to pin down just what these people are up to. After months of hearings, of reading through hundreds of reports and recommendations, we still have no clear idea of just what Mentotechnists believe. We don't know if it's a religion or a college or a commune. Or a bunko operation. Can you tell me if the Temple really is a religion?

LAMBERT: Well, sir...

THOMPSON: Do you know how many people we've had to interview? How many so-called experts? Doctors, psychiatrists, lawyers, police detectives, students, even accountants! Do you have any idea of the extent of Evanston's financial holdings? In North America? Around the world?

LAMBERT: Well, sir, I...

THOMPSON: And can you tell us if there's anything to what Evanston's therapy promises? Why do so many people seem to accept these outrageous claims? How can any parliamentary commission be expected to make any kind of useful recommendations about something so strange? How...

WEISS: Perhaps if you would allow Dr. Lambert to actually say something she might address some of your concerns.

LAMBERT: What I can tell the Commission is where Evanston gets the ideas and symbols that make the Temple of Mentotechnics such a unique system of beliefs and practices. I also have a few theories about why people follow Evanston's teachings with such devotion.

THOMPSON: I'm all ears, professor.

LAMBERT: (to the Page) Can you please distribute my first exhibit?

PAGE: Yes, ma'am.

SOUND: <u>FOOTSTEPS OF THE PAGE WALKING AROUND THE TABLE. HE DEPOSITS BUNDLES OF MAGAZINES IN FRONT OF EACH M.P.P.</u>

THOMPSON: What are these, professor?

LAMBERT: What we've just passed around are some old science fiction magazines... some of them contain stories written by D.H. Evanston. It is in these stories that we find the key to unlocking the puzzle of

	Mentotechnics.
WEISS:	Oh really?
LAMBERT:	Definitely. I've marked some of the pages where you might find some familiar ideas. Such as a fleet of airships in which a secret society operates...
SOUND:	<u>FLIPPING OF PAGES AS THE M.P.P.S CHECK OUT THE PAGES.</u>
McPHERSON:	(muttering) Good heavens.
LAMBERT:	...or a special mind-enhancing machine which gives people advanced intelligence and telepathic powers...
THOMPSON:	Oh, yes, here it is.
LAMBERT:	...or how about an evil world-wide conspiracy by government and the medical profession to suppress scientific progress and the evolution of mankind?
WEISS:	That does sound very much like the Temple's anti-FDA literature.
McPHERSON:	Which is all very interesting...
SOUND:	<u>WEISS TOSSES HIS MAGAZINE ASIDE.</u>
WEISS:	But what does it tell us?
LAMBERT:	A number of things. First, it indicates the state of mind of Mentotechnics' creator: that he has trouble distinguishing between fantasy and reality. Also that he leans toward megalomania. Many of the Temple's institutions and practices—mobile headquarters, mind-machines, fleets of airships—can be seen as attempts by D.H. Evanston to actualize the ideas from his fiction.
WEISS:	I suppose that's something an academic would find very profound. But what else does it tell us?
LAMBERT:	The similarities to science fiction are also what gives Mentotechnics its power and tremendous ap-

peal.

THOMPSON: Religious power? From this nonsense?

LAMBERT: Almost certainly. Science fiction stimulates the imagination... many of its stories promise enhanced mental powers and happiness through advanced science and technology. Mentotechnics is a religious version of science fiction. The Temple promises the same things as science fiction: guaranteed salvation and gratification in the material world. And this conviction is validated by wider society's widespread faith in the power of science.

THOMPSON: You're raising more questions than you're answering, professor. Regardless of where Mentotechnics came from, thousands of people accept it as gospel truth!

LAMBERT: Yes, sir, many of these people really believe that Mentotechnics is a form of gospel.

WEISS: Are you suggesting that any level of government can rule on whether this, or any, religion is valid? None of us have that kind of insight or authority.

THOMPSON: But what if that so-called religion is guilty of fraud and felony?

WEISS: Where do we draw the line to maintain the rights of society to be protected from criminal acts...

McPHERSON: ...and the need to protect individual rights for freedom of expression and religious belief? This is a real problem—at least in Ontario, where we feel some obligation to protect even unpopular religions!

THOMPSON: I still think we're being played for suckers.

WEISS: We've already been around and around on this!

McPHERSON: Do you see our problem, Professor? You may be able to enlighten us on a few points of background, but you haven't been able to help us past this fundamental difficulty.

LAMBERT: Please consider: Mentotechnics makes some extraordinary claims for a religion—claims that it can generate real success in the material world. Surely this is now an educational problem; not only does the Temple claim to be a religion, it also states that it has scientific infallibility.

THOMPSON: Yeah, well, so what? I think most religions say they are infallible.

LAMBERT: But Mentotechnics also claims to be hard science. But the hard lesson of modern research is that science conveys no such magical powers. So we now have an educational problem: why can't you teach people to question those who promise miracle health cures? Or instant wealth? Or the easy solution to complex social problems? This critical attitude would be a boon to society, that is, if you agree that a democracy would benefit from the presence of intelligent, questioning minds...

THOMPSON: (a little embarrassed) Of course we do, Professor Lambert! We are democratically elected officials!

WEISS: I'm skeptical if we can solve all these problems by simply telling more people just what science really is.

McPHERSON: (dryly) Particularly when most of us don't know either.

LAMBERT: (irritated) Do you honestly believe that the people associated with the Temple are consistently mentally unbalanced or pathologically stupid?

THOMPSON: Well, not all of them.

McPHERSON: Actually, I'd say none of the people we've interviewed were crazy.

LAMBERT: That's what I thought. My experience suggests that many of the members of the Temple are, in fact, above average in intelligence and more sensitive than most people. The danger of Mentotechnics is not posed by its adherents, but stems from the deviant personality characteristics of D.H. Evanston and his inner circle.

THOMPSON: This is all one man's fault? That seems a little hard to believe.

LAMBERT: Powerful charismatic leaders often tend to paranoia, and they also tend to establish organizations that become authoritarian and confrontational. There is plenty of historical precedent. Unstable sociopaths and borderline psychotics can exert tremendous influence over their followers. I mean think of... of... (she struggles to think of an example) ...think of Hitler!

Scene Fourteen

Stage 17, Summit Studios, Hollywood, California. They are shooting a scene in the bedchamber of the Priest-Queen ruler of Planet Bikpen IV. The same day.

QUEEN DORXINDRA: (huskily) Brave Captain Hughes, you have saved our planetary system!

HUGHES: Yes, that is true...

DORXINDRA: Even though it is my sacred duty to abstain from all forms of physical congress...

HUGHES: Queen Dorxindra...

DORXINDRA: ...I am strongly tempted to abandon my life-long training as a spiritual celibate and to abandon myself to a wild frenzy of interstellar passion!

SOUND: A BIG WET KISS.

HUGHES/KYLE: Your Royal Space Highness, you honour me with your affections. And it is with the greatest humility and deepest respect that I convey the following message from all the people of Earth... (giggles) *Honk! Honk!*

DORXINDRA/LEA: (angry) *Ouch!* Get your hands off my—

HOLMES: (on megaphone) *Cut!*

KYLE: (sheepish) Oh, hi, Mr. Holmes.

HOLMES: (very angry) *What do you think you're doing?!*

JOQUIN: Yes, Kyle, why don't you tell our executive producer what you were doing?

KYLE: (laughs feebly) Well... it was like Mount Everest. Her chest was right there and, heh, and isn't our mission to "cross over into experiences unknown to man?"

HOLMES: You know, you are a complete and utter moron. Did you know that, Kyle?

KYLE: Well...

HOLMES: (to Lea) Did the utter moron hurt you, honey?

JOQUIN: (also to Lea) Are you going to be all right? Do you need shots or anything?

LEA: (irritated) He just surprised me. Can we just get on with the shoot?

HOLMES: Sure thing, sweetie. (calls) Okay, places! Stop laughing, damn you! (to Kyle) And no more nonsense from you, do you hear?!

SOUND: CAMERAS ROLLING INTO PLACE. FOOTSTEPS AS HOLMES AND MICHELLE WALK AWAY FROM THE ACTORS.

JOQUIN: I'm sorry, Mr. Holmes. He just seems to get worse every day.

HOLMES: Fondling my niece... after they finish this scene, I want you to get me Clyde on the phone.

JOQUIN: With pleasure, Mr. Holmes.

STUDIO TECHNICIAN: (in the distance) Take eighteen!

Scene Fifteen

<table>
<tr><td></td><td>The lobby of the Erewhon Inn. Late in the evening.</td></tr>
<tr><td>SOUND:</td><td>A TELEPHONE RINGS DOWN THE HALL.</td></tr>
<tr><td>CLYDE:</td><td>(VO) I really ought to say something clever. About how science fiction in the 1960s was a literature of creative speculation and cultural revolution and all that shit.</td></tr>
<tr><td>SOUND:</td><td>THE PHONE KEEPS ON RINGING.</td></tr>
<tr><td>CLYDE:</td><td>(VO) But it wasn't. Frankly, the second American Revolution was fought in the 1930s, lost in the 40s and the purges were conducted in the 50s. By the 1960s, we were so disconnected from everything, we didn't know what was really going down... and hell, I had a lot of personal stuff happening on this trip...</td></tr>
<tr><td>SOUND:</td><td>THE PHONE STOPS RINGING. CLYDE DROPS INTO A LARGE EASY CHAIR.</td></tr>
<tr><td>CLYDE:</td><td>(VO) Maybe I'm feeling too pessimistic to be a good narrator right now. If anything important occurs to me I'll get back to you, okay?</td></tr>
<tr><td>CROSS:</td><td>Your visual acuity will improve if we turn on the lamp.</td></tr>
<tr><td>SOUND:</td><td>CLICKING OF A SWITCH.</td></tr>
</table>

CLYDE AND McREADY: (startled) *Hey! Aiee!*

<table>
<tr><td>CLYDE:</td><td>(shaken) Cross! McReady! W-what the-the-the hell are you two lurking around in the dark for?</td></tr>
<tr><td>McREADY:</td><td>(breathless) W-we're j-just hanging out in the lobby, as the youngsters like to say.</td></tr>
</table>

CROSS: (cryptic) Maintaining a low profile.

CLYDE: What for? Who's here to avoid?

McREADY: (rueful) You might be surprised.

CROSS: There are certain developments to the North... that we are very interested in avoiding.

CLYDE: Unless you're talking about snow flurries, I don't think I want to know about it.

CROSS: Good. We are not particularly interested in discussing the matter.

McREADY: (calmer) But it is good to see you, Robert. You're still working for that silly TV show, aren't you?

CLYDE: Yes, I tried to get a job on the sensible one, but you know how it is.

McREADY: (earnest) Well, I've got a great merchandising idea, make us all millionaires!

CLYDE: (stonily) Oh, goodie.

McREADY: You've still got that alien character on the show? The one with the piggie nose who can levitate objects?

CLYDE: Chief Technology Officer Zagar. Gets the most fan mail on the show.

McREADY: Remember how popular those coonskin hats were when the Disney show came out? You know, Daniel Boone?

CLYDE: I think I still have one of those hats.

McREADY: (struggling for breath a little)

CLYDE: Are you feeling okay, Mac? You look a little tired.

McREADY: Never mind me, just listen to this idea: you can sell a toy based on this Dagar character. You make a big pig nose mask and attach a bugo, or a bozo at the end of it...

CLYDE:	A bugo?
CROSS:	A bozo? Do you mean a clown's nose?
McREADY:	(irritated) No! No, those things that gauchos use in South America.
CROSS:	A bolo?
McREADY:	Yes, that's the thing. Anyway, you hang this thing like a yo-yo at the end of a string at the end of the pig snout. The string oughta be a good yard long, and the yo-yo, bolo thing should be a pretty substantial weight...
CLYDE:	Are you serious?
CROSS:	Yes, he is. I have observed McReady when he was being serious in the past.
McREADY:	Anyway, the kid puts on the mask and he can whip the bolo thing up and down, and around and around...
CLYDE:	They whip the thing around and around?
McREADY:	Like they can levitate it... they can even do tricks.
CROSS:	Yes, levitation tricks.
McREADY:	So, whaddya think?
CLYDE:	It's great. There might be a tiny problem with some kid getting the occasional concussion, but that shouldn't be a big obstacle.
McREADY:	(pleased) Wonderful! When can we start selling them? I want 60% of all profits!
CLYDE:	I don't think it's quite that easy, Mac. This is such a good idea that you'd better take some steps to protect it, so that nobody steals your profits.
McREADY:	(shocked) Is that possible? Somebody would ac-

tually do that?

CLYDE: Oh yeah. Happens all the time. Here's the card of our executive producer, Jason Holmes. What you should do is put your idea down in writing and send it off to him. I'm sure he'll be fascinated to hear all about it.

McREADY: Thanks, I'll do that.

SOUND: <u>MCREADY RISES OUT OF HIS CHAIR.</u>

McREADY: But that's enough creative work for one night. See you in the morning, Jay.

SOUND: <u>THE OLD MAN SHUFFLES AWAY.</u>

CLYDE: Wow, did he really used to be Stewart D. McReady, the world famous editor of *Tremendous Stories*?

CROSS: Even he isn't sure. He just heard from Hayden MacArnold's agent; the sequel to *Martian Messiah* will be moving to either *Analog* or *Galaxy*.

CLYDE: You mean Mac hasn't got a single big name left? They'll toss him off the magazine for sure.

CROSS: A formality, I fear. Pamela McReady has assumed most of the editorial responsibilities since the Mentotechnics fiasco.

CLYDE: (sighs) Poor bastard. (pause) But it's good of you to stand by the old guy in his hour of need.

CROSS: Interesting interpretation, Clyde.

CLYDE: But I'm a little surprised. I thought you two broke off years ago.

CROSS: Accounts of our differences may have been exaggerated.

CLYDE: So are you thinking about writing again? That might help him out.

CROSS: No, that is not possible.

CLYDE: So, if you aren't going to write anything, what are you doing here?

CROSS: An associate informed me that both McReady and I would be well advised to be unavailable for a week. There is a government inquiry in Canada regarding the Temple of Mentotechnics...

CLYDE: (with dread) Oh, man, not them again.

CROSS: ...and I felt that both McReady and I could indeed function quite happily without the stress.

CLYDE: Really? I thought you might enjoy publicly testifying against Evanston.

CROSS: You are correct. But I was advised to arrange my absence for professional reasons.

CLYDE: What is your profession, by the way? You haven't written anything for almost twenty years now.

CROSS: After the first federal investigation into the original Evanston Foundation, I was placed in direct contact with certain security branches of our national government. I discovered I had a surprising compatibility with the personnel and structures of these organizations. Very soon, I was retained on contract by an agency.

CLYDE: A rather central agency? You're a spy?

CROSS: I advise certain civil servants on a range of topics: future trends, likely technological breakthroughs, new methods of mind control, abuses and applications of consciousness-altering substances, deviant ideologies...

CLYDE: (snorts) You mean you're still writing science fiction, but the taxpayers are directly subsidizing you?

CROSS: (laughs) Another interesting interpretation, Clyde.

CLYDE: Lords of the Galaxy! This may be the first time you've betrayed any evidence of human emotions in front of a witness.

CROSS: (amused) For reasons of National Security, I can neither confirm nor deny your claim.

CLYDE: I knew there was something different about you. You almost sound like a real person... you're less... less...

CROSS: Robotic? It is true. Perhaps it is an outcome of my change in occupation.

CLYDE: Maybe. (pause) Man, it's dark out there.

CROSS: My employers are so concerned with global trends, the world-view, fluctuations in continental economies, shifts in planetary belief-systems...

CLYDE: Big picture stuff, huh?

CROSS: They were drawing on the very essence of my science fiction vision. Huge, complex organizations using subterfuge and advanced technology in a covert struggle to control the future of the human race.

CLYDE: Sounds like a bundle of laughs, Cross.

CROSS: Well, it all became quite mundane. Even ridiculous. Every one of our grand strategies demanded an absolute certainty of purpose, but every scheme was founded on an incomplete accounting of the facts. Every master scenario to control society ended with a new, unexpected, and usually undesirable outcome. A new generation of conventional weapons for Europe leads to a new war in the Middle East, a new truth drug for the interrogation of double agents leads to a counter-culture movement in San Francisco. We seemed to be doing things that had such strange results.

CLYDE:	Well, the 1960s certainly seem to be turning out to be pretty strange times.
CROSS:	I suppose I've grown out of science fiction. I don't seem to need to live it anymore.
CLYDE:	Thanks to guys like you, the world seems to be turning into science fiction.
CROSS:	Oops.
CLYDE:	And you have to venture into the wilderness in order to gafiate. You really have to get away from it all.
CROSS:	So it would seem.
CLYDE:	It's probably your own damned fault. (sighs heavily) Well, I'd better get back to my room.
SOUND:	<u>CLYDE WALKS HALFWAY ACROSS THE LOBBY AND STOPS.</u>
CLYDE:	And welcome to the human race, Cross.
CROSS:	Thank you. It's been an interesting experience so far.
SOUND:	<u>CLYDE WALKS AWAY. THE PHONE IN THE DISTANCE STARTS RINGING AGAIN.</u>

Scene Sixteen

Clyde's hotel room, a few minutes later.

SOUND: THE TELEPHONE IS RINGING. DOOR OPENS, CLYDE WALKS OVER AND ANSWERS THE PHONE.

CLYDE: Hello?

HOLMES: (on telephone receiver throughout) Robbie! Sorry to butt in on the old creative sanctum, but I've got "Egos in Collision" over here. Worse than the last quake.

CLYDE: (irritated) What did Kyle do this time? Bite somebody? Set fire to the scenery?

HOLMES: Worse, Rob-man, he felt up my niece on camera. We're going to see that that on blooper reels at every studio Christmas party until the 23rd Century.

CLYDE: Be sure to save me a copy.

HOLMES: Shut up, Bob-san. Anyway, that moron is ruining the series. Not only are Michelle and I forced to ruin your vacation, he's upset my sister's kid! Bob-guy, what can we do about him?

CLYDE: (thoughtful) What's Kyle's contract situation?

HOLMES: Oh, legally I can dump him; he's up for renewal this season, just like everybody else. But there's only the slightly major continuity problem of the star of a show suddenly disappearing.

CLYDE: Why not do a *Mission Impossible* on him?

HOLMES: Are you suggesting I have him secretly assassinated or trade him to another series? This isn't Cuban baseball, Robber.

CLYDE: No, it's nothing like that. Desilu Studios had to change the star of their show at the end of the first season. Everyone thought it would kill an already weak series. But when they put in the new actor as the star...

HOLMES: (excited) The show became a monster hit! Do you think we could do something like that here, B.C.?

SOUND: <u>CLYDE SITS DOWN AT HIS DESK.</u>

CLYDE: Yup.

SOUND: <u>CLYDE LOADS A PIECE OF PAPER INTO HIS TYPEWRITER.</u>

HOLMES: Great!

CLYDE: Mr. Holmes, you have inspired me, sir. I'm about to end my vacation and write a treatment for the surprise season opener... which will feature the tragic death of the brave space captain Hughes.

HOLMES: Courageous solution, Mr. Bob! Outstanding stuff! I'll remember this when your contract comes up.

CLYDE: Well, it's just that some things just have to come to an end.

SOUND: <u>CLYDE HANGS UP. CLYDE STARTS TYPING EARNESTLY.</u>

Scene Seventeen

McReady's hotel room. A few minutes before Clyde's telephone conversation with Holmes.

SOUND:

DOOR OPENS, MCREADY WALKS IN SLOWLY, TURNS ON THE LIGHT.

FREAK:

(nerdy voice) Hi, there, Mr. McReady!

McREADY:

(gasping in fear) *Awk!* Oh, my god, a hippie freak! Please! Please, don't hurt me! Please!

SOUND:

MCREADY FALLS ONTO THE BED.

FREAK:

Gosh! I'm sorry, Mr. McReady. I hope I didn't scare you.

McREADY:

(very frightened) What do you want?! You aren't going to kill me in some sort of Negro-panther flower-power sex ritual, are you?!

FREAK:

Golly, no, Mr. McReady. I couldn't find no other place to wait for you and I'm sorry I was so late, but they only run one bus a night out here, ya know?

McREADY:

(still scared, but now a little angry) What do you want from me, you hemp-fiend?

FREAK:

I know you're real busy being a world-famous science fiction editor and everything, Mr. McReady, but *The Martian Messiah* is my absolutely favourite book...

McREADY:

So why aren't you hiding in Hayden MacArnold's hotel room? He wrote the thing.

FREAK:

Because you were his editor... so I know you'd really wanna see the *manuscript for my new science fiction novel!*

SOUND: THE FREAK DROPS A MASS OF PAPERS ON THE BED BESIDE MCREADY.

McREADY: Listen, kid. It's really late and I'm not feeling that well.

FREAK: (tone of menace creeps into his voice) Mr. McReady, I've been waiting a very long time and I really don't think you want to disappoint a young writer, do you now?

McREADY: (shaken) O-okay, let's take a look here...

SOUND: PAPER SHUFFLING AS MCREADY PICKS UP A SINGLE SHEET FROM THE PILE.

FREAK: (effusive) Oh, thank you, Mr. McReady! I just know that you can appreciate what I'm trying to express in my work!

McREADY: Lust beasts and mind monsters? Evil aliens employed by the government? Cripes, your stuff reads just like a writer I knew back in the 1940s...

FREAK: Does my work remind you of...

SOUND: SOUND OF SPIRIT GUM AND TAPE BEING STRETCHED AS THE FREAK PULLS OFF HIS WIG AND A FALSE BEARD.

FREAK/EVANSTON: (with an evil laugh) ...the great and lamented D.H. Evanston?

McREADY: (gasps) Dear God! Donald, what in heaven's name are you doing here?

EVANSTON: Same as you, just hanging out.

SOUND: HE SITS ON THE BED BESIDE MCREADY.

McREADY: But how did you know I'd be here?

EVANSTON: Oh, connections. My organization is very powerful, and I'm very rich, my friend. I can find things out.

McREADY: (pain in his voice) But what are you sneaking around like this for?

EVANSTON: From time to time, a king should walk among his people. My airfleet will drop me off for the odd little field trip, which I conduct incognito to avoid over-exciting my followers.

McREADY: Or getting nailed by the IRS for back taxes.

SOUND: <u>MCREADY FEEBLY WAVES A PIECE OF PAPER IN THE AIR.</u>

McREADY: Is this for real, Donald? Have you really written a new novel?

EVANSTON: Of course this is for real. I've been living a science fiction epic for years, it was time to set it all down.

McREADY: Oh, god, my chest... I'm sorry, I don't follow you.

EVANSTON: (expansively) I'm in control of a world-wide organization with thousands of mind-soldiers—every one of them utterly loyal to me! I'm in command of a squadron of advanced aircraft, I'm the mayor of the world's first aerial community! I'm controlling a battle, the fate of which will determine the future of the planet!

McREADY: (irritated but in great pain) Oh, yeah? Well, so what?

EVANSTON: Okay, I never could B.S. you for long, Mac. With all that time and money at my disposal, I figure I could finally get it together and write another book. I mean, hell, I'm so famous, millions of my fans must be waiting to read my latest work, right?

McREADY: No way, bub! Everyone in the science fiction world has either forgotten you or is anxious to say they never knew you. You make all the other lunatics in this crank factory look like insurance salesmen.

EVANSTON: (very angry) *You stupid old man! I was your king! Your ace! God of the pulps!* I was the first *Tremendous* writer to hit the bestseller list!

McREADY: (calmer but still in pain) As the author of a book of lies, not of fiction. The only way you'd sell a million D.H. Evanston books today is if you and your team of trained loonies bought them all yourself.

EVANSTON: You pompous ass! (raving) I always knew that you were really against me... always jealous of my genius... always secretly plotting against me... constantly trying to keep me from getting ahead... always thwarting my aspirations...

McREADY: (snorts) *Thwart* your aspirations? Always with the melodramatic dialogue. (sighs) Look, Donald, I'm on the verge of becoming science fiction history myself. I'm in no position to get anyone... or help anyone for that matter...

SOUND: CREAKING OF BED SPRINGS AS MCREADY TURNS AWAY FROM EVANSTON.

McREADY: Now, please go away. I'm not feeling very well.

SOUND: RUSTLING OF PAPER AS EVANSTON TAKES HIS MANUSCRIPT BACK.

EVANSTON: Well, I'm not surprised. You never had the guts to try and really live the Dream. (hisses with rage) *You weakling!*

SOUND: EVANSTON STORMS OUT OF THE ROOM AND SLAMS THE DOOR.

McREADY: (weeps with pain) Somebody, please help me...

SOUND: THE STRANGE WINDS OF NON-TIME RISE.

CLYDE: (VO) There was never a record of that conversation. I only know about it because I'm also the narrator. Stewart D. McReady was in no position to tell us about his bizarre encounter with the mysterious D.H. Evanston because he died of a heart attack later that night.

SOUND: THE ALIEN HOWLS TAKE ON A VAGUELY MOURNFUL TONE.

CLYDE: (sadly) Some things just have to end.

**End of
Disappointing Success**

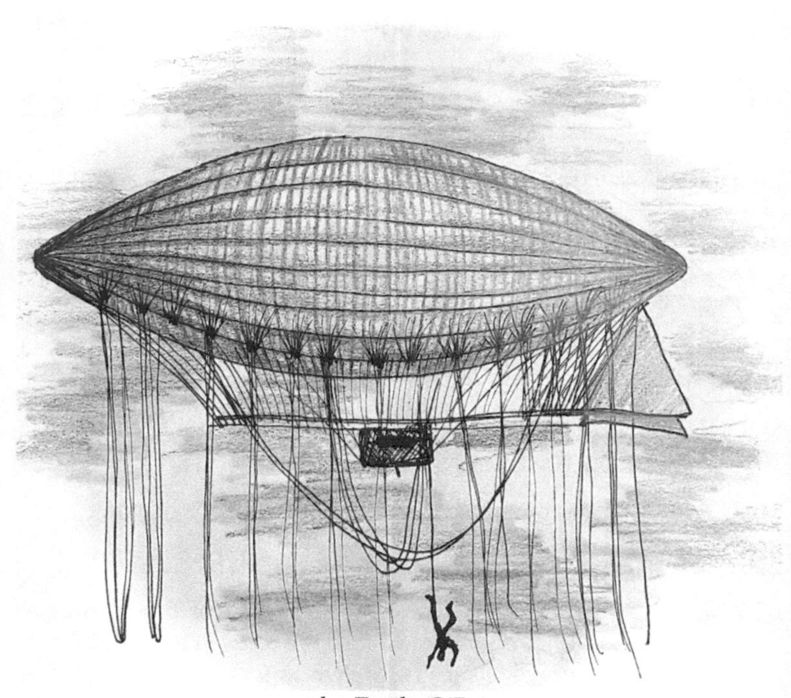

art by Emily O'Brien

Disappointing Success
Part II

Play Four:
Disappointing Success Part II

Characters – In Order of Appearance

CAPTAIN ZAGAR/
SHECKLEY
: Now the lead character in the *Space Spanners* film franchise. Played by actor Leo Sheckley.

DR. STURGEON/CLARK
: Still chief medical officer on the starship "Astral Arrow" in the *Space Spanners* films. Played by actor Sybil Clark.

SHIPMAN JANSEN
: Minor character in the latest *Space Spanners* film.

SHIP COMPUTER
: Artificial intelligence that controls the "Astral Arrow".

LARRY HOLMES
: Executive producer and occasional director of *Space Spanner* films.

BOB CLYDE
: Our protagonist and narrator. Also executive story consultant in the *Space Spanner* films.

LAURA WILLIAMS
: Co-host of the network morning show *Rise-Up America!*

DAN BRIFF
: Co-host of the network morning show *Rise-Up America!*

RONALD REAGAN
: President of the United States from 1981 to 1989.

BARBARA ZEBROWSKI
: A journalist. Sheldon Isaacs's ex-wife.

FANS #1 AND #2
: Participants at a *Space Spanners* convention held at EPCOT/Disney

	World.
MONORAIL VOICE	A pre-recorded information system.
JACK WEBB JR	A Happiness Officer employed by Disney World.
JOY DICKINSON	A Joy Agent employed by Disney World.
DR. SHELDON ISAACS	Now an extraordinarily successful science and science fiction media phenomena. President and founder of Sheldon Isaacs Inc.
DR. HEATHER ATKINSON	Chief Operating Officer of Sheldon Isaacs Inc. Wife of Sheldon Isaacs.
ROLF DENSEN	Now a somewhat more successful science fiction writer.
FRANCIS FREEDMAN	Also a somewhat more successful science fiction writer.
DAVID POOLE	A semi-retired science fiction writer and editor with a surprisingly good reputation. One of Ray Ann Sparks' ex-husbands.
RAY ANN SPARKS	A reasonably popular but essentially frustrated science fiction writer, anthologist and editor. One of David Poole's ex-wives.
LUCILLE RIPLEY	One of the marketing directors and vice presidents of Omega Global Communications.
VOICE ON WALKIE-TALKIE	A control technician at EPCOT.
STEVE SUTTON	A *Space Spanners* fanatic.
JAY E. CROSS	Former science fiction writer and CIA consultant. A rather mysterious fellow.
GREG DANIELS	Graduate student in social anthropology at McMaster University.
AGNES MILGORE	Mother of a recent recruit to the

	Temple of Mentotechnics.
D.H. EVANSTON	The recently dead founder/director of the Temple of Mentotechnics.

Scene One

Stage 22, Summit Studios, Hollywood, California. Mid-March 1983.

SOUND: STEADY THROB OF THE STARSHIP *ASTRAL ARROW*'S MIGHTY ION ENGINES. VARIOUS ELECTRONIC SOUNDS OF THE SHIP'S CONTROL CENTER.

CAPTAIN ZAGAR: Situation report, Doctor.

STURGEON: I don't know, Captain. I just don't like the look of these readings from that moon...

ZAGAR: That is regrettable, Doctor. It seems that we are forced to investigate further. (calls out) Shipman Jansen, prepare a shuttle for immediate planetfall.

SOUND: BEEPS AS JANSEN PRESSES A FEW BUTTONS.

JANSEN: Yes, sir!

SOUND: BRIEF ELECTRONIC BLARE OF SHIP'S AUTOMATIC ALARM SYSTEM.

SHIP COMPUTER: We have just entered Emergency Condition Delta.

STURGEON: Captain Zagar, you can't be serious! We can't go back to that moon! You know how dangerous those caverns can be, they're still filled with evil and subversive mutants!

ZAGAR: Yes, after all these years, I still remember. But we must go! The security of the Galactic Alliance is at stake.

SHIP COMPUTER: Neutron cannons are fully armed and ready.

ZAGAR: Once again, we must face the wrath and treachery

of the Nevadasnobs!

HOLMES: (on megaphone) *Cut!*

SHECKLEY (AKA ZAGAR): (impatient) Oh, what is it now?

HOLMES: Sorry, sorry, everybody. Bobbie's flagged a blooper.

SHECKLEY: So?

HOLMES: So, he is the Exec. Story Consultant so we're paid to better listen to him.

CLYDE: (sarcastic) Thanks for the vote of confidence.

SHECKLEY: Well?

CLYDE: This is just a small point—but the aliens—your main adversaries in this film? They are called *Zephulons*. Remember them?

SHECKLEY: (sighs) Yeah, yeah, I remember. I've just had a bit of a mental black about Z-Zephulons for the last 15 years (fades).

<u>SOUND</u>:   <u>WINDS AND EERIE MUSIC OF NARRATIVE NON-TIME.</u>

CLYDE: (VO) Greetings. It's the year 1983 and I'm still writing for *Space Spanners*. Right now we are shooting the third in a seemingly infinite number of movie sequels.

<u>MUSIC</u>:   <u>MOCK HEROIC ORCHESTRAL SCORE RISES. ANY SIMILARITY TO ANY PARTICULAR SCIENCE FICTION TV SERIES AND FILM FRANCHISE IS COMPLETELY INTENTIONAL.</u>

CLYDE: (VO) The network cancelled the original series in 1970. They said that America was sick of space, so a science fiction show with marginal ratings and a questionable rep just had to go.

<u>MUSIC</u>:   <u>GETS BRIEFLY SCARY, THEN SAD.</u>

CLYDE: (VO) Made sense to me. By then I was sick of the show, anyway. But the network was only partly right; people were indeed, completely fed up with words like "lunar excursion", "command module", "separation sequence" or "Congressional funding allocation". It sounded like divorce proceedings! It was a subtle point, but what the public hated was the *reality* of space exploration.

MUSIC: <u>GETS HEROIC AGAIN.</u>

CLYDE: But everybody still loved the *dream* of space travel... the fantasy of the promise of the future. And in our show the future was dead easy. We didn't take ten years to design our spacecraft, and we didn't spend 35 billion to build and launch the thing. Oh, no! And we didn't settle for dinky destinations like the moon. We'd just push a couple of buttons, intercut with a couple of special effects shots, and hell! There we were, on the other side of the galaxy!

After we got cancelled, the show went into reruns on syndication... and it became a monster hit! By 1983 the show is played 50 times a day, every day, somewhere in the world. People were dreaming up costumes, organizing conventions, printing up amateur *Space Spanner* newsletters... like the old fanzines we were writing out of Camp Fantastic! We'd created a new religion! (sighs) Unfortunately I wasn't smart enough to pick up any points on the reruns so I had to really hustle for a living.

I tried to write some novels. (sighs again) It didn't work out. While my Fabulist colleagues were mutating from weird nerds and dorks into the grand old "elders" of science fiction, I had the scarlet letters "Tee" and "Vee" burned into my forehead. It wasn't until they let me novelize some of the old *Space Spanners* episodes that I was looking at any kind of money. And when the studio finally decided to produce some movies starring the original cast... (delighted) ...well... I was living in *style* again!

MUSIC:	<u>ORCHESTRA GIVES WAY TO WEIRDNESS OF NON-TIME WINDS.</u>
CLYDE:	It didn't bother me *too* much that in the 1980s we were re-making a show from the 1960s which were just re-hashings of old pulp stories from the '30s and '40s. Although, sometimes, in the middle of the night, I wondered that we conducting dangerous experiments... like we were re-cycling time... and that we'd somehow cause the universe to implode on itself.
HOLMES:	Okay, everybody! The bard is satisfied! Let's do some serious work. Places!
SOUND:	<u>CAST AND CREW TAKE THEIR PLACES.</u>
HOLMES:	(whispers to Clyde) Have you changed your mind, yet? You have to go to the convention! It's Florida! It's EPCOT! It's fun!
CLYDE:	(snorts) It's marketing!
HOLMES:	(concerned) Don't laugh, Spannies are powerful, the studio's afraid of them. You have to go to that convention and talk to them. We're in the program book!
CLYDE:	(laughs) It's okay, I'm going.
HOLMES:	(relieved) Really? That's great! (suddenly suspicious) Why?
CLYDE:	Got a call from Sheldon Isaacs' agent, he's going be there too.
HOLMES:	I thought you two hated each other.
CLYDE:	Oh, I hate a lot of people. But his people want to talk some business, what can it hurt?
CLYDE:	(VO) And as far as Sheldon Isaacs was concerned, that was absolutely the *worst* decision I have ever made!

Scene Two

The action alternates between Studio C, WBS-TV New York City and a cafe at the EPCOT A-Frame Hotel in Orlando, Florida. 8:30 a.m. EST, late March, 1983.

MUSIC: <u>(ON TV SPEAKER) DRAMATIC NEWS FANFARE.</u>

WILLIAMS: Good morning. And it's time for the news update on *Rise-Up America!*

BRIFF: And the lead story this half-hour is the death of Donald H. Evanston, the mysterious and controversial founder of the Temple of Mentotechnics. According to Temple representatives, Evanston died of complications following heart surgery.

WILLIAMS: A former science fiction writer and a recluse since 1973, Evanston, and his organization, have been the subject of hundreds of government investigations and legal actions. According to the Department of Justice, the Temple still faces ongoing charges of fraud, tax evasion, harassment of elected officials and the theft of IRS files.

BRIFF: The most recent court action was last year's sentencing of five leading Temple organizers to 17 years in federal prisons for theft of classified CIA computer records. Charges against Evanston were dropped owing to lack of evidence.

WILLIAMS: While Evanston was strongly criticized by medical doctors, psychiatrists and theologians, he had thousands of devoted followers all across the country, with an estimated three million Temple members around the world. Some prominent Mentotechnists are Hollywood celebrities, and we have on-line that television and film star, John Tra—

BRIFF: Sorry to interrupt that story, but we have that tape of last night's Presidential address... we'll get back to Hollywood right after this message about the future of our global defence policy.

WILLIAMS: (smile in her voice) Ladies and gentlemen, the President of the United States...

REAGAN: ...Many people might think that a 10% increase in defence spending is excessive in terms of this administration's policy of fiscal restraint. But I want to share with Americans a vision of hope:

MUSIC: <u>SCARY ORCHESTRAL MUSIC, REMINISCENT OF THE OPENING SCENES OF A 1950S GIANT INSECT MOVIE.</u>

REAGAN: I am showing you previously classified intelligence photographs which clearly demonstrate the Soviet Union's efforts to build up an offensive military force around the world...

MUSIC: <u>THE SCORE CONTINUES, STARTS TO SOUND A LITTLE MORE HOPEFUL.</u>

REAGAN: This may seem to be a hopeless situation to many of you, but I ask you: what if free people could live secure in the knowledge that their security did not rest upon the threat of instant retaliation to deter a Soviet attack; that we could intercept and destroy strategic ballistic missiles before they reach our own soil or that of our allies?

I hereby appeal to the scientists of America to turn their great talents to the development of an anti-ballistic missile system capable of destroying enemy missiles before they could reach their targets...

MUSIC: <u>IS NOW DOWNRIGHT HEROIC—LIKE THE THEME TO THE SUPERMAN TV SHOW.</u>

REAGAN: Wouldn't it be better to save lives rather than to avenge them? Are we not capable of demonstrating our peaceful intentions by applying all our abilities and ingenuity to achieving a truly lasting stability?

There will be failures and setbacks just as there will be successes and breakthroughs. But it is worth every investment necessary to free the world from the threat of nuclear war.

MUSIC: <u>GETS CHEERFUL.</u>

REAGAN: I am taking an important first step. I am directing a comprehensive and intensive effort to define a long-term research and development program to begin to end the threat posed by nuclear missiles.

MUSIC: <u>TURNS INTO A MEDLEY OF 1950S TV THEMES. GETS TINNIER AND EVENTUALLY FADES INTO THE BACKGROUND.</u>

SOUND: <u>VOICES AND CLATTER OF CUTLERY IN AN EATING ESTABLISHMENT.</u>

CLYDE: (VO) I loved it. Evanston dedicated his life to selling the world a giant science fiction story and his obituary gets interrupted by an even bigger one.

CLYDE: (mutters) D.H. Evanston, what an ass...

BARBARA: Excuse me, but did you know I met him years ago? My ex-husband introduced us.

CLYDE: (surprised) My god! *Barbara Isaacs!* I didn't recognize you! You look terrific!

BARBARA: Actually, it's Barbara Zebrowski these days.

CLYDE: It's really good to see you, Barbara. I wondered how you were doing ever since—

BARBARA: The divorce? Well, I had to get the kids safely packed off to university, and then I decided to go myself. I finished my degree in journalism and now I write magazine articles.

CLYDE: You're a writer, too? (with mock sorrow) Please accept my deepest sympathies.

<u>SOUND:</u>	<u>TWO SETS OF FOOTSTEPS SHUFFLING PAST.</u>
FAN #1:	Okay, Episode 33: what did Captain Zagar say to Dr. Sturgeon in the alien death camp?
FAN #2:	"Doctor, you can suck the brains out of a space officer, but never the human spirit!"
FAN #1:	Okay, then what did she say—
FAN #2:	(whispering to Fan #1) Shhh! Do you think it's him?
CLYDE:	(quiet) Damn!
BARBARA:	What is it, Bob?
CLYDE:	There's been a sighting.
FAN #1:	Hey, Bob Clyde! Famous movie writer! *We really hate your stuff!*
CLYDE:	I don't know if I can handle all this adoration from my public.
BARBARA:	Never mind. I'm here doing a story on this convention. I've seen a lot of that sort of behaviour.
CLYDE:	You're doing some anthropological study of the future?
BARBARA:	Supposedly, but I'm not getting anything very interesting. I'm thinking of doing a piece on this place.
CLYDE:	On EPCOT? A travel piece?
BARBARA:	Into a future that could never exist. I've been having some heavy thoughts, like comparing how the subliminal message of EPCOT and the vision of Reagan's new defence policy reflect a fundamental confusion of science fiction with reality.
CLYDE:	Yeah, this is quite the place. You know, it seems very familiar, I don't know why... (he listens) It's the music... do you...?
<u>MUSIC:</u>	<u>FROM THE SPEAKERS RISES AND REACHES</u>

<u>A DRAMATIC CRESCENDO, THEN FADES.</u>

BARBARA: (laughing) Arthur Bliss. One of the great British symphonic composers of the 20th Century. That is his soundtrack score to the 1936 film *Things To Come* directed by William Cameron Menzies, based on the novel by H.G. Wells...

CLYDE: Wow! Where did you pick all that up?

BARBARA: You Fabulists used to play it all the time at Camp Fantastic. When you broke up, Sheldon lifted it from the apartment. He used to play it incessantly. For inspiration, he said.

CLYDE: (suddenly excited) *That's what this place is!* They've finally built Camp Fantastic! As we saw it in our minds! This is our vision of the future... back in 1937. (something between a laugh and a sob) We were so... despised back them. Everyone thought we were such losers and fools... we *were* losers and fools... but they still took our dreams and made them into... into...

BARBARA: An amusement park? The most successful tourist attraction in history?

CLYDE: I feel used.

BARBARA: I don't think you can copyright collective visions, Bob.

CLYDE: No, guess not.

BARBARA: So, what are you doing here?

CLYDE: Oh, I'm just speaking at this silly convention and I've got a business meeting—(embarrassed)—uh, listen, did you know that Sheldon and Heather are staying at the hotel here?

BARBARA: No. Nor do I really care. Listen, Bob, I have to go and make a few calls, why don't we get together to-night? We could talk and eat.

CLYDE: (surprised but delighted) I'll call you.

SOUND: <u>BARBARA STANDS UP AND WALKS OUT.</u>

CLYDE: (VO) This is good. Actually, this is very good! I've always liked Barbara. She's smart, she looks *great*, and she's not crazy. This is all very promising. I'm even getting over having some giant faceless corporation steal the creative spirit of my generation.

Scene Three

Inside a Disney World monorail. About ten minutes later.

SOUND: <u>ELECTRIC MONORAIL ROLLS TO A STOP. THE DOORS "SWISH" OPEN AND CLYDE STEPS INTO THE MONORAIL. THE DOORS "SWISH" SHUT.</u>

MONORAIL VOICE: Welcome to the Walt Disney World Monorail Ride! The next stop is the Walt Disney World Resort Hotel, followed by the Magic Kingdom!

SOUND: <u>WHINE OF THE ELECTRIC ENGINE.</u>

CLYDE: (hums) Zippidee-do-dah... zippidee-ay...

WEBB JR.: Don't move, sir.

CLYDE: Excuse me, is there something I can for you?

WEBB JR.: Check him against the Polaroid, Dickinson.

DICKINSON: This looks like our man.

CLYDE: (offended) Now, this can't be the magic of Disney...

WEBB JR.: Mr. Clyde? Mr. Robert Clyde?

CLYDE: That's me.

WEBB JR.: I'm Happiness Officer Jack Webb Jr., this is my associate Joy Agent Joy Dickinson. We are on-site operatives for the Walt Disney World Security Force.

CLYDE: (astonished) The what?!

DICKINSON: We've been sent to locate you.

WEBB JR.:   Mr. Clyde, please keep your voice low, do ex-
                   actly what I tell you, and come with us.

CLYDE: What's going on here?

DICKINSON: It is vital that you speak to someone.

SOUND: THE MONORAIL ROLLS TO A STOP.

MONORAIL VOICE: (cheerful) Welcome to the Walt Disney
                   World EPCOT Terminal! Be sure to take all
                   personal belongings with you as you leave!

Scene Four

	An executive meeting room at the EPCOT A-Frame Resort Hotel. 30 minutes later.
MUSIC:	<u>THERE IS A DEEP ORCHESTRAL CHORD, WHICH BUILDS INTO A BROODING, ALMOST MENACING MELODY.</u>
SOUND:	<u>FAN OF A SLIDE PROJECTOR.</u>
ISAACS:	Why don't we hold on this slide for a moment?
DENSEN:	Wow! Look at that big gun!
FREEDMAN:	Look at that chest!
ATKINSON:	(annoyed) Oh, please, let's keep the conversation at an adult level.
ISAACS:	Humph! I see that my former associate Mr. Clyde has not seen fit to join us yet.
DENSEN:	I think I saw him heading toward the monorail a little while ago. Bob is a pretty quick study, why don't we just proceed and fill him in when he gets here.
ISAACS:	Very well. It's not vanity that requires me to show you this book cover.
SPARKS:	(sarcastic) Oh, god! Of course not, Sheldon!
ISAACS:	(doesn't seem to notice) No, this illustration is part of a proposition I have for all of you.
DENSEN:	A proposition?
ISAACS:	Most of you are aware that over the last 10 years or so, I've been enjoying a certain amount of diversification. In addition to my fiction and non-fiction

writing, I am the editor of the *Sheldon Isaacs' Best Science Fiction in the Universe* anthologies, I'm publisher and editor-in-chief of *Sheldon Isaacs's New Tremendous Stories*, I'm the principal referee for the *International Journal of Science Fiction Studies*, I have a daily syndicated newspaper column, I host *Sheldon Isaacs's World of Peculiar Events* on many syndicated television stations, and I've recently been approached by Summit Studios to be the scientific advisor for the new *Space Spanners* film.

POOLE: (muttering) That ought to make Bob ecstatic.

ISAACS: ...and I'm currently developing a Saturday morning cartoon series with strong merchandising links to a new line of toys and comic books.

SPARKS: (again sarcastic) We are so happy for you, Sheldon. Was this career update why you asked us here?

ISAACS: There's no need to get jealous, Ray. What I'm trying to explain to you is that Sheldon Isaacs Inc. has become something of a growth industry. And like many promising enterprises, I was the subject of a very attractive take-over bid.

POOLE: Are you saying that you've been bought out?

ISAACS: (smile in his voice) Yes. By the Omega Communications Group.

SPARKS: (horrified) They bought your name?

ISAACS: They have rights to use my name on their products, it's rather complicated.

DENSEN: (also horrified) You mean they *own* you?

FREEDMAN: (really horrified) It sounds awful!

ISAACS: Not at all. I have a very beneficial working relationship with Omega.

RIPLEY: (clears her throat) Hello, everyone.

ISAACS: And accordingly, I want to introduce you to Lucille

Ripley, one of Omega's marketing directors who will further explain this arrangement and how it could be relevant to you!

SOUND: <u>CLICK OF THE PROJECTOR CONTROL.</u>

RIPLEY: My job as a marketing director is to target Sheldon Isaacs's books to as many different audiences as we possibly can. With a high recognition name like "Sheldon Isaacs" backing a line of quality science fiction products, we feel we have the best possible chance of gaining maximum penetration of the widest possible range of consumer markets... provided Omega's experts are free to package and deliver the product.

SOUND: <u>RIPLEY CLICKS ON TO ANOTHER SLIDE.</u>

RIPLEY: This close-up of the same book cover reveals some of our marketing "hooks". Our surveys indicate that the main audience for the Alexander Steel books are adolescent white males from middle-class backgrounds.

SPARKS: You mean heavy metal fans in the suburbs of Seattle?

RIPLEY: This cover is calculated to best appeal to our *target markets*—through the application of strategic psy-chographic data.

DENSEN: "Psychographic"? Like an insane illustration?

SOUND: <u>RIPLEY CLICKS ON TO ANOTHER SLIDE.</u>

RIPLEY: Please, it is a serious technical term. Now in this even closer view we can see that the gun is mod-elled after the male member and it is extremely technological in nature. This responds to emerging male sexuality and any latent *homosexuality*. The technical detail answers older boys' more prevalent interests in machines and science.

SPARKS: (amused) Right...

RIPLEY: The breasts of the female character are deliberately exaggerated and exposed to nurture potential *heterosexual* drives—by demonstrating mastery over the opposite sex.

POOLE: Now, there's a fantasy for you.

RIPLEY: The exploding planet and spaceship are also targeted to positive values toward science and technology. One of our survey findings was that this kind of imagery helps readers feel comfortable with science without actually having to go the trouble of understanding it.

FREEDMAN: (giggles) Oh, man...

POOLE: I don't believe this.

RIPLEY: You should, sir. Our surveys and focus groups are quite accurate.

POOLE: Oh, I didn't mean to question your infallibility.

RIPLEY: In total, this illustration, like all SF covers published by Omega Communications, conveys the themes of personal power and mastery of the universe—these are themes which appeal tremendously to our readers—

SPARKS: (disgusted) And can be summarized in the phrase: "How I saved the universe with my gun!"

Scene Five

A service elevator in one of the EPCOT "Solutions of Technology" Pavilion. A few moments later.

SOUND: MOTOR OF THE ELEVATOR AS IT ASCENDS TO A GREAT HEIGHT.

CLYDE: Could somebody tell me what is going on here? Am I going to be interrogated by Mickey Mouse? The frozen brain of Walt Disney?

DICKINSON: Not today, sir. This is the south service elevator in the "Solutions of Technology" Pavilion.

CLYDE: Well, that doesn't tell me a hell of a—

WEBB JR.:   Just a moment, sir.

SOUND: THE OFFICER ACTIVATES HIS WALKIE-TALKIE.

WEBB JR.:   (into walkie-talkie) Central Planning, this is Webb Jr., we have located subject and are bringing him to the *event point*.

VOICE ON WALKIE-TALKIE: We copy, Agent Webb. Verify expertise of subject. Check for faulty experience.

CLYDE: Sounds like you're talking to an artificial intelligence. Is Disney World run by a giant robot brain?

VOICE ON WALKIE-TALKIE: Repeat message, Agent Webb?

WEBB JR.:   (into walkie-talkie) Disregard, Central: uncodable response from subject. Will contact later. Out.

SOUND: WEBB JR. TURNS OFF HIS WALKIE-

	<u>TALKIE.</u>
WEBB JR.:	Mr. Clyde, you are currently employed as Executive Associate Story Consultant for *Space Spanners III*?
CLYDE:	Yes, and I wish I could say I was proud of it.
WEBB JR.:	You were also story editor and head writer of the *Space Spanners* television series broadcast on American television from 1966 to 1970?
CLYDE:	(exasperated) Yes! Has that become a crime? Is Disney World deporting me for bad writing?
DICKINSON:	Were you the credited writer of episode #26 of *Space Spanners*, titled "The Glorious Ending", broadcast on September 17, 1967?
CLYDE:	That was a very long time ago, but yes, I think that's correct.
WEBB JR.:	And in this episode, was a certain character, a *Star Commander Hughes*, killed?
DICKINSON:	Was this character killed by having his emergency escape pod crash into an exploding planetoid which was hurtling into a black sun?
CLYDE:	Are you arresting me for the murder of a fictional character? (laughs feebly) Besides, I have witnesses, I was nowhere near any black suns that night.
SOUND:	<u>THE ELEVATOR COASTS TO A STOP. THE DOORS OPEN.</u>
WEBB JR.:	There's someone we want you to explain that to...

Scene Six

The meeting room in the A-Frame Hotel. A moment later.

POOLE: This lecture on modern marketing methods is all very interesting, but why are you telling us this?

RIPLEY: Omega Communications is attempting to consolidate all our SF entertainment resources into an overall packaging strategy—Dr. Isaacs's stories and his reputation are integral to our corporate master plan.

FREEDMAN: Sounds kind of sinister.

RIPLEY: There's nothing sinister about it, Mr. Freedman. It's just that our audience research revealed something quite paradoxical about your genre—

DENSEN: What do you mean?

RIPLEY: While science fiction pretends to be involved with invention and originality, your audience doesn't want to explore any new ideas. They read sci-fi because they want to continually experience the same escapist themes, over and over again.

SPARKS: (angry) *Why, thank you!*

POOLE: (sarcastic) I thought I was just a hack for all these years, and I really appreciate your audience surveys confirming it.

ISAACS: The truth is often a painful thing, my friends. Look at that book jacket of mine. Is it any different from the 1937 cover of *Amazing Stories*? We are writing about a future that's been, gone and never was!

FREEDMAN: (irritated) So, what exactly is your point?

RIPLEY: The Omega Group also wants to buy your names, rights to all of your published works, and to market your names and work in the same fashion that we promote Sheldon Isaacs's products.

POOLE: And?

RIPLEY: *And* we want to help you develop new projects for Omega, at the same scale as we have been doing for Dr. Isaacs.

DENSEN: Ha! No way I'm working like a slave for you guys!

POOLE: I think I speak for all of us when I say that we are all getting on a bit. There's no way we could match Sheldon's output.

ATKINSON: You'd better tell them, Sheldon.

Scene Seven

	The roof of the "Solutions of Technology" Pavilion. Moments later.
<u>SOUND:</u>	<u>BRISK BREEZE BLOWING, METAL DOOR SWINGS OPEN.</u>
SUTTON:	(yells) *Stop right there!* Keep back or I'll jump!
DICKINSON:	Hold on, Mr. Sutton. We aren't going to come any closer. We still want to help you.
WEBB JR.:	We brought you a visitor... the man you said you wanted to see.
<u>SOUND:</u>	<u>CLYDE'S FOOTSTEPS ON THE GRAVEL SURFACE OF THE ROOF.</u>
CLYDE:	(to Sutton) Hi, nice costume. Do you know what's going on?
SUTTON:	You're Bob Clyde? You're the monster who murdered the greatest hero in modern science fiction?
CLYDE:	I'm just a writer, buddy.
DICKINSON:	We know you're very upset, Mr. Sutton...
WEBB JR.:	...so we brought Mr. Clyde here...
DICKINSON:	...to explain how Star Captain Hughes will return in the next *Space Spanners* film.
CLYDE:	(very surprised) *What?!*

Scene Eight

The meeting room. A moment later.

ISAACS: Er, as some of you may recall, I had a mild heart attack several years ago...

FREEDMAN: Yeah, we remember.

POOLE: ABC and CNN both did spots on you.

SPARKS: (disgusted) They referred to you as the "father" of science fiction.

ISAACS: After the attack, it became apparent that I would not be able to maintain the same level of creative output.

ATKINSON: I refused to let him continue writing day and night.

ISAACS: The situation was simply unacceptable, just the drop in income...

POOLE: That's B.S., Sheldon. With just books sales and movie options, alone, you knew you'd never have to work again.

ISAACS: I admit that the possibility of seeing my work slowly disappear from public attention was not an appealing one.

SPARKS: You mean, you couldn't stand not to see your name in every bookstore in the planet? My god, what an ego.

RIPLEY: Omega was also concerned about the potential loss of product visibility—which we were enjoying through the regular supply of Dr. Isaacs's books in the marketplace.

POOLE: Uh huh.

RIPLEY: Therefore we supplied Dr. Isaacs with certain re-
               search, editorial and creative services, and staff
               support... to help him with his new creative pro-
               jects.

POOLE: Let's see... Omega bought out Steadman back in
               seventy-six, so that means that their people have
               been ghost writing for you for almost seven years.

ISAACS: The term "ghost writing" is a little harsh, David. All
               the basic concepts are developed with my consulta-
               tion and I read every draft before it goes out with
               my name on it.

SPARKS: But that means you haven't written a word for
               nearly ten years. (laughs bitterly) I thought your
               style had gotten a little impersonal.

ISAACS: (a little hurt) I was only trying to serve the in-
               terests of my readership.

FREEDMAN: Is this some kind of confession? Are you asking us
               to exonerate you?

POOLE: I doubt that our opinion is that important to
               Omega Communications.

SPARKS: No, but I think I know where all this is heading.

RIPLEY: (beaming) I want you to know that I feel it an hon-
               our to be with you today. You are among those
               writers most responsible for the development of
               today's science fiction: a genre, which through new
               media advances and marketing techniques, has be-
               come a *billion-dollar industry*.

POOLE: Oh, think nothing of it...

SPARKS: ...because that was never our intent!

RIPLEY: Nevertheless, your names, your reputations, your
               visions... are part of the consciousness of America...
               and the world! With the intellectual authority of
               your previous works, new books carrying your
               names... would have tremendous sales potential!

POOLE: (weary) But what if we don't feel like writing a zillion sequels to stuff we wrote over 30 years ago?

RIPLEY: If any of you are unable to personally deliver the literary product, we will provide you with the same support services we offered to Dr. Isaacs.

SPARKS: I've moved on. I don't even write science fiction anymore.

SOUND: <u>SPARKS GETS OUT OF HER CHAIR.</u>

SPARKS: You people are free to go ahead and recycle yourselves, but I'm going home and then I'm going to write something.

SOUND: <u>SPARKS WALKS ACROSS THE ROOM, OPENS THE DOOR AND IS GONE.</u>

FREEDMAN: Well.

DENSEN: Gosh.

POOLE: Hmmm.

SOUND: <u>RIPLEY SNAPS OPEN AN ATTACHE CASE.</u>

RIPLEY: So, gentlemen... shall we discuss contractual arrangements?

Scene Nine

	The roof of the "Solutions of Technology" Pavilion. Moments later.
<u>SOUND:</u>	<u>WHISTLING OF THE WIND.</u>
CLYDE:	Get off this ledge, right now. I have my first date in half a century coming up and I can't hang around here with you.
SUTTON:	That's exactly what I thought a callous fiend like you would say. You don't care how you affect people, do you?
CLYDE:	How do you know what kind of person I am? Now, get real, kid, we're halfway through shooting the movie and there's no way we could do a re-write like that!
<u>SOUND:</u>	<u>SUTTON WHIPS OUT A CRUMPLED PIECE OF PAPER AND HANDS IT TO CLYDE.</u>
SUTTON:	I prepared that agreement when I heard you were going to attend the convention. It's a contract that says that unless Star Captain Hughes is included in the next *Space Spanners* project... I will jump or otherwise kill myself in some violent fashion.
CLYDE:	This is the dumbest thing since *The Partridge Family in Space*. I'll never agree to sign this!
SUTTON:	Then my horrible death will be on your hands. (sighs) But why should I be surprised? You've already destroyed my dreams.
CLYDE:	You really can't waste your life because of some decision made in Hollywood! I was just doing my job.

SUTTON: Only a job, huh? *Space Spanners* is everything to me! (choking back tears) They used to run the show every Sunday afternoon at home. I'd hear the theme song and I'd come running in from the back yard. When I watched the show, I really thought I was in space.

CLYDE: Well, that was mostly your own imagination. The sets were really cheesy... you could drive a car on some of the matte lines in our effects shots.

SUTTON: (sniffs) I *had* a great imagination. Dad got an old furnace crate... one of the really big ones... he painted it up into a recreation of Captain Hughes' Command Pod. Dad did a great job. I played there for hours. All that summer I was fantasizing in that silly crate while I waited for the second season to start...

CLYDE: Please don't tell me about this.

SUTTON: That day in September was one of those beautiful early autumn days. I had all my favourite comics out on the floor, *The Atom*, *Doom Patrol*, the original *X-Men*... and some really great picture books on dinosaurs...

CLYDE: (miserable) Please kid, stop it...

SUTTON: Then it was time, Dad and I sat around the TV... and there it was. You killed him. His escape pod hits a moon and gets sucked into nothingness. Kind of a coward's death, really. We didn't even get to hear his voice one last time. My dad tried to tell me it was okay... that Captain Hughes was still a real hero... and died a hero's death...

CLYDE: But why didn't your dad say that it was only a story, that you shouldn't take it so seriously...

SUTTON: My dad died a few months later.

CLYDE: (whispers) Kid, I'm really sorry.

SUTTON: Did you know I'm one of the few serious Captain Hughes fans? I do what I can to honour his memory at these conventions. A lot of the younger spanners don't even know who he was.

CLYDE: Look, you have to believe me, I didn't write Hughes out of the series because I wanted to destroy your childhood. We had a serious creative problem on the set. It was either lose the lead actor or lose the whole show.

SUTTON: At first, *Space Spanners* opened up a whole new world of visions and possibilities... when I watched the show I was inspired! I wanted to be an astronaut, an astronomer, a scientist... I wanted to explore the universe... understand everything around me...

CLYDE: Well, I'm happy to hear that the show was able to reach young kids in a positive way...

SUTTON: But I gave up hoping real quick after you killed off my hero. Why try to be anything when the universe is a cruel and irrational place? When everything you love can be ripped away without warning?

CLYDE: (upset) You can't lay that emotional blackmail on me.

SUTTON: Oh, I see, you're happy to accept credit for any good influence but no responsibility for the bad stuff, huh?

CLYDE: That's not fair!

SUTTON: Having somebody blow away your boyhood hero isn't fair either! Now if you'll excuse me...

SOUND: GRAVEL CRUNCHING AS THE FAN JUMPS TO HIS FEET. THE WIND RISES.

SUTTON: ...I really have to be going...

CLYDE: (screams) *Wait! Think about this!* For God's sake, don't kill yourself for a stupid reason!

	Think! For just one damn minute! Why is this all so important to you?!
SUTTON:	(takes a long deep breath) I've memorized every first season script. I can recite Captain Hughes' lines word for word.
CLYDE:	(carefully) I'm afraid I can't say the same... and I wrote most of those words.
SUTTON:	Name an episode, one with Hughes in it.
CLYDE:	Uh, first season? Um, how about the "Beings of Decapodia", second last scene?
SUTTON:	(voice similar to Kyle playing Hughes) "Your blind decision to suppress individual choice has forever destroyed your chance of becoming a truly advanced democratic planetary society."
CLYDE:	(impressed) Wow!
SUTTON:	(himself again) Pretty good, huh?
CLYDE:	Yeah, great. If I knew people would be reciting it years later, I would have felt better about it when I wrote it.
SUTTON:	Give me another.
CLYDE:	Okay, how about the love scene from "The Moon is Shattered and It Strikes the Earth?"
SUTTON:	(as Kyle/Hughes) "Princess Zintrixtra, I know that your chastity represents the virtue of your people... but if I pleasure you... will you free my crew?"
CLYDE:	Hey, that's great, but careful with the blocking, you'll fall off the building.
SUTTON:	Holy doodle, the famous Bob Clyde actually does care.
CLYDE:	Yes, he cares. Which is likely to be the downfall of the famous Bob Clyde.

SOUND: <u>MORE GRAVEL CRUNCHES AS CLYDE STANDS UP.</u>

CLYDE: Look, there's no way I can give in to this demand... but if that character means that much to anybody, I clearly haven't explored all its potentials yet. I'll look at it and see if there's one more Captain Hughes story somewhere.

SUTTON: (ecstatic) Really?! *That's fantastic!*

SOUND: <u>GRAVEL CRUNCHES AS SUTTON EMBRACES CLYDE.</u>

CLYDE: Yes, really...

SOUND: <u>SUDDEN GUST OF WIND.</u>

CLYDE: Now careful, watch out for the ledge—

CLYDE AND SUTTON: (scream as they fall off the building)

Scene Ten

Clyde's afterlife.

SOUND: <u>STRANGE HOWLS OF THE WINDS OF NARRATIVE NON-TIME.</u>

CLYDE: (echoes, somewhat like a VO) And so I died. (matter-of-factly) No sense getting upset about it now. Although the circumstances were a little strange. Some of my boyhood friends died fighting evil and tyranny. I'm done in at EPCOT by a bad case of reality failure.

SOUND: <u>WARPING EFFECT.</u>

CROSS: (echoes) Hello, Robert.

CLYDE: (surprised) Cross! What are you doing here? Are you dead, too?

CROSS: (calm) Oh, no. I am currently communicating with you via my astral projection.

CLYDE: You mean that Mentotechnics stuff actually works?

CROSS: Not as such. Come with me, Robert.

CLYDE: Okay.

SOUND: <u>ANOTHER WARPING EFFECT.</u>

CLYDE: So you eventually did develop advanced mental powers.

CROSS: Of a sort. I am escorting your soul across the various levels of the astral plane.

CLYDE: (impressed) You can do that?!

CROSS: Well, you'd be going through this anyway, but I thought you might enjoy some company.

CLYDE: Thanks. (pause) Is there anything we should be talking about, Jay?

CROSS: Okay... I've conquered the boundaries of time and space, and I'm reasonably omniscient. Is there anything you'd like to know before you move into eternity? Some profound truth about life? A little gossip, perhaps?

CLYDE: Jeez, if I knew I was going to be in this situation, I would have prepared a few questions. (pauses) How did things work out for the other Fabulists?

CROSS: Your ex-wife returns to Minnesota to her job as an editor of a local newspaper. She tries to write an autobiography about her life in science fiction—she never gets past writing about David Poole.

CLYDE: I suppose Ray actually was a nice person—for a victim of inexplicable sexual and aesthetic obsessions. And what happened to Poole?

CROSS: He got my old job in the intelligence community. He found the bureaucratic environment very comforting. Unfortunately, he was laid off with the end of the Cold War in 1990.

CLYDE: The Cold War ends? Who wins?

CROSS: We're not sure.

CLYDE: What about Freedman and Densen?

CROSS: They sell their names to Omega Communications, form a partnership and move to California. Summit Studios award them a contract as executive story consultants for the next seven *Space Spanners* films.

CLYDE: You mean they get *my* old job?

CROSS: I'm afraid so.

CLYDE: And what about Sheldon?

CROSS: (sighs) An interesting case. Through the miracle of artificial surgical implants, Sheldon Isaacs lives for

	another 250 years. And he writes at an even greater rate. By the year 2083, Sheldon has produced so many books that numerous environmental groups view him as the single greatest threat to the world's forests.
CLYDE:	You're kidding, aren't you? It's not polite to fool a dead person, Jay.
CROSS:	Happily, in the fifth global energy crisis of 2132, the true value of Sheldon's work is finally realized. His books become the primary source of heat and light throughout a nuclear winter triggered by an accidental exchange of atomic weapons.
CLYDE:	(laughs) So what about the people on the other side? Am I going to spend eternity listening to Mitchell and McReady argue about how to edit magazines?
CROSS:	Why don't you ask them yourself?
CLYDE:	*Wait a minute!* Speaking of dead people, didn't Evanston just kick off the other day? Am I going to have to deal with that bozo?
CROSS:	Not if you don't want to. But there is one thing you could do...
CLYDE:	(suspicious) Yeah...
CROSS:	...before you leave Earth forever. It would be of great service to some essentially innocent people... (fades)
<u>SOUND:</u>	<u>THE SHIFTING WINDS OF THE ASTRAL PLANE GROW STRONGER.</u>

Scene Eleven

	The office of a graduate student at McMaster University, Hamilton, Ontario. September 1984.
SOUND:	<u>DANIELS IS PACKING HIS BOOKS AND FILES INTO CARDBOARD BOXES. THERE IS A KNOCK AT HIS OFFICE DOOR.</u>
DANIELS:	Come in.
MILGORE:	(nervous) Mr. Daniels? I'm Agnes Milgore, I telephoned yesterday.
DANIELS:	Yes, sorry things look a little disorganized right now; I'm in the middle of moving.
MILGORE:	May I sit down?
DANIELS:	If you can find a clear spot.
SOUND:	<u>SHIFTING OF FURNITURE.</u>
MILGORE:	I heard that you just finished some research project on the Temple of Mentotechnics.
DANIELS:	Just my thesis research, and it's all over now—
MILGORE:	(abruptly) My daughter has joined the Temple.
SOUND:	<u>TRANSDIMENSIONAL/ETHEREAL WARP.</u>
CLYDE:	(echoes) What's this place?
DANIELS:	I see.
MILGORE:	I'm so worried!
CLYDE:	(echoes) These people don't seem to even notice that I'm here!
SOUND:	<u>ANOTHER TD/E WARP.</u>

CLYDE: (annoyed, echoes) *You!* I never thought I'd see you again!

EVANSTON: (to Clyde, echoes) Well, well. Lightweights in the afterlife.

DANIELS: Mrs. Milgore, I get three or four calls a week from concerned parents and families. I don't know how people found out I was studying the Mentotechnics organization, but aside from offering my sympathies, there isn't much I can do.

MILGORE: (upset) But Josie's changed so much! We hardly see her anymore, I think she's giving them all her money!

EVANSTON: (to Milgore, echoes) It's none of your business! It's your daughter's *right* to become a Mentotechnist!

CLYDE: (echoes) And what business is it of yours, Evanston? *You're dead!*

EVANSTON: The Temple is my claim to immortality on Earth; her child's dedication to my teachings is a tribute to my genius.

CLYDE: You know, it's really too bad you're already dead.

MILGORE: Mr. Daniels, you are my last hope. If you can't help me, I don't what to do!

DANIELS: At times like this I truly appreciate the limitations of human knowledge.

MILGORE: I beg your pardon?

CLYDE: (disgusted) Man, what a wimp.

DANIELS: I'm a pretty lucky person, I have access to the best libraries and journals, and your tax dollars allow people like me to sit around and think up new things to study. So I now know quite a few things— and people like you helped me to do that.

MILGORE: I don't quite see your point, Mr. Daniels.

DANIELS: Actually, as of last week it's Doctor Daniels.

CLYDE: (even more disgusted) *Oh, soooorrrieeee!*

DANIELS: But here's where the limitation comes in: after all that education, I still don't know what I can tell you.

EVANSTON: And what could you possibly tell this woman? How can some snot-nosed grad student possibly understand my philosophy?

MILGORE: Oh... (starts to cry)

DANIELS: The only reason people like me can even start their research is because we live in a place where we are free to believe and think as we like...

EVANSTON: (triumphant) *Exactly!* The freedom of thought, the freedom of expression, and the freedom of religion are absolutes! Those freedoms are the sacred foundations of progressive movements like Mentotechnics... people have the *freedom and the right* to follow me!

CLYDE: (outraged) You mean they have the right to be lied to? The freedom to be *ignorant and exploited?* You are—er—you *were* nothing but a con artist, Evanston!

EVANSTON: And you, Clyde, were irrelevant, even before you died.

MILGORE: (still crying) There's nothing you can do?

DANIELS: Some people would say your relationship with your daughter was a regrettable, but necessary, sacrifice to living in a free and open society.

MILGORE: (bitter) *Oh, thank you very much!* I suppose I should try and find one of those deprogrammers.

DANIELS: You probably respect your daughter too much to have her kidnapped.

MILGORE: So what can I do?

CLYDE: Yeah, kid! All that research and you can't help this poor woman?

EVANSTON: Of course he can't. He had no right to investigate the Temple in the first place. It's an invasion of privacy.

CLYDE: Oh, I see, freedom of thought only applies to those people whose thoughts you control? Is that it, Evanston?

DANIELS: I'm sorry, but I just don't see...

CLYDE: (exasperated) Oh, hell, man!

SOUND: <u>BREEZE AND RUSTLING OF PAPERS.</u>

CLYDE: There must be something on this desk that can help... there's something here that she can use...

SOUND: <u>RUSTLING OF PAPERS CONTINUES.</u>

CLYDE: *Aha!*

DANIELS: Well, here's something, I was wondering where I put it...

MILGORE: (sniffs) Yes?

DANIELS: It's an article published in an old science fiction magazine by a writer named Bob Clyde. He used to know Evanston and he's quite blunt about the man's ethics and where he got his ideas for a new religion.

EVANSTON: (angry) Don't show her that stupid article! (to Clyde) I knew I should have sued you for that damned thing! And Zeigler never should have printed it!

CLYDE: Right now, I think it's the best thing I ever wrote.

MILGORE: What am I supposed to do with this?

DANIELS: Read it. Let yourself know what you're dealing with. Also, you could let your daughter see it, it might stimulate a few questions. Remember, the author was writing in the early 1950s, before the Temple was founded. And Clyde had no reason to slander Evanston—he was just another writer.

MILGORE: Isn't there anything else we can do?

DANIELS: Just the simple stuff, keep in touch with your daughter... don't give her very much money until you're sure everything is okay.

MILGORE: Why not?

DANIELS: Because every cent of it will go to the Temple.

EVANSTON: (furious) *This is an outrage!*

DANIELS: If your daughter is in financial trouble, buy her food, offer to pay her rent, even make her car payments for her. Just let her know that you have no intention of subsidizing Evanston's organization.

EVANSTON: (horrified) *I need that money!*

CLYDE: You *needed* that money, you're dead. Remember?

EVANSTON: How can Mentotechnics survive without cash?!

CLYDE: Well, I think that reveals the true priorities of D.H. Evanston. Now why don't you just take a flying leap to your ultimate fate?

SOUND: WARP EFFECT.

EVANSTON: (screams mightily and fades away)

MILGORE: Thank you, Mr. Daniels.

DANIELS: Also... (hesitates) I'll write you an outline, a summary of my research. It might help when you're talking to your daughter, or at least it might help you to understand what's going on... you can pick it up tomorrow.

MILGORE: I will. Goodbye.

SOUND: DOOR CLOSES.

DANIELS: Where did I put my typewriter?

SOUND: THUMP AS DANIELS PUTS HIS PORTABLE TYPEWRITER ON HIS DESK AND LOADS A SHEET OF PAPER INTO THE MACHINE.

CLYDE: An apparently quiet outcome for such a long story, but I think we did some good. I wish I could leave you all with a definite moral here. Almost everything I, and my Fabulist friends, predicted in our stories was wrong. There were no inflatable planets, no thought-driven starships, no aliens in the closet, and no safe, cheap nuclear power.

SOUND: <u>DANIELS STARTS TYPING.</u>

CLYDE: It wasn't that the future was less incredible than we thought it would be—it was *far stranger* than any of us could have possibly imagined. We were expecting space travel and ended up with satellites beaming *Star Trek* re-runs around the planet a thousand times a day. (sighs) Oh well, I feel that I've paid my dues as far as that's concerned. And I may have helped some innocent people and that may count for something.

SOUND: <u>WARP EFFECT RISES.</u>

CLYDE: In spite of it all, I'm still an optimist. The imagination and the vision we had back in 1937 is still out there, and maybe... *maybe...* we're getting smart enough to make good use of these gifts.

SOUND: <u>WARP EFFECT FADES. THE TYPING CONTINUES.</u>

DANIELS: (muttering) ...by 1937, science fiction enthusiasts... were well... on the way... to forming a... distinct... subculture... which was to... provide among... other things... the symbolic... breeding ground... for... Mentotechnics...

Scene Twelve

A segment from *Spandex in Amsterdam*, a contemporary cyberpunk novel by Alan Glib.

MUSIC AND SOUND: POUNDING SCREAM OF ELECTRONICA FADING INTO AMBIENT PULSE OF A DECAYING INDUSTRIAL COMPLEX.

SOUND: CLICKS AND BEEPS AS GLIB TYPES ON HIS PC KEYBOARD.

GLIB: (echoes) Carbon Karx jacked himself off the Collective Unconscious Netrix and found himself somewhere in Real-World Sprawl. It was night. It was gloomy.

SOUND: SOFT CRUNCH OF KARX STEPPING ON SMALL BITS OF RUBBLE.

KARX: If this is Thursday, then this must be Arkansas.

GLIB: (echoes) Karx knew that Arkansas was not a good place for even the most accomplished cyber-cowboy to reality crash...

SOUND: STRANGE SCREAM OF A FARAWAY ELECTRONIC ALARM.

KARX: Damn, AI-Drones!

SOUND: PULSING THROB OF THE AI-DRONES' HOVER JETS RAPIDLY CLOSE IN.

GLIB: (echoes) Picking up any organism on their flesh-scopes would put them into extermination mode...

AI DRONES: (bellow through loudspeakers) *Die, meat-scum!*

MUSIC: SCREAM OF ELECTRONICA BURSTS ON.

<u>CONTINUES FOR A TIME, THEN FADES.</u>

**End of
Disappointing Success
Part II**

art by Emily O'Brien

Cult Stories

Cult Stories
Episode I: "Student"

Cast – In Order of Appearance

CHARLES TSUTSHI	A graduate student at the Anthropology Department at McMaster University.
ETHAN DANIELS	Also a graduate student at the Anthropology Department at McMaster University. He shares an office with Charles Tsutshi.
SUBJECT #3	A member of the Temple of Mentotechnics and the object of Daniel's research.
NINA BROWN	Computer systems operator at McMaster University. Also a major *Star Trek* fan.
CALLER	A member of the Temple of Mentotechnics.
SUBJECT #18	Also a member of the Temple of Mentotechnics and the object of Daniel's research.
MILGORE	The parent of a member of the Temple of Mentotechnics.
POLICE OFFICER	On the Hamilton Police Force.
SIRKOWSKI	Daniels's thesis supervisor.

Scene One

Graduate student office at McMaster University, 1979.

SOUND: <u>THE DEEP BELL OF AN OLD ROTARY PHONE RINGS. SOMEONE PICKS UP THE RECEIVER.</u>

TSUTSHI: Hello?

SUBJECT #3: (filter) Is this Professor Ethan Daniels?

TSUTSHI: No, I'm sorry, there's no Professor Ethan Daniels here.

DANIELS: (distant) Hey!

SOUND: <u>WHEELS OF DANIELS'S CHAIR ROLLING TOWARDS TSUTSHI.</u>

TSUTSHI: Now, there's a Mr. Daniels—

SOUND: <u>BRIEF BUMPING AS DANIELS GRABS THE RECEIVER.</u>

DANIELS: This is Ethan Daniels speaking.

TSUTSHI: (Distant. Laughs.)

SUBJECT #3: (filter) I'm calling in regards to an advertisement you placed in the university paper.

DANIELS: Yes, I'm looking for people to interview for my research.

SUBJECT #3: (filter) And this is research into Mentotechnics. Correct?

DANIELS: The ad doesn't specifically say so but yes.

SUBJECT #3: (filter) That's what I figured.

DANIELS: You must be pretty closely affiliated with the

Temple to have worked this out.

SUBJECT #3:   (filter) Is your research in any way hostile to the Temple of Mentotechnics?

DANIELS: No, this is an objective study.

SUBJECT #3:   (filter) And the identity of your research subjects?

DANIELS: Will be completely confidential. You don't even have to give me your name.

SUBJECT #3:   (filter) What do you pay?

DANIELS: Officially I can't offer any remuneration.

SUBJECT #3:   (filter) Unofficially?

DANIELS: Three-fifty an hour. Five dollars an hour if you can prove you're an actual member of the Temple.

SUBJECT #3:   (filter) Is Wednesday afternoon okay with you?

Scene Two

Second-hand bookstore. Hamilton, Ontario, near McMaster University, 1979.

SOUND:	<u>POP MUSIC PLAYS IN THE DISTANCE ON A PORTABLE RADIO IN THE SHOP. SOMETHING FROM THE MID TO LATE 1970S LIKE PRISM OR GERRY RAFFERTY.</u>
NINA:	(fades in) Excuse me—
DANIELS:	Yes?
NINA:	Are you going to buy that book?
DANIELS:	No, please, take it. I was just looking at the cover.
NINA:	Thanks! I've been looking for this one for ages!
DANIELS:	*Spock Must Die*?
NINA:	It's a rare classic.
DANIELS:	A classic? Like *Heart of Darkness* or *Crime and Punishment*?
NINA:	It's the very first original *Star Trek* novel.
DANIELS:	So who is this Spock? And why must he die?
NINA:	(shocked) Are you telling me that you've never heard of *Star Trek*?
DANIELS:	That's a television show, right?
NINA:	(still shocked) Good god! If you don't know about *Star Trek*, what are you doing here in the science fiction section?
DANIELS:	I was looking for books by D.H. Evanston.

NINA: Never heard of him.

DANIELS: (fades) He used to be a science fiction writer.

Scene Three

Cinema. Two hours later.

SOUND:	DISTANT MUSIC FROM THE PROJECTION ROOM, VERY ORCHESTRAL AND HEROIC.
DANIELS:	(VO) After some initial miscommunication, my repartee with Nina Brown rapidly improved and she invited me to the local cinema where they were showing a marathon of *Star Trek* episodes.
NINA:	(laughs) Think of it as a crash course.
DANIELS:	I approve of education.
SOUND:	VOICES OF ACTORS, FAMILIAR BUT INDISTINGUISHABLE, ECHO THROUGH THE MOVIE THEATRE.
NINA:	(whispers) What do you think? Isn't this great?
DANIELS:	(whispers) Well... it certainly is... interesting.
NINA:	(whispers) Have you ever seen anything like it?
DANIELS:	(whispers) Oh, no.
MUSIC:	FAMILIAR TV THEME MUSIC RISES.
DANIELS:	(VO) I could tell that my new friend really liked *Star Trek*.

It would take months for me to realize that if *Star Trek* had been a church then Nina Brown would have been one of its most devoted saints.

Scene Four

Nina's apartment. A few hours after the *Star Trek* marathon.

DANIELS: Bring Back *Star Trek*?

NINA: Drink up.

SOUND: <u>NINA SNAPS THE CAP OFF OF A BOTTLE OF BEER.</u>

DANIELS: You say this is a movement?

NINA: Big time.

DANIELS: A political movement?

SOUND: <u>NINA TAKES A LONG DRINK AND PUTS HER BOTTLE DOWN.</u>

NINA: It kind of transcends politics.

SOUND: <u>DANIELS ALSO TAKES A LONG DRINK.</u>

DANIELS: You do know this is Hamilton, Ontario, don't you? That we have things like factories and steel mills and trade unions in this city?

NINA: (laughs) Yes, I have read the occasional newspaper, Professor Daniels.

DANIELS: Mr. Daniels. I'm not a professor yet. (drinks again) So, Miss Brown...

NINA: Ms. Brown.

DANIELS: So Ms. Brown, you do know that politics, next to money, is the most serious thing around here, right?

NINA: Oh, yeah.

DANIELS: So politics is not something all that easily "transcended."

NINA: Cheers!

SOUND: <u>THE TWO CLINK BEER BOTTLES.</u>

NINA: I stand by my statement. (bold) *We must move forward as a species or face extinction!*

DANIELS: (almost gasps) *My god!*

NINA: (giggles) Have I just impressed you or do you just think I'm crazy?

DANIELS: What you just said... it fits in with my research.

NINA: Then you must be doing some very important research.

DANIELS: I'm not sure everyone thinks so but thank you.

SOUND: <u>NINA STANDS UP, WALKS ACROSS THE ROOM.</u>

NINA: I don't know if I should do this...

DANIELS: Do what?

SOUND: <u>NINA OPENS A DRAWER, PICKS SOMETHING UP AND WALKS BACK TOWARDS DANIELS.</u>

NINA: I've never shown this to anyone before.

SOUND: <u>NINA DROPS A HEAVY FILE FOLDER ONTO A TABLE.</u>

DANIELS: What is it?

SOUND: <u>NINA SITS DOWN.</u>

NINA: Read it and find out.

SOUND: <u>RUSTLING OF PAPER AS DANIELS STARTS LOOKING THROUGH THE FILE FOLDER.</u>

DANIELS: Did you write this?

NINA: Yes.

SOUND: NINA HAS ANOTHER DRINK OF BEER.

DANIELS: (VO) What I was reading was fiction. Nina's fiction. I later learned that it was called "fan fiction."

SOUND: PAPER RUSTLING AS DANIELS TURNS THE PAGES.

NINA: So, what do you think?

DANIELS: (VO) By the time I reached page five I was able to recognize it as incredibly pornographic fan fiction.

It's very... *interesting.*

(VO) Most of her stories focused on a long-standing homoerotic affair between Captain Kirk and Mr. Spock.

NINA: You don't think it's sick or anything?

DANIELS: No, no. The imagination must go where it must.

NINA: Would you like some more?

SOUND: NINA POPS THE CAPS OFF TWO MORE BEER BOTTLES.

DANIELS: (VO) Had I been in a more objective and analytic mood, I might have started asking questions about fan subcultures and homosexual symbolism, but to be completely candid, Nina and I had both consumed rather a lot of alcohol at this point.

Cheers.

SOUND: BOTTLES CLINK.

NINA: Drink much, live long and prosper!

DANIELS: (VO) Events ensued... and my physical? Romantic? My relationship with Nina began.

DANIELS: What does that mean?

NINA: (smile in her voice) It's a joke, silly.

SOUND: NINA KISSES DANIELS.

DANIELS: (VO) When we first got together I didn't think Nina's passion for *Star Trek* made her crazy. I thought it just made her fun.

NINA: I'll explain later.

<u>SOUND:</u>   <u>MORE KISSING.</u>

DANIELS: (VO) Later, I was forced to revise my opinion.

Scene Five

	Daniels's office at McMaster University. A few months later.
<u>SOUND:</u>	<u>DANIELS PRESSES THE RECORD KEY ON AN OLD AUDIO CASSETTE MACHINE.</u>
DANIELS:	It is October 23, 1979 and this is my interview of Subject #3.
<u>SOUND:</u>	<u>CHAIR LEG SCRAPING ACROSS A TILED FLOOR.</u>
DANIELS:	How long have you been practising Mentotechnics?
SUBJECT #3:	Just about two years.
DANIELS:	Have you noticed any benefits?
SUBJECT #3:	You bet! Back when I started I could hardly read.
DANIELS:	You had literacy problems?
SUBJECT #3:	Big time!
DANIELS:	And you think Mentotechnics changed that?
SUBJECT #3:	No kidding! Now I can read really fast and I really love reading!
DANIELS:	What was the last book you read?
SUBJECT #3:	Ummmm...
<u>SOUND:</u>	<u>DANIELS PRESSES THE STOP KEY.</u>

Scene Six

Daniels's apartment. Very early in the morning.

SOUND:	TELEPHONE RINGS.
DANIELS:	(distant, groggy) Oh, god…
SOUND:	TELEPHONE CONTINUES RINGING. BED-SPRINGS AND FOOTSTEPS AS DANIELS GETS OUT OF BED.
DANIELS:	(mutters) Don't these idiots ever learn?
SOUND:	RINGING STOPS AS DANIELS PICKS UP THE RECEIVER.
DANIELS:	She doesn't live here anymore.
SOUND:	FAINT CRACKLING ON THE OTHER END OF THE LINE.
DANIELS:	She hasn't been at this number in over a year.
SOUND:	MORE CRACKLING, THEN BREATHING.
DANIELS:	I wish the landlord would get the number changed but if you're one of her clients I'm afraid you're out of luck.
SOUND:	CRACKLING STOPS, AS IF THE CONNECTION HAS SUDDENLY IMPROVED.
CALLER:	(filter, on phone) Hello?
DANIELS:	You do know that it's almost three in the morning, right?
CALLER:	(filter) Is this Ethan Daniels?
DANIELS:	(surprised) Uh, yes.
CALLER:	(filter) Ethan Daniels, the graduate student?

DANIELS: (annoyed) Yes, can I help you with something?

CALLER: (filter) You better stop what you're doing.

DANIELS: Well, ah... (pause)

SOUND: <u>TICKING OF DANIELS'S ALARM CLOCK GROWS LOUDER TO FILL THE SILENCE.</u>

DANIELS: Stop what, exactly?

CALLER: (filter) D.H. Evanston is the greatest man who ever lived.

DANIELS: (laughs a little) Oh! This is about Mentotechnics!

CALLER: (filter) Yes.

DANIELS: Mr. Evanston is certainly a remarkable person, but you have to admit—

CALLER: (filter) He's going to save the world.

DANIELS: That's a really interesting opinion. It would be great if you could come by my office and we could dis—

CALLER: (filter) People like you are working out of fear and ignorance.

DANIELS: I don't know about the fear part but you're right—there's a lot about Mentotechnics that many of us don't understand.

CALLER: (filter) No kidding.

DANIELS: That's why we conduct research.

CALLER: (filter) Bad things will happen if you don't stop.

SOUND: <u>CALLER HANGS UP. DIAL TONE.</u>

Scene Seven

<table>
<tr><td></td><td>Daniels's bathroom. Just past 08:00 on the same morning.</td></tr>
<tr><td>SOUND:</td><td>ALARM RINGS FOLLOWED BY RUNNING WATER.</td></tr>
<tr><td>DANIELS:</td><td>(softly) What an incredibly ineffective threatening phone call.</td></tr>
<tr><td>SOUND:</td><td>WATER STOPS AS DANIELS TURNS OFF THE TAP.</td></tr>
<tr><td>DANIELS:</td><td>I must remember to tell Professor Sirkowski when we discuss the committee's comments on the latest chapters of my thesis. I also need to stop by Mill Memorial to see if the inter-library loans have come in.</td></tr>
<tr><td>SOUND:</td><td>DANIELS OPENS HIS MEDICINE CABINET.</td></tr>
<tr><td>DANIELS:</td><td>And I must stop by the drugstore and pick up a new box of condoms.</td></tr>
<tr><td>SOUND:</td><td>HE CLOSES THE MEDICINE CABINET.</td></tr>
<tr><td>DANIELS:</td><td>Alternatively, and perhaps more responsibly, I could always break up with Nina Brown.

Nina... to use an appropriate folk-culture termino-logy... is going seriously nuts.</td></tr>
</table>

Scene Eight

<table>
<tr><td></td><td>Daniels's office. Later that week.</td></tr>
<tr><td>DANIELS:</td><td>(VO) I trace the disintegration of her personality to the premiere of Star Trek: The Motion Picture.</td></tr>
<tr><td><u>SOUND:</u></td><td><u>DANIELS PRESSES THE RECORD SWITCH ON HIS TAPE MACHINE.</u></td></tr>
<tr><td>SUBJECT #18:</td><td>I'm pretty sure I shouldn't be talking to you.</td></tr>
<tr><td>DANIELS:</td><td>Why do you say that?</td></tr>
<tr><td>SUBJECT #18:</td><td>Because you could be writing something that's hostile to Mentotechnics.</td></tr>
<tr><td>DANIELS:</td><td>No, this will be an objective study.</td></tr>
<tr><td>SUBJECT #18:</td><td>I guess I should look on the bright side.</td></tr>
<tr><td>DANIELS:</td><td>You mean that Mentotechnics might benefit from scientific study?</td></tr>
<tr><td>SUBJECT #18:</td><td>Hell, no! I mean that I can use the money you're paying me to buy more therapy sessions.</td></tr>
</table>

Scene Nine

<table>
<tr><td></td><td>Nina's apartment. November 1979.</td></tr>
<tr><td>DANIELS:</td><td>(breathless) Dear god!</td></tr>
<tr><td>NINA:</td><td>(laughs) Are you okay?</td></tr>
<tr><td>DANIELS:</td><td>W-what is it with you these days?</td></tr>
<tr><td>NINA:</td><td>What do you mean?</td></tr>
<tr><td>SOUND:</td><td>BEDSPRINGS CREAK AS DANIELS SITS UP.</td></tr>
<tr><td>DANIELS:</td><td>It's just that you have so much more... energy.</td></tr>
<tr><td>NINA:</td><td>It just goes to show, baby, that Star Trek lives!</td></tr>
<tr><td>DANIELS:</td><td>No kidding.</td></tr>
<tr><td>NINA:</td><td>Are you complaining?</td></tr>
<tr><td>DANIELS:</td><td>No, no. (takes a deep breath) It's great.</td></tr>
<tr><td>SOUND:</td><td>MORE SPRINGS CREAKING AS NINA SITS UP.</td></tr>
<tr><td>NINA:</td><td>It's going to be incredible!</td></tr>
<tr><td>DANIELS:</td><td>Darling, I've got to get some sleep tonight.</td></tr>
<tr><td>NINA:</td><td>I was talking about the movie.</td></tr>
<tr><td>DANIELS:</td><td>It's coming out soon, isn't it?</td></tr>
<tr><td>NINA:</td><td>It's going to be incredible.</td></tr>
<tr><td>DANIELS:</td><td>(VO) Like a lot of Trekkers at the time, Nina took a lot of pride in the fact that they were finally producing Star Trek: The Motion Picture.</td></tr>
<tr><td>NINA:</td><td>Fourteen days, fifteen hours and a bunch of minutes and seconds.</td></tr>
<tr><td>DANIELS:</td><td>I'm sure you'll figure it out.</td></tr>
</table>

NINA: Of course, we'll be at the first showing.

DANIELS: When's that?

NINA: Five in the afternoon. At the Tivoli.

DANIELS: (VO) Nina believed she was part of a world-wide grassroots movement motivated by love and idealism that was changing the course of the monolithic American entertainment establishment.

NINA: (sighs) really incredible...

DANIELS: (VO) I don't like to use simplistic Freudian concepts but they seemed to apply in this situation.

               (VO) There definitely seemed to be some powerful cathartic psychosexual link between the *Star Trek* universe and Planet Nina.

NINA: Are you sure you want to go to sleep?

DANIELS: (VO) I probably should have talked to her about it.

               Well...

               (VO) But the pathology was so much fun.

Scene Ten

Daniels's office. A few days later.

<u>SOUND:</u>	<u>KNOCK AT THE DOOR.</u>
DANIELS:	Come in.
MILGORE:	Excuse me, I'm sorry to drop in like this. Are you Ethan Daniels?
DANIELS:	That's right.
MILGORE:	I was told that you are doing a research project on Mentotechnics.
DANIELS:	Did Professor Sirkowski send you?
MILGORE:	My daughter has joined the Temple.
DANIELS:	I see. Have a seat.
<u>SOUND:</u>	<u>MILGORE SITS DOWN.</u>
MILGORE:	(upset) I'm so worried!
DANIELS:	Aside from offering my sympathies there isn't much I can do.
MILGORE:	There's *nothing* you can do?
DANIELS:	Some people would say that the loss of your relationship with your daughter is a regrettable, but inevitable, sacrifice to living in a free and open society.
MILGORE:	(sarcastic) Oh, thank you very much! I suppose I should try and find one of those deprogrammers. (starts to cry)
DANIELS:	I'm sorry. I know it's difficult... but you probably respect your daughter too much to have her kid-

	napped.
MILGORE:	(sniffs) So, what *can* I do?
DANIELS:	It's probably not much...
MILGORE:	I'll try anything, Professor Daniels.
SOUND:	<u>DANIELS OPENS A FILING CABINET.</u>
DANIELS:	I wonder where I put it...
SOUND:	<u>RUSTLING OF PAPER.</u>
MILGORE:	Put what?
SOUND:	<u>HEAVY BOOK DROPS ON DANIELS'S DESK.</u>
MILGORE:	What can I do with that?
DANIELS:	You can educate yourself, let yourself know what you're dealing with.
MILGORE:	Isn't there anything else I can do?
DANIELS:	Just the usual. Keep in touch with your daughter as much as you can. Don't give her very much money—all of it will go to the Temple.
MILGORE:	Thank you, Professor Daniels.
DANIELS:	Mr. Daniels. I'm not a professor yet.
	(VO) Most of the people who walked through my door just wanted to vent. The best thing to do was to be polite, sympathetic and try to pass on some useful history.

Scene Eleven

Daniels's office. Two days later.

SOUND: <u>(FADES IN) DANIELS TYPES THE KEYS ON AN IBM SELECTRIC. HIS TYPING IS NOT TERRIBLY BRISK.</u>

DANIELS: (VO) It started out as a pretty good day. Saturdays were usually good because the department offices were just about empty, which made it a very good time for catching up on my interview transcripts.

SOUND: <u>HE PULLS A SHEET OF PAPER OUT OF THE TYPEWRITER.</u>

DANIELS: (VO) This particular Saturday was even better than usual. I had just finished the first draft of my thesis. At 1:15 p.m. I typed in the last entry on my index card, boxed the 300 plus pages...

SOUND: <u>DANIELS DROPS A HEAVY PACKAGE ON A WOODEN SURFACE.</u>

DANIELS: (VO) ...and deposited the manuscript in Professor Sirkowski's mailbox.

SOUND: <u>DIAL TONE AS DANIELS PICKS UP A TELEPHONE RECEIVER.</u>

DANIELS: (VO) Now all I had to do was wait for my thesis committee's comments.

SOUND: <u>WHIRRS AND CLICKS AS DANIELS DIALS A NUMBER.</u>

DANIELS: (VO) I had the unexpected gift of free time.

SOUND: <u>RINGING.</u>

DANIELS: (VO) But I had some ideas about how I might fill

it.

SOUND:	<u>NINA ANSWERS THE PHONE.</u>
NINA:	(filter, on receiver) Hello, McMaster security.
DANIELS:	Hi, sweetheart. Are you hungry?
NINA:	(filter) Not yet, are you?
DANIELS:	All of my appetites are very active right now.
NINA:	(filter) You pig.
DANIELS:	They're showing *Alien* at the Student Union tonight and we could get some dinner at that new Greek cafeteria.
NINA:	(filter) I hear their souvlaki is really good.
DANIELS:	If you can pull yourself away from that mainframe, we'd have a few hours to kill this afternoon.
NINA:	(filter) Oh? And what would you like to do? Shop? Go check out the new exhibits at the art gallery?
DANIELS:	I was thinking we could go to your place.
NINA:	(filter, sighs) I figured.
DANIELS:	I guess we could go to the art gallery.
NINA:	(filter) No. I'll see you in an hour.
DANIELS:	Great.
NINA:	(filter) Don't forget to bring some condoms.
SOUND:	<u>NINA HANGS UP. DIAL TONE.</u>

Scene Twelve

Outside Nina's apartment. 45 minutes later.

DANIELS: (VO) I decided not to use public transit and walk the five miles to Nina's place.

SOUND: <u>TRAFFIC.</u>

DANIELS: (VO) For late January it was pretty nice weather and I seemed to have energy to burn. Maybe it was because I had just reached a major milestone in my studies. Maybe it was the prospect of a few hours of fun with Nina.

SOUND: <u>DISTANT ROAR OF A POWERFUL AUTO-MOBILE ENGINE.</u>

DANIELS: (VO) I felt like I was radiating light and bouncing down the street.

SOUND: <u>ENGINE GROWS CLOSER AND LOUDER.</u>

DANIELS: (VO) It was like the whole city had suddenly been teleported to the moon.

SOUND: <u>SCREECH OF TIRES. ENGINE RACING—VERY, VERY CLOSE.</u>

DANIELS: (VO) This is probably why I didn't notice that car bearing down on me.

SOUND: <u>HORRIFIC CRASH AS THE CAR SMASHES INTO A CONCRETE WALL.</u>

DANIELS: (VO) I still have no idea how it managed to miss me.

SOUND: <u>CAR HORN BLARES. SOMEONE SCREAMS. SOUNDS SLOW AND DISTORTED.</u>

DANIELS: (VO) But then I have no idea about a lot of things that happened in the next ten minutes.

SOUND:	AMBULANCE SIRENS, ALSO AT VERY SLOW SPEED. STEADY THROB OF DANIELS'S HEARTBEAT RISES.
DANIELS:	(internal) Help.
SOUND:	HEARTBEATS CONTINUE, STEADILY GROWING LOUDER.
DANIELS:	(VO) It was like trying to think through an ocean of frozen mud.
SOUND:	MORE HEARTBEATS.
DANIELS:	(internal) I should.
	(VO) Good god! *I should try and help!*
SOUND:	HEARTBEATS STOP. SUDDENLY WE HEAR THE HORNS AND THE SIRENS—AT NORMAL SPEED AND VERY CLOSE.
DANIELS:	(VO) What kind of flayed, bleeding mass of human suffering was I going to find in there?
SOUND:	SIRENS CUT OUT. DANIELS'S FOOTSTEPS ECHO IN SLOW MOTION.
DANIELS:	(VO) It felt like it took me a geological age to get to what was left of the car door.
SOUND:	CREAKING OF TWISTED METAL AS DANIELS STRUGGLES TO OPEN THE DOOR.
DANIELS:	(VO) I was completely unprepared for what I saw on the other side of that shattered windshield.
	(screams) What *the hell?*
	(VO) What I saw was... absolutely nothing.
SOUND:	SIRENS AND CAR HORN CUT IN AT NORMAL SPEED.
DANIELS:	(internal) Nobody. No one.
	(gasps and sobs)

Scene Thirteen

Daniels's apartment. Soon after the car crash.

DANIELS: (VO) Things got pretty spotty after that.

SOUND: <u>ALARM CLOCK TICKS.</u>

DANIELS: (VO) I'm not sure how I got home but I do recall lying down for rest of the weekend.

SOUND: <u>TICKING RISES.</u>

POLICE OFFICER: (echoes) Just tell us what you saw, Professor Daniels.

DANIELS: (echoes, shaky) That's Mr. Daniels.

(VO) I have no memory of talking to the police but I suppose I must have at some point.

SOUND: <u>MORE TICKING. SIRENS ECHO IN THE DISTANCE.</u>

DANIELS: (VO) Of course I had found a pay phone and called an ambulance. Of course I had made a complete statement to the police. I may have even administered first aid. I just had no memory of these events because of the shock.

SOUND: <u>DISTANT CRASH OF THE CAR.</u>

DANIELS: (VO) I was familiar with this kind of stress reaction but as a social scientist I was annoyed that I was a participant in this pathology rather than an observer.

SOUND: <u>TELEPHONE RINGS. DANIELS PICKS UP THE RECEIVER.</u>

DANIELS: (groggy) Hello?

SIRKOWSKI: (filter, on receiver) Outstanding draft, Mr. Daniels.

DANIELS: Uh, what? Professor Sirkowski?

SIRKOWSKI: (filter) Lots of revisions needed, mind you, but at the end of this process you might have something publishable here.

DANIELS: (coughs) Forget it.

SIRKOWSKI: (filter) I beg your pardon?

DANIELS: Forget the whole thing, sir. I'm changing my thesis topic.

**End of
Episode I**

Cult Stories
Episode II: "Lover"

Cast – In Order of Appearance

ETHAN DANIELS	A graduate student at the Anthropology Department at McMaster University. Nina Brown's boyfriend.
NINA BROWN	Computer systems operator at McMaster University. Also a major *Star Trek* fan and Ethan Daniels's girlfriend.
REPORTER	Host of a television news magazine.
EVANSTON	Founder of the Temple of Mentotechnics and former pulp science fiction writer.
TREKKER #1	One of Nina Brown's friends and an active member of the *Star Trek* fan community.
TREKKER #2	One of Nina Brown's friends and an active member of the *Star Trek* fan community.
TREKKER #3	One of Nina Brown's friends and an active member of the *Star Trek* fan community.
TREKKER #4	One of Nina Brown's friends and an active member of the *Star Trek* fan community.
STUDENT #1	One of Ethan's students.
STUDENT #2	Another one of Ethan's students.
DELIVERYMAN	Works for a courier company that services local cinemas.
WELLESLEY	Dean of Arts and Sciences at McMaster University.
SIRKOWSKI	Ethan Daniels's thesis supervisor. Senior

faculty member at McMaster University.

NEWSCASTER #1 — On one of the Buffalo TV stations that can be received in Hamilton.

NEWSCASTER #2 — Also on one of the Buffalo TV stations that can be received in Hamilton.

TSUTSHI — A graduate student at the Anthropology Department at McMaster University. He shares an office with Ethan Daniels.

RECORD STORE CLERK — Works at the Sam the Record Man outlet on James Street in Hamilton.

SPOKESPERSON — Official representative of the Temple of Mentotechnics.

Scene One

Daniels's bedroom. Hamilton, Ontario. 5:30 a.m., December 1979.

SOUND: TELEPHONE RINGS. FUMBLING AS DANIELS PICKS UP.

DANIELS: (groggy) Hello?

NINA: (filter, on phone) Ethan.

DANIELS: Nina? (coughs) Are you all right?

NINA: (filter) Do you know what today is?

DANIELS: Nina, it's not even six in the morning.

NINA: (filter) Do you know what today is!

DANIELS: Uh... it's Friday?

NINA: (filter, annoyed) Today is the Premiere!

DANIELS: Of course, sorry, I'm just waking up.

NINA: (filter) Well, don't go back to sleep.

DANIELS: No, no. I love being up before the sun.

NINA: (filter) Listen: my security training class ends at noon. I will be in my office for two hours and then I will be at New Hall to meet you at 2:30.

DANIELS: Nina, my lecture doesn't finish until three at the earliest.

NINA: (filter) We will then go directly to the movie theatre for the 5:00 show.

DANIELS: Nina, I can't just...

NINA: (filter) Ethan, if we are going to get a good position in line we will need to get there in plenty of time.

DANIELS: Nina, what's wrong with the 7:00 show? We can get something to eat—

NINA: (filter) Ethan, we are *not* going to miss the first showing.

SOUND: <u>NINA HANGS UP. DIAL TONE.</u>

Scene Two

Television program. Early 1980s.

<u>SOUND:</u>	<u>SOMEONE TURNS ON A TV SET.</u>
REPORTER:	What do you say to those who are critical of you and your organization?
EVANSTON:	I'm always surprised by these supposed critical people. Who are they?
REPORTER:	Those people who say that your work is a lie and that you are a fraud.
EVANSTON:	What can I say, Mike? We have measurable, scientifically proven, results. We have the hard evidence.
REPORTER:	*Scientific* evidence that Mentotechnics works?
EVANSTON:	Absolutely. Astonishing evidence. People's lives have been changed in ways that are truly miraculous.
REPORTER:	Scientific miracles?
EVANSTON:	Beautifully put, Mike.

Scene Three

Lecture theatre, McMaster University. Early December 1979.

DANIELS: (VO) Friday, December seventh, nineteen hundred and seventy-nine. The great day had finally arrived.

(echoes through lecture hall) It would be a mistake to assume that everyday life in our modern-day society is exempt from the sorts of rituals that anthropologists like Malinowski and Firth describe in their ethnographies of South Pacific natives.

SOUND: <u>LOUD, SHARP COUGH IN THE DISTANCE.</u>

DANIELS: (VO) Nina appeared at the door of the lecture theatre. It was about half an hour before the end of my class.

Okay, folks...

(VO) Preemptive action was needed.

...We've been talking about marginal social states and liminal conditions in a range of different cultures...

NINA: (coughs again)

DANIELS: ...so let's have an unscheduled research assignment.

SOUND: <u>GROANS FROM THE STUDENTS.</u>

DANIELS: I want you to write a paper, at least five—no, ten pages in length for next Thursday.

SOUND: <u>EVEN LOUDER GROANS.</u>

DANIELS: Okay, seven pages. I want you to analyze your weekend as a liminal state where you encounter and practice different mores and social conventions.

STUDENT: (timid) How are we going to do that, Mr. Daniels?

DANIELS: I want you to make a logbook of all your activities for the next 48 hours. Then compare what you do on the weekend with your behaviour on Monday.

ANOTHER STUDENT: Do we have to type our notes?

DANIELS: Double-spaced handwriting will be fine, but please use blue or black ink.

STUDENT: But we can type it if we want to?

DANIELS: Yeah, sure. Now, I know this a quite a challenge to spring on you by surprise, so we're going to adjourn a little early to give you more time for your assignment.

SOUND: STUDENTS RISING OUT OF THEIR CHAIRS.

DANIELS: (VO) Nina was appeased. At least for the moment.

Scene Four

TV documentary. Early 1980s.

SOUND: <u>SOMEONE TURNS ON A TV SET.</u>

REPORTER: If you have this "hard evidence", why is the Department of Justice impounding your files and therapy machines?

EVANSTON: Good question, Mike.

REPORTER: Do you have a good answer?

EVANSTON: I don't think that the Justice Department would say that we don't have evidence.

REPORTER: Really? What would they say?

EVANSTON: They just don't know what they have evidence of.

SOUND: <u>SOMEONE TURNS OFF THE TV.</u>

Scene Five

<table>
<tr><td></td><td>Outside the Tivoli Theatre. Just over an hour after Daniels's lecture.</td></tr>
<tr><td><u>SOUND:</u></td><td><u>DISTANT TRAFFIC. A FEW EXCITED WHISPERS.</u></td></tr>
<tr><td>DANIELS:</td><td>(VO) Standing in line outside the cinema I was starting to feel the December wind.</td></tr>
<tr><td>NINA:</td><td>Hey guys! You made it!</td></tr>
<tr><td>TREKKER #1:</td><td>Not before you!</td></tr>
<tr><td>DANIELS:</td><td>(VO) Nina, on the other hand, seemed oblivious to all physical discomfort.</td></tr>
<tr><td>TREKKER #2:</td><td>(distant) Live long!</td></tr>
<tr><td>DANIELS:</td><td>(VO) Speaking of liminal states, the Trekkers were definitely existing outside of normal social space and time.</td></tr>
<tr><td>TREKKER #2:</td><td>And prosper!</td></tr>
<tr><td>DANIELS:</td><td>(VO) This was definitely an instance of "communitas"—the breaking down of social barriers and distinctions as part of the celebration of a greater ideological or spiritual collective expression.</td></tr>
<tr><td>NINA:</td><td>So what's the latest?</td></tr>
<tr><td>TREKKER #2:</td><td>Doesn't sound good.</td></tr>
<tr><td>DANIELS:</td><td>(VO) Except that this wasn't a holy communion or the rite of passage for the youth of a West African village, or even a sacred ritual orgy. No, this communitas involved people wearing rubber ears.</td></tr>
</table>

NINA: You think they might cancel?

TREKKER #2:   I was on the phone to the LA club yesterday. The lights have been on at the Paramount *Star Trek* Building all night for the last three weeks.

DANIELS: (VO) Nina had told me what they were worried about: there had been some problems with the special effects. The original special effects studio had been fired and two new technical teams had to start work just a few months ago.

                   (VO) There had been a lot of speculation that the film just wouldn't be ready for its scheduled release. Or that the special effects would look really terrible, especially in comparison with *Star Wars*.

NINA: We've got to keep the faith.

DANIELS: (VO) Things like this were really important to Nina and her friends.

SOUND: <u>VAN ROLLS UP TO THE CURB. REAR DOOR SLIDES OPEN.</u>

TREKKER #2:   That's it? That's the movie?

TREKKER #3:   It's here?

TREKKER #4:   On time?

DELIVERYMAN: (grunts as he lifts the film canisters) Goddamned prints are still wet. I heard they pulled the things right off the editing machines at Paramount.

TREKKERS: (cheer)

DANIELS: (VO) I looked at Nina as she watched the last of the film canisters disappear through the glass doors of the Tivoli. I wondered if she would look as happy at the birth of her first child.

MUSIC: <u>THUMPING ORCHESTRAL SOUNDTRACK RISES AND FADES.</u>

Scene Six

<table>
<tr><td></td><td>Valentino's coffee shop. Three hours later.</td></tr>
<tr><td></td><td><u>CLINK OF CUPS AND SPOONS, MUTED CONVERSATIONS.</u></td></tr>
</table>

Valentino's coffee shop. Three hours later.

<u>SOUND:</u>   <u>CLINK OF CUPS AND SPOONS, MUTED CONVERSATIONS.</u>

DANIELS: Nina?

NINA: (low) Yeah?

DANIELS: What did you think of the film?

NINA: (grunts) What did you think of it?

DANIELS: Honestly? (sips his coffee) I found it really hard to follow. (sips again) Interesting special effects though.

NINA: (softly) Interesting special effects?

DANIELS: Would it be fair to say that *Star Trek: The Motion Picture* was not quite the experience that you had expected?

NINA: (starts crying) The world has lost a great opportunity.

Scene Seven

Office of the dean of graduate studies. January 1980.

SOUND: KNOCK AT THE DOOR.

WELLESLEY: (calls) Come in!

SOUND: DOOR OPENS.

DANIELS: Uh, hello?

SIRKOWSKI: Take a seat, Ethan.

DANIELS: Thank you, Professor Sirkowski.

SOUND: SQUEAKS AND CREAKS AS DANIELS LOWERS HIMSELF INTO AN EXPENSIVE LEATHER CHAIR.

SIRKOWSKI: Ethan, I don't believe you've met Dr. Wellesley, the Dean of Graduate Studies.

WELLESLEY: I'm always pleased to meet one of our student body.

DANIELS: Actually, Dr. Wellesley and I did meet at last year's departmental dinner.

WELLESLEY: (snorts a little) Really?

DANIELS: Yes, we discussed my grant from the Social Sciences and Humanities Council.

SIRKOWSKI: (surprised) Really?

WELLESLEY: (snorts again) We did? I'll be damned.

DANIELS: Yes, you expressed some incredulity that the Council would fund research into something as trivial as "science fiction".

WELLESLEY: Perhaps you didn't describe your thesis in its best light.

DANIELS: Perhaps you weren't paying—

SIRKOWSKI: (interrupts) Perhaps it would be best to address the purpose of today's meeting.

WELLESLEY/DANIELS: Yes.

SIRKOWSKI: Your decision to change your thesis topic has caused a certain amount of concern among the Faculty.

DANIELS: Really?

WELLESLEY: Really.

DANIELS: Some members of faculty have described people like me as just one of many completely disposable PhD candidates; why would anyone care what I was researching?

WELLESLEY: Look Daniels, you're not going to get very far if you go around with some chip on your shoulder.

SIRKOWSKI: Even if the Department was to accept that you no longer wish to research the history and social structure of the Temple of Mentotechnics, we have some serious reservations about your new thesis proposal.

DANIELS: Yes, I'm very excited about it.

WELLESLEY: Fine, let's waste everyone's time.

DANIELS: I would expect a more objective attitude from an academic of your stature, Dr. Wellesley.

WELLESLEY: Up yours, punk.

SIRKOWSKI: (loudly) "Fishnet Technologies and Techniques in 19th Century Ojibwa Communities".

DANIELS: Yes. Important research that needs to be done.

WELLESLEY: You're fucking kidding me, right?

DANIELS: I have a fierce intellectual passion to understand more about how aboriginal peoples obtained their fish.

WELLESLEY: This is bullshit!

SIRKOWSKI: Dean, please. There is no reason to doubt Mr. Daniels's sincerity—

WELLESLEY: (angry) We have every reason to doubt his sincerity!

DANIELS: And why is that, Dean?

WELLESLEY: I've reviewed this kid's academic record. He's never shown any interest or aptitude for any sociological phenomena before 1949. And he sure as hell doesn't give a rat's ass about aboriginal issues!

SIRKOWSKI: That assessment might be a little extreme, Dean.

DANIELS: Indeed.

WELLESLEY: The feds have sunk thousands of dollars into this twerp's research and now he wants to shut it all down and write about how people in northern Ontario used to fish?!

DANIELS: Yes. That's it exactly.

WELLESLEY: (screams) Give me a fucking break!

SIRKOWSKI: (sighs) Why don't we all try and calm down for a moment?

DANIELS: I agree.

WELLESLEY: Better yet, why don't we stand up and all piss in the wind for ten or fifteen minutes?

SIRKOWSKI: Dean Wellesley, please.

WELLESLEY: (sighs) Fine.

SIRKOWSKI: Ethan... (pause) ...being as objective and fairminded as I can... I have to tell you that there are two central flaws in your new thesis proposal.

DANIELS: Could you please enlighten me with regards to these flaws, Professor?

SIRKOWSKI: Don't get cute with me, Ethan. We are in a very serious situation here.

DANIELS: I'm sorry, sir.

SIRKOWSKI: The first problem is that while I do agree with you that this is potentially useful research, there are archaeologists and ethno-historians who are far better qualified to carry out this research than you will ever be.

DANIELS: I believe that I can develop the necessary expertise as I conduct the research.

WELLESLEY: (exasperated) Right, sure.

SIRKOWSKI: My second concern is that yours must be the safest and least controversial research proposal that I have encountered in the last 25 years.

DANIELS: I beg to differ, sir. There are critical social justice issues associated with native technologies and the use of natural resources—

WELLESELY: Coming from someone else, that might be true. But coming from you? Total bullshit.

SIRKOWSKI: (shocked) Dean!

WELLESLEY: Sorry.

DANIELS: This is deeply relevant research.

SIRKOWSKI: Possibly, but you will never be the one best suited to carry it out.

WELLESLEY: Plus, I have the RCMP and the U.S. Department of Justice crawling up my ass because they are very interested in what you might find out about Mentotechnics.

DANIELS: I had no idea that interest in my work extended to such high levels.

WELLESLEY: Well, happy fucking birthday, kid! Those people at "such high levels" have been paying for your research and they're expecting to get some results.

DANIELS: Interesting, but I'm not feeling much of a sense of obligation right now.

WELLESLEY: Why don't you try working on that?

SIRKOWSKI: Ethan, both Dr. Wellesley and I are aware that you experienced a rather traumatic event recently.

DANIELS: I suppose some might interpret the car crash in that manner.

SIRKOWSKI: Most people would understand if your brush with mortality caused you to question all manner of things in your personal and academic life.

SOUND: (DISTANT) CAR SMAHING INTO A BRICK WALL.

WELLESLEY: Exactly! That car almost turned you into a pancake!

DANIELS: (softly) That's true.

SOUND: (DISTANT) CAR HORN BLARING.

SIRKOWSKI: But Ethan, we can't allow these regrettable events to deter us from our greater purpose.

WELLESLEY: That's right, Daniels. You have to pick yourself up, dust yourself off, and get back to fucking work!

SOUND: (DISTANT) POLICE SIRENS. FADES.

DANIELS: Professor Sirkowski, Dean Wellesley. I appreciate what you are telling me, but there is more to the situation than just a car crash.

SIRKOWSKI: You will have to explain that, Ethan.

DANIELS: This may sound as though it defies rational explanation... but... the car that nearly hit me... (pause)

WELLESLEY: Well?

DANIELS: It had no driver.

SIRKOWSKI: What are you saying, Ethan?

WELLESLEY: (snorts) Right! Some kind of ghost car tried to run you down.

DANIELS: Amusing as it may seem to you, Dean, it is my conviction that somehow, someone from the Temple of Mentotechnics was in control of that vehicle.

WELLESLEY: So you're saying that somehow these wackos found a way to throw a car at you?

DANIELS: Mentotechnics doctrine does state that telekinetic ability is one of the outcomes of their training.

WELLESLEY: (incredulous) So you're saying that they really did find a way to throw a car at you?!

DANIELS: (takes a deep breath) What I'm saying is that the car accident was some kind of directed action and that I am convinced that my life was in danger.

WELLESLEY: (mutters) Jesus H. Christ.

SIRKOWSKI: (sighs) Point taken, Ethan. No one should die in pursuit of their doctorate degree.

DANIELS: Thank you for your understanding, Professor.

WELLESLEY: Just a minute. I'm not sure I'm at the "understanding" point yet.

DANIELS: What evades you, Dean? They found about my research, they threatened me and then used

	some unknown means to try and kill me.
SIRKOWSKI:	Perhaps this was just another warning.
DANIELS:	If so, I intend to heed that warning. I'm very sorry but I have no intention of putting myself in danger just to appease your masters.
SIRKOWSKI:	Well.
WELLESLEY:	Okay, Daniels. (sighs) These people scared the living hell out of you and if it were me I'd be wearing brown trousers right now too.
DANIELS:	Thank you for your understanding, Dean.
WELLESLEY:	Don't fucking thank me, kid! These Mentotechnics types may be absolute bastards but they aren't the only ones who can make your life miserable.
SIRKOWSKI:	Listen to what he's saying, Ethan.
WELLESLEY:	You don't want to research Mentotechnics anymore? Fine. But you better come up with something better pretty goddamned quick!

Scene Eight

Television news broadcast. A few days after Daniels's meeting with Sirkowki and the dean.

SOUND: SOMEONE TURNS ON A TV SET.

NEWSCASTER #1: (fades in) ...and reports from California inform us that D.H. Evanston, founder and leader of the controversial Temple of Mentotechnics, died today from what Temple representatives describe as "natural causes". They made no reference to the ongoing investigation of the Temple by the US Department of Justice, the IRS or the FDA. They did, however, urge people to buy the first instalment of Evanston's 12-novel science fiction series *Universal Conflict.*

NEWSCASTER #2: Gosh, Sheila. Any idea how he's going to finish the rest of the series now that he's dead?

NEWSCASTER #1: That's a great question, Bob!

SOUND: SOMEONE TURNS OFF THE TV SET.

Scene Nine

Chester New Hall, home of the anthropology department at McMaster University. A week after the meeting with the dean and a day after the preceding TV broadcast.

TSUTSHI: Ethan, haven't seen you since the big meeting.

DANIELS: I've been camping out at the reference library.

TSUTSHI: Hiding from your thesis supervisor?

DANIELS: Maybe a bit.

TSUTSHI: But you survived?

SOUND: <u>SOFT PING AS DANIELS PRESSES THE ELEVATOR BUTTON.</u>

DANIELS: They didn't cut off any part of my body if that's what you mean.

SOUND: <u>ANOTHER PING AND THE ELEVATOR DOORS ROLL OPEN. THEY STEP INTO THE ELEVATOR.</u>

TSUTSHI: I hear that hardly ever happens these days.

SOUND: <u>ONE MORE PING AS TSUTSHI PRESSES A BUTTON.</u>

DANIELS: Lucky for me.

SOUND: <u>ELEVATOR DOORS ROLL SHUT.</u>

TSUTSHI: So the discussions with the Dean didn't go well.

SOUND: <u>RUMBLE OF THE ELEVATOR MOVING.</u>

DANIELS: (calm) Oh, it was pretty terrible. It's hard to believe that a person as stupid and foul-mouthed would ever be given any kind of position of responsibility at a major university.

TSUTSHI: He was quite direct, was he?

DANIELS: Or even a minor one.

TSUTSHI: And he failed to impress you?

DANIELS: Or even a correspondence school.

TSUTSHI: You hated him that much?

DANIELS: You know, one of the ones you find in those old *Blackhawk* comics.

TSUTSHI: I know the ones. Lots of hitting in them.

DANIELS: (sighs) How did an idiot like that get to be Dean of Graduate Studies?

TSUTSHI: He is very tall.

DANIELS: (thoughtful) Indeed. And he has steely blue eyes.

TSUTSHI: As well as thick grey hair that always seems to be very nicely combed.

DANIELS: That man will be President of the University in less than two years.

SOUND: ONE MORE PING AS THE ELEVATOR REACHES ITS DESTINATION.

TSUTSHI: Inevitable, really.

SOUND: ELEVATOR DOORS ROLL OPEN.

DANIELS: Sure wish I was tall.

SOUND: THEY STEP OUT INTO A CORRIDOR.

TSUTSHI: So is it fair to deduce that they were not well disposed to your new thesis proposal?

DANIELS: It would be fair to say that if my proposal was food and they had eaten it, they would have projectile vomited it right back at me.

TSUTSHI: So what happens now?

SOUND: <u>FOOTSTEPS STOP.</u>

DANIELS: Wish I knew.

SOUND: <u>DANIEL UNLOCKS AN OFFICE DOOR.</u>

DANIELS: But if I'm going to still be sharing an office with you next week, I must come up with a topic more to their liking.

TSUTSHI: So that's what you were doing in the library.

DANIELS: Oh, yeah.

SOUND: <u>DOOR OPENS.</u>

DANIELS: Chuck? (pause) Was anyone in the office while I was away?

TSUTSHI: What the hell is that?

DANIELS: I... (another pause) ...I really don't know.

TSUTSHI: Whatever it is, it's covering your desk!

DANIELS: It's extremely ornate. I think it's supposed to be beautiful.

SOUND: <u>A FEW FOOTSTEPS AS THEY APPROACH ETHAN'S DESK.</u>

TSUTSHI: I think it's some kind of shrine, made of construction paper and doilies. What's this photograph at the centre?

DANIELS: Read the caption.

TSUTSHI: D.H. Evanston: Founder of the Temple of Mentotechnics and former science fiction writer. Oh... (pause) It says here that he died yesterday.

DANIELS: I suppose it had to happen sometime.

TSUTSHI: But why put it here?

DANIELS: Looks to me like they are trying to send me some kind of a message.

TSUTSHI: But what are they trying to tell you?

DANIELS: With any luck, I won't have to find out.

Scene Ten

Bedroom in Daniels's apartment. Night, 1980.

<u>SOUND:</u>	<u>SQUEAKING OF BEDSPRINGS GRADUALLY STOPS. A RADIO IS PLAYING FAINT POP MELODIES THROUGHOUT THE FOLLOWING CONVERSATION:</u>
NINA:	(a little breathless) That was better than it's been in a while!
DANIELS:	(also somewhat winded) Can't disagree with you there.
<u>SOUND:</u>	<u>SHIFTING OF SHEETS AS NINA PRESSES UP AGAINST DANIELS.</u>
NINA:	(sighs) I'm sorry I've been such a cow lately.
DANIELS:	I've been a bit off myself.
NINA:	It's just been tough trying to figure out what I believe in these days.
DANIELS:	Nina, there's something I have to tell you.
NINA:	You're not breaking up with me, are you?
DANIELS:	I have to tell you for ethical reasons.
NINA:	Tell me what, for god's sake?
MUSIC:	(sound from the radio becomes more distinct) *In your mind, you have capacities you know...*
DANIELS:	I submitted a new thesis proposal to Professor Sirkowski today. He approved it almost immediately.
NINA:	That's great, Ethan!

MUSIC: (from the radio) *...to transmit thought energy far beyond the norm...*

DANIELS: I told him I want to study the beliefs and behaviours of *Star Trek* fans.

NINA: Really?

DANIELS: I want to use you and your friends as my subject group.

MUSIC: (from the radio) *...Please close your eyes and concentrate with every thought you think...*

NINA: Are you serious?

DANIELS: Completely.

NINA: (calmly) Ethan, you are such an asshole.

SOUND: <u>NINA GETS OUT OF BED.</u>

MUSIC: (from the radio) *...upon the recitation we're about to sing...*

DANIELS: Nina! Where are you going?

SOUND: <u>DOOR SHUTS.</u>

MUSIC: (from the radio) *...Calling occupants...*

Scene Eleven

Daniels's (and Tsutshi's) office at McMaster University. A few days later.

SOUND: <u>TYPING SLOWS AND STOPS. DANIELS HITS THE RETURN KEY AND PULLS A SHEET OF PAPER OUT OF HIS TYPEWRITER.</u>

DANIELS: (satisfied) Done!

TSUTSHI: Is that your new thesis proposal?

DANIELS: How does this sound? "Just as the Trobiand Islanders evoked all manner of ritual and spiritual aid to ensure success and survival when they venture in their fishing boats from the known safety of the lagoons to the chaotic riches and unknowable dangers of the open seas—immersive science fiction worlds and communities of ants provide a comforting intellectual cushion against the personal risks and unpredictable societal terrors of an exponentially rapid and complex future."

TSUTSHI: That's an extremely long sentence and a little melodramatic but I think you have a valid argument there.

DANIELS: Well, you have to get your reader's attention.

TSUTSHI: True. What else do you have?

SOUND: <u>DANIELS FLIPS TO ANOTHER PAGE.</u>

DANIELS: "The Cargo Cult phenomena of Melanesia is well documented by ethnographers. Here natives build "aircraft" and "cargo ships" from tree leaves and branches in the attempt to emulate and evoke the technological and political power of industrialized colonial states."

TSUTSHI: Everybody in this building knows that, Ethan.

DANIELS: It goes on: "The costumes and props so prevalent at science fiction conventions can be viewed as analogous beliefs and behaviour: where citizens of the 20th Century, buffeted by vast and seemingly overwhelming social and economic forces, can acquire a fleeting measure of false control over their tiny destinies by representing the processing simulacra of the superior science and technology."

SOUND: DANIELS RUSTLES THE PAPER.

DANIELS: Well?

TSUTSHI: Once again, the writing's a bit purple.

DANIELS: Once again, once I have the reader's attention I have to do something to maintain it.

TSUTSHI: Setting aside your uncertain approach to dramaturgy, you may indeed, have another valid insight.

DANIELS: I don't care if it's valid or even particularly true.

TSUTSHI: No?

DANIELS: I just want the Dean and Sirkowski to buy into it.

TSUTSHI: Your intellectual integrity is just a little less than inspiring, Ethan.

DANIELS: I'm a desperate man, Chuck.

TSUTSHI: That much is very apparent. (pause) So why do you want to study *Star Trek* fans?

DANIELS: Three reasons.

TSUTSHI: Three? That is impressive.

DANIELS: Reason one: It is more or less consistent with the original application that got me my research grant in the first place.

TSUTSHI: Respect for bureaucracy. Good.

DANIELS: Second reason: the new proposal allows me to use at least some of my earlier research into the Temple of Mentotechnics.

TSUTSHI: Really? That surprises me.

DANIELS: At least with the early history of both movements.

TSUTSHI: Even better.

DANIELS: Third: I have an inside track into the fan community.

TSUTSHI: Through Nina? (pause) Could be dangerous, my friend.

Scene Twelve

	Daniels's apartment. Two days later—morning and evening.
<u>SOUND:</u>	<u>TELEPHONE RINGS. DANIELS ANSWERS.</u>
DANIELS:	Hello?
NINA:	(filter, on receiver) I feel badly about leaving things the way I did.
DANIELS:	It was kind of sudden.
NINA:	(filter) I know how important your work is to you and I really believe that things like social science research are important to human progress.
DANIELS:	We certainly agree on those points.
NINA:	(filter) And I know that you really didn't mean to sound so condescending.
DANIELS:	Well...
NINA:	(filter) Ethan?
DANIELS:	Why don't you come over for dinner and we can discuss it more?
<u>SOUND:</u>	<u>DANIELS AND NINA MAKING OUT ON HIS COUCH. POP MUSIC PLAYING ON THE STEREO IN THE BACKGROUND. SAME SONG AS PREVIOUS SCENE.</u>
MUSIC:	(from the stereo—song) *...calling occupants of interplanetary craft...*
DANIELS:	(echoes) So you recommend this album?
RECORD STORE CLERK:	(echoes) If she's into sci-fi, then she'll love this one.

DANIELS: (echoes) Oh, that she is.

MUSIC: (from the stereo) *...calling occupants...*

RECORD STORE CLERK: (echoes) Some people think that these guys are really The Beatles.

MUSIC: (from the stereo) *...calling occupants...*

DANIELS: (gasps a bit) Do you like the music?

NINA: (softly) It's very nice.

MUSIC: (from the stereo) *...calling occupants...*

SOUND: <u>NINA GETS OFF THE COUCH.</u>

DANIELS: What's wrong?

NINA: I can't stay the night.

SOUND: <u>SHE WALKS TOWARDS THE DOOR. DANIELS FOLLOWS.</u>

DANIELS: Why not?

SOUND: <u>NINA OPENS THE DOOR.</u>

NINA: I just have to go.

DANIELS: Don't forget your record.

NINA: Keep it. It's just some silly stuff about UFOs and alien contact.

DANIELS: Silly?

NINA: That's not what I care about.

DANIELS: I thought you liked it.

NINA: I guess you really don't understand me.

SOUND: <u>DOOR CLOSES.</u>

MUSIC: (from the stereo) *...We are your friends!*

Scene Thirteen

Television program. Early 1980s.

SOUND: <u>CLICK OF SOMEONE PRESSING THE REMOTE.</u>

REPORTER: How do you respond to rumours that D.H. Evanston really isn't dead? That he's gone into hiding to avoid legal difficulties?

SPOKESPERSON: That's just not the case. The death certificate is a matter of public record and some of us were present at the time of his passing.

REPORTER: Who was present?

SPOKESPERSON: Close family members and senior Temple officials. Myself included.

REPORTER: This must be a tremendous loss to all of you.

SPOKESPERSON: It's a loss to all sentient life.

REPORTER: Uh, yes. So how are you all coping? Will this lead to the end of your organization?

SPOKESPERSON: Not at all. We're completely prepared for this and our movement will continue to flourish.

REPORTER: Is this a time of great change for Mentotechnics?

SPOKESPERSON: There's been some change and there's been some continuity.

SOUND: <u>CLICK OF SOMEONE PRESSING THE REMOTE. STATIC.</u>

**End of
Episode II**

Cult Stories
Episode III: "Tourist"

Cast – In Order of Appearance

ETHAN DANIELS	Now a professor of anthropology at McMaster University. Nina Brown's ex-boyfriend.
NINA BROWN	Now a senior operative for the Canadian Security Intelligence Service (CSIS). Ethan Daniels's ex-girlfriend.
TSUTSHI	Now a professor of anthropology at the University of Ottawa. He shared an office with Ethan Daniels when they were graduate students at McMaster University.
WAITER	At the University of Ottawa's Faculty Club.
SUBJECT #140	A member of the Temple of Mentotechnics and the object of Daniels's research.
ALEXANDER STEEL	Fictional character from a 1930s science fiction story written by D.H. Evanston, founder of the Temple of Mentotechnics.
EVIL ALIENS	Also fictional characters from the same 1930s science fiction story.
GUIDE	Works at the World Headquarters of the Temple of Mentotechnics in Orange County, California.
TRUCK DRIVER	Services roads in central and northern Saskatchewan.

Scene One

Daniels's office at McMaster University. 1993.

SOUND: <u>TELEPHONE RINGS. DANIELS PICKS UP.</u>

DANIELS: Professor Daniels. How can I help you?

NINA: (filter, on receiver) Ethan. We need you to go to Los Angeles.

DANIELS: (snorts) Nina Brown! I'm flattered that you think I'm so essential.

NINA: (filter) Don't feel too flattered.

DANIELS: So why do you want me to go to Los Angeles?

NINA: (filter) You do know they opened up the new World Headquarters for the Temple of Mentotechnics, don't you?

DANIELS: I might have read about that somewhere.

NINA: (filter) We want you to go down there and take a look for us. See what they're up to.

DANIELS: That's fascinating... but why does CSIS care about what the Mentotechnologists are doing in California?

NINA: (filter, sighs) Because they are bad people, Ethan! Or rather their leadership is.

DANIELS: Yes, but why your employers, Nina? Why is a Canadian law enforcement agency concerned about what's going down there?

NINA: (filter) Let's just say that there have been a series of transactions that have crossed the border.

DANIELS: Nina. (pause) I haven't been researching minority

religious movements for quite a while.

NINA: (filter) I doubt that. You're a determined scientist and (slightly nasty laugh) ...one sneaky bastard.

DANIELS: I'm so glad you're not bitter.

NINA: (filter) Bitter about us? Christ, Ethan! I can barely remember what happened last week, let alone over ten years ago.

DANIELS: Maybe that's good.

NINA: (filter) We'll courier down a background package that you can look at.

DANIELS: Nina, I haven't agreed to go yet.

NINA: (filter) But you're going to, aren't you?

DANIELS: (sighs) Yes.

Scene Two

Faculty club at Carlton University, Ottawa. A few weeks earlier.

DANIELS: (VO) Getting that phone call from Nina was definitely a surprise. Not a complete surprise, however. I had just received news about her a few weeks earlier.

SOUND: <u>QUIET TALKING, CLINK OF GLASSES AND CUTLERY.</u>

TSUTSHI: It's nice to see you again, Ethan.

DANIELS: It's good to have an excuse to come up and see you in your new situation up here in Ottawa.

TSUTSHI: Carlton University seems to be a good place for resolving First Nations repatriation issues.

DANIELS: That's very reassuring.

WAITER: Excuse me? A Molson's?

TSUTSHI: That's me.

WAITER: And the gin and tonic?

SOUND: <u>GLASSES BEING SET DOWN.</u>

DANIELS: Thanks.

TSUTSHI: How's the conference going?

DANIELS: "Folklore and Pop Culture" is going very nicely. My paper on Football Fan Symbolism and Classic NHL Hockey Magic Rituals was well received.

TSUTSHI: Really?

DANIELS: Well, nobody walked out on me anyway.

SOUND: <u>TSUTSHI TAKES A SWIG OF BEER.</u>

TSUTSHI: That's always an encouraging sign.

DANIELS: Preston is editing a new journal of the social history of sport and I thought I might re-work it as an article and send to him.

SOUND: <u>DANIELS SIPS HIS DRINK.</u>

TSUTSHI: Thrift, Horatio! Thrift!

DANIELS: (chuckles) So why haven't I seen you at the conference?

TSUTSHI: I've been too goddamned busy! I've got all this security paperwork to deal with.

DANIELS: Security paperwork? You're doing archaeological digs in B.C. for god's sake!

TSUTSHI: I know! I mean, I was expecting that we might have some problems with the aboriginal community but nothing like this! One afternoon last month, some people from CSIS showed up and debriefed me and my grad students for over five hours!

DANIELS: What the hell for?!

TSUTSHI: You might have heard on the news that there's been some protests going on regarding the lumber industry and some of the forest lands out there.

DANIELS: Isn't there always? They're nuts out there.

TSUTSHI: According to the Canadian Security and Intelligence Service, there may have been a connection between the local protesters and international eco-terrorist groups.

SOUND: <u>DANIELS TAKES ANOTHER DRINK. SETS DOWN HIS GLASS.</u>

DANIELS: That sounds just a bit paranoid to me.

TSUTSHI: They seemed like very serious people.

DANIELS: So what did you have to do for them?

TSUTSHI: We went through hundreds of photographs, trying to determine if we'd seen any of those people near our campsite.

DANIELS: Sounds *very* paranoid to me.

SOUND: DANIELS TAKES ANOTHER DRINK.

TSUTSHI: (suddenly excited) Oh, I know! There was something I wanted to tell you!

DANIELS: What?

TSUTSHI: The leader of the CSIS team, she was your old girlfriend.

DANIELS: (shocked) My what?

TSUTSHI: You know, the one from McMaster. The *Star Trek* fan!

DANIELS: (even more shocked) Nina? Nina Brown?!

TSUTSHI: That's right!

DANIELS: Nina Brown is an agent for the Canadian Security and Intelligence Service?

TSUTSHI: A senior agent according to the identification she showed me.

DANIELS: I'll be damned.

TSUTSHI: She seemed very competent.

DANIELS: (thoughtful) Nina in CSIS? (pause) Actually that does make an odd kind of sense.

TSUTSHI: Are there a lot of science fiction fans in the intelligence community?

DANIELS: I have no idea. But Nina was extremely well-organized, highly intelligent, extremely dedicated and very idealistic.

TSUTSHI: If she was so great, why did you break up with her?

DANIELS: Political reasons I suppose.

TSUTSHI: Really?

DANIELS: Well, *Star Trek* politics. Hard to explain.

TSUTSHI: But why join up with CSIS?

DANIELS: At one level, she probably had many of the necessary skills. She was doing very advanced data processing and analysis and some of that involved
campus security. There's a nuclear reactor at Mc-
Master University—they have very serious security
there.

TSUTSHI: And at the other level?

DANIELS: *Star Trek* fans want to create a better world. Maybe
Nina thought CSIS was a way to do that.

SOUND: <u>TSUTSHI TAKES A LONG SWIG OF BEER.</u>

TSUTSHI: (burps slightly) I don't know, Ethan. She didn't
come across as particularly idealistic to me.

Scene Three

Daniels's office, McMaster University. One month later.

<table>
<tr><td><u>SOUND:</u></td><td><u>DANIELS PRESSES THE RECORD SWITCH ON A TAPE MACHINE.</u></td></tr>
<tr><td>DANIELS:</td><td>Were you ever concerned that D.H. Evanston was a science fiction writer before he founded the Temple of Mentotechnics?</td></tr>
<tr><td>SUBJECT #140:</td><td>No, not at all.</td></tr>
<tr><td>DANIELS:</td><td>You mean it didn't raise any doubts?</td></tr>
<tr><td>SUBJECT #140:</td><td>Why would it?</td></tr>
<tr><td>DANIELS:</td><td>I don't know; it might be like hearing that Mother Teresa wrote Harlequin romances or that John the Baptist was a contributor to Cousin Mort's Flying Saucer Quarterly.</td></tr>
<tr><td>SUBJECT #140:</td><td>Your statements are even more biased than usual. You must be tired.</td></tr>
<tr><td>DANIELS:</td><td>Thanks, I'll watch out for that.</td></tr>
<tr><td>SUBJECT #140:</td><td>In answer to your question, once again, no. Evanston's work as a science fiction writer didn't bother me at all. I thought it made a lot of sense.</td></tr>
<tr><td>DANIELS:</td><td>Made sense? In what way?</td></tr>
<tr><td>SUBJECT #140:</td><td>It takes tremendous vision and imagination to comprehend the enormity of what Mentotechnics really is.</td></tr>
<tr><td>DANIELS:</td><td>I guess that's one way of looking at it.</td></tr>
<tr><td>SUBJECT #140:</td><td>And besides, science fiction is the only truly rel-</td></tr>
</table>

evant literature left.

DANIELS: But you told me earlier that you had some concerns about the Temple that some people were there for the wrong reasons.

SUBJECT #140: Yes. Some people, like the ones at the Training Centres, were just there for personal advancement.

DANIELS: And that's a problem?

SUBJECT #140: They're so close to the truth, but they're missing the big picture. While they are worrying about ways to pass auditions they can't see that the human race is evolving into something new and wonderful!

DANIELS: Sounds terrific.

SUBJECT #140: It's beyond terrific! It's beyond infinity! We are on the verge of a whole new relationship with the very essence of the Universe.

DANIELS: Yeah.

SOUND: <u>DANIELS PRESSES THE STOP SWITCH ON THE TAPE MACHINE.</u>

Scene Four

Daniels's office, 1993.

NINA: (filter, on receiver) Come on! You must still be doing some kind of research.

DANIELS: (sighs) Okay, okay.

NINA: (filter) Ha! I knew it!

DANIELS: But nothing much, just a few interviews and collecting some newspaper stories on the microfiche from the local library. The Temple has been buying up a lot of real estate over in western New York and it made me curious.

NINA: (filter) Good. So you're more or less up to speed with Mentotechnics?

DANIELS: What do you want, Nina?

NINA: (filter) You may be able to give us some context.

DANIELS: Context?

NINA: (filter) Yeah. We need to make an assessment of the current criminal probability of the organization.

DANIELS: Uh, you want me to write a report?

NINA: (filter) Yes. We want you to go there and afterwards write a report.

Scene Five

An excerpt from a science fiction story written by D.H. Evanston, circa 1937.

DANIELS: (VO) So science fiction is profound and prophetic? The only relevant literature ever written? Let's dial back to the 1930s and explore some of the brilliant writings of D.H. Evanston...

SOUND: ROAR OF ROCKET SHIP ENGINES GROW LOUDER AND THEN SUBSIDE AS WE HEAR ITS MASSIVE LANDING FINS DIG DEEP INTO THE ALIEN SOIL. THERE IS A HISSING SOUND AS THE HULL OF THE ROCKET COOLS AND A DEEP METALLIC ECHO AS THE MAIN HATCHWAY OPENS.

STEEL: (to himself) So here I am on one of Jupiter's moons...

SOUND: A SOFT CRUNCH AND DUSTY FOOTSTEPS AS STEEL JUMPS DOWN AND WALKS OUT ONTO THE SURFACE OF THE MOON.

STEEL: ...I just hope the readings from my mentaloscope are accurate. Otherwise...

EVIL ALIENS: (a bunch of them) *Die, terrestrial scum!*

SOUND: TINY DYNAMOS POWER UP AS STEEL ACTIVATES HIS WEAPON.

STEEL: Get back, you inhuman, slavering hordes! I have an atom blaster here—capable of imploding your nucleic structure even from distances exceeding 700 zardons...

EVIL ALIENS: We have no fear of your pathetic human toys!

SOUND:	<u>EERIE HOWL RISES AS THE EVIL ALIENS MOVE CLOSER.</u>
STEEL:	In the name of Science, I'm warning you! Stay back, you mutated monstrosities, you!
EVANSTON:	(echoes) ...even though... it seemed as if certain doom...
SOUND:	<u>THE SOUND OF RAPID TYPING IS HEARD IN THE BACKGROUND.</u>
EVANSTON:	...leaked from every... fissure... of... the Jovian caverns... Space Patrolman... Alexander Steel... felt fear... sorry! Felt... *no*... fear... as a leader of the... United Earth States... Solar Police... he knew he... could fail... damn! Could *not*... fail...
STEEL:	*Die, subversive beings!*
SOUND:	<u>RAPID BURSTS OF ATOMIC FORCE AS STEEL FIRES HIS BLASTER. THE ALIENS SCREAM AS THEY IMPLODE.</u>
STEEL:	Such is the fate of all who oppose the rule of Technology!
SOUND:	<u>SCREAMING FADES.</u>
DANIELS:	(VO) Inspiring, isn't it?

Scene Six

Orange County, California. Summer 1993.

SOUND:

DANIELS: The World Center for Mental Technology is located in the grounds of what was once a Navy blimp hangar in Orange County, which the literature at my hotel described as "one of the world's largest wooden structures."

SOUND:

DANIELS: Popular belief is correct in the assertion that it is essentially completely impossible to get around southern California without a car.

I hate driving, but here I am stuck behind the wheel of a rental, trying to find my way to the Center.

SOUND:

DANIELS: I've been driving around the general area for over an hour. I can see the huge golden spire that marks the place, and once in a while I can even get a glimpse of the great wooden hump of what was once the hangar. But I cannot find the actual entrance.

SOUND:

DANIELS: If I actually believed Mentotechnics doctrine, I would conclude that this was some kind of telepathic defence system—somebody knows I'm coming and is using the power of illusion to prevent it.

SOUND: ENGINE CONTINUES.

DANIELS: But really, it's just the unique quasi-urban geography of Orange County.

Scene Seven

Nina's office at CSIS headquarters, Ottawa. Three months earlier.

NINA: I advised my people that you have a unique combination of experience.

DANIELS: Thanks. But you probably know as much about this phenomenon as I do.

NINA: Since I left the university I've become a pretty good cop.

DANIELS: I was recently told that you're one of the country's best intelligence officers. I really don't know what you need me for.

NINA: And I emphasized that you are a highly credible source on this matter.

DANIELS: I'm flattered.

NINA: Ethan, a portion of the World Mentotechnics Center is now accessible to the general public.

DANIELS: Given their rather secretive nature I would say that is... unusual.

NINA: Yeah, ain't it just?

DANIELS: What are they doing? Guided tours?

NINA: You got it. They put up an exhibition honouring Evanston on the anniversary of his death.

DANIELS: Exhibition?

NINA: The U.S. Department of Justice has run into some political problems with the Mentotechnics organization.

DANIELS: They made an exhibition about Evanston?

NINA: Isn't that what I said? Now, because there's a Canadian connection, the Americans have asked us to take over the investigation.

DANIELS: You want me to go and see this exhibition?

NINA: (attempting to sound patient) *Yes.* All you have to do is show up and tell us what you think.

Scene Eight

World Center for Mental Technology, Orange County, California. 1993, right after Daniels has parked his car.

<u>SOUND:</u>	<u>HEAVY DOOR OPENS IN THE DISTANCE. FOOTSTEPS ECHO OFF THE MARBLE FLOOR AND WALLS.</u>
DANIELS:	Hello?
GUIDE:	What do you want?
DANIELS:	(flustered) I, uh, I—
GUIDE:	(impatient) *Well?*
DANIELS:	I, uh, just came to see the exhibition.
GUIDE:	*Really?*
DANIELS:	I can leave if I'm not welcome.
GUIDE:	Do you mean you're not a mental technologist?
DANIELS:	No.
GUIDE:	You're sure?
DANIELS:	The man at my hotel said that the Temple was open to the general public.
GUIDE:	(intense) *Yes!* Yes, it is! (laughs feebly) I thought you might be part of a bus tour of members from our Albuquerque branch.
DANIELS:	Oh...
GUIDE:	But I guess they must be late.
DANIELS:	Is it okay for me to see the exhibition?

GUIDE: Of course! I'll give you the guided tour.

SOUND: <u>HEELS CLICK AS SHE WALKS TO THE GALLERY ENTRANCE.</u>

DANIELS: (VO) My guide was wearing six-inch heels and a metallic mini-dress that looked as though it had been applied with a spray can. She looked like one of Captain Kirk's girlfriends from the third season.

GUIDE: (echoes) Follow me, please.

DANIELS: (VO) I am slightly disgusted with myself because I like the effect so much.

SOUND: <u>ELECTRIC DOORS ROLL OPEN.</u>

DANIELS: (VO) The first display was pretty validating, because it was almost exactly as I had imagined. It was a recreation of the offices of *Tremendous Stories of Super Science*.

    (VO) There were two figures: one represented the editor Stewart D. McReady, and the other the then youthful D.H. Evanston. They were leaning over McReady's large oak desk, presumably discussing Evanston's latest submission.

GUIDE: It was at this stage in his career that Donald Evanston quickly became one of the most popular and prolific writers in the Golden Age of science fiction.

DANIELS: (VO) She spoke very well. As though she'd memorized every word but wasn't bored with the material yet.

GUIDE: People say that Donald Evanston could produce at least three short stories a day.

DANIELS: (VO) My guide pointed to an artifact display: a very early model electric typewriter connected to a hefty roll of newsprint.

GUIDE: He wrote so quickly that he didn't want to wait

to change pages.

DANIELS: Sounds like real creative flow.

GUIDE: Yes. (pleased) I've never heard it put that way, but yes.

SOUND: <u>ANOTHER ELECTRIC DOOR OPENS. FOOTSTEPS.</u>

DANIELS: (VO) We walked down a huge tunnel—it was a collage of four-colour print. The walls were lined with thousands of science fiction magazine and paperback covers. The floor and ceiling were lined with mirrors that created a room-sized kaleidoscope effect.

SOUND: <u>MYSTERIOUS ENO-LIKE SYNTH THROBB-ING.</u>

DANIELS: (VO) It was sort of like the trip sequence from Kubrick's *2001* but with much worse art direction.

GUIDE: Donald Evanston went on to become a major influence on the genre of science fiction.

SOUND: <u>ELECTRO-THROBBING CONTINUES.</u>

GUIDE: The Temple is still a patron of important new work.

DANIELS: (VO) We entered a room that looked like another set from a movie or a TV show. Maybe something like *The Time Tunnel* or *Lost in Space*. There were flashing lights everywhere with lots of reel-to-reel tapes and shelves of electrode-covered skullcaps.

GUIDE: And this is our Therapy Machine timeline.

DANIELS: (trying to sound innocent) I've heard of these.

(VO, very excited) I'd never seen this much Mentotechnic paraphernalia. It was the Holy Grail of post-modern religious/popular culture studies!

GUIDE: The T-Machine is the foundation of everything we do in Mentotechnics.

DANIELS: (VO) Damn right.

GUIDE: And this is a complete collection of every unit issued by the Temple. From the 1952 prototype to next year's model.

DANIELS: How do they work?

GUIDE: Well, T-Machines operate on the principle that we can monitor and record every human thought.

DANIELS: (VO) Of course, that is not possible. You can measure various clusters of electrical activity in the human brain but nobody can track specific interior meanings. In terms of accurate, provable science we were essentially in a room full of animated Etch-A-Sketches.

GUIDE: Could you stand over there?

SOUND: GUIDE FLIPS A SWITCH. ELECTRICAL HUMMING STARTS.

GUIDE: Once we've traced a thought, we can repair it and eventually enhance the abilities of the thinker.

DANIELS: (VO) What a lovely, and hopelessly naive, notion.

                Gosh.

GUIDE: And in some ways it helps us to think more effectively together.

DANIELS: (VO) That's odd, I didn't know of anything about collective telepathy in Mentotechnic doctrine.

GUIDE: Would you like a demonstration?

DANIELS: Sure.

                (VO) Nina was going to love this!

GUIDE: Now lean forward while I put on the electrodes.

DANIELS: Ooh! Those are cold.

GUIDE: At the advanced levels we believe that we can record entire human personalities and sustain their intellects in artificial environments.

SOUND: <u>GUIDE CLICKS A FEW SWITCHES ON THE T-MACHINE.</u>

GUIDE: This is how we've been able to maintain continuity of leadership in our organization.

SOUND: <u>SHARP ELECTRICAL TWANG.</u>

DANIELS: *Huh?*

GUIDE: Would you like to meet the living mind of D.H. Evanston?

DANIELS: *Duh!*

SOUND: <u>RUSH OF VOICES AND SYNTH-SURGES.</u>

DANIELS: (VO) Then everything went very dark and for an indeterminate time I felt like I was weightless in the presence of something very ambitious with an Arkansas accent.

SOUND: <u>CACOPHONY OF WORDS AND NOISE CONTINUES.</u>

DANIELS: (VO) Billions of words and images were floating around me but I could only understand one voice.

META-EVANSTON: (echoes) Well, look at what we have here.

DANIELS: (terrified) That voice... I recognize it...

META-EVANSTON: (echoes) Of course you do.

DANIELS: (VO) I floated upwards into the dome of what looked like an infinite crystal cathedral. I was surrounded by thousands of human specimens. Representatives of all races, cultures and ages of history. All connected together by twisting cords of energy.

DANIELS: (incredulous) D.H. Evanston? But you're dead!

META-EVANSTON: (echoes) Big deal.

DANIELS: (VO) The living glow of the crystalline structures suffuses their naked bodies and makes them perfect. We drift into a loose helix pattern as we turn toward a massive corridor that stretches out into the Universe.

META-EVANSTON: (echoes) Why are you bothering my people, Daniels?

DANIELS: How do you know my name?

META-EVANSTON: (echoes) The size and power of my consciousness is greater than the Sun's. I know every fucking thing on the planet.

DANIELS: That's incredible!

META-EVANSTON: (echoes) Even boring shit like the fact that burnt-out academics like you are still wandering around out there.

DANIELS: (VO) I saw myriads of life forms of every conceivable configuration lining the inner walls of the enormous passageway.

                (VO) Intuitively I sensed that this was the gateway to the collective knowledge and experience of all intelligent life in creation. A Galactic Super-Culture.

META-EVANSTON: (echoes) Now, I repeat the question: what the hell do you want?

DANIELS: I-I—I want to understand why you believe what you believe—

SOUND: ROAR OF ELECTRO-CEREBRAL ENERGY RISES.

META-EVANSTON: (echoes, laughs) *Why?* Look around you, man! We're occupying a realm completely outside normal human values!

DANIELS: What are you?

META-EVANSTON: (echoes) Like the lady said, I am the living mind of D.H. Evanston—dynamic, growing and enhanced a billion times by technologies beyond this world. (chuckles) Pretty impressive, eh?

DANIELS: (gasps) Then what does all of this mean?

META-EVANSTON: (echoes) You and that idiot girlfriend of yours would really like to know, wouldn't you? (snorts in derision) *Star Trek!*

DANIELS: Nina is not my girlfriend!

META-EVANSTON: (echoes) Sure, whatever you say, pal.

SOUND: <u>ROAR SUBSIDES INTO A DULL PULSATION.</u>

META-EVANSTON: (echoes) So you're the big seeker of truth? You want to understand what all this means?

DANIELS: (screams) *Yes!*

META-EVANSTON: (echoes) Okay, then I have a message for you.

DANIELS: A message?!

META-EVANSTON: (echoes) Yeah, from the Galactic Super-Culture directly to you.

DANIELS: To me?

META-EVANSTON: (echoes) Personally.

DANIELS: Okay...

EVANSTON: (reverberates) *YOU ARE A COMPLETE MORON!*

SOUND: <u>ROAR OF ELECTRO-CEREBRAL ENERGY RISES AGAIN.</u>

Scene Nine

Prince Albert National Park, Saskatchewan. Some time later.

SOUND: <u>THE SOUND OF META-EVANSTON'S MIND FADES INTO WAVES LAPPING ON A LAKE SURFACE. LOONS CALL OUT IN THE DISTANCE.</u>

DANIELS: (VO) When I regained consciousness I discovered that I was lying next to a very cold lake, on a pile of leaves, twigs and muskeg.

(groans)

SOUND: <u>TWIGS BREAK AND MUSKEG CREAKS A LITTLE AS DANIELS STRUGGLES TO HIS FEET.</u>

DANIELS: (VO) I was cold and alone. The sun was just over the horizon.

(mutters) What on Earth?

(VO) I was in a landscape that was populated with pine trees, a lake with a beach of stones and what might be a disused dirt road.

DANIELS: I'm going to freeze to death!

(VO) Hugging myself I followed that road until I could hear what I hoped was the sound of vehicular traffic.

SOUND: <u>OLD TRUCK APPROACHES AND BRAKES TO A STOP. DOOR OPENS.</u>

TRUCK DRIVER: Hey, stranger! You're a bit off the beaten path.

DANIELS: Thank you for stopping!

TRUCK DRIVER: You better get in.

SOUND: DANIELS CLIMBS INTO THE TRUCK AND SHUTS THE DOOR.

TRUCK DRIVER: I'm going as far as North Battleford. Does that suit?

DANIELS: As long as they have telephones there I am completely fine with it.

TRUCK DRIVER: You want me to turn up the heat? Looks like you put on your summer clothes this morning.

SOUND: FANS OF THE TRUCK'S HEATER TURNING ON.

DANIELS: I'm certainly not dressed appropriately for this climate.

TRUCK DRIVER: So are you up here camping? The main site in the park won't be open until the end of May.

DANIELS: Park? We're in a park?

(VO) Trying not to sound completely insane, I was eventually able to piece together enough information to determine that I had landed in Prince Albert National Park, somewhere in central Saskatchewan.

TRUCK DRIVER: How did you manage to get over to this side of the lake? You're lucky I found you—nobody comes here!

DANIELS: Bit of a misunderstanding. I got dropped off at the wrong place.

(VO) How and why the Temple of Mentotechnics had gotten me to subarctic wilderness was, and still is, a total mystery to me.

META-EVANSTON: (echoes, distant) *Moron.*

**End of
Episode III**

Cult Stories
Episode IV: "Survivor"

Cast – In Order of Appearance

ETHAN DANIELS	A professor of anthropology at McMaster University. Nina Brown's ex-boyfriend.
DOCENT	Retired farmer at the Museum of Pioneer History in St. Paul, Alberta.
SGT. FERGUSON	Works for the Royal Canadian Air Force at CFB Trenton.
NINA BROWN	A senior operative for the Canadian Security Intelligence Service (CSIS). Ethan Daniels's ex-girlfriend.
WAITER	At the Vulcan Visitors Centre in Vulcan, Alberta. Probably dressed as an Andorian or Romulan or some such alien from *Star Trek*.
TEAM LEADER	Heads up the CSIS SWAT team under Nina Brown and advised by Ethan Daniels.
TEAM MEMBER	Part of the CSIS SWAT team.
IT SPECIALIST	Also a part of the CSIS SWAT team.
FULL TEAM	CSIS SWAT team.
SHOOTER	Part of the CSIS SWAT team.
SUBJECT X	A member of the Temple of Mentotechnics and the object of Daniels's research.
TSUTSHI	A professor of anthropology at the University of Ottawa. Long-time friend of

Ethan Daniels.

SPEAKER #1   Gives a eulogy at a funeral. A member of the *Star Trek* fan community.

SPEAKER #2   Also gives a eulogy at a funeral. A member of the *Star Trek* fan community.

Scene One

Museum of Pioneer History, St. Paul, Alberta. Morning, 2009.

SOUND: <u>MOBILE PHONE RINGS. DANIELS ANSWERS.</u>

DANIELS: Hello? (pause) I'm at the Museum of Pioneer History. It's the only thing open this time of day. (pause) Sure, I can stay here for a while.

SOUND: <u>HANGS UP.</u>

DANIELS: (VO) The CSIS team said they were running late, so I had a couple of hours to kill. Not the easiest thing to do in central Alberta.

SOUND: <u>HIS FOOTSTEPS ECHO THROUGH THE GALLERY.</u>

DANIELS: (VO) This was definitely farm country. Even the docents were dressed in those denim bib overalls that nobody makes anymore. But according to Nina's briefing notes, this part of western Canada was also a "hot spot"—a region with numerous UFO sightings and encounters. My favourite was the memo about the town that started: "RE: ROSWELL NORTH."

DOCENT: Do you have any questions?

DANIELS: Gosh, I don't know. Where did you get all this farm equipment?

DOCENT: Well, the combine and the two tractors over there used to belong to me. I worked them for over 40 years.

DANIELS: They look brand new.

DOCENT: If my kids hadn't left for the city they could still use them.

DANIELS: Gosh. (pause) So what was that big platform out there with all the flags?

DOCENT: That's the town's Centennial project.

DANIELS: Is it some kind of art installation?

DOCENT: (laughs) That's the world's first flying saucer landing pad.

DANIELS: That's pretty unique.

DOCENT: Now if you check the guidebook... (pause) ...aha! This is what you find written at the base of the landing pad: "The area under the World's First UFO Landing Pad was designated by the Town of St. Paul as a symbol of our faith that mankind will maintain the outer universe free from national wars and strife. That future travel in space will be safe for all intergalactic beings. All visitors from Earth or otherwise are welcome to this territory and to the Town of St. Paul."

DANIELS: Those are very noble aspirations.

DOCENT: Back when they opened it, the Minister of Defence flew all the way down from Ottawa.

DANIELS: Really? That far?

DOCENT: Set down right there on the pad.

DANIELS: (surprised) What? In a flying saucer?

DOCENT: Just a helicopter.

DANIELS: That's a little disappointing.

DOCENT: Some people did swear they saw a couple of spaceships back in '67.

DANIELS: Did you ever see anything?

DOCENT: Naw. The furthest visitor we've ever had was from Halifax.

DANIELS:	Halifax is pretty far away.
DOCENT:	Of course, I'm not counting those folks over at the Mentotechnics Institute.
DANIELS:	(trying to sound casual) What are they like?
DOCENT:	They're okay. Very polite.
DANIELS:	Polite?
DOCENT:	Must be real busy because we don't see them very much.
SOUND:	<u>MOBILE PHONE RINGS. DANIELS ANSWERS.</u>
DANIELS:	Yes?
NINA:	(filter, on receiver) Meet me at Vulcan.
SOUND:	<u>SHE HANGS UP.</u>
DOCENT:	Everything okay?
DANIELS:	I gotta go.

Scene Two

Tarmac at Canadian Forces Base, Trenton, Ontario. 6:00 a.m. Three days earlier.

DANIELS: (VO) Odd as it was to be in central Alberta, waiting for them to unroll the sidewalks, it was not nearly as strange as the events that took me there.

SOUND: <u>JET ENGINES REVVING UP, GRADUALLY GROWING LOUDER.</u>

SGT. FERGUSON: (calling out over the engines) Dr. Daniels! It's good to see you here!

DANIELS: (calls out) Is it?!

SOUND: <u>FOOTSTEPS ON METAL AS THEY CLIMB THE STEPS INTO THE JET.</u>

DANIELS: I'm not exactly sure why I'm here!

SOUND: <u>HATCH SLAMS SHUT. JET ENGINES BECOME MUFFLED.</u>

SGT. FERGUSON: I'd say welcome to Trenton but I can see the van with your team coming up to the terminal.

DANIELS: Team?

SOUND: <u>DUAL CLICKS AS FERGUSON OPENS HIS ATTACHE CASE.</u>

SGT. FERGUSON: If you could read these briefing documents from Agent Brown while you're en route, it would be extremely helpful.

SOUND: <u>CRACKLE OF FAKE LEATHER AS DANIELS TAKES A SEAT.</u>

DANIELS: Are you authorized to tell me where we're going? My driver claimed to have no idea.

SGT. FERGUSON: Your immediate destination is CFB Edmonton. After that, ground transportation will take you to the town of St. Paul, Alberta.

DANIELS: What the hell for?!

SGT. FERGUSON: My orders say that it's very important.

DANIELS: Important?

SGT. FERGUSON: And that's all they say.

DANIELS: Your driver woke me up at three in the morning and that's all you can tell me?

SGT. FERGUSON: Your team is here.

DANIELS: I don't have a team!

SOUND: <u>SGT. FERGUSON OPENS THE HATCH. SOUND OF THE JETS GROWS LOUDER.</u>

SGT. FERGUSON: (calls) *You do now!*

DANIELS: (calls) What am I supposed to do with these people?!

SOUND: <u>BOOTED FOOTSTEPS HAMMERING ON THE STAIRS.</u>

SGT. FERGUSON: (calls) *Tell them what you know!*

SOUND: <u>ENGINES GROW LOUDER.</u>

Scene Three

Tourism visitors' centre, Vulcan, Alberta. Four hours later.

SOUND:	<u>LOW RUMBLE OF DANIELS'S RENTAL CAR.</u>
NINA:	(echoes) Meet me at Vulcan.
DANIELS:	(VO) I wonder how many times Nina had wanted to say that to me, or anybody for that matter.
SOUND:	<u>DANIELS BRAKES THE CAR TO A STOP.</u>
DANIELS:	(VO) But the circumstances and the meaning were very different from what she might have imagined all those years ago. Nina meant Vulcan, Alberta, not Vulcan the planet.
SOUND:	<u>DANIELS OPENS THE CAR DOOR.</u>
DANIELS:	(VO) This Vulcan was a fairly small town a couple of hours' drive from Calgary and another four hours' drive from the Mentotechnics compound.
SOUND:	<u>DANIELS'S FOOTSTEPS CRUNCHING ACROSS THE PARKING LOT.</u>
DANIELS:	(VO) The Vulcan Visitors' Centre has a giant sculpture of the USS Enterprise looming over the highway. The centre itself is modelled after a United Federation of Planets space station.
SOUND:	<u>DANIELS PUSHES THE DOOR OPEN.</u>
DANIELS:	Hi, Nina.
NINA:	(sullen) Cheers. Sit down.
SOUND:	<u>DANIELS SLIDES INTO THE BOOTH.</u>
DANIELS:	You're looking well.

SOUND: NINA PUTS HER GLASS DOWN.

NINA: You're still a terrible liar.

DANIELS: Truth is relative. (laughs feebly) And we're all getting older.

NINA: (still sullen) Ha. Ha.

DANIELS: (calls out) Drink? A blue one like my friend's?

WAITER: Right, sir. One Romulan Ale coming up.

DANIELS: What kind of alien is he supposed to be?

NINA: (swallows and burps) Andorian.

DANIELS: (VO) Nina was right. She really did look awful. Pale, red-eyed, and her business suit was hanging off her like combat fatigues. She looked the way I felt when I'd woken up in northern Saskatchewan 15 years ago. But I'd been drugged and shipped halfway across the continent—I had an excuse.

DANIELS: You've been here before?

NINA: Couple of times. (she takes another drink) The Klingon group from Great Falls comes up here every spring. They do a nice music festival.

WAITER: Your Romulan Ale, sir.

SOUND: WAITER SETS GLASS ONTO THE TABLE.

DANIELS: Thanks.

NINA: It's just blue beer, really.

DANIELS: So are you getting back into *Trek* culture?

NINA: Not really. (empties her glass) You can't recapture that kind of a feeling. (calls out) Waiter? (normal) But I still respect what they're trying to do.

DANIELS: A positive vision for the future?

NINA: (very serious) A *human* vision for the future.

WAITER: Ma'am.

SOUND: <u>PLACES A GLASS DOWN. WAITER WALKS AWAY.</u>

DANIELS: I assume you want to talk about what they're doing with that radio telescope at the compound?

NINA: (slightly nasty chuckle) Do you know that they think they're picking up intelligent signals from outer space?

DANIELS: (matter-of-factly) Probably from a confederation of star systems from the galactic core. (takes a drink) At least that would be consistent with Temple doctrine.

NINA: And what do you think they're doing in that aircraft hangar?

DANIELS: Most likely building a flying saucer. Every once in a while one of their branches builds a mock-up spacecraft, hoping that they can get out there and commune with their maker.

NINA: (takes a very long drink) Yeah.

DANIELS: It's not a big deal, Nina. It's like those cargo cults in the South Pacific that used to build airplanes out of palm trees.

NINA: Palm trees? (burps menacingly) You think this is all about *fucking palm trees?*

DANIELS: (carefully) I'm just saying that there's precedent for this in the ethnographic literature.

NINA: (irritated) Ethan, we got the Americans to do a flyby with one of their surveillance drones and I have three pieces of information that you might find somewhat interesting.

DANIELS: Really.

NINA: First. (takes a drink) They have two connected super-computers in there.

DANIELS: Maybe they have picked up some interesting astronomical data and need something to process it

	with.
NINA:	(nasty laugh) Do you really think so?
DANIELS:	Why not? There's nothing in Mentotechnics that precludes some kind of legitimate scientific inquiry. Even if they've come across the data accidentally.
NINA:	That's mighty liberal of you, Ethan. (takes a long drink) But there's more news, and it goes from bad to worse.
DANIELS:	Let's hear it.
NINA:	We also think they've got some plutonium in there.
DANIELS:	That's terrible. But... (weakly) ...what do you want me to do? I'm no expert on nuclear bombs and—
NINA:	(impatient) I want you to go back there with some of my people and pick up one of their members.
DANIELS:	Why?
NINA:	I want you to interrogate that person. *Thoroughly.*
DANIELS:	(offended) Nina, I'm a social scientist, you know I don't do de-programming.
NINA:	This is serious shit, Ethan!
WAITER:	(distant) Is there a problem, ma'am?
DANIELS:	(calls back) No problem, we're fine!
NINA:	(loud whisper) This is plutonium! And I'm not asking you to de-program anybody.
DANIELS:	No? Sounds like it.
NINA:	I doubt that's even possible.
DANIELS:	So, what do you want me to do?
NINA:	Just try and behave like a real anthropologist and get us some information about what's happening in that compound.

DANIELS: Observation and analysis? That's all you want?

NINA: Just get me the lay of the land. That's all that's use-
                ful to me.

DANIELS: Okay.

NINA: (now calm) Okay.

DANIELS: Nina?

NINA: Yes?

DANIELS: What's the worse news? (voice trembles a little)
                What could be worse than a bunch of crazy Mento-
                technologists having the makings of an atomic
                weapon?

NINA: Oh. (giggles, a little crazy) Nothing much. We just
                think that Mentotechnics... or some aspects of it,
                might actually work.

Scene Four

Portable classroom at CFB Edmonton. Eight hours later.

SOUND:	

SOUND: COUGHS AND SHUFFLING OF FEET BEHIND DESKS.

DANIELS: Hello everyone.

SOUND: MORE SHUFFLING.

DANIELS: I imagine that some of you are as in the dark as I am about why exactly we are all here today.

TEAM LEADER: All we were told was that you are the S.A.E. and would give us the background we needed.

DANIELS: S.A.E.?

TEAM LEADER: (sighs) Subject Area Expert.

DANIELS: Okay, that makes sense. (coughs) I haven't had any time to prepare, but I think I have a way we can get through this.

SOUND: PAPER RUSTLING.

DANIELS: How many of you have watched the *Star Wars* movies? Raise your hands.

SOUND: DESKS SHIFTING AS SOME VERY BIG PEOPLE RAISE THEIR HANDS.

DANIELS: All of you. That makes sense when you think about it. Now, how many have you watched any of the versions of *Star Trek*?

SOUND: FEWER DESKS SHIFTING.

DANIELS: About half of you. All right, how many of you regularly read science fiction novels or short

	stories?
SOUND:	<u>SOMEONE COUGHS AT THE FAR END OF THE ROOM.</u>
DANIELS:	Two of you. Let me guess, you two are the IT specialists on the team.
SOUND:	<u>MILD LAUGHTER.</u>
TEAM MEMBER:	(distant) Busted!
DANIELS:	Never mind. As the 21st century progresses it is becoming increasingly apparent that nerds make the world go around.
IT SPECIALIST:	(distant) All right!
DANIELS:	Now, how many of you have read science fiction written by a man named D.H. Evanston?
SOUND:	<u>DEAD SILENCE.</u>
DANIELS:	Nobody. That's not unexpected.
SOUND:	<u>DANIELS FLIPS THROUGH SOME LECTURE NOTES.</u>
DANIELS:	Now, the reason I've been giving you this science fiction trivia quiz is that science fiction—even though 99.9% of it turns out to be total fiction—is sometimes far from trivial. In short, we will be investigating the activities at a compound just east of the town of St. Paul, Alberta. The compound is populated with members of a group called the Temple of Mentotechnics.
TEAM LEADER:	So this is like some kind of *Star Trek* or comic book convention?
DANIELS:	It would be much more agreeable if it was.
IT SPECIALIST:	Or like a commune?
DANIELS:	That might be closer but not exactly. Religious and ethnic communes like the Dukabors and Hutterites are the opposite from the Mento-

technologists in that they are essentially paci-fists and limit their use of technology.

TEAM MEMBER: So we got high-tech Hutterites here?

DANIELS: What we have is a group of religious zealots—who are following the teachings of the late science fiction writer D.H. Evanston.

TEAM LEADER: Why does it matter that he was a science fiction writer?

DANIELS: Mentotechnics can be seen as the attempt to make D.H. Evanston's science fiction world a reality: extra-terrestrials, time travel, space travel, intergalactic civilizations, and extra-sensory perception—the whole thing, the Mentotechnics believe it, they try to live it out.

TEAM LEADER: So what's the big deal? I have one cousin who's a Catholic and another who's a Mormon. Both of them believe some pretty strange stuff when you look at it closely.

DANIELS: I'm inclined to agree with you. However, if you went into the basement of the cathedral over at St. Paul's or the Mormon temple down in Cardston, you probably wouldn't find super-computers, advanced electronics, ammunition or automatic weapons. We do have evidence of such things inside the compound.

TEAM: (gasps, impromptu) What the hell? What the fuck? That's crazy!

DANIELS: (calls out) What we could be looking at is something more akin to the Heaven's Gate and Waco phenomena. Let me read some excerpts from our CSIS operative's situation report: "It is not an exaggeration..." (fades out)

NINA: (fades in) ...to regard the Mentotechnics community in central Alberta as a classic doomsday cult. Under normal circumstances, or at least as normal as these kinds of circumstances get, precedent would suggest the following options:

Scenario One: Containment. Based on expert advice it is possible that the commune will eventually self-destruct—much like Jonestown or Heaven's Gate. The leaders can't handle the disconnect between their vision and the real world and eventually they and all their followers end up killing themselves. The procedure here is to stand back, prevent the cult from harming the surrounding community and let events take their course.

Scenario Two: Intervention. This when we have to go in there and take out the cult leaders. Waco and David Koresh is one of the most recent examples here. The group in question has acquired weapons and other means to try and beat the world into the shape that their ideology dictates. We're in a much messier situation here. While the idea of going in there and sorting these people out seems very satisfying, we usually end up killing some people and often the victims didn't do anything worse than exerting poor judgment in deciding what they believed.

Ideally the Mentotechnics commune in Alberta would be more like Scenario One. We could just sit back and watch them collapse under financial and social pressure and mop things up later. However, the large amounts of equipment they've accumulated suggests that they are planning something and we will have to take action.

The directive from CSIS and the Armed Forces is to intensively observe, continually report and be prepared to take extraordinary action.

DANIELS: Any questions?

Scene Five

Inside CSIS van. St. Forte, Alberta. A day after the conversation at Vulcan.

<table>
<tbody>
<tr><td>SOUND:</td><td><u>BEEPS OF RADAR SCANNER.</u></td></tr>
<tr><td>TEAM LEADER:</td><td>Just remember, keep that toque on your head at all times.</td></tr>
<tr><td>DANIELS:</td><td>Why?</td></tr>
<tr><td>TEAM LEADER:</td><td>Orders, Professor. If you lose your hat, sir, I'll have to give you one of these darts.</td></tr>
<tr><td>DANIELS:</td><td>No thanks.</td></tr>
<tr><td>SHOOTER:</td><td>Target in sight.</td></tr>
<tr><td>DANIELS:</td><td>How old is that kid? Sixteen? Seventeen?</td></tr>
<tr><td>TEAM LEADER:</td><td>Doesn't matter. Take the shot.</td></tr>
<tr><td>SOUND:</td><td><u>PUFF OF AN AIR RIFLE.</u></td></tr>
<tr><td>SHOOTER:</td><td>Got 'em.</td></tr>
<tr><td>TEAM LEADER:</td><td>What a freaking mess.</td></tr>
<tr><td>DANIELS:</td><td>Apparently even highly evolved super-beings like their daily fix of doughnuts.</td></tr>
<tr><td>SOUND:</td><td><u>VAN DOORS ROLL OPEN.</u></td></tr>
</tbody>
</table>

Scene Six

CSIS field office, Alberta. Two hours after the previous scene.

SUBJECT X: Oh, it's you again.

DANIELS: I don't think we've met.

SUBJECT X: We know all about you.

DANIELS: Really?

SUBJECT X: Really. We've been keeping tabs on so-called "researchers" like you for quite a while.

DANIELS: Pick up anything interesting?

SUBJECT X: Not from you, but some people have been making surprising progress.

DANIELS: What do they know?

SUBJECT X: You, on the other hand, provide entertainment.

DANIELS: Thanks.

SUBJECT X: Don't worry about it. None of it matters any more.

DANIELS: Why doesn't it matter?

SUBJECT X: We don't believe we'll tell you right now.

DANIELS: *We?*

SUBJECT X: That's what "We" are. The Therapy Machines, the hypnotic training processes, all those expensive courses, everything in Mentotechnics was designed to bring us all together.

DANIELS: All together? With a collective political ideology?

SUBJECT X: You're thinking too small.

DANIELS: A unified consciousness?

SUBJECT X: Very good! You remember the doctrine!

DANIELS: But that's scientifically impossible.

SUBJECT X: All minds at the compound are governed by the recorded thought patterns of D.H. Evanston... and we say you're wrong.

DANIELS: Do you know that you're part of a profoundly delusional community?

SUBJECT X: Do you know that you're really pissing us off right now? Not a great idea, Professor!

TEAM LEADER: (off mic, partly unintelligible) *...about the plutonium!*

DANIELS: These gentlemen want to know why you have plutonium on the compound.

SUBJECT X: I'm sure they do. But they already know more than you do.

DANIELS: What do you mean?

SUBJECT X: Those silly hats you have to wear. We can read minds if you don't have telepathic protection.

DANIELS: (sighs) Fine, since we're protected and we have you here, why not answer the question? What's the big plan at the compound?

SUBJECT X: You're supposed to be the expert. What's the ultimate goal of Mentotechnics?

DANIELS: To bring about the ultimate transformation of the human race?

SUBJECT X: By creating the ideal consciousness.

DANIELS: And that's a hive-mind, based on its founder's personality?

SUBJECT X: Sort of. But you forgot the most interesting

	parts. We also plan on transcending the boundaries of this tiny world and taking our place among the stars!
DANIELS:	Okay, but what does that have to do with plutonium?
SUBJECT X:	We used the radio telescope to ask for help.
DANIELS:	Help, as in help from outer space?
SUBJECT X:	They suggested that we needed the plutonium to help things happen.
DANIELS:	You think you can use it to power that flying saucer and go out and see these aliens?
SUBJECT X:	The saucer isn't any kind of a spacecraft. It's more of a catalyst.
DANIELS:	You mean it's a bomb?
SUBJECT X:	Bomb is such a pejorative term.
DANIELS:	You—
SOUND:	EXPLOSION. FADES.

Scene Seven

<table>
<tr><td></td><td>Daniels's office at McMaster University. One week later.</td></tr>
<tr><td>SOUND:</td><td><u>TELEPHONE RINGS. DANIELS PICKS UP THE RECEIVER.</u></td></tr>
<tr><td>DANIELS:</td><td>(subdued) Hello?</td></tr>
<tr><td>TSUTSHI:</td><td>(filter) Ethan.</td></tr>
<tr><td>DANIELS:</td><td>(laughs feebly) Chuck.</td></tr>
<tr><td>TSUTSHI:</td><td>(filter) Heard you were back.</td></tr>
<tr><td>DANIELS:</td><td>Yeah. Two days ago.</td></tr>
<tr><td>TSUTSHI:</td><td>(filter) Are you okay?</td></tr>
<tr><td>DANIELS:</td><td>Yeah, yeah. Got all my fingers and toes.</td></tr>
<tr><td>TSUTSHI:</td><td>(filter) I also hear that Nina Brown—</td></tr>
<tr><td>DANIELS:</td><td>(sighs) Didn't make it.</td></tr>
<tr><td>TSUTSHI:</td><td>(filter) Listen, if you want to talk about it...</td></tr>
<tr><td>DANIELS:</td><td>If I did, I think we'd both be up on charges.</td></tr>
<tr><td>TSUTSHI:</td><td>(filter) Jesus. (pause) Well, if there's anything I can do...</td></tr>
<tr><td>DANIELS:</td><td>When are you coming down this way?</td></tr>
<tr><td>TSUTSHI:</td><td>(filter) Next month. My kid's got a recital.</td></tr>
<tr><td>DANIELS:</td><td>Let's crash the Student Union pub and drink it dry.</td></tr>
<tr><td>TSUTSHI:</td><td>(filter) Sounds like a plan.</td></tr>
<tr><td>DANIELS:</td><td>I have to go, Chuck. Report to file.</td></tr>
<tr><td>TSUTSHI:</td><td>(filter) Sure.</td></tr>
</table>

SOUND:	DANIELS HANGS UP AND TURNS ON HIS TAPE MACHINE.
DANIELS:	(VO) When I heard the explosion I thought that the Mentotechnists had detonated their nuclear device.
SOUND:	EXPLOSION AGAIN. THIS TIME FAR MORE DISTANT.
DANIELS:	(VO) I was wrong. It was just Nina driving an armoured truck full of plastic explosives through the compound and blowing up the saucer.
	(VO) So, if Evanston's mind had been recorded in there, it wasn't any more.
SOUND:	BITS OF DEBRIS HITTING THE GROUND, FLAMES, DISTANT SCREAMS AND MOANING.
DANIELS:	(VO) Neither were Nina and 22 residents of the compound. (sighs) None of the CSIS team knew about her plan. They had been told that the explosives were going to be used to destroy the radio telescope after they had made all the arrests.
SOUND:	CRACKLE OF FLAMES GIVES WAY TO PRAIRIE WINDS. FADES.
DANIELS:	(VO) There wasn't anything they could have done.
SOUND:	AN IRRITATING CHEERFUL MUSICAL TONE AS DANIELS TURNS ON HIS COMPUTER.
DANIELS:	(VO) There wasn't anything I could have done either. Not much I can do now.
SOUND:	FINGERS CLICKING ON KEYS AS DANIELS STARTS TO TYPE.
DANIELS:	(VO) Except write a report for whoever replaces her. (echoes over typing) None of the events convince me that any aspect of Mentotechnic practice or belief has any basis in empirical fact. It is likely that the intensity of the operation caused your

team leader to become one more subscriber in the cult's delusional world-view.

SOUND: TYPING STOPS.

DANIELS: (VO) Poor Nina. Once again she got caught up in the fantasy and went off the deep end.

SOUND: HE STARTS TYPING AGAIN.

DANIELS: (VO) Nevertheless, her actions were correct, though perhaps somewhat extreme, in spite of her warped frame of reference. She recognized the strong possibility of nuclear terrorism and took direct steps to stop it. If the pathology of similar "communities of unreason" is any indicator, then we can assume that the group at the compound was planning to use the detonator as a vehicle of mass suicide. Your team leader's actions undoubtedly saved the lives of over 200 Mentotechnologists on the compound as well as the residents in the nearby town.

SOUND: TYPING STOPS.

DANIELS: (weary sigh) Dear god.

Scene Eight

Unitarian meeting hall. The next day.

MUSIC:	<u>ORGAN MEDLEY OF *STAR TREK* SOUNDTRACKS AND SOMETHING THAT SOUNDS SUSPICIOUSLY LIKE "CALLING OCCUPANTS."</u>
DANIELS:	(VO) Another thing I could do was attend the funeral.
MUSIC:	<u>MEDLEY CONTINUES.</u>
DANIELS:	(VO) Nina's *Star Trek* friends had arranged the service at a Unitarian meeting hall that looked like it had been built in the 1970s. They all put on their convention uniforms so it looked a lot like they had all gathered on a set from the original series. Two people gave the eulogy.
SPEAKER #1:	(fades in) ...I know everyone here knows what a wonderful, loving person Nina was.
DANIELS:	(VO) Well... mostly, I suppose.
SPEAKER #1:	But what you might not know is how lucky, how deeply blessed I felt, to have Nina as my partner for the last fifteen years.
DANIELS:	(VO) That last statement surprised me. I had trouble imagining Nina with any other significant other than me. Silly, I know.
MUSIC:	<u>FADES IN AND RECEDES TO THE B.G.</u>
SPEAKER #2:	Being Nina's spiritual counsellor was a tremendous privilege and a true joy because she helped me approach and understand the world, if not the whole universe, in new and exciting

ways.

Nina... (pause) ...Nina represented everything that was fine and noble in *Star Trek*. How she respected the unique potential of the individual. How she understood the importance of a strong sustainable world community, and how she strove for our species to create its own best possible future.

MUSIC:	<u>SWELLS. IT IS NOW DEFINITELY "CALLING OCCUPANTS."</u>
DANIELS:	(VO) One of the speakers was dressed like Captain Kirk. The other looked like Mr. Spock.
MUSIC:	*We are your friends!*

End

I don't think history can possibly be true. Possibly!
—Orson Welles

Evolution of a Fabulist Cycle

This material began as a connected set of proposed stage plays titled **Amazing Struggles, Astonishing Failures and Disappointing Success**, which I wrote from 1989–1990. I am grateful to the members of the Cecil Street Writers Group for expanding the scope of their discussion to include such scripts, as well as for their insights into the different forms of science fiction over the decades.

Eventually I arrived at the conclusion that my original vision for **ASAFDS** was simply not feasible as a stage production[1] and I am grateful to my fellow Cecil Street-er, David Nickle for the suggestion that I re-conceive the works as a radio mini-series.

Amazing Struggles, Astonishing Failures and Disappointing Success (plus **Disappointing Success II**, also known as **Eternal Disappointing Success**) was produced and performed by Shoestring Radio Theatre over several months in 2004. The radio plays were broadcast on KXSF 102.5 FM - San Francisco and carried over the Public Radio Satellite Network.

Cult Stories is not so much as a sequel to **ASAFDS**, but more of an intersecting narrative—which may be why it started as a short story that was first published in 2012 as part of the *Tesseracts Sixteen* anthology and was later included in my collection *Why I Hunt Flying Saucers and Other Fantasticals* (available from Brain Lag).

Laura Nordin, Emily Andrews and the extraordinarily gifted voice actors of The Film Coop were invaluable in helping me to transform a story from a rather long and not-as-good-as-it-needed-to-be radio play into an audio serial of four episodes whose structure and pacing still make me very happy. I was also delighted that Shoestring Radio Theatre performed and broadcast **Cult Stories** in 2014–2015.

I believe that both **ASAFDS** and **Cult Stories** have been rebroadcast by Shoestring but I'm afraid I have misplaced the record of when that was.[2]

---

1   I guess I enjoyed *Les Miserables* so much that I forgot that all those actors, sets, and giant stages cost money.

2   This sort thing happens when writers get older. What was I talking about?

Please note that the scripts in this volume are in the form as they were originally written and do not include any revisions or re-interpretations in the broadcast versions. My reasons for this are important only to me and should not be interpreted as any kind of commentary on the contributions of my many brilliantly talented and generous collaborators.

We live in strange and sometimes terrifying times—but I am astounded and thankful that I am active as a writer in an era when projects such as these are possible.

Hugh A. D. Spencer
October 2023

Hugh A. D. Spencer's short fiction has been published in magazines and anthologies such as *Descant, Interzone, On Spec* and the *Tesseracts* series. Most of these stories are now available in *Why I Hunt Flying Saucers* and *The Progressive Apparatus* from Brain Lag Publishing. His novel *Extreme Dentistry*, also from Brain Lag, was  released in 2014. Hugh developed a passion for aural performance by listening to the 1938 *War of the Worlds* "panic broadcast", the BBC Radio serial of *The Day of the Triffids*, as well as every Firesign Theatre LP he could get his hands on. He went on to adapt much of his own work into audio dramas which have been performed by Shoestring Radio Theatre for the Public Radio Satellite Network.

Hugh was twice nominated for the Aurora Award in Canada for best short story (English) in 1992 and as media curator and writer for the National Library of Canada's exhibition on science fiction and fantasy (1996). His story "(Coping with) Norm Deviation" received an honourable mention in *The Year's Best Science Fiction* (2007). In May 2019, his play "The Triage Conference" was performed at the Scripted Toronto Theatre Festival. His second novel, *The Hard Side of the Moon*, was released in hardback in 2021 and in paperback in 2023. All of the plays in this volume were performed by Shoestring Radio Theatre from 2004 to 2016.

Hugh's research into the origins of contemporary religious movements in science fiction fandom was funded by the Social Science and Humanities Research Council and is available online from McMaster University or through the reference collections of the Toronto Public Library. He is also the president of The Museum Planners Group, an international cultural consulting firm, and lives in walking distance of Lake Ontario in Toronto, Canada—which is very convenient for walking dogs and admiring ducks.

www.ingramcontent.com/pod-product-compliance
Lightning Source LLC
Chambersburg PA
CBHW061219190726
48288CB00001B/239